To Live Again
Arelia's Story

by

Cam O'Keefe

DORRANCE
PUBLISHING CO
EST. 1920
PITTSBURGH, PENNSYLVANIA 15238

Copy editor: Lisa Ducote
Cover Art by Austyn Schwartzbeck
Cover Typography by Sabrina Blackwell, Sabrina Design & Production

Dorrance Publishing Co
585 Alpha Drive
Pittsburgh, PA 15238
Visit our website at *www.dorrancebookstore.com*

ISBN: 978-1-6495-7264-6
eISBN: 978-1-6495-7768-9

Table of Contents

PART II—HEALING OF MEMORIES

1. Ravenshire: Home of Margaret Davidson and Edward F. Davidson

2. Benedictine Monastery: First place of refuge for Arelia after leaving Ravenshire

3. Hamptonshire: Village where Arelia lived with Camellia, Cornelius and baby Cornelius

4. Faircastle: Home of Sir Daniel Fairchild, Lady Marisa and Sir Edward Fairchild

5. Fairchild Manor: Manor Home of Sir Daniel Fairchild

6. Havenshire: Home of John and Joan Wingate, and Miriam

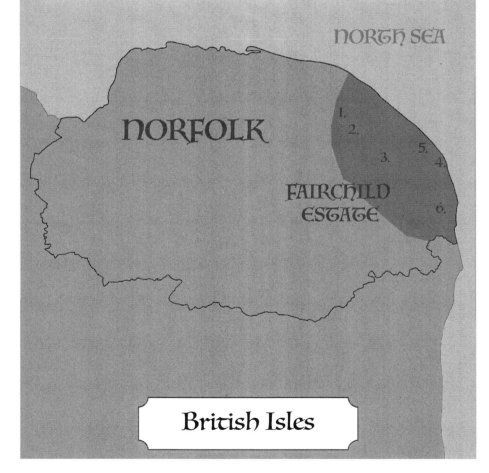

NORTH SEA

NORFOLK

1.
2.
3.
5.
4.

FAIRCHILD ESTATE

6.

British Isles

Nothing of historic proportion happens in a vacuum.

The Medieval Plague, Black Death,

was an event of historic proportion.

The Plague impacted social, economic,

and religious institutions across Europe.

The resulting changes can be seen in our world today.

PART I

CHAPTER 1

1348 AD, ENGLAND
Ravenshire, Norwich County

Normal did not exist anymore.

Arelia awoke slowly, not knowing where she was and not really caring. There was no moonlight coming through the shutters to give her a hint, no glow from dying embers. What time was it—early morning, late night? Did it really matter?

Reality forced itself into consciousness as unexpected cold began to pierce through to her aching bones. The room was quiet, too quiet; no whimpering, no moans, no rasps of forced breath strained through swollen tissue. No popping of flaming embers turned to darkened ash. Something was wrong, desperately wrong.

Fear gripped her. "Mother," she whispered. No answer. Louder, "Mother?"

Before now, either her father or brother had kept the fire stoked against the cold. Daniel had been buried weeks earlier, and her father, whose appearance seemed to become more grossly distorted by the minute, had not gotten out of bed in days. It hadn't occurred to her to keep the fire. She poked at an ashen log to spark a small flame in order to light a slender twig to hold to the lantern's wick, a simple, familiar process which seemed oddly difficult. Her mother was at the table, hopefully only sleeping, with her head resting on her crossed arms. "Mother," she coaxed, afraid that there would be no response. "Mother," again, gently shaking her arm as she set the lantern on the table.

Her mother squinted against the light. "He is gone, Arelia. Your father is gone," she repeated as she reached for her daughter's slender and quivering hand.

She lifted the lantern as if it were too heavy to bear and led Arelia to the bed where she and her husband had slept together for nearly twenty years, the bed where she had conceived and delivered their five children. The face was unrecognizable, covered with black patches and bulbous growths, and even his clothes were unfamiliar. "Father," Arelia said, more as a question than a statement of despair. She studied the grey-blue tunic and large medallion. "What is he wearing?"

"This is what he was wearing all those years ago when he came to me. I thought he should leave me in the same way."

Arelia shed no tears for the body which looked nothing like her father; confusion raced through her mind. Her mother shuffled haltingly to the heavy log mantle over the fireplace and came back with her dark wooden sewing box, handing it to Arelia. With great reverence and care, she pulled the rough-woolen blanket he was lying on over him, lapping one side over the other.

As if in a dream, Arelia watched as her mother folded the blanket over unfamiliar boots. "Should we take those boots off?"

"They will serve us no purpose. There is no one left to wear them," she said as she opened her sewing box and threaded a long, tarnished needle with coarse woolen thread that she and Arelia had spun themselves.

"Mother, are you going to stitch the blanket shut?" Everything had become strange over the past several weeks, but now she had to question her mother's odd behavior, maybe even her sanity.

"He does not even have a coffin. Oh, Arelia." She moaned as she touched his cocoon-like shape. "This is not right. I will not have people staring."

"We will stay inside today. Do not tell anyone. I do not want them taking him. I need one more day with him." Her eyes clouded over in tears as she looked into her daughter's dark eyes, pleading for time that did not exist.

"Oh, Mother, I would keep him here forever if we could."

As her mother stood over his body to stitch the cloth coffin closed, she recited the familiar burial psalm. *The Lord is my Shepherd; there is nothing that I want. In green pastures you let me graze; to safe waters you lead me; you restore my strength. You guide me along the right path for the sake of your name. Even when I walk through a dark valley, I fear no harm for you are at my side; your rod and staff give me courage.*

Arelia had heard that psalm read and recited many times in her life, but she listened to the words, as if for the first time, as they fell softly from her mother's lips. Pulling a chair from the fireplace for her mother to sit, she asked, "Do you really believe that?"

"Believe what?"

"Believe that the Lord is your Shepherd, and there is nothing you should fear."

Her mother pushed the needle through the cloth, leaving it as a rusty nail in a coffin and then, with apparent pain, slowly settled into the chair. Her face was grave, an expression unfamiliar to her daughter. Arelia sat on the floor and rested her hand on her mother's lap. "Arelia, you have seen much in twelve short years and most of the pain of it in the last two or three weeks. We are in the dark valley which the psalm talks about. I do not know why we are here or how it came to be, but we are. Your father came to me for the first time when I was just a few years older than you." She smiled. "He had been very sick, and I guess you could say that he came to me from the valley of death all those years ago.

"Somehow he survived that terrible illness and went back to his family and then, unexpectedly, returned to me as in a dream. We have walked together through green pastures most of our lives. You and your brothers and sister came out of those happy times.

"Do I still believe?" She wrinkled her brow and rubbed her temples as if to dislodge a sharp pain or maybe buried memories. "It has been so terribly difficult lately. I could have never imagined burying three of my children and now my husband." She laid her arm across his legs and breathed a deep sigh.

"We are deep into the valley of death, you and I. If you and baby John survive, you will experience green pastures again. They will seem greener for you after all this."

Arelia corrected, "If we *all* survive."

Margaret stroked her daughter's dark silky hair and rested her hand on the back of her neck. Their eyes met with a sadness neither had ever experienced before. There was a painful and unfamiliar knowing.

"Mother, what are you thinking?"

"I am thinking about Mary."

"Mary?"

"Yes."

Arelia's expression showed she did not understand why their neighbor would be on her mother's mind at this time. "I am sorry, Mother, I do not understand. Mary?"

"Yes. Oh, Arelia, I held three of my children and watched them die. I never knew pain could cut so deep. Mary held her son, too." Her words were heavy with grief.

"Mary lost her son, too?"

Margaret, looked questioning, "Yes, child, you know that. As I held each of our children, I realized how much she understood my pain, maybe better than anyone. And then last night, for the first time, I realized she also lost Joseph, just as I have lost my Edward." Tears filled her eyes. "We have so much in common. She understands me."

Arelia was completely lost. "Mother I am here for you, too." Pain and grief clearly had have taken her mother's mind.

"Oh, dear Arelia, of course you are. You have been so precious to me since the first time I looked into your little eyes; my first baby girl.

"And now, you have stood with me so bravely tending to our family right by my side." She stopped with a sad realization. "Oh, my child, you have lost your brothers and sister and now your father. I have overlooked your own grief!"

"No, Mother, we have not had time to stop and grieve," she consoled.

"Arelia, take comfort in Mary. She lost her son and her husband, and certainly her mother and father. She understands our pain."

"I am sorry, Mother. Are you talking about our neighbor?"

"Our neighbor?"

"Yes, Mary."

Margaret's confused expression turned to unexpected, yet weak, laughter. Arelia was stunned and realized that, in fact, her mother had lost her mind.

"Oh my. No dear, Mary, the Mother of Jesus." She smiled.

Arelia laughed at the misunderstanding but mostly from relief that her mother's words made sense after all.

"Arelia, Jesus gave us His mother from the cross. Both Mary and Jesus are always here for us, and they understand everything we are going through. We are living, and now dying, through terrible times, but we are never alone. I shudder to think it, but it may become even worse for you, and there is nothing I can do to help you."

"Oh, Mother, it could never get worse."

A shadow washed over Margaret. Letting go of her daughter's hand, she hesitated and then said, "I suspect you have noticed the swelling on my neck, and it is getting painful under my arm now." She opened the collar of her dress to reveal a dark patch of skin creeping onto her breast. "You know as well as I do that I am short for this world and that you and John may be left on your own. Tomorrow we will talk to Kempra and Mr. Jackson about taking in the two of you."

Arelia went to rest her head on her mother's lap, but instead, her mother lifted her to her feet as she stood, and then she reached under the blanket, covering her father's face and chest. Removing a large medallion, she explained, "This is an amulet of your father's heritage, his bloodline. Place it on John, and if he survives, you both will be cared for.

"Let us say the Angelic Salutation together for one last time."

"Mother, not the last time, but *one more* time."

Margaret's voice was little more than a whisper. "Hail Mary, full of grace, The Lord is with thee. Blessed art thou among women, and blessed is the fruit of thy womb, Jesus."

Arelia lifted the heavy pendant. "What is this? You and Father have never told us about Father's family or how you met. Why have you and Father always avoided our questions? Mother, I do not understand. Tell me now." Arelia, near to pleading, began to cry.

"Oh, Arelia," she said weakly, suppressing a cough, "I have no strength for it. Let me sleep a while, and then I will tell you it all. But what could it matter now?" She slowly shuffled across the room to lie down on Daniel's narrow cot. For the first time, she noticed her mother wasn't wearing her boots but rather her husband's larger work boots; hers rested unattended on the hearth next to Daniel's, Prudence's, and Marcus's boots.

Arelia leaned over her father's body to finish the work her mother had begun, remembering happier times in green pastures. "Our Father, Who art in heaven, hallowed be Thy name . . . .."

Arelia sat alone. How could it have come to this? It had only been two months since the man had come from London, as he had done so many times before, his wagon filled with grain, seeds, cloth, and wares. He had even remembered to bring her mother another small bale of soft raw wool for spinning. Now, all of her family but she and John were dead. How was this possible?

He had also brought rumors of Black Death in London and other parts of England—hundreds dying—bodies being thrown out of windows for the burying wagons to carry off—the dead being buried in pits—children walking the streets with no parents to care for them. They had heard rumors before, but now he said that it was spreading all over England, and it had been for over a year. Not everyone believed what he had to say, but some did and hid in the woods with what little they could tie to the back of a horse or fit into a wagon. Like Arelia's family, most stayed.

When the peddler had leaned down from his wagon to hand her mother the small bale of wool, Arelia had wondered about the large swelling on his neck and the dark bruise that peeked out from the collar of his shirt. It was only a few days later when Father Jerome, deeply concerned for the man, went to wake the trader from sleeping under his wagon to bring him a loaf of bread that he found him dead. Fear spread, but it was too late. The plague had taken hold of their village like wildfire.

She sat on the porch rocking her baby brother, sleeping against her chest, finally calmed by her heartbeat, as their neighbors carried her mother and father toward the fire. No cry left her lips; no tears fell—the well was dry.

In the beginning of the blight, after having found the trader dead from Black Death, days had turned to weeks as she lost her brothers and sister. First, little Prudence had shown the unusual, egg-shaped swelling in her groin and under her arm. A deep cough had followed with gut-wrenching dry heaves that had startled her awake at the beginning. The putrid smell drove everyone out of the house with the exception of Margaret who clung to her tiny daughter. The day before Prudence died, her oldest brother Daniel developed dark, livid patches that showed first on his fingertips and toes and then crawled across his entire body, and then Marcus died only two days after the first swelling appeared under his arm. She had begged her prayers be answered, but they seemed to fall on deaf ears, and they had all died nonetheless, one at a time like candles being snuffed out around an altar. Arelia had believed they would be spared, but in little over a month, only she and John remained.

Her mother had never awakened from her rest. The story of her father's upbringing and parents' memories had died with them, lost for all eternity. The men had come, not even surprised that both her mother and father were dead. Nothing was surprising anymore. Nothing was as it had been; nothing was normal. Now they were being laid together in a pile of ashes waiting for new logs and a flaming torch. There was nothing she could do.

At first the villagers had buried their dead as prescribed by the Church, but as the pile of corpses had grown, and more people took to the forest in order to hide from the scourge of disease, there were no longer people who were strong enough or willing to dig the graves. Being among the first to die, her brothers and sister had the grace of a Christian burial in the village graveyard with consoling prayers, songs of hope, and a deep cradle dug from the earth to hold their bodies, resting in the wooden caskets her father had quickly crafted. Even before that, Fr. Jerome had anointed their darkened bodies, but to no avail for their bodies, only for their souls. After attending to the sick and burying the dead day after day and night after night, Fr. Jerome himself was taken, leaving the villagers without the consolation of their Priestly Shepherd for Sacraments and Christian burial. Only Fr. Jerome's beautifully hand-written Scripture was left for consolation.

It was just days after Marcus was buried that her father and several men had taken to digging large pits, but soon there were not enough men to keep up with even that. The men who had survived and stayed to dig the pits and carry the bodies on the clumsily built litter seemed to mock their own inevitable death. No one had wanted to burn the bodies—it was sacrilegious—

the smell of rotting corpses was more than people could stomach, and the fear of poisonous vapors emitted from ravaged flesh, searching for the next victims, caused certain alarm. Often a fetid corpse would have to be set on the ground outside a hut overnight, waiting to be carried away. The first time wolves ventured into the clearing and tore the bodies apart, the men decided burning the dead was the only choice that remained. They relied on the promise of a loving and merciful God. *Father, forgive them. They know not what they do.* In fact, this was all they could do.

The morning air was frosty as she watched men gather wood for the cremation fire. John had finally fallen asleep in his cradle after she had wrapped her mother's body in a rough woolen blanket and stitched it shut, just as she and her mother had done for her father earlier that morning. Arelia wanted to grant her mother the same tender care that she had given to her husband. She had rolled her mother's lifeless form onto its side while she slid the blanket under her and then carefully folded it over her like a baby being swaddled for slumber. John's cries had often interrupted her stitches, but she persisted throughout the night until the last knot was tied. Somehow, it didn't seem morbid that she had let their father and mother stay with her and John one more day. They were her parents. She needed them. Time seemed to stop as Mr. Jackson and Mr. Shomocker lifted the bodies onto the litter. Mother and Father disappeared into the smoke-filled haze of eternity. Now she and John were alone.

CHAPTER 2

 "No!" Her scream seemed to hit no ears but her own. Horror froze in the cold, frigid air like the icicles hanging from her family's hut. "Not John! Please, Lord, not John!"

Poor little John, not yet one. She felt the growth under his arm as she lifted him from his little cradle. His cries seemed to echo the pain of those who could no longer cry. His little face, once so bright and mischievous, with eyes that laughed at the sight of his sisters and brothers, was now distant and dark—dark with impending death.

It was John's brightness that Arelia was fighting to retrieve from death's door. Her mother said that her father had once escaped death to be with her years ago; now she was determined to rescue John. He was her last connection to the once happy family that was now turned to ashes and dust just outside the village square. He had to survive.

Arelia had placed the large, cold medallion around John's tiny neck as her mother had instructed. She had told Arelia that it was not just a sentimental notion but would identify him if no one else in the family remained. The amulet looked so large against his small heaving chest. His eyes were dull compared to the brightness of the light reflecting from the gold medallion. She carried her little brother for what seemed like miles to the closest inhabited hut across the clearing. "Kempra," she pleaded through her tears, "I cannot lose John."

"Let me help you," Kempra offered as she took the baby, trying to conceal her shock on seeing his blackened and distorted little face. "Fix tea, and I will rock John for you."

Arelia sipped the steamy, hot brew on the porch as she studied her family's empty hut across the clearing. *Alone* was a condition that had never existed in the Davidson household. When Father was out working in the field or animal pen, the house stayed busy with baking, sewing, and washing. Games, story-telling, and Scripture reading were saved for the quiet of evening only after everything else was done.

After dinner Father would read and talk about a verse or two from his meticulously hand-written Psalter and then tell stories by the fire as John and Marcus fell fast asleep. Arelia and Daniel would listen to his stories night after night and imagine distant places and noble adventures. They would ask questions, and Father would always exaggerate with even more fantasy than in the story before: castles and knights, ladies and lords. The same old stories came alive. Prudence always found Mother's lap after John was tucked into his cradle. She would sew with Mother's sure hand patiently guiding each tiny stitch.

Now there was only John in a little plight-ridden body, unrecognizable except for the heavy metal amulet. He had to live. He was the family now—not just company but their name and family heritage.

"Arelia," called Kempra's soft voice. "John is sleeping. You must sleep while you can. I will sit with him."

Where had the day gone? Was it just this morning that my parents' bodies were burned? Could that possibly have been today? No, yesterday or maybe the day before.

Sleep, not death. Is there a difference? Where does the mind go as the body lies so still? Will they think me dead, not asleep, and cast me into the flames still lit by my parents' bodies? Will John follow with his tiny body tossed on the fire like a fallen log in the woods? Not sleep, but death. Dark men with dark hoods, walking, carrying bodies into flames . . . wolves howling in the distance . . . babies crying in the woods . . .

"Arelia, you must awaken quickly before it is too late. They have come for John. I could not stop them," Kempra cried, shaking the sleeping child.

Poor Kempra. Why did I sleep?

Frozen in disbelief, she watched the man carry her little brother's body to the fire. It didn't seem like a child being carried, so dark, still, and quiet. *Where is the crying that carried through the night? I want to hear the crying!*

Is that John flying into wildly burning flames or a log casually tossed into the fire to burn the bodies before him?

"John!" She screamed as she ran toward the clearing.

"Someone stop her. She will catch fire herself. Hold her back!"

The smell and sound of death was unrelenting. Some would never say it— they likened the sound and smell of it to a roasting pig or chicken—it was death burning finally into ashes.

"Oh, God, my God, no!" Arelia sobbed. Tears rose from an unknown pit of grief. Her body remained crouched by the fire, guarded from self-destruction by one silent man.

Was it hours that passed or days? Arelia dug insanely, savagely, through the warm ashes. "Where are the bones? Which bones are mine? Where is my family?"

"Arelia, you must come away from the fire. Your family is gone." The man came with his rake, starting at the edge of the burn pile, working his way toward the center, gathering remains into a wagon that would be dumped into a large pit of bones with others who had been burned before.

Arelia continued to claw through the ashes, oblivious to pitiful glances and silent stares from neighbors who were now onlookers lost in their own misery and confusion, with no energy left to care.

"What are you looking for, girl?"

Arelia did not respond. She felt a strong hand on her shoulder. "Arelia! Arelia!"

Dark, cloudy eyes looked into a pitying gaze. "Arelia, we do not know whose bones are whose. There is no way to know. Go home."

"You should not have burned them." She moaned.

With stooped shoulders and eyes downcast, he consoled as best he could, "Arelia, we are gathering the ashes and bones to bury in a pit. We could not keep up. Your family will be there on the last day for the resurrection of the dead.

"I am sorry. My wife and sons are in there too. We ask the merciful God to forgive us and to bring them to heaven and everlasting life. We will be reunited on the last day. Go now."

She fell back on her legs folded below her and began to cry, "Dear Father, help me.

"Wait!" she yelled. "Baby John wore a medallion from my father."

One man answered from the opposite side of the ring of ashes and smoke. "Something flew from him when I tossed him into the flames. It went somewhere over there." He motioned to an undetermined area.

She nearly jumped to her feet and stumbled toward where he motioned. She knelt into a crawl and began to dig under dried leaves in one direction and then another. Soon, her hand glanced against something warm. Afraid of what it would be, she lifted her hand and saw the now familiar disk, dangling from the end of a chain. Tears puddled on the medallion, washing dust and grime into a muddy pool in the palm of her hand. She clutched it to herself with gratitude that something of her family was left to hold.

To sleep on the edge of the ashes may have seemed insane to some, but others understood. No one dared to disturb her. Someone mercifully covered her with a blanket during the night. Pounding hammers brought nightmares of nails being slammed into soft blanket coffins with blood pouring from rusty nail holes. Gradually the pounding became stark reality as she opened her eyes to the noise.

"Why are you boarding up our hut?" she yelled as she ran toward the men.

"Arelia, you know this was your father's home. He needs no home now. Be on your way. You need to find a man, if death spares you. Then you will have a home."

"I will take her," called a rough voice.

"Arelia is too young for you. See if death spares her first. It may find her next. If it does pass her by, then she might be yours to take. No one else will be able to care for her with no property, name, or dowry."

"Arelia, you must come away from the ashes. Your family had friends, and others need your help," someone coaxed.

"Arelia, your father would not want you standing out here alone."

"Where do I go?" questioned Arelia. "Who will have me?" She sunk to the steps of her family's hut, not knowing where to turn.

"Go where you are needed. There is so much to be done. You cannot take time for yourself. Others need you." Distant voices with no answers came out of nowhere.

The plague seemed to stop as quickly as it had begun, like a wildfire having run its course. The first deep freeze seemed to bring relief. Not many were left, and those who survived the Black Death were consumed with inconceivable grief. Somehow, news spread, and people began to return from the forest—one family one day, a mother or children alone the next. Within weeks a few of the huts began to come alive again.

Arelia wanted to stay with Kempra, but she had lost her husband and had her and her sister's children in a tiny, one-room hut. She tried staying for a short while, but there was no space and not enough food. Eventually, she made her way to the home of Mr. Jackson, a friend of her father. Mr. Jackson was one of the men who had carried the bodies into the flames. Remarkably, both he and his wife had been saved, and they had taken in many orphaned children, having only one daughter of their own.

Arelia was of service to the family, bringing water, making soup, and keeping the fire lit. When she could leave without notice, she would take Kempra a potato or bunch of carrots. Mr. Jackson's wife, Rebecca, showed her appreciation through tired, sad eyes, but Arelia didn't need gratitude. Activity was all she needed to numb her grief and to distract her from the memories of her own family and her fear of knowing what would become of her without them.

Now that the threat of dying was behind them, months had passed without a death fire in the village. The few remaining men cleared the fields of livestock that had fallen victim to the same pestilence that had laid waste to the farmers and their families. What the wolves and wild dogs hadn't eaten or dragged away, they burned. The smell of burning animal flesh was a sad reminder of their own cremation fires. Everyone cautiously began normal chores. Doors opened, and dust flew from the tips of brooms. Parentless children were taken in by childless parents. Rags and furniture were burned; clothes were washed and hung. Boards were pried from empty huts, and furniture was distributed where needed. The ground was tilled. Mouldboard ploughs that had been idle for months came to life, cutting deep grooves into thick, fertile soil. There would be fewer crops this year with fewer hands for planting and harvesting but also fewer mouths to feed. Much of the livestock that provided wool, meat, and milk had also fallen victim. It would be difficult to pay the landowners' levies, if possible at all.

Arelia watched as families of two or three picked up their lives—one without a father or mother, others without sons and daughters—and Arelia alone.

Why have I survived?

Mr. Jackson and Rebecca had been kind to Arelia and to several younger children who had lost their parents, yet she sensed that there was tension between them. Mr. Jackson came in tired and angry every night, and he and Rebecca had started to argue.

"We cannot keep all of the children, Rebecca. I just cannot do it anymore." Mr. Jackson moaned. Arelia listened quietly, pretending to be asleep.

"We have room. If we do not keep them, where will they go?" Rebecca pleaded.

"We do not have room. We have given up our own bed to three of them, and there is little food for all of us. Maybe she can stay while it is still warm, but once the cold comes, we will not have enough food. I am short of seeds and can barely plant enough to feed us all now, and the livestock is nearly gone. We also have levies to pay. I talked to Joseph. He and Ruth can take Andrew's sons. And Mr. Honeycutt will take Arelia as his wife."

"Wife! Arelia is just a child. She is only twelve. You cannot expect her to be his wife," Rebecca objected.

"Arelia has seen a lot. She is a good worker and will serve him well. In a couple of years, she will grow into the role of a wife and mother," assured her husband.

"Oh, I grew into a woman as you grew into a man, and that was nearly impossible, even when we loved each other. Mr. Honeycutt is at least four times her age, and he is not a good man."

"Rebecca, Arelia is not my child. I cannot care for her. I have made no promise to Edward to care for her. Unfortunately, in weakness, I pledged care for Timothy's children, but I have no responsibility toward Arelia." He was firm in his decision.

Arelia was gripped with fear. Rebecca had become like a mother to her—both a mother and a friend. She had watched Rebecca's delicate fingers mend worn dresses with the same even stitches that her mother made. She cooked potatoes just as her mother had and made weak tea at the same time every day. There was normalcy with Rebecca, like trees shedding their leaves every fall and plants sprouting in spring. Life was becoming familiar and predictable again.

Rebecca could never completely replace the love of her own mother, yet they worked well together and often talked late into the night. She knew Arelia's family and allowed her to talk out her memories, both joys and sorrows. There was so much comfort from this woman who knew the grief of losing her own daughter. Only someone like that could truly understand Arelia's broken heart.

Rebecca was right; Mr. Honeycutt was not a nice man. Everyone knew of his cruelty. Arelia had often overheard her father tell her mother stories about Mr. Honeycutt's immoral ways. She was even frightened by his looks, not to mention his behavior. Once she had seen him watching her mother from behind a tree. The intensity of his stare brought chills to the young girl, and so she had called Margaret inside with the excuse of Prudence needing her. Arelia feared that he would look at her in the same way. This man could not and would not replace the love of her father. He didn't even know what love was.

In reality, Arelia knew from Mr. Jackson's tone that his decision was final, and, to be honest, he was right. Three children were enough in their small hut, and he had made no promises to her father. He seemed to be willing to give her a little time so that she could help in the garden, but she knew her time was short.

Placing her hand over the disk hidden under her bodice, she whispered, "I know there is a place for me somewhere." Sleep was peppered with dreams of flames and screams, fireside stories and laughter, and images of each precious body being tossed into the flame.

Rebecca appeared nervous as she prepared breakfast for a house full of children. Arelia knew that the cause of her concern was not the rambunctious household, and so she was not surprised when Rebecca asked, without turning from the hearth, "Arelia, have you met Mr. Honeycutt?"

"Yes," answered Arelia, trying to calm the panic arising within her chest.

"And what do you think of him?"

"I do not *think* of him at all, Rebecca," she answered, trying not to be rude. Arelia could see the concern on Rebecca's face and realized she would be required to follow Mr. Jackson's verdict, although unwillingly. Arelia understood that Rebecca cared deeply for her but could not go against her husband's will. Her mother had often disagreed with her father, but in the end, her father always prevailed. Arelia recognized the same struggle within Rebecca's mind and heart.

"As it warms up, we will spend more time in the garden and help tend the livestock. I do not even know who is back since . . . now that things are normal again. I wonder if the Whitaker boy is back. Did his family take to the woods? What was his name?"

"Gabriel."

"He is Daniel's age if I remember correctly. Is that right?"

Even at age twelve, Arelia was keenly aware of where the conversation was leading, in light of the reference to Mr. Honeycutt, but she also knew that Gabriel Whitaker was not a potential match for her and that there was no time to develop such a relationship before she would be forced to leave. Although her thirteenth birthday was in less than a month, marriage was the last thing on her mind right now. She made an excuse to go outside in order to escape the conversation.

Unlike previous days that had begun to seem normal, this day was filled with tension. Arelia knew that Rebecca had the best of intentions and that she wanted to tell her of her husband's plans but just couldn't bring herself to it. Fear began to fill her at the thought of living with Mr. Honeycutt. She could hardly breathe with the thought of it. She could not and would not let it happen, and she couldn't bear putting Rebecca through the hard decision.

Late that night, as the house became quiet and the embers died in the stove, Arelia left quietly. She wanted to awaken Rebecca to thank her for the time that she had given her to rest and to feel a part of a family, but she knew it would be best to leave quietly.

Although icicles no longer hung from the eaves, the night air was bitterly cold. "I know there is a place for me," Arelia repeated softly. She was drawn to her family's hut. The door had been unbarred to air out from the stench of death. She walked quietly into the familiar dwelling for the first time since it had been boarded up months before. Strangely, everything was as it had been. The bowl and rag still sat on the table next to the bed that had held each sick body. The stove was open with long-since-cold coals. Chairs sat empty around the table with the handwritten Psalter at Father's place. "Father sat here, and Mother here with Baby John, Daniel and Marcus next to them, and my chair with Prudence next to me," she said as if introducing them to guests, walking around the table and touching each chair with each introduction.

But everything was eerily quiet now. Even when she had awakened at night, it had never been completely quiet. It seemed that just days before she'd heard Father's deep, relaxed breaths and occasional snore, Marcus tossing restlessly on his cot, and John's occasional whimper. But it was never quiet. Even the wind had died.

I know there is a place for me.

Arelia walked to the hearth near Daniel's bed and picked up her mother's heavy boots. She pulled her mother's chair from the table and sat on the edge of it as she slipped her feet into the large shoes and tied the laces. Unaccustomed to the weight of such heavy boots, she walked to the hook next to the door and took down the bulky woolen cape with deep pockets and an oversize hood that she and her mother had laboriously woven and lovingly stitched. It had been for both of them. If Mother went out in the cold, she wore it; if Arelia went out, she wore it. But, if they went out together, Mother insisted that Arelia have it. It still hung long on Arelia, but she would grow, and it would fit her as it had Mother. When Prudence argued to wear the warm cape, Arelia wrapped it around her tiny shoulders. Everyone would laugh as Prudence tripped over the length of it. Mother always promised her that she would get to wear it when she grew, and then she and Arelia would spin enough wool to make a new cape to share. The wool that had come with the peddler from London just months earlier was to spin the yarn to weave two new capes, one for Arelia and one for Prudence.

"Mother would want me to have this now," Arelia announced to the empty room.

She took the amulet that she had recovered from her family's ashes and placed it on top of the Psalter at her Father's place at table. "This is yours, Father." Then, turning sadly, she looked around the room for one last time and passed through the doorway. As she stepped onto the porch, the cold breeze that brushed against her face could not compare to the chill that cut through her small frame at the sight of the dark forest that was to become her world. The warm cloak could shut out night's cold but not fear's chill. Daylight's warmth would be a relief from both.

"I know there is a place for me." She pulled the cape tightly around her, clutching it against her chin. "I am on my own now." As she walked slowly away from their home to the edge of the woods, she turned hesitantly back toward the village for one last glance. A full moon shone on their hut, giving it an eerie glow. Running to the door, she paused and then walked to the table, picked up the amulet, and placed it around her neck and then tucked the Psalter into the pocket of her cloak.

"Father, I take back your name. Please help me find my place." She cried as she stepped into the dark woods, disappearing into the dark, foreboding canopy of trees.

CHAPTER 3

Arelia walked until morning's light, not so much to get far from the village, but for fear that wild animals would find her asleep. She had left the village only twice before, with her father and brother to trade chickens for wool from a monastery, but she didn't exactly know where. They'd brought back the same wool that had been made into the blankets which had become her parents' coffins. She had been younger then and did not clearly remember where they traveled, but she thought that they had ridden two days pulling a wagon. They had seen a pack of wolves in the distance when they stopped to rest the horses. She and her brother had sat very still until they had passed, while her father kept an arrow pointed at the animals. She had never forgotten how frightened she had been.

Although there was a main road, she didn't feel safe following it and kept to paths just off at a distance. There were turns and forks that contributed to her confusion, but because she didn't have any particular destination, it didn't seem to matter which path she took. She remembered the monastery was somewhere off the main road but had no idea how to find it and only hoped to stumble upon it.

Wind blew through the oaks overhead, creating dark shadows and soft light on the narrow path. She froze in her footsteps at an occasional wolf's howl or owl's hoot, wanting to run back to the safety of Kempra's warm hearth, but she set one foot in front of the other determined by her fear of Mr. Honeycutt, even more than of wolves.

Occasionally, she rested on the bough of a low branch or in a leafy nest hidden amongst a gathering of boulders only to imagine what lay ahead of her, realizing that without a father or brother, she would not be acknowledged or helped by strangers, and she could be in danger from passersby. She had seen what had happened to older women in the village whose husbands had died without leaving a son to care for them. More often than not, a kind family would take them in to help care for the house and children, but on rare occasions, they were left to work the soil alone, and died soon after. Neighbors would sometimes help at first, but widows were sometimes left on their own as people became busy with their own families. She knew from hearing stories that she was in danger from both man and beast. She would have to find a place for herself alone, possibly an abandoned hut in the woods.

As the morning air began to warm, Arelia felt it safe enough to sleep, being too exhausted to go on any longer anyway. She saw a gathering of rocks among a cluster of small trees that provided a private place to sleep away from the path.

As she crawled behind the rocks, tension began to fade from her tired, aching body. The trees made a secure yet gentle canopy over a thick bed of dried leaves, while the circle of rocks provided a cradle. Her mother's cloak provided both a cushion and a cover as she arranged it over dried leaves into a cozy bed. Once comfortably settled, she thought how quickly her life had changed. She could not determine how long it had been since the first person died in the village or when Prudence first got sick. She remembered that it was very cold and damp the day Prudence's small body was buried, but she was not sure if the air was really cold or if it was only horror that had chilled her. Her mind had not been able to grasp why her little sister had been taken from her, and she could never have imagined what was yet to come.

As she reviewed the past days, weeks, and months, she realized that now it was getting warmer, and yet there was no memory of the last Christmas; she had lost all track of time. Thoughts of previous Christmases blocked out memories of the past many months as she slipped into a deep and comfortable sleep, exhaustion taking over. Wind rustled the trees, providing a familiar, comforting sound as she dreamed of cutting a Christmas tree, of walking with Daniel and Marcus through the woods, and of picking berries for her mother to prepare pies and bread. She dreamed of walks with Father as he identified different trees and nuts. She dreamed of collecting flowers with Mother and Prudence.

The howl of wolves in the distance startled her awake. For a few seconds, she didn't know where she was or even who she was and couldn't imagine why she would be alone in the forest. Memory returned with a painful jolt. The sky was nearly dark, chillingly cold and still. *Have I slept through the day?*

Tears began to fall—not a flood of tears or even a river, simply a soft trickle. *I do not want to die here alone*, she thought. *I should never have left the village.* Slowly, she lifted her hand to feel her neck under her ears. Her breath caught in her throat as she felt for any swelling under her arm; no swelling, not even tenderness. She lifted her sleeve and searched for dark patches in the soft light of dusk—no patches, not even an unfamiliar spot.

"God, why have you not taken me, too? I do not want to be alone." Only nature responded with an owl's hoot and the whisper of wind through the trees. God appeared to be silent.

The thought of dying alone sent a shiver through her. "Please let me die with people. I do not want to die here. The animals will eat me and scatter my bones. No one will know, and no one will be around to pray over me. Please, Lord. Why have you left me here?"

She lay back onto nature's bed until hunger cut through her thin body, but she was too afraid to leave the safety of her cradle. She decided that she would find nuts and berries in the morning light as she had done so many times before, and prayed that no hungry animals would find her during the night.

Lying there, she remembered stories her father had told—stories of wars, knights, princesses, and kings. Many times he ended his stories by saying, "Soldiers often fight battles they do not understand, but they fight because they have faith in their king."

She often wondered if he had fought any battles. He explained, "There are many battles in life we fight and do not understand. We do not always see the king or understand why we are fighting. We do not always fight with swords." She never understood what he meant. Mother would look at him lovingly and seemed to understand. *They have a secret*, she often thought.

As Arelia lay there, she felt she had been through a battle, and wondered if it was over. She wanted to ask Father if she had been through the kind of battle of which he spoke. She cried softly, longing to hear his voice but knowing he would never be able to answer. She cried herself back to sleep. *The Lord is my Shepherd; there is nothing I shall want. He will lead me to safe paths. Please take away my fear.*

※

"Father's book!" Her own voice woke her with a start. It was as if she had never fallen asleep, but the sky was waking to morning. *Maybe his secrets are here*, she thought as she lifted the cape from her leafy bed and reached deep into the pocket. As the book fell open to Psalm 139, she read:

1　LORD, you have probed me, you know me:

2　you know when I sit and stand;
　　you understand my thoughts from afar.

3　You sift through my travels and my rest;
　　with all my ways you are familiar.

4　Even before a word is on my tongue,
　　LORD, you know it all.

5　Behind and before you encircle me
　　and rest your hand upon me.

6　Such knowledge is too wonderful for me,
　　far too lofty for me to reach.

7　Where can I go from your spirit?
　　From your presence, where can I flee?

8　If I ascend to the heavens, you are there;
　　if I lie down in Sheol, there you are.

9　If I take the wings of dawn
　　and dwell beyond the sea,

10　Even there your hand guides me,
　　your right hand holds me fast.

A quick movement on the rock behind her caused her to jump and let out a little scream. A small squirrel holding a fat nut in his mouth appeared more startled than she. He jumped onto a tree near the rock and ran into a hole in its bough. He had already begun his day's work. Arelia laughed, thinking that if she could, she would follow him safely into the tree. Food, nuts! Father had often told her the birds and squirrels would lead her to berries and nuts. She and Daniel had startled many squirrels foraging for food. Today she would do as Father taught and let the wildlife lead her to her breakfast, and she would move about assured from the words of his Psalter that God knew everything about her: where she was, her thoughts and feelings, fears, battles, and even how she would escape. The little squirrel motivated her to get out of her cradle and look for food.

She remembered that her father teased her by saying that squirrels were smarter than she was, because they opened their shells without mallets or stones. When she asked how they cracked the shells, he said they really carried their nuts into the holes in trees when no one was looking and cracked them with little hammers that they had hidden there. Daniel and Mother would laugh at her because, when she was younger, she believed all that Father told her.

After roaming around within sight of her little cradle, bending and standing, filling her cloak's deep pockets with nuts and berries in the morning light, she climbed back over the rocks and settled into her leafy bed for a quiet breakfast. The entire day was spent snacking on fresh nuts and berries, sleeping, crying, remembering her family, and watching the curious little squirrel who checked on her occasionally.

When darkness crept in again, she slept soundly to songs of rustling leaves, raspy crickets, and noisy frogs. The air was not as cold as the night before, and so her cape provided enough warmth to keep her comfortable. One of her mother's heavy boots rested on its side serving as a pillow under the hood of her cape. It dawned on her just before falling asleep that if there were croaking frogs, there might be a pond nearby.

She awakened early, unexplainably happy to see sparkling dew on the leaves and to hear birds chirping as they gathered seeds and insects for their hatchlings. She had developed a love of nature because Mother always took her for walks when she was upset, and they would sit and look at the trees and wildflowers. "Trees and flowers have no worries or fears. We can learn from them.

If they could talk, they would tell us to be quiet and stop all our noise. They would tell us, 'Our roots are deep and strong, and the sun is warm.'" Arelia thought about what her mother had said so many times. She was very quiet and took comfort in the warm patches of sunlight that made their way through the leaves. How many times had she walked with her mother and sat quietly listening to the rustling of trees and singing birds? She could hear her mother's reassuring voice. "You will walk through green pastures again."

At a frog's croak, she spent part of the day searching nearby for a pond. Leaving broken branches behind, she found a shallow pool and fell to her knees, filling her cupped hands with thirst-quenching gulps of water. Between finding water and foraging for food, the day passed quickly.

"I know there is a place for me," Arelia said aloud as she settled into her new bed. Both from fear and exhaustion, Arelia rested for another day and night, but the fourth night brought cold rain with crashes of thunder and blasts of lightning that kept her hidden under her cloak, snuggled as close to the protective rocks as she could manage. Thankfully, the morning sky was clear, as if the violent storm had been a dream. She hung her cloak to dry on an overhead branch, but there was nothing she could do to dry her clothes.

Around midday, her cloak was nearly dry, and she had collected enough nuts and berries to fill her pockets and move on. In spite of the rain, or maybe because of it, four days of rest and reflection had renewed her both in mind and body. She continued along the path that had brought her from her home leading to an unknown destination, walking on a carpet of wet leaves, avoiding puddles and patches of mud. She was not nearly as afraid as before her rest; she was hopeful, yet cautious, about the next village.

Had the plague been there, too, or was it there now? Would there be happy children and loving parents? Would there be whole families?

Her thoughts were interrupted by movement off the path in the trees; something big and brown rustled fallen dry leaves in the distance. As quietly as possible, she stepped behind a tree, trying to focus on the strange beast, bending and standing, bending and standing. It was a man who spotted her as he stood. "Hello," he called out. His long dark robe gave him away as a monk from the monastery.

"Hello," was her cautiously happy reply.

"I am gathering nuts. Are you hungry?"

"Yes, very"

"Do not be afraid. I will not bite. Are you alone?"

Her first thought was, *Of course I am not alone*, and then she remembered. "Yes," she replied fighting back tears of both grief and relief.

"Step up. You can come with me. I have bread baking and tea brewing." His smile encouraged her to step forward.

"I am Brother Ambrose, and may I ask who you are?"

"Arelia."

"Arelia, wonderful! You must be hungry."

Brother Ambrose had seen enough people in the woods to not ask why she was alone. He'd heard the same story time and time again from many children and parents who were running from horror to the unknown.

"I am happy to have stumbled upon you. It gets awfully cold and dark out here at night. You must have been caught in the rain last night. It was a frightful storm."

"Yes, I was soaked through last night, and night is not a quiet place in the forest. I have learned that in the last four nights."

Brother Ambrose trudged ahead through the thicket as she followed until they came to a clearing surrounding a large stone wall.

"Come along. We will go inside and find something to eat." Once inside he didn't comment on the dark circles under her eyes, her sunken cheek bones and thin arms, neither the twigs nor leaves in her hair and on her cloak nor her damp skirt. He knew the story only too well. So many who stumbled onto the monastery had been out for much more than four nights.

After getting her settled at the table near a large oven in the warm kitchen, Brother Ambrose placed a plate with a thick slice of bread and a slathering of butter in front of her. "Let me get you some hot tea, and then you can tell me where you are from if you like."

Arelia was more comfortable than she could remember being in a very long time. Brother Ambrose placed a few more logs on the fire and went about busily preparing tea and warming more bread. She didn't want even the sound of her own voice to disturb the peace.

"Are you here alone?" she asked, noticing the size of the kitchen.

"Almost, now; there used to be about fifty of us before the plague. Most of the priests and brothers went out to help the sick in the villages, and only a few have returned. About twenty of us stayed to be here for travelers who frequent our doors. We have lost all but ten of us now."

"We lost Fr. Jerome, our priest. My parents and baby brother did not even receive last rites. My sister and two brothers were anointed before Fr. Jerome died."

"Arelia." He smiled reassuringly. "I am sure your parents sacrificed for all of you before they passed. God has a very special place for all your family with Him and all those who were called so quickly.

"With the great loss of priest, the Church, too, will suffer for a long while, but we will survive just as you will. Jesus promised us so, although it probably does not seem like it right now. We will all help each other." He smiled.

Arelia blew gently into her cup to cool her tea, fighting back tears.

"There are a few others here who are traveling to find a new place. In fact, we have a young family who has been here only a few days. They have a baby and are getting a good rest before they move on. In a while, I will bring you to a room with a wash basin and let you rest before introducing you. But first, finish your tea and bread. Give your skirt a little time to dry near the fire."

Arelia stood in a small stone room with only a table, a basin, a small chair, and a bed. It was very stark compared to the warmth of her family's hut. Even with that, she was so thankful to be inside, warm and comfortably full from bread and butter. It somehow seemed miraculous, an answered prayer.

Brother Ambrose poured the water he had heated for her into a basin and handed her a small cloth. "Get washed up and then have a little rest. About dusk, I will come back for you to have a little dinner and meet the other guests." As he closed the heavy door behind him, she said a silent prayer of thanksgiving for this caring monk and the safety of the stone walls surrounding her.

Warm, clean water felt wonderful, miraculous. Running her fingers through her hair, she was embarrassed to find it thick with leaves and twigs, realizing that she must be a sight. The bed was hard but safe. She stepped out of her still damp dress and draped it over the chair. Crawling under the covers in only her long chemise, sleep quickly overtook her.

> 10 Even there your hand guides me,
>   your right hand holds me fast.
>
> Psalm 139

CHAPTER 4

Benedictine Monastery

After allowing Arelia a long rest, Brother Ambrose knocked on her door and told her that he would be back to escort her to dinner in ten minutes. It took several knocks, calling her name to wake her from a deep sleep, and then she had no idea where she was when she opened her eyes. He had learned to be very patient with weary-worn travelers fleeing the blight, and so he waited patiently until she responded through the heavy door.

When he returned, she and Brother Ambrose walked down a long hallway where she heard talking and laughing bouncing off stone walls. When she peered into a large dining room, she spied a mother holding a baby and a man talking to a small group of people, sitting at a long table. There were other brothers and two priests among them and several people who appeared much like herself. She wondered if she looked as tired and thin as they did, with recognizable grief lining their faces.

Brother Ambrose announced, "Greetings, everyone. This is Arelia. She has just joined us this morning."

The man who appeared to be the father of the baby stood and extended the first greeting, and one of the priests who was sitting with the group got up to meet her. After their warm welcome, Fr. Clement introduced Arelia to everyone at the table, but none of the names stayed with her. It was too much and too unfamiliar.

Conversation flowed around large bowls of steamy soup filled with potatoes, carrots, onions, and tiny bits of lamb. To all it was the best meal they had had in months. The stories were the same: black blotches, bulbous growths, deep breathless coughs, and then quick death. Tears flowed, knowing looks were exchanged, and deep grief was shared. The night ended with hugs and prayers for peaceful and restful sleep with a better tomorrow.

Crying awoke Arelia the next morning, bringing about dreams of John fruitlessly clinging to life. After splashing cold water on her face and quickly getting dressed, she ventured into the hallway following the cry, which echoed off hard-stone walls, and then she heard the soothing hum of a mother's voice. She found the young family sitting alone in the dining hall near a roaring fire.

"Good morning."

"Hello, Arelia. Please join us. You probably do not remember, but I am Camellia, and this is baby Cornelius, named after his father and grandfather." Cornelius nodded a greeting as Arelia stifled her tears, pushing away images of baby John.

"You seem terribly young to be alone for such a distance. Is anyone with you?"

For the first time, Arelia explained what had happened. She had not spoken of it aloud and in such detail and was almost surprised at her own story. Her voice cracked and broke as she fought off tears of overwhelming grief. Somehow none of it seemed real. Although she was certainly alone, there seemed to be no believable reason in her young mind to be by herself, and the story seemed just that—a story.

"Our stories are like so many others," Camellia said as she offered her a piece of bread, which Arelia gratefully accepted.

"We heard about the sickness about a year ago from gypsies who came through our village. They had come all the way from Italy to escape the disease only to find it here. Actually,"—she smiled with a distant memory—"we had only been married a few weeks when they brought the news. Cornelius was wary of strangers and kept a close watch for anyone who might bring the disease.

"One day a man came up in a wagon filled with grain. Everyone crowded around to buy what he had. Cornelius noticed that he was sweating even though it was a cool day. He suspected a fever. He ran home, and we packed up everything and hid in the woods. It was not long before others started to leave. We had to move deeper into the woods as others came to hide. We have been in the woods over a year now. It has not been easy, but we are alive. Cornelius delivered our baby himself," she explained, smiling at her cooing son.

31

Cornelius cut in, "Our parents were devastated when we told them of our plan to move into the woods at the first sign of the sickness. We were leaving our families, but I would not risk losing my new wife and the family I knew we would have one day. No matter how we tried to persuade them, none of them left with us."

Tears fell as Camellia explained, "It was the hardest thing either of us have ever done in our lives."

"We watched the road. As travelers picked up to return home, we heard that the sickness had run its course, and so we lived on the outskirts of our village until there were no more cremations or burials. We moved back into our old hut but decided to move on soon after. Only Camellia's grandmother had survived. It was too sad without all the family and neighbors we had known."

"My grandmother refused to come with us. She stayed behind to help other families." Camellia took a deep, calming breath. "I understand, but I wish she had come with us."

She continued, "It was only a few days ago that we thought it safe enough to come here. We plan to move on soon. Cornelius believes it is safe to settle somewhere. He is a carpenter but plans to also tend and shear sheep. We are looking for a place where he can do that. Brother Ambrose is giving us a few sheep to get started."

"And where are you headed?"

The question caught Arelia off guard. "I do not know." Camellia patted her hand, wanting to sooth away Arelia's wrinkled brow.

"I am sorry. It took Cornelius and me months to decide what to do. It seems that this is all new for you."

"Yes, I left only days ago."

"Not to worry. There will be a place for you."

Camellia, the baby, and Arelia spent most of the morning together in the large dining hall, playing with baby Cornelius while Cornelius went to offer his assistance wherever needed. Brother Ambrose recruited Arelia to help in the kitchen for a few hours while the baby had a late morning nap.

Brother Ambrose proudly introduced her to Brother Thomas, who ran the kitchen and planned wholesome meals with care and precision. She actually enjoyed her time peeling potatoes, washing turnips, and cracking nuts. It was familiar work that made life feel almost normal. Soon she caught herself singing familiar hymns along with the brothers and a few women as they prepared dinner.

Over a dinner of fresh baked nut bread, turnips, and shepherd's pie, Brother Thomas explained that they were accustomed to having travelers regularly stay at the Benedictine monastery. Lords often found lodging in the city to be unseemly and not always safe for ladies. Priests and brothers provided secure lodging for the ladies at the monastery—good food, wine, and ale. Even more than hospitality, their greatest treasure was the library with a huge collection of books that had been copied and preserved for the ages. Many learned men frequented the library, borrowing a book or two to return them only for the opportunity borrow other writings. Many lively debates and discussions had taken place around the dinner table with priests, monks, and their visitors. The brothers appreciated travelers' payments, which provided more to share with tenant farmers, often being the main source of help to families nearby. In addition to temporal assistance, many tenants walked miles to celebrate Mass and hear Scripture with these holy men. Both commoners and aristocrats often came for cures for both physical and spiritual ailments. The monastery served as a source of hospitality, care and healing, learning, lively discussion among scholars, and prayer. "But now, with the plague, lords and ladies are not venturing out of their estates nor allowing others in, and so the monastery is a refuge for all who need rest, healing, food and prayer—people such as yourself."

"You have a collection of books here?" Arelia asked, interrupting Brother Thomas's description of life in the monastery.

He laughed at the sudden change of topic. "Yes, a real library. It took years of painstaking work to amass the books we have here." He laughed at such enthusiasm coming from a young girl. "Before duty called me to the kitchen, I was librarian in charge of collecting, copying scrolls, organizing works, and preserving books and scrolls. I spend most of my time away from the kitchen in the library or in our chapel. Come, I will show you.

"Can you read?" he asked after clearing the table and then walking around the courtyard to the library.

"Yes, Fr. Jerome taught all the children in our village to read from the

Scriptures. May I go back to my room on the way to the library? I have something to show you!"

Arelia handed Brother Thomas her father's psalm book as soon as she stepped out of her room.

"Young lady, this is a treasure! Where did you get it?"

"My father copied it from a psalm book that Fr. Jerome had. He spent almost every night for nearly a year with an ink well and a candle. Mother sometimes had to wake him to go to bed because he had fallen asleep. Sometimes, he was forced to stop to wait for the peddler to bring more paper and ink from London." He carefully turned the pages, too interested to continue toward the library.

"Well, you hold on to this and make use of the beautiful words which your father has left for you. These words are hundreds, and some even thousands, of years old and have helped people who have suffered throughout time just as you are now." He continued turning the pages. "Your father did painstaking work with this. It is rare to see this quality of workmanship. The care he took indicates his love of the text recorded."

"Yes. It is now a gift to me, which I keep safely wrapped and tucked deep in the pocket of my cape."

"You must keep it safe." He studied the pages a little longer before continuing down the hall. "Now, let me show you some of our treasures."

He opened a large wooden door at the end of a long corridor, revealing an amazing sight. Arelia took a step back and gasped. "I have never seen anything like this. My Father would sit here for hours if he knew all these books were here."

"Yes, indeed. That is why so many learned gentlemen come from miles around. Some have even gifted a volume or two."

"You must have a hundred volumes."

"Well, young lady, that is a relatively good guess. Just under one hundred at this point." He pulled a volume from the shelf. "I think I will enjoy a few pages of this tome that I have been trying to make my way through. Take a while and look through any of the books you would like." He settled into a straight-backed chair and rested the book on a long table to read.

"You did all this?!" Arelia interrupted.

Brother Thomas laughed. "Absolutely not! At the peak of our days here, we had ten scribes and even copied entire Bibles for kings and princes. It took years for one Bible. Only three scribes remained before the sickness. They left to minister to the sick and to give the final anointing. Of all the priests and brothers who left, none have returned." He turned his teary eyes back to his book.

As Arelia walked slowly before the bookshelf reading titles, she wondered if this was the same monastery where her father had gone to buy sheep, and if he had ever seen this same library during his trips. He had often stayed a night or two; had he sat at this same table reading?

Brother Thomas occasionally looked up from his book, inspired by Arelia's obvious love of books and learning. A thought struck him.

"Arelia, may I ask you a question?"

"Yes, of course, although I have tired of telling my story."

"No, it is not about your story, rather it is about your present condition."

She wrinkled her brow in response.

"You are different from the others. Although you have experienced the same horrors in your life, you do not seem to have the same sense of despair and hopelessness. You are young and alone and yet you seem to still have a ray of hope. You even smile occasionally."

She smiled.

"There you are, a smile. Do you have hope?"

"There is always hope. Is that not right?"

"Yes, of course, but not many people can hold on to hopeful thoughts and feelings through such difficult times. You seem to. Do you know why?"

The question seemed to puzzle her. Brother Thomas waited while she pondered her response. "God. Jesus."

Brother closed his eyes and tilted his head back. The name seemed to resonate among the volumes lining the shelves.

"Yes, God, Jesus," he repeated. "And how have you come about such a strong faith after all your sorrows?"

"Father Jerome's favorite season was Lent and Easter. He brought us to understand how deeply Jesus was persecuted and suffered for us. What struck my family is a sickness; no person turned against me like they did Jesus. Easter proved the true strength and purpose of God. He will not forsake me, even though it seems like it now. I read verse ten of Psalm 139 from my father's book. It tells me, 'Even there your hand guides me, your right hand holds me fast.' I believe that God guided me into the woods where Brother Ambrose found me."

"Arelia, please keep your faith no matter what happens to you and hang on to hope. You have inspired me."

"Brother Thomas, I do not know all my mother and father experienced, but I think that my father had hard times. He shared a psalm with us every night and told us that we need to memorize them as best we could because the words would help us through hard times. I suspect that is the reason he spent months and months writing this book." She smiled a wistful smile. "I have it now. It is from him."

"I have a verse or two for you which I am sure you know from Psalm 22." Brother Thomas recited the well-known passage.

> I   2   My God, my God, why have you
> abandoned me?
> Why so far from my call for help,
> from my cries of anguish?

"Because your Fr. Jerome's favorite season was Lent and Easter, you are probably familiar with that verse?"

Arelia smiled as though she had passed a test. "Yes. Fr. Jerome surprised all of us with that verse. He explained that the Jewish people memorized the Psalms as poetry but mostly as songs."

"That is correct."

"He told us that Jesus was so crafty that he knew the Jews who were responsible for his death would hear the first line of the verse and know that Jesus was proclaiming His victory over them, not to mention that He pointed out their sin." Arelia smiled. "Fr. Jerome said that even at the end, Jesus was outsmarting them by teaching and telling them who He was."

"Yes, and He used Scripture to do it. We forget that Jesus was not only divine, but He was a person, and one smart person at that!" Brother Thomas smiled. "I can only imagine how angry, or maybe frightened, they were when the rest of the psalm continued in their minds. The Romans likely heard only words of despair, but the learned Jews knew exactly what He was telling them."

Arelia was so refreshed by talking about Jesus and the Psalms as Fr. Jerome and her father had done. There were many times when she had sat on the steps of the porch, listening to the two men share ideas about Scripture.

Brother Thomas picked up his book as Arelia walked along the shelves reading titles of the volumes. Even many titles were beyond her understanding. She wondered what treasures rested within their covers and who had shared their ideas. *My father would have loved these books and discussion with Brother Thomas*, she thought.

After a few days, Camellia offered Arelia the opportunity for company walking to the next village. It was only now that they felt safe enough to settle into a community of people again. After having rested with plenty of good food and a comfortable place to sleep, even baby Cornelius seemed strong enough to travel. For the previous few months of living in the woods and only seeing people pass through, Camellia marveled that most people were overwhelmingly generous with what little they had, and they were most appreciative, especially to the monks for giving them substantial food a place to sleep.

Realizing that she couldn't stay at the monastery forever, Arelia accepted their offer to walk with them to the closest village, thinking that there might be a family who would need her help.

They planned to leave early the next morning, but before a hearty breakfast, Fr. Clement offered Mass for their lives which were spared, for safe travels, and that they quickly find the perfect village. All the families gathered for the familiar liturgy shared in each of their villages. Beautiful Scripture passages spoke of strength through suffering and salvation through the cross. Fr. Clement explained that Jesus Himself understood suffering better than anyone, and that His love and redeeming grace would carry them forward. During the Eucharistic Prayers, the familiar Latin words soothed and calmed her in body, mind, and spirit.

Pater Noster . . .

Sanctus, sanctus, sanctus . . .

Agnus Dei, qui tolis peccata mundi, Miserere nobis.
Agnus Dei, qui tolis peccata mundi, Miserere nobis.
Agnus Dei, qui tolis peccata mundi,
Dona nobis pacem.

After Communion she became aware that baby Cornelius had fallen asleep against Camellia's breast, and she was deep in prayer, feeling the same sense of healing grace that Arelia felt. Oddly, Camellia held a hint of a smile. Arelia realized that they were not just joined by common suffering but also by common faith. With the death of so many priests, she wondered how long it would be before she had the opportunity to receive Communion again. She glanced around at the few people in the pews who had survived the plague. Most knelt with eyes closed; she closed her eyes, resting in the peace which surrounded her, experiencing a strange sensation which almost felt like joy. *Jesus, I trust You.*

Breakfast of eggs, cheese, and hard bread followed. As they gathered to leave, Fr. Clement led them in an Our Father and Angelic Salutation.

Those guests remaining at the monastery followed them out as the monks packed their cart with supplies. Brother Ambrose led a nursing sheep and her lamb out to Cornelius, encouraging him to start his own herd. It was a loving send off, unlike when she had stolen away from her village.

As they walked along together, Camellia explained that Cornelius had been an apprentice carpenter to his uncle. He had learned his trade well and was beginning to work on his own. Camellia cared for the baby and helped Cornelius by sweeping the work area and carrying wood. They were hoping the next village would be a good place to work his trade. The monks had told them that it was spared the worst of the devastation and was growing in population, and so people there could probably use a good carpenter. The sheep would offer a livelihood, just in case.

Arelia felt comfortable traveling with Cornelius and Camellia and enjoyed playing with the baby along the way. While at the monastery, Cornelius had built a sturdy cart to carry baby Cornelius and their few possessions, along with bread and cheese that the monks had provided. Camellia and Arelia took turns sitting in the cart to rest while Cornelius pulled almost untiringly with the sheep ambling along behind.

It wasn't long before they saw newly thatched roofs and wisps of smoke rising from well-worn chimneys. Arelia was excited as they approached the familiar setting of a village and saw children playing happily while mothers worked outside their huts. A number of men were tilling and planting in a large clearing away from the huts. Dogs ran among the children, barking for attention. It was like a memory come alive. The sights and smells of new thatch, tilled soil, and activity spoke of hope.

"Arelia, what will you do now that we are in the village?" asked Cornelius.

"I will find a place," she replied hesitantly, thinking that she would really find some place in the nearby woods.

"Baby Cornelius really likes you," said Camellia. "You could be a great help to Cornelius and me if you would stay with us for a while. You can help me with the house and baby, and that will give me more time to help Cornelius get set up." It did not take Arelia any time to accept their generous invitation. She was embarrassed by her tears of relief, but Camellia reassured that she understood with a hug.

Many of the women in the village approached them to get news from other villages. Other travelers at the monastery had provided information that seemed to satisfy the most curious. The plague had passed through their village many months earlier, but they seemed to have been spared the toll that many other villages had suffered. Only a few of the huts were empty, needing repair. Unlike other villages, in order to stop the spread of the plight, these people had burned huts of those left empty after entire families had died. They expected that as other people came, they might need to rebuild what they had burned. One of the women took Cornelius to meet the men in the field while the others stayed to hear the tragic news from Camellia and Arelia of what other villages had experienced. The story was the same from village to village, but gratefully, theirs seemed to have been spared the worst of it.

Arelia watched as Cornelius walked toward the field. She recognized the familiar mounds of fresh graves, which remained as a cruel reminder of the killer that had passed through. The square was dotted with black ground and ashes that marked the places of huts that had been burned to rid them of the sickness.

Within a short time, Cornelius returned, walking into the few empty huts which remained from families who had fled. She watched him approach with a smile on his face and got excited about the prospect of a new home. She would no longer be alone.

Arelia and Camellia spent the short time before dark sweeping out a dusty hut that was left vacant by a family who had gone into the woods to hide from the plague and had never returned. They unloaded their few possessions. One of the men in the village brought wood for the stove, another brought hay for the beds, and several women brought gifts of bread and cheese. The mood was warm and welcoming for the travel-worn strangers.

Once Cornelius lit the stove, the room of the tiny hut took on a warm, familiar glow. Arelia lay peacefully on a small cot. Sleep came quickly yet gently; there were no dreams to interrupt her sleep this night. She had finally found her place.

CHAPTER 5

Hamptonshire, Norwich County

Thankfully for everyone, months passed uneventfully with no sign of illness or fear of abandonment. Arelia found the villagers friendly and helpful. Everyone had lost friends and family, and so they were happy to have a new family join them. The women were especially kind to Arelia. In some ways, she replaced the daughters many had lost.

As baby Cornelius began to walk and make sounds that resembled words, Arelia found herself playing with him and remembering John almost constantly. So many things about him were the same. She seemed to absentmindedly call him John as often as she called him Cornelius. Camellia frequently heard the mistake but never corrected her error. Baby Cornelius began to fill the void that baby John had left.

Laughter returned to her life as she and Camellia shared stories of their childhood antics and memories of kinder times. Light and hope returned to Arelia's experience-wise eyes, and color returned to her pale cheeks. Camellia was only four years older than Arelia and not far removed from playing chase and kickball in their village clearing. On more than one occasion, Cornelius demanded that the two young women stop their chattering and giggles so that he could get some sleep before sunup. He affectionately called them the "Ellias," a name that caught on in the small village.

But giggles hadn't come first for the *Ellias*. Many afternoons, during little Cornelius's nap-time, many tears were shed over memories of what was lost.

"In some ways it was easier for me than most," Camellia began one day. "I was a new bride with new hopes and dreams that were not about my parents and sisters and brothers. There were six of us. Two of my older sisters and one brother were already married, and so only my two brothers were left with Mother and Father. Mother had been sick on and off for several years and had almost died before.

She had received Last Rites twice and then recovered. Father and the boys spent most of their time with the crops or the sheep. Her sister was a widow with three married children, and so she spent most days with my mother. My grandmother was still alive, and so the three ladies took care of the families together.

"I felt guilty leaving Mother when we got married, but she would not tolerate worry and guilt. She encouraged me to make my own home and start my own family without concern for her. It seems strange now, but at the time, moving into the woods just seemed like another move after getting married." She laughed softly. "I think Cornelius could have led me into the ocean. All I could think about at the time was him.

"When we went back, my mother had died, and Father and my younger brothers had left shortly after. No one knew where they went. One of my sisters had gone into the woods with her family and never returned. After my oldest sister died, her husband and little son left. Cornelius said that we would go back one day and see if they had returned. I suspect that will never happen."

Her voice cracked as she dabbed a solitary tear. "One day, as we were moving farther into the woods, we smelled the stench of something dead. I stayed back, but Cornelius walked a little closer. He did not know for sure but thought there were two or three bodies. We went in the opposite direction." She covered her face for a minute and then wiped her eyes with the back of her hand. "Ever since I heard my father and brothers had left, I have wondered if it was them. . . . I can still smell the rotting bodies."

Cornelius's story was different but with the same sense of loss. One rainy day, sitting around the fire with a cup of tea, Cornelius shared his story. "We had four brothers in our family with one sister." He laughed. "And did we give my poor mother a time!"

"Your mother was perfectly capable of handling every one of you," Camellia said in awe of the woman who raised him.

Cornelius laughed even harder. "There is no doubt about that, but we did our best to outwit her.

"Our father died of the croup when I was just five. I had two older broth-ers, one younger, and a baby sister. My little sister died of the croup, too. My oldest brother was ten and pretty much took over, along with Mother's brother who lived next door. My uncle and his wife never had children, and so we pretty much moved between their home and ours." He laughed again. "It made Mother's life a little easier, and it was fun for us. We could go off for hours, and they would just think we were next door." Laughter bubbled up from deep inside. "Did we have fun times!

"Anyway, when I turned twelve, my uncle asked my mother if he could take me on as an apprentice carpenter. He actually sold furniture to other fam-ilies, and a couple of times, a traveling salesman bought chairs to sell along the way. He was developing quite a reputation and more requests were coming in—so many he could not keep up. That is what I was doing when we got mar-ried. Shortly after, we heard about the plague.

"A few days later, I knew we had to leave. I had lost my father and sister to the croup, and I was not going to lose my wife." He stared into the fire for a long time. Arelia refilled their teacups and stoked the waning embers. He looked at Camellia with tear-filled eyes. "I was young and impulsive. I did not even try to convince my mother to go with us. I just left her. I did not understand how serious it would be. Both my brothers were married, and I just left her. God, forgive me." He cried. Camellia walked over to him and cradled his head against her.

He took a deep breath and exhaled heavily. "My brother said she lingered for two months, taking care of my grandmother and uncle before they died. It was probably harder because she was so strong." About that time, little Cor-nelius started to stir from his nap, giving Arelia a chance to go outside and give the couple time alone.

Because Cornelius and Camellia were more like friends than parents, Are-lia felt that she was becoming more of a woman than a child. Late one evening she complained to Camellia about a pain and small knot in her breast. Camellia just laughed and hugged her saying, "Not to worry, you are becoming a woman now." That was both an exciting and scary revelation. Arelia knew that she was only months into her thirteenth year with adulthood soon to follow.

She was not sure she was ready to give up her childhood. She felt so much of it had been taken from her. She had had only a few months to play with other children in the village since their arrival and was enjoying her childlike freedom. Every afternoon when Cornelius took his nap, Arelia would leave the hut to give Cornelius and Camellia time to themselves. Kickball was a favorite with all the children, but Arelia most enjoyed long walks exploring the terrain around the village. She'd found a shallow cave with signs of some kind of animal living there. Gilbert, a fifteen-year-old who had become her friend, and his little sister often accompanied her on her explorations.

After one particular search which revealed no new discoveries, Arelia and her new friends sat on a rock outcropping and watched a herd of sheep graze in a nearby field. No one talked as private thoughts and memories played on their minds. A silent tear of relief fell as Arelia realized that she, in fact, was walking in green pastures, no longer alone. She visualized little Cornelius, asleep in his cradle, and Camellia possibly cutting potatoes for stew. This was her family now—somehow, she had found a family, or rather, a family had found her. She had many days like this—normal, happy.

Travelers passing through town brought news of areas that had nearly been destroyed by the plague. Many of these people were relocating because only a few people in their village remained, and they needed others in order to survive. Their lives depended on it. Empty huts in the village were soon filled with newcomers just as Arelia, Cornelius, and Camellia had filled theirs. More travelers stayed, and new huts were built. Cornelius was busy with new construction from sun-up until dark, while the Ellias tended the garden and the sheep, cared for little Cornelius, prepared meals, washed clothes, hauled water, swept the hut, and help Cornelius when necessary. Life was busy, fun, and completely normal at last.

Along with people passing through came news from other areas. A growing concern in the wooded areas was that wild dogs that had taken up with wolves. These animals had been left by families who had died or by those who could no longer care for them. Many dogs had taken to the woods for food and joined packs of wolves. The dogs, being familiar with people, would venture near the village at night, often killing chickens and sheep. Some wolves had begun to come nearer too. None of the feral animals had actually come into their village, but many travelers had encountered them in the nearby woods. There were many stories about near-fatal attacks.

Other stories surfaced of women begging for food with no family to care for them and of children found dead along wooded paths from hunger or wild-animal attacks. Some told of entire villages that were ghost towns with not a soul in sight. One family reported that a monastery had only one monk left who had given away the sheep, cows, chickens, and farm equipment to needy villages. Churches were without a priest and unkept. A common tale was of people still hiding in the woods with no intention of coming out. Robbers and vandals were the order of the day in some wooded areas. The news was not good outside of the village.

Christmas was a real celebration for the entire village intent on celebrating the birth of Jesus. There were whispers of Christmas lost in the tragedy of the year before, missing people at the table, and the scarcity of traditional foods, but those who had survived the plague were determined to revive the tradition for children and adults alike.

Cornelius and several other men brought in a tree to decorate with nuts and berries. They placed it in the clearing surrounded by huts. A large pit was dug for a yule log where they gathered every evening to share stories of St. Nicholas and the story of Mary, Joseph, and the birth of Jesus.

Each family brought a special dish with the few ingredients available to them. Potatoes, carrots, and eggs were plentiful, but the biggest treat was the two large geese roasted with turnip roots and onion. There were different variations of plum pudding, without the raisins, but all were delicious.

It wasn't exactly as Arelia remembered, but the stories, fire, delicious food, and family filled the crack in her broken heart.

One rare, bright, sunshiny, spring morning, Arelia and several children decided to gather berries, herbs, and wild onions. Their parents cautioned them to be aware of the wild dogs and robbers and sent two of the older boys along carrying spears for protection. Excitement over warm weather and adventure beyond the first row of trees made the children throw caution to the wind.

Arelia was as excited to explore the woods as she had been with Daniel and Marcus, but she also looked forward to time to herself as she had with her mother when they listened to the quiet chatter of animals, flowers, and trees. She remembered how healing her time in the leafy cradle had been before she met Brother Ambrose, and she longed for a few minutes of time alone with nature. Since the day she met Cornelius and Camellia, she had not had much alone time to remember her family. Memories were still painful, but today she wanted time to think of her family and to talk to them without anyone hearing. She tucked her father's Psalter into her cape, hoping to have time with her favorite passages.

She would tell them all that had happened since she was alone in the world. She would tell them how afraid she was that she would have to live with Mr. Honeycutt and about why she ran away. She would tell them about the healing time in the woods and about Brother Ambrose taking her to the monastery for rest and, more importantly, for food. She would describe the library in the monastery with nearly a hundred books. She would tell them about her new friends, Cornelius, Camellia. She would tell them about little Cornelius. She would tell them about the psalms she had read.

She would tell them how Cornelius, Camellia, and little Cornelius were beginning to fill the empty places in her heart. She would tell them that she was beginning to laugh again, and that she did not cry as often anymore. As she walked into the woods with the other children, she knew she would have a lot to say.

"Where is Arelia?" she heard the boys calling from a distance. Gilbert's voice was most clear.

She had walked farther than she realized, lost in her thoughts and distracted by the beauty of a variety of green buds popping through bare branches and fallen leaves. With a late and unexpected storm brewing, it would probably turn cold again soon, delaying the bloom of wildflowers and tender leaves just starting to bud. As the wind picked up, clouds blocked the warm sun. Squirrels gathering nuts for the next cold snap took to the trees to crack them open with their little hammers before the rain began to fall.

She moved away from their calls because she felt the need to pass water. As she squatted near a rock to relieve herself, she noticed a smear of blood on her leg. She had not cut herself and wondered why she was bleeding.

Could this be the blood that Camellia said women have that comes and goes with the moon? Does this mean I truly am a woman now? Her mind raced with questions that she would ask Camellia when she got back to the village.

Distracted by blood and the possibility of more unfamiliar womanly changes, Arelia walked a short distance before realizing she had lost her direction. Billowing clouds blocked the sun, as she turned from one direction to another unable to determine which way to go, nor could she hear the other children through the wind in the leaves no matter how hard she strained. A small clearing in the distance caught her attention. Hoping to get a better look at the sun, she pulled her cape around her face and shoulders to block out the chill as a whirlwind coaxed a cluster of leaves playfully around her feet.

Just as the rising wind announced approaching rain, she heard a low growling noise and turned to see a pack of wolves and wild dogs with backs arched and teeth bared staring at her. She wanted to run but remembered Daniel yelling at Marcus to stay still as a stray wolf watched him.

The blood. They smell the blood. Her mind raced with fear. Terrified, she ran toward the lowest branch of a tree. As she jumped, the lead dog grabbed her heavy boot in his teeth and pulled furiously. She was able to kick him with her other foot as she screamed for help. Another dog grabbed at her long skirt, ripping the hem and nearly pulling her from the limb. Her long cloak fell to the ground. She could not get a good grip of the branch and fought not to lose her hold. She screamed over and over, calling to the boys for help. Her plea was carried away in the wind as the children ran back to the village, hoping to beat the rain.

The wolves and wild dogs leapt higher, catching her skirt and ripping it with each jump. She tried to wrap her legs around the branch but would nearly lose her grip each time they tugged at her skirt. Her arms grew tired as she struggled to lift her weight from the jaws of the hungry animals below. A warm trickle of blood flowed slowly down from her hands torn by the rough bark of the tree, and she could feel a warm trickle of blood flowing down her leg. As she lost her grasp of the branch that cut into her flesh, she felt sharp, savage teeth tear into the flesh of her leg. Only one animal attacked her when she landed with a thud on her back while the others stood back growling and barking.

She kicked furiously with her hard boot, aiming at the dog's nose. She managed to get to her feet and jumped, trying to grab the branch with both hands again, but she lost her footing and fell to the ground. She continued to kick at the wild animals, but each time she missed, one would catch her bleeding flesh. She sat up hoping to run onto an outcropping of rocks.

Suddenly a scraggly wolf leapt into the air, aiming for her throat. As she saw him fly toward her, an arrow pierced him in the chest. He yelped and fell heavy and hard on her trembling body. The other wolves and wild dogs quickly ran into the woods, yelping and barking as they ran. Warm blood formed a pool on her stomach, soaking though her dress. When she tried to get to her feet, the weight of the wolf stopped her, and she could not stand from the pain in her torn legs.

A voice from the woods called out, "Stay down. Do not move." She did not recognize the voice and was startled to see two men running into the clearing. They were right out of her father's stories. *I must be dreaming a very bad dream.*

Her surprise was outdone only by the pain from her wounded legs, and sobs kept her from speaking. The first warrior that reached her, seeing her exposed legs, covered her with his surcoat and then her cloak for warmth.

"Lie still and do not move. The wolves are gone now and will not come back." *This seems so real,* she thought.

The two men quickly began to cut long, thick branches. They took their tunics, ripped them, and devised a pallet on which to place her pained body, lifting her carefully onto the pallet, avoiding her open wounds. The sky had turned dark, as did her world.

CHAPTER 6

Soldiers' Camp
Faircastle, Norwich County

 It was dark when the soldiers returned to camp. Many of the men gathered around to see what the two were carrying on the pallet. They were surprised to see a young, battered woman.

"Men, who is this girl?" demanded their officer.

"She was attacked by wolves and wild dogs in a clearing just over the ridge. We frightened them away but could not leave her there. They would have killed her. Her legs have several serious bites that need bandages. We tied off her leg, but she is still losing blood."

"Bring her into my tent and lay her on the cot. Donald will bandage her legs."

As two young knights gently lifted Arelia from the pallet, her metal amulet reflected the light from the fire.

"What is this medal?" the officer asked, approaching the girl. "This is the Fairchild emblem. How did she get it, and why is she here? I have never seen her, but we need to bring her back with us. They will be happy that we found her."

Intense pain and loss of blood brought Arelia in and out of consciousness. Donald washed and bandaged the wounds on her legs and hands and wrapped her loosely in warm blankets. Her eyes moved rapidly under closed lids from the pain of torn flesh and from trauma. Frightening images shattered her mind: fire, graves, snarling animals, dead, bloated bodies, shrieking babies—all images of her short past. She yelled out occasionally until he gave her a potion for pain.

At first light, Arelia opened her eyes to see that she was in a small, stuffy tent. She could not remember where she was or how she had gotten there and wondered if she was still dreaming. Feeling pain in her legs and hands brought the memory of the animal attack. Checking her legs, she could see tightly wrapped bandages and several bruises, scratches, and cuts. Her wrapped hands throbbed as she tried to touch her aching legs.

She remembered the attack and calling for the boys, but she didn't know how she had come to be in a tent. *Where would Cornelius have gotten a tent, and why did I not stay in the hut so Camellia could tend to me?* Unfamiliar voices approaching the tent frightened her. *Who are these men? What will they do to me?*

Memories came back—the wolf lunging and being struck by an arrow with two soldiers running toward her. They would surely bring her back to the village.

"What is your name, young woman?" the officer asked.

"Arelia, sir." Fear and confusion overwhelmed her. She studied the chain mail covering his chest and remembered her father's description of the knights in his stories.

"I see that you possess an amulet," he replied.

Arelia thought the comment strange but was too confused and pained to be concerned. *How would he know?*

"How is it that you were in the woods alone, Arelia?" he questioned.

"I got separated from my friends and lost my direction. I was trying to find my way, but they must have gone without me."

"Well, young lady, we will return you to your family. We leave shortly and will be there by nightfall."

Arelia didn't realize that she had wandered so far. Maybe the men had carried her a long way on horses throughout the night to reach their camp. She didn't have the energy to explain that her family was gone, and she was with Camellia and Cornelius now.

"I am very appreciative of the transport, sir. I am afraid I would be unable to walk."

"The men have made you a sturdier pallet so you will not have to walk. We have a mild potion for pain that will help you bear the journey and allow you to sleep." When the officer left the tent, a somewhat familiar man entered. He was also dressed in chain mail over his tunic, but his reached to his knees.

"My lady, drink this potion, and I will help you to your pallet. It will be better for you if you do not feel pain so you can sleep. It could be a very painful journey for you."

"Do I know you, sir?" Arelia asked.

"I found you in the woods and brought you here," he replied.

"If I do not see you again, I want to thank you for your bravery," Arelia said.

"Let me take you to your pallet now." The young man seemed embarrassed as he gently lifted her from the cot and carried her to the pallet outside the tent. He didn't speak again, and once he got her settled and covered her snuggly with blankets and her cloak, he left quickly. He carefully placed her father's worn book beside her.

The wolves—was it knights or angels who stopped the wolves? She was very groggy now. She was aware of horses and men—mumbling and shuffling around in the distance. *This must all be a dream. Baby John will cry soon, and I will awaken. I must be there for John.*

There was a sound of women's voices in a distant place. "She is very pretty."

"She certainly does not look like royalty."

"She is very thin."

"She is dressed like a commoner."

"Her wounds are deep."

"Bring me hot water and that rag."

"She needs a pain potion and clean sleeping gown."

Another dream.

Arelia opened her eyes slowly to yet more unfamiliar surroundings—large stone walls and log beams held aloft a high wood ceiling. Brightly colored rugs made into pictures hung on tall, whitewashed walls. Large dark-wood furniture tried to fill an immense room. A breeze blew through a large open window near a raging fire. Women were talking quietly in the corner, sewing.

"Oh, look, she is awake," said one of the women. "Arelia, are you in pain?" the woman asked as she walked toward her bed. She turned toward her young friend. "Tell Sir Daniel the girl is awake and bring me some clove oil to help numb the pain."

Arelia looked at the lovely older woman. Her graying hair was pulled into a tight knot away from her face, but soft wisps of gray escaped the knot and gentle curls softened the austere style. She was not much taller than Arelia herself and slightly plump, especially for a woman fighting the plague. Her crystal-blue eyes gave her the appearance of being too naïve and gentle to handle the difficult task at hand.

"Yes, madam, I am in some pain. Where am I?"

"You can rest now, my child. You are at Faircastle. Sir Daniel will be here with you shortly."

Faircastle? Why would I be in a castle? I cannot be in a castle. This must be a dream.

"Is this a *castle*?"

"No." She laughed. "Kings live in castles. I have never been in a castle, but I understand they are very large."

"This is very large."

"Yes." She smiled. "I guess you could say it is a castle, a small one, but not as big as where King Edward III lives. *Lord* Daniel lives here. He is a lord, not a king.

"Sir Daniel's castle has only two towers," she continued.

"Towers?"

"Yes, to look out to see if enemy is approaching."

Enemy. I must be dreaming. She closed her eyes briefly and then opened them again, but she was in the same place.

As Arelia looked around the room she was reminded of her father's stories. Knights, women dressed in lovely fabric, large rooms made with heavy stones rather than logs and thatch. *Did the dogs kill me, and now I am living in some sort of fantasyland? What am I doing here?*

A tall, stately man opened a door across the room and started toward her. In spite of her pain, Arelia jumped up. "Father!" As he came closer with an inquiring look on his face, she saw that she was mistaken—or was she? His hair was lighter than her father's and graying at the temple. His nose was long and his jaw narrow, just as her father's, and his eyes seemed to see right through her as she had experienced so many times as a child. The man appeared to be her father but older and dressed in odd-looking stockings, trousers, and a pleated surcoat. *Had the sickness changed him? No—the fire? Is he in heaven? Am I?*

"I am sorry to have startled you, young lady. You were hoping for your father?"

"I was mistaken, sire; my father is dead. Can you tell me why I am here?" Arelia asked, grimacing with pain as she sat back onto the bed.

"Do I understand that Arelia is your name?" He extended his hand to help her as she slid back onto the tapestry pillow propped against a massive wooden headboard.

"Yes, sire." Even talking was exhausting.

"Is this amulet yours, Arelia?" He opened his hand and gave Arelia the amulet her mother had placed on John. She had not even realized that it was no longer around her neck. She felt her chest and, not finding the disk, answered, "Yes, thank you, sire. It is mine," she said as she slipped it around her neck.

"Can you tell me how you have come by it, child?"

Arelia explained, "This is the amulet of my father's family. My father and mother died in the plague. Before my mother died, she put the amulet around my baby brother's neck to identify him as my father's son. When he died, I kept it for myself, as it is all I have left of my family. Please forgive me, sire, if it is improper for a girl like me to wear it."

The man seemed to have tears in his eyes. "No, child, if it was your father's, you should wear it proudly. Rest now. I will return shortly."

Arelia watched as the man left, downcast. She was surprised that her story would bring him to tears. *Did he really look like my father, or do I miss him so desperately that the potion made me see him?*

Arelia lay back in the huge, dark-wood bed and closed her eyes. She wanted to shut out all the confusion she was feeling. *Why was I brought here? Where am I? Who are these people? Why did the man have my amulet and be brought to tears? Where are Camellia and baby Cornelius?* Nothing could stop her thoughts. All of her questions were unanswered.

She dozed on and off until the door opened again. The old man walked in with a younger man who seemed very upset.

"Arelia, this is my son, Edward. This is now his home, and he wanted to meet you."

Confused by her previous conversation, Arelia asked, "Are you King Edward?"

Sir Daniel laughed. "No, Arelia, this is my son Edward."

"Thank you, Sir Edward, for letting me stay until Cornelius comes for me," Arelia replied.

"And who is Cornelius?" asked Sir Edward, his blue-grey eyes focused, as if the answer were very important.

Arelia explained her chance meeting with Cornelius and Camellia as briefly as she could.

"Arelia, my father told my wife and me that this amulet belonged to your father. I do not understand how you came to have it and why you are alone," the younger man said somewhat irritably.

For yet another time, Arelia told the story. She was tired of repeating the same details over and over. Everyone here seemed so curious about her history. But, politely, she gave the same account, struggling to get the words out, hoping it be the last time anyone would ask. She couldn't understand why they didn't listen if they were supposedly so interested.

The younger man studied her a moment and then replied, "I find it curious that you have come *here*. What is it you want from *me*?"

"From you, sire?" repeated Arelia. "I want nothing from you, except possibly help getting home."

"To your father?" asked the young man.

"No, sire. I have told you *all* of my family is dead—killed in the plague. My home is now with Cornelius and Camellia."

"What is your father's name, Arelia?"

"The same as yours, sir, Edward."

"And his surname?"

"Davidson, sir."

Edward pressed on, "Who sent you here?"

"Enough!" interrupted Sir Daniel. "Arelia has told you her story. She needs to rest. You are tiring her with your persistent questioning."

The older man continued, leaning toward Arelia, "You must be hungry. Would you like food brought here to you, or would you like to join me for a meal in the dining room?"

"I would like you to join me here, sire, if you do not mind. I am weary from being alone and lying in this bed, but I do not think my legs will carry me."

"Very well, I will send a maid with fresh clothes to help you dress. She will call for me when you are ready." The man seemed genuinely pleased that Arelia had agreed to have dinner with him.

"Father, if you will not be offended, Marisa and I will not be joining you this evening. We will eat lightly and retire early. I am sure you and Arelia will be good company for each other," said Edward curtly.

Arelia noticed that Sir Daniel smiled and thought it strange that he would be pleased that his son and his wife would not be joining them for dinner. Although he had light colored eyes like his father's, Sir Edward's hair was much darker and his complexion almost sickly pale. He was a good three inches shorter than Sir Daniel in both stature and presentation. Their appearances were so different that Arelia would not have guessed they were father and son; their attitudes and manner also seemed to be poles apart.

Shortly after Sir Daniel left, the maid came in with a dress more beautiful than any Arelia had ever imagined, made from soft, fine, deep-green threads. Arelia and her mother had spun wool for most of their dresses and only occasionally traded chickens for other fabric. Even traded fabric was heavy and dull compared to the cloth in this dress.

The maid spoke only when spoken to, and Arelia was relieved that the woman didn't ask any questions so she wouldn't have to tell her story again. Her behavior struck Arelia as strange. She seemed to think Arelia didn't know how to dress herself. She brushed her long dark hair, brought her water and clean clothes, and actually held the dress for Arelia to step into. Back at the village, when Camellia and Arelia had dressed in the mornings, one would bring the water to share, but neither "dressed" the other, and they certainly brushed their own hair. "You are very nice to help me. It is difficult with the bandages, and I feel very weak."

"Yes, my lady," was her simple response.

The maid's dress was similar to Arelia's but made of much simpler fabric. Her tunic seemed new and the wimple, which covered her grey hair, was clean and white. Arelia was relieved to see her mother's heavy cloak draped over a chair. Arelia noticed her dress hanging on a hook on the wall near a very large chest. It was coarse and dull in comparison and covered with splotches of dried blood, and the shape of it was straight—nothing compared to the gathers and overlays in the one that the woman brought for her to wear now. Arelia wondered why this lady would bring her such a beautiful dress and keep such a simple one for herself. Why would she dress like that to eat in her room? Her father never described what the women in his stories wore, but she imagined that this would be the dress fit for a queen or princess.

Once the dress was buttoned, the maid led her to a "looking glass." Arelia was truly startled. She had seen her reflection in a pond or a bucket of water but never on a wall. Even more startling was her appearance. She didn't look like the little girl looking back from the bucket; rather, in that dress, she looked like the ladies she imagined in her father's stories. The deep green was as the dark thick leaves at the tops of the trees but bright as when the sun shined on them. And then she saw her neck and face. She leaned into the mirror, thinking something was on the strange glass, but no, it was her real image. A scratch extended from her chin into the neckline of the dress, and there were several bruises on one side of her face. She leaned away and took in the whole image, a wounded girl with dark straggly hair in an elegant dress. It was mismatched, a contradiction.

The older woman watched Arelia's expression change as she noticed the bruises and ran her fingers along the long scratch. She touched her hair, but when tears formed in her eyes, the maid interrupted, "Arelia, let me knot up your hair. We are not finished yet," she said as she led her to a chair facing a view of the forest. "You can take another look once your hair is done."

"Thank you, but I always do it myself."

"Well, today I do it for you."

It was relaxing to have someone comb and arrange her hair. She closed her eyes and could almost believe that it was her mother who combed her hair as she had done so many times before. The maid would stop occasionally for a second or two and then begin again. Arelia opened her eyes and noticed a little pile of broken leaves and twigs on the table. "What is that?"

The older woman said somewhat sadly, "I am finding bits of the forest in your hair. You must have had a terrible time of it. I am so happy that you are here with us now."

Gentle tears fell down Arelia's pale cheeks as she basked in the love expressed for her. "Now, we are done. Take another look."

Once again she walked to the looking glass but more hesitantly this time. If she looked beyond the bruises and long scratch, she saw something she had never seen before. She gasped at the image before her. Once again, she wondered how her father knew so much about castles and finery. She always thought that he just described pictures from his imagination in a type of fairy-tale. Travelers would pass through with news about knights and battles, but she thought her father had made up the stories to entertain her mother and the children. Looking back from the looking glass was a young woman, dressed as a princess, who appeared to have stepped out of one of his stories. She was very confused, and if she hadn't been in a safe and comfortable place with such nice people, she would have been frightened, but now she was gripped with curiosity.

CHAPTER 7

Arelia turned to the woman. "Are we ready for dinner now?"

The woman looked down quickly and smiled. "I will call for Sir Daniel."

A young woman came in with a cloth and pitcher, followed by two men with large trays of plates and bowls filled to overflowing, Arelia thought how strange it was. She was glad her father had told all the stories, or she would have been sure she had died. No one was supposed to be in pain in heaven, so she determined that she could not be in heaven. Her pain was real. Hell was supposed to be the painful place, but she thought that hell could not hold such beautiful things and caring people, and so she could not be in hell. In either case, she figured that she could not be dead.

Her legs were very sore under the bandages, even with clove oil to soothe them. The rags around her hands showed in sharp contrast to the beautiful gown, but she enjoyed being out of bed, and she especially enjoyed the prospect of company—especially company who reminded her so much of her father. She almost felt she was stepping into one of his stories with him at her side. *Were Father's stories real?*

She could hear an unfamiliar noise coming from the window and asked what it was. The young woman laying the cloth said it was the ocean. *The ocean!* She walked slowly to the window. The old woman joined her and helped her lean slightly out and look into the distance. She saw something startling, which she had never seen. Just to the side of the trees and off a rocky cliff was the ocean, with waves breaking on the rocks. She was startled, having never seen such a wide expanse of water, and she had no idea how she had gotten to its shore. The house was situated on a cliff and provided a view of both the forest and the ocean. When Sir Daniel walked in, he seemed dwarfed in the large room with an ocean outside its window.

She almost shouted, "I have never seen an ocean before. My father spoke of it, but I have never seen it!"

Sir Daniel laughed. "Yes, it is amazing! That is the North Sea. Faircastle is in Norwich County." He walked to the window.

Arelia felt foolish with her childish outburst. She suddenly became shy and felt out of place. She wanted to turn and run back into her warm hut with Cornelius and Camellia.

"Arelia, I am glad you are strong enough to allow me to join you." He seemed genuinely pleased and surprised to see her looking so well. He helped her to a chair, being especially careful of her bandaged hands and legs. Arelia's anxiety melted away as she looked into the face of the man who seemed so familiar. She wanted him to put his arms around her while she cried and then tell him all the horrible things that had happened, hoping that he would tell her that it had all just been a terrible nightmare.

The food, like her dress, was much more elegant than anything she had ever seen. At home she would have had hard bread and a bowl of potherbs, which consisted mainly of cabbage and onions. This evening, she and Sir Daniel feasted on fresh vegetables seasoned with fine herbs, pork and chicken, and beautiful cakes for dessert. It seemed absurd that someone had prepared all this food for only the two of them.

Sir Daniel was very interested in her family, especially her father. She wanted to tell him of their resemblance but thought he might find her silly.

"Where did your father grow up, Arelia?" asked the gentle old man.

"He grew up far from our village, near the ocean. I do not know that he ever told me the name of his village or which ocean," Arelia responded with a slight chill as she looked toward the window.

"Did you ever visit his family when you were younger?" he probed.

"No, sire. We did not have a way to go such a long distance, and we could not leave our crops and chickens. Father said his parents were no longer alive, and so there would be no one to visit. Mother's mother and father lived in our village, but they both died even before the plague."

The rest of the evening was spent talking about Arelia's large family and happy experiences in her childhood. Sir Daniel laughed often at stories about her brothers and sister and said that he had had similar experiences with his brother, who was now dead. He regretted that he had only one son because his son missed out on the fun of brothers and sisters.

Arelia was becoming very tired, but she was enjoying Sir Daniel's company and didn't want him to leave her alone.

"Arelia, I think you should rest now. I am going to meet with my son and his wife early in the morning. I would truly enjoy having lunch with you. There are some things I would like to tell you about myself. I will leave you for now."

Once the dishes were stacked, the tablecloth folded, and the people quietly left her room, the same woman came in to help her undress and get into bed. It seemed strange, but Arelia was glad of it as she needed help getting out of the huge dress, and she certainly enjoyed the company.

As she lay in bed reviewing her evening, once again pain took second place to curiosity and feelings of peace. *It really seems like one of Father's stories. The big stone walls, the good food, the ocean. But Sir Daniel did not say anything about himself.* She fell asleep thinking about Sir Daniel and looking forward to their next meeting when she would hear his story.

Sir Edward and his wife had spent a much different evening. "Do you really believe that this girl is your *cousin?*" Marisa asked.

"Why else would she have the amulet, Marisa?" he responded sarcastically.

"This cannot be true. And now your father is getting to know her. You should have insisted that we join them for dinner." Marisa paced the room like a caged animal.

"Marisa, calm down. He has missed his brother for years and has talked about finding him as long as I can remember. Now that Grandfather is dead, you know he would have begun the search soon anyway. Neither you nor anyone else could stop him."

"Well, at least her brothers are dead," she answered snippily with a satisfied grin.

"What a horrible thing to say! I do not understand you sometimes." Edward poured himself a full goblet of stout port.

"*You* are the one *I* do not understand, Edward. How can you *not* understand? Those brothers would have a share of our property. You said there were three of them. That would not leave much for us. Surely your father will not give anything to Arelia just because she is wearing that amulet. Who knows if it is even real?"

"Marisa, you are being ridiculous. I saw it myself. It is definitely real." Edward sat in a massive chair, watching his wife pace, her figure cinched as tightly as an hourglass, her eyes and brows pinched in deep thought, plotting.

"When your father leaves, we must insist the girl stay with us. We do not want him to get any closer to her than he already has. We can send her back to her hut and be done with her," she said, wagging her finger as to a naughty, ignorant child.

"This girl is my family. I am named after her father—my uncle, whom I never met. She cannot be a threat to what *I* have. She is a girl. We cannot send her back unless she wants to go." His words were stronger than his whiny tone, almost asking permission to express his opinion. He took a gulp from the goblet.

"She may be no threat now, but she is nearly a woman. What happens when she has a son of her own?" Marisa stared at him, waiting for a response as she threw out her high card with a triumphant smirk.

Edward was quiet now.

"For God's sake, Edward! Be a man for once in your life. You have a family to protect."

He had not thought about providing for his own future family but only of his father's welfare. Ever since his mother and baby sister had died in childbirth, his father seemed different. Everyone had known his mother was too weak to have another child and had been advised against it. Considering two previous miscarriages, her pregnancy seemed to be both a miracle and a threat. Edward had enjoyed his family with just the three of them and had not wanted a new baby to share his parents' attention. He had been jealous at the prospect and was secretly relieved when the baby died at birth but then deeply grieved when he lost his mother, too. His father's attentions waned with his own personal loss. Guilt, grief, and seeming abandonment was a hard pill for a twelve-year-old boy to swallow.

Now it seemed his father was somewhat renewed with his paternal feelings toward Arelia. Now an adult himself, Sir Edward didn't begrudge his father that, but he hadn't thought about his cousin Arelia's offspring.

Marisa was very important to him. A distant cousin five years older, she was related by blood as well as marriage; they shared the same great-grandparents. Although she was not naturally beautiful, she certainly held everyone's attention. She demanded it. Her biggest asset was that she was shrewd in business. He didn't want his father to know how much Marisa controlled his dealings, because Sir Daniel often complimented him on his shrewdness. His father often compared him to his grandfather in business. Sir Edward didn't want him to know this was the result of Marisa's management skills rather than his own.

For now, he didn't want to think about any of this. Everything had been going so well since his grandfather's death. Marisa had been thrilled when Sir Daniel told them that he was leaving his estate to them and that he would be moving to his father's manor house. Actually, Edward realized, Marisa and his grandfather were very much alike in business knowledge, and he knew their assets would grow under her guidance. As Marisa was the oldest girl in a family, with only one son who became a priest, her grandfather had taught her everything he knew about business. She would be his only heir with the potential of marrying well and increasing her family's holdings. The match between young Sir Edward and Marisa had seemed perfect at the time. Edward valued Marisa for her attractive appearance and business sense, especially because he really didn't enjoy all the business dealings himself. So much was expected of him. No one needed to know who had the real expertise; the important thing was to keep the property in the Fairchild family.

If Marisa said Arelia should stay with them, then she would stay. Sir Edward didn't know how she would arrange it, but he knew it would happen.

He drained his goblet of wine in one final gulp and then poured another.

Arelia eased into deep, peaceful sleep, uninterrupted until late in the morning. The maid who had helped her prepare for bed the night before had bathed her legs and hands and then had coated them with a soothing lotion of herbs and butter which relieved the pain. Combined with a relaxing evening with Sir Daniel, she slept comfortably for the first time since the wolf attack.

The same woman appeared shortly after Arelia awakened to bathe her wounds again and help her dress in another beautiful gown. This gown was not as elegant as the one the night before but beautiful nonetheless; straight-cut, royal blue with a pale blue tunic. The dresses were slightly large on Arelia but not too noticeably so.

When she walked into the large dining room, she was surprised at how wonderful it was with rugs and wall hangings dancing with color, while the breeze from the ocean cooled the room and gave it a scent of sea spray.

Sir Daniel rose to greet her, and although he smiled at seeing her, he looked tired.

"Are you all right, Sir Daniel?"

"Yes, Arelia, I did not sleep well after our evening. I had a lot to think about. I spoke with my son and his wife for some time this morning. Lady Marisa and Sir Edward are eager to meet with you."

"I look forward to meeting with them too, sire."

Arelia thought of the quiet woman who helped her dress and of Camellia. She hoped that Marisa was more like Camellia, and they could be friends, at least until Cornelius arrived to take her home.

He took her hand to escort her to a large chair near the fireplace, and then he sat opposite her. "I notice that you are wearing your amulet," he said as he eased into his chair.

"All I have left of my family is right here," she said, grasping the medallion. "I do not want to risk losing it."

"Arelia, a family is more than a medallion. It is a history of people. It is the parents of your parents and their parents before them."

"All of my grandparents are dead, sire," said Arelia.

"Did you have grandmothers and uncles?"

"Yes, my mother had one sister and two brothers who lived in a nearby village. I do not know how many survived the sickness."

"And your father?"

"I do not know about my father's side."

Sir Daniel looked down at the floor for several seconds, got up from his chair, and walked to the window. Arelia watched him, knowing what he would say. His likeness to her father was not a coincidence—even his mannerisms were the same. *The stories Father told were not fantasies, and the amulet Father wore is also Sir Daniel's.* Arelia walked over to the window and looked into his face. His eyes showed the same grief she felt from losing her family. She stepped toward him, put her head on his chest, and cried as he wrapped his arms around her and wept.

Marisa walked quietly down the hall and slowly opened the door to the dining room. She had come to see if Arelia and Sir Daniel were together. Spying through the small opening, she watched the girl being comforted by her father-in-law. She knew now she was right; Arelia must stay with her and Edward. She had to protect her estate. Marisa pulled the door shut quietly, without notice.

Arelia looked up at the old man through dark, teary eyes and asked, "Who are you, sire?"

"Arelia, was your mother's name Margaret Peterson?"

Arelia, stepped back, startled. "Sire, how would you know my mother's name?"

"I am your uncle, Arelia, your father's only brother."

They stood at the window for some time, both sorting through their own thoughts, trying to put the pieces together.

"Sir Daniel, I do not understand. Why have I never met you or even heard of you?"

"It is a long, long story, Arelia, which began before you were even a thought in your father's mind. He was considerably younger than I, by eight years. As long as I can remember, he wanted to be a knight, although he and I were heirs to Father's estate and he had no need to do so. While growing up, he often sat with my father during meetings and followed the knights around in the field.

"To humor him, my father let him go on an exploration under the care of his soldiers. He knew it would be safe as it was simply for surveillance. The troops were to be gone for several months. Needless to say, my mother was upset with Father's decision, but she honored his wishes.

"Edward was thirteen at the time of his first exploration and was excited about the adventure ahead of him. Unfortunately, during the time they were away, he became very ill. The officers were deeply concerned about his health as heir to their lord, and so they brought him to the nearest village to be cared for by a woman who had knowledge of healing herbs. I now understand this to be the home of your grandfather and grandmother, also the home of your mother.

"Edward stayed with them for several weeks until he was well enough to return to the estate. As time passed, my brother remembered being confined in the small hut and the loving care he received from the tenant family. One of his fondest memories was of the couple's daughter, Margaret, who often brought his meals and talked with him. They had spent long hours talking about how differently they lived.

"When Edward turned fifteen, he asked to go back. Mother was aware of his intentions and refused to let him go. It seems she had already arranged his marriage and did not want anything to get in the way of her plans.

"In spite of what my parents said, Edward left during the night. My father immediately sent a troop after him when he realized that he was gone. They found him in the village with the peasant family.

"Edward refused to return unless Margaret came with him. The two children were very strong in their desire to be together. Margaret and her parents traveled back to my father's estate with Edward and the soldiers. My parents coolly, but politely, received them. Mother and Margaret's mother discussed the situation, came to an agreement, and her parents were escorted back to the village. My parents were relieved that the ordeal was over and that Margaret's parents agreed with them.

"What they did not bargain for was Edward's will. At seventeen, only months before his eighteenth birthday and arranged marriage, he left, leaving behind a note and this amulet."

He reached down and gently tapped Arelia's amulet.

"I was devastated. Even though Edward was much younger, I admired his nature. He was becoming a very good friend to me—not just a brother. I was afraid I had lost my only brother and friend forever.

"Father and Mother were furious and humiliated. They had to cancel his wedding. They refused to do anything to find him and declared him no longer a part of the family. Shortly after that, Mother died.

"I had taken Edward's amulet the night we discovered him gone. After my parents' reaction, I realized there was no chance for reconciliation on their part, and so I sent a knight with the amulet to return it to Edward. I included a letter describing my parents' strong feelings and asked him to return. When Mother died, I hoped that he would return to see our father.

"Originally, he had sent a brief note with the knight, who told me he was living in the village like a peasant, under a different surname, and that he had gratefully accepted the amulet. Another note came when Mother died." He laughed. "Oh, and there was one other letter sending advice about my marriage. I thought I could lure him back by needing his help, but he was not about to fall for that! I never heard from him again. Rumor was that he and Margaret had moved to a different village, but I never discovered where.

"I always anticipated that he and his new wife would return, but I did not account for his stubbornness.

"My father has just recently died, and with the plague . . . I was going to send a party to locate Edward as soon as I settled my father's estate." Sir Daniel looked out the window quietly, fighting back his tears, shaking his head sadly. "I should have acted sooner. He and his sons are as much heirs as I. I shall always regret it. I named my son after him; it was all I could do."

There was a knock on the door announcing Lady Marisa and Sir Edward. Marisa was aware that they had interrupted an important conversation but acted excited to "finally meet" Arelia. Arelia had never seen anyone quite like Lady Marisa. Her appearance was perfect, not necessarily pretty, but perfect. Arelia remembered her first image of herself in the looking glass as she stood in the beautiful dress. Although she and Marisa were dressed in similar clothes, Arelia felt that she looked more like the quiet woman who had helped her dress and bathe her legs rather than the woman standing before her. She could not imagine Marisa bathing her own legs or even dressing herself. Now she understood the maid.

She watched as Marisa approached the large dining table, marveling at how any woman could have a waist no bigger around than a small log. Her reddish hair was pinched into waves that flowed into a funnel pinned to the back of her head. Arelia had never seen anything like it and wondered how it had ever come to be. Her beautiful red hair contrasted with pale, transparent skin which framed strangely light sage-green eyes. In every aspect of description, Marisa would be portrayed as beautiful, but something was very wrong; somehow it wasn't all put together exactly right.

As Marisa had offered her greeting, Arelia realized that she no longer saw through the eyes of a child. Her experiences had changed that. A child would have been mesmerized by Marisa's being perfectly dressed and by her composure. As a child, she would have thought her hair and dress beautiful; she would have been captivated by her bright eyes, porcelain skin, and generous smile with unusually colored lips. But Arelia saw something different; she saw eyes that said something contrary to her words and an appearance that defied nature.

She remembered that her mother had warned her about that kind of person years ago. Arelia had a friend who had hurt her deeply. She soon realized the girl had befriended her only to get close to her older brother. She'd had a long cry, and her mother warned, "Not everyone talks from the heart. Sometimes words do not match intentions. Do not trust these people." Arelia thought she would use this advice in regard to Marisa. This woman would never take her mother or Camellia's place in her life. Instinctively, she knew not to trust her.

Sir Daniel helped Arelia to her chair while a manservant helped Lady Marisa.

Marisa said all the right things, "We are *so* happy to have found you. It would have been *tragic* if those animals had been the end of you. It's *wonderful* to find you have family you did not even know you had. You *must* stay with us." Her eyes did not agree with her words, or perhaps she said too much, too quickly. She only glanced at Arelia as the servers held trays of meats, vegetables, and creamy sauces, but her smile never changed.

Sir Edward, on the other hand, seemed sincerely happy about having found Arelia but somehow seemed to hold back. "My father has talked so much about his brother, my legacy. I am sorry that will never have a chance to meet him, but all is not lost because we have found you." He glanced nervously at Marisa. His appearance was only slightly similar to her father's. Perhaps that was why she was more comfortable with her uncle.

"Have you lost anyone from here to the blight?" Arelia asked in order to get the attention off herself.

"Thanks to the king, we have lost only a few," Marisa enthusiastically interjected.

"The king?" Edward questioned.

Marisa jumped in with an explanation in an arrogantly conspiratorial tone. "Of course! Arelia, there is no way *you* could know, but King Edward and Queen Philippa lost their daughter Joan to the plague. She was on her way to seal a most *beneficial* alliance by marrying Peter I of Castile. The king, not wanting to lose anyone else, sealed off Windsor Castle to anyone coming or going. He sent word that any messengers would need to be in quarantine before meeting with him or anyone in the household. After we received the message, *I* persuaded Sir Daniel and Edward that we should do the same. We had lost only a few servants up to that point and no one of importance, but then lost no one afterward. It was obviously a very good decision on my part."

Wondering how and where Marisa acquired all the information about the royal family distracted Edward from her words. She hardly took time for a breath between sentences.

"Of course, with four other daughters and *five* sons, the king—"

Sir Daniel cut in quickly, "On the contrary, Marisa, every life lost was of importance, and you have not even mentioned good Fr. Martin." Marisa's stone-cold stare demonstrated that she did not appreciate his interrupting her knowledge of the royal family.

Sir Daniel continued, "Thankfully, when I heard that occurrences of deaths had ceased, I sent a party of troops out to watch for burials and to talk to tenants in order to determine if it was safe to open the gates. I say *thankfully* because that is when they found you and brought you here." He reached over and gently patted Arelia's hand. "We can all thank God that we are here together and have survived death. Every night I pray for those who are lost to us."

The meal continued in strained silence until Marisa offered, "Well, dear Arelia, we will not keep you. I know you need your rest. I hope you find your room comfortable and not too overwhelming. I know you are accustomed to much simpler surroundings."

Sir Daniel saved Arelia the answer, "Thank you, Marisa," and turning toward his son, "and Edward. I am taking good care of Arelia. You do not need to be concerned. Maybe we shall meet at dinner."

As the door closed behind them, Sir Daniel apologized, "Oh, Arelia, I am sorry for that display. I fear it was my duty to arrange my son's marriage, and I seem to have failed the task. I thought business sense was a great asset, but I overlooked the most basic element of love in marriage. I can only blame myself. My dear Ruth would not have made the same error."

Arelia had gone to bed so many nights with a great deal on her mind. Tonight was no exception; the revelation of her heritage deeply confused her. Until today, she knew she would go back to the village, live with Cornelius and Camellia until she married, and then settle into a home of her own with a young man from the village. Now she did not know what the future held.

Her father's stories began to play in her mind, but this time, knights had faces, stone walls held tapestries, and chandeliers cast rainbows on the walls.

"I know there is a place for me," she repeated as she fell asleep. "Could this be the place?"

CHAPTER 8

Arelia awoke early, wanting to see her uncle. Somehow, the woman who dressed her always came in just minutes after she awakened, but Arelia still wasn't able to get to know her. The gentle woman bathed and wrapped her legs, brushed her hair, brought fresh water, and helped her put on a clean shift, which she brought in for her every day. She rarely talked, and when she did, it was about what Arelia needed, her clothes, and plans for the day. Her quiet demeanor kept Arelia from asking questions or even from making casual conversation. Strangely, she didn't even know her name.

She sometimes wore the same dress over her straight undergarment, but the woman gave her a new surcoat to change the appearance of the dress each day. The surcoat was long and sleeveless and made of beautiful fabric often embroidered with silken threads, although not as elegant as the dresses she had worn at dinner.

Arelia didn't understand how someone could help her so much and yet be so distant. There was so much about all of this that she didn't understand. She didn't understand why there were so many large rooms and so much food for so few people. She didn't understand why there had been so much love between her father and his brother, and so many secrets. She didn't understand why anyone would get married and not love each other. She didn't understand why she would be dressed so elegantly and the woman who dressed her dressed so plainly. She didn't understand why with so much to do to keep a large house, she sat idle. She didn't understand why the people she wanted to talk to the most, those she saw who were most like her, did not talk to her; they seemed kind but did not talk.

After Arelia was dressed, the woman brought hot tea into her room. For the first time in weeks, she picked up her Father's Psalter to read some of his favorite passages, the ones he shared with his family in the evening around the warmth of the fire.

The first verses of Psalm 49 made sense to her for the first time. It was one her father had read often. She read.

2 Hear this, all you peoples!
   Give ear, all who inhabit the world,
3 You of lowly birth or high estate,
   rich and poor together.
4 My mouth shall speak words of wisdom,
   my heart shall offer insights.
5 I will turn my ear to a riddle,
   expound my question on a lyre.

I

6 Why should I fear in evil days,
   with the iniquity of my assailants surrounding me,
7 Of those who trust in their wealth
   and boast of their abundant riches?
8 No man can ransom even a brother,
   or pay to God his own ransom.
9 The redemption of his soul is costly;
   and he will pass away forever.
10 Will he live on forever, then,
   and never see the Pit of Corruption?
11 Indeed, he will see that the wise die,
   and the fool will perish together with the senseless,
   and they leave their wealth to others.
12 Their tombs are their homes forever,
   their dwellings through all generations,

<blockquote>
"They named countries after themselves"

13   —but man does not abide in splendor.

He is like the beasts—they perish.
</blockquote>

She stared at the page, dumbstruck. It all made sense now; the fairy tales, the psalms. She grasped the heavy medallion around her neck. "The amulet," she whispered. In fact, he had been telling them about his life all along, but she had never seen the amulet; so much had been hidden.

A quiet knock on the door interrupted her reverie. The door opened slightly, "Good morning, Arelia. May I come in?"

"Oh, of course, Sir Daniel!" She nearly jumped up and took his hand. "I love seeing you." Her eyes filled with tears as she looked into her uncle's face, a man she had already come to love. "Do you have time to stay with me?"

"Yes, of course, but I am not sure you are up for it, and so I came here. You have been through so much in your young life. How are your wounds today?"

"Oh, they are so much better, being cleaned and salved every day."

"Good, we do not want any trouble developing there.

"I see you have a book."

"Yes, it is a Psalter." Arelia offered it to him. He opened it and said, "This is your father's handwriting. He must have spent many hours copying this!"

She smiled. "Yes, but I am surprised that you would recognize his script from so long ago."

He let out a small chuckle and shook his head, slowly rubbing the writing on the pages. He handed her the book. "I take out those three letters which he sent occasionally. Although much younger than I, he was much wiser in many ways. I suspect this book might have something to do with that.

"I miss the Scripture and having Mass here. Since Fr. Martin died, there has been a great absence. No one is feeding our spirits."

"I know what you mean. When Fr. Jerome died, we lost so much, too. Mass at the monastery was a great treat. How did your Fr. Martin die? Was it the plague?"

"That is what we assume, but we do not really know. He wanted to go out to tend to the tenants, and Lady Marisa told him if he did, he could not return until long after the plague passed. I assume it took him because there has been no word. He is probably in one of those mass graves."

Tears fell quietly. "My parents and baby brother were burned." Sir Daniel gasped. "My father had helped dig the big graves, but soon there were not even enough people to do that."

"So, my brother's bones are in with many." They were quiet for a while, speechless.

"Arelia, read some of the passages that my brother read to all of you."

"Only if you also read to me, sire."

"Arelia, you must call me *uncle* now."

Arelia smiled, shyly, and read Psalm 49. They talked about what it must have meant to her father to have left his wealth behind. "Sire, . . . I mean, Uncle, there is something that I am very curious about but hesitate to ask."

"Please go ahead."

"You said my mother and grandmother came here. Did you see my mother? Did you meet her?"

He burst into a grin. "I am glad you would ask. Yes, I did. Of course, she was much younger, probably about your age now. By the way, how old are you?"

"I am fourteen now." She smiled.

"Yes, well, you are quite grown up. Your mother was probably sixteen when we met. In fact, now that I think about it, you look very much like your mother at her age.

"I would not have known you as my niece, but with the amulet and having seen your mother, there is no mistaking that you are my family.

"My brother—your father"—he smiled and patted her hand—"asked me to go into the parlor with our family and your mother's family. It was very tense, but your mother was beautiful, and I understood immediately why your father wanted to marry her; not for her looks alone, but for the person she was. Of course, she was beautiful, but young. You look so much like her with your straight dark hair, your dark eyes, and fair complexion. But, more importantly, it was her demeanor. She was confident and very poised. My mother could be intimidating, and she asked many questions. Your mother never faltered. She looked straight into my mother's eyes, sat very straight, and gave excellent and honest answers. I never understood why my mother would not welcome her into our family. She was exactly the kind of lady every family would have wanted in order to enhance their estate and position. Sadly, it was only because she was not in the royal class. It was definitely our loss.

"There is no doubt that you have received so much from both your mother and my brother. I am so proud to call you family, my niece. You are from good stock."

Arelia winced.

"Have I offended you?"

"Sir, you use the word *stock* as if my parents were nothing more than cattle."

His brows wrinkled and then he threw back his head and laughed. Tears escaped his eyes, increasing the humiliating offense. Arelia was close to running out of the room but did not know where she would go.

"Oh dear, Arelia, on the contrary, you are nothing like cattle. You are lovely and pure of heart. There is such irony here." He pulled a handkerchief out of his pocket and dabbed his eyes.

"I do not understand."

"Of course not, and I pray you never will. This will be very hard to explain. With our family, and other so-called *royal* families, there is a great deal of fear of losing our wealth. We focus on it in almost everything we do, including marriage. There are a limited number of families, and so the choice of a spouse is also limited. We often have large families in order to increase our chance of a beneficial alliance with others of wealth. We all want sons in order to be in the best bargaining position in order to establish an alliance that will expand our estates. It is a complicated and highly manipulated process. In fact, we talk about *breeding*, which in this perspective seems ridiculously obvious. We also talk about *bloodline*, which now does lead me to think about horses and cattle. Strangely, I have never put it together that way." He chuckled and wiped his eyes once more, taking a very deep breath as he studied her confused expression.

Arelia was taken aback by his explanation and was clearly bewildered. "You said that my father was to be married within months of leaving. I do not understand. If he loved someone enough to marry, how could he leave? Was this a planned breeding of which you speak?"

Daniel rubbed his eyes and leaned back in his chair, carefully considering his words before speaking. He shook his head as his smile vanished. "Hearing you refer to it as *planned breeding* sounds reprehensible, but of course, that is exactly what it is. I shall never see arranged marriages the same. Oh, so much of our position does not make sense. My mother had arranged your father's marriage as she had for me."

"I do not understand," she repeated.

"Of course not, because it does not make sense; it is not understandable. There are relatively few in our class—the royal class. Marriage is not anything about love; it is strictly about property and wealth. Parents negotiate an agreement in order to ensure the continuance of property or in order to expand property. It is both a business and political arrangement."

Arelia was speechless. "Is that why my father left?"

"Yes, and he was smart and brave to do so. I, on the other hand, was not so brave. I had an arranged marriage. Fortunately for me, we grew to love each other, but that does not always happen."

"Is that why you feel guilty about your son's marriage to Marisa? Was Marisa's family in the royal class?"

"Marisa's heritage is woven from ours. Her great-grandparents were my grandparents. One of their sons was my father, and one of their daughters was her grandmother. Edward and Marisa have the same great-grandparents. Her grandmother was a Fairchild until she married, and then she had a daughter, who is Marisa's mother."

"Oh, dear. That is too confusing. Marrying for love is so much simpler."

"The Fairchild bloodline came to Marisa though her grandmother and mother," he tried to explain.

"And so . . .? She is royal because she is a Fairchild?"

"Well, yes, and also through the arranged marriages to the men of other royal families. Even though she was several years older than Edward, her father and mother wanted to renew the Fairchild name with their grandchildren and return the Fairchild property to her bloodline. It made sense to me at the time."

"It may make sense to a royal family, but it makes no sense to me," she said with wrinkled brows. "Was her name *Marisa Fairchild* before she and Edward married?"

"No . . . Well, yes and no. Her name was *Marisa Fairchild Pearce*, from the House of Pearce."

"And so, you are saying that she married Edward to become Marisa Fairchild Pearce Fairchild?" Arelia shook her head in confusion.

"Oh dear, yes, I can see that now. It sounds absurd in the telling. I wish my Ruth had been here. She would not have made the mistake I did. I doubt that Edward and Marisa will ever love each other. I suspect that she is incapable of loving anyone but herself. I have unintentionally taken so much from my son." He put his head back, took a long, deep breath, and closed his eyes, rubbing the bridge of his nose between thumb and forefinger. Arelia wondered if he was trying not to cry.

"Sir," she interjected quietly. "Do you think my father loved my mother? He seemed to."

Sir Daniel smiled, "Loved her? Oh, yes! That is why he left here. He gave up everything to be with her. I have never witnessed such sacrificial love. When he left, my mother ordered that he would not leave with anything except what was on his back, not a change of clothes or even a coin for his pocket. My father insisted that he be given a horse and a blanket; otherwise, he would have been on foot. I sneaked him a loaf of bread. Mother thought he would head home if he had nothing. Happily, she was wrong; she underestimated his commitment to your mother."

"I remember a time when my father was talking to Daniel, my oldest brother. Oh, Daniel! That is your name!" She laughed.

He smiled broadly. "I guess he did care for me as much as I loved him. We named our sons after each other."

"Yes, anyway, he told my brother that he would know when he was in love because he would do anything for his beloved."

"Well, that is certainly how he felt about your mother."

"Father also told Daniel that St. Paul said that a man should love his wife as Christ loved the Church, a self-sacrificing love. He told him that a man is to leave his father and mother and cling to his wife! Oh my! Now I understand!"

"Arelia, I told you earlier that your father was much wiser than I. He evidently not only read Scripture but followed it. He actually had written those same words to me, giving me advice about my marriage. That, along with other words of wisdom, helped me learn to love my wife."

They were interrupted by a servant with large bowls of hearty, steaming soup and hot bread and butter. The midday meal passed quietly as each considered all that had been said.

"Sir, I have another question that I may be too shy to ask."

He smiled and suggested, "Well, follow the lead of your father and mother and put that aside. You may ask me anything."

"Sire,. . . Uncle, one day I would like to marry and have a family of my own, but I must marry for love as my parents did. If I were to stay with you, would I be allowed to marry for love and not be forced into a planned breeding?"

He leaned forward with a soft smile and took her hand with such tenderness, "Oh, my dearest Arelia, I have ruined my son's life. I have no heart to ruin yours. I do not know how you will find your love to marry if you stay with me, but I will assist you to the best of my capability. After meeting you, I know your father made the best choice, and I know you will be the best one to make that choice for yourself. No one will interfere."

CHAPTER 9

Sir Daniel suggested that Arelia take time to rest and have dinner in her room after a long nap. She gladly accepted his suggestion. He was the only one she wanted to spend time with anyway, and they had had such a wonderful time together. Uncle Daniel mentioned that he would need to be away for a time and suggested that he would like her go with him to his father's estate, but he worried that because so much had happened to her, another change seemed more that she should consider. He promised that there would always be time for her to travel with him in the future.

As she fell asleep that night, she reflected on their conversation and on what she hoped to accomplish; actually, she wasn't sure what that was, because she didn't know what people did in castles, and she didn't know anyone other than Marisa and Edward. She couldn't imagine that Marisa, dressed as she did, milked cows or tended a garden, and she determined that, because she was dressed similarly to Marisa, she probably would not tote milk buckets and dig potatoes either. With that consideration out of the way, she had no idea what she would do while her uncle was away.

She did know that she wanted to see Cornelius and Camellia again. They must be very concerned by her disappearance. No one would suspect that she had found an extended family as the result of a wolf and wild-dog attack.

She also knew she wanted to spend more time with her uncle. He had mentioned that he was moving to his father's estate, but she hadn't asked any questions. She wanted to know how far away he would be and when he was leaving. It would make sense for her to return to the village when her uncle left.

Meanwhile, Marisa was also planning, or rather plotting. She knew that she had to keep Arelia and Sir Daniel separated, and so she had to devise a plan to keep Arelia at Faircastle when her father-in-law left, and yet maybe she should allow Arelia to return to the peasants' village as she wished. Neither of these choices were clear to her as of yet, but she had no doubt that a plan would come to her.

Sir Edward had awakened with foreboding late that same morning and with a slight headache. He listened to Marisa's long gown drag the floor as she paced back and forth in her adjoining room, obviously devising a plan to destroy his pretty little cousin, who brought light to his father's eyes. He pretended to sleep, not wanting to get caught up in destroying this new relationship between uncle and potential heir. On first seeing Arelia, he was captivated by her seeming innocence and wanted to get to know her—his only known cousin. But an obvious threat stood between him and any possible relationship, and that threat paced as he pretended to sleep.

Sir Daniel had had the most fulfilling day. For the first time in many years, he looked forward to life. He would actually have someone who was interested in what he had to say and someone in his life who wanted a husband and family. Finally, his remaining years held hope.

Earlier, he had been amused and warmed when Arelia walked into the parlor wearing one of his wife's dresses. It was a little large on her, but she was still refreshingly beautiful. She had a certain look that reminded him of her mother and, oddly, of his. Fortunately, Arelia had not been ruined by manipulative people as had others in his family, namely Edward; she had a disarming innocence about her. Of course, she was still young. It was easy to see that she had been raised with a great deal of love, care, peace, and laughter.

There was something of a contrast between her innocence and her depth of feeling and experience. Although her life situations had been cruel to her, she still seemed to retain trust and concern for people, and she also exhibited great maturity. Sir Daniel hoped she would be able to keep all those beautiful qualities, and that others would not take advantage of her.

When Arelia awoke from her nap, the kindly old woman came in with a dinner tray. "I have your dinner. Sir Daniel thought you might like to rest this evening. He is planning to also eat in his room this evening.

"I will come back later to tend to your wounds."

"Thank you"—and gathering courage—"Before you leave, I would like to ask your name. You have helped me for days, and I do not even know your name."

"My name is Sarah, miss," she replied, smiling.

"Do you live in the house, Sarah?"

"Yes, miss, I live here with my son and daughter and husband." She seemed surprised and embarrassed by Arelia's questions.

"What do your children do while you are here with me?" continued Arelia.

"My daughter helps with the clothes, washing and mending. My husband and son work in the stable with the horses. You will meet my daughter soon, as Sir Daniel has asked that his wife's clothes be altered to fit you."

"Lady Ruth's clothes?"

"Yes, my lady. Those were the only clothes we had for you."

Arelia did not realize that she had been wearing Sir Daniel's wife's clothes. She had wondered where all the lovely dresses were coming from and could not imagine that they belonged to Marisa.

But now she wanted to learn more about Sarah. "How have you and your family come to live here, Sarah?"

"I have always lived here. My father tended the stables when I was a young girl. I have never been away from here."

Arelia thought how interesting it was that she had never been away from her village until her parents died. She realized what a small view she had of the world. Sarah had been as sheltered as she but from the perspective of the castle. Sarah was a common woman, who was familiar with the fairytale life, although not part of it. Arelia was unaware of such a life yet was unknowingly a part of the fairytale family.

She was not sure where she fit. Although she wanted to be part of her uncle's life, she also wanted to return to Cornelius and Camellia. She would talk with her uncle, hoping that he could help her decide what she should do.

"How are your legs feeling?"

"Most of the soreness is gone, thanks to you. I never thought that I would recover so quickly."

"I am so happy that you are doing so well.

"Sir Daniel requests that you join them for breakfast in the dining room in the morning."

Morning came much too early. Sarah came in early to change her bandages and help her to dress and to arrange her hair. Arelia entered the dining room with the others already at table having tea. It was obvious that she had interrupted a dispute. Marisa hardly gave her time to sit down before speaking her mind.

"Well, Arelia, I am so happy to have you with us. I suspect we will have many good times together in the future."

Arelia was shocked by Marisa's assumption and hoped it didn't show as she took time to gather herself while they served their plates from the butler's tray. She had no intention of staying with Marisa and Edward. She intended to go back to Cornelius and Camellia as soon as her uncle left. Now she could see that it was critically important to speak to her uncle about returning to her friends as soon as possible.

"Arelia, I will be leaving for my father's estate late next week. I am getting things in order now. I was hoping that you would move with me. You do not have anything to pack. I have instructed Sarah to prepare clothes for you that will be ready in time to leave with me. I had considered your staying here until I return, but now I believe that you are well enough to make the trip with me." They seemed to be in a tug of war.

Arelia was more stunned and confused than before. She had never considered anything but returning to the village or staying at the castle with her uncle for some time. Although she was happy, she didn't feel she fit into their storybook life. She hesitated while quietly buttering a piece of bread, not knowing what to say. She knew Sir Daniel understood her circumstance and her wishes, and she was growing increasingly anxious.

Marisa, seeing her hesitance, seized the opportunity to respond in her place, "Father, I do not think that Arelia is well enough to travel. After she has had sufficient time to heal, we will send her to you." She smiled sweetly toward Arelia.

This was becoming more confusing. Marisa had never even asked what her wishes were.

"Uncle," she said hesitantly, trying to calm panic, "I was hoping to return to my village as soon as I could or to stay with you here a while longer before I returned."

Everyone in the room seemed surprised by her comment, and Marisa did not miss her addressing Sir Daniel as *Uncle*. "I thought you were happy with us, Arelia." Marisa feigned hurt.

"Oh, I am, but I know everyone in the village must be very worried about me."

"We can send word that you are safe," Marisa suggested.

"I thank all of you so much, but I know that they will not rest until they see me. Camellia and Cornelius both need my help. I feel I need to return to them."

Arelia's uncle was obviously hurt and disappointed. After his initial thought of leaving Arelia, he realized now that it would be better if she left with him. For the first time in years he was happy, having found family that he didn't even know existed. He had lost his brother and didn't want to lose Arelia. His assumed dream was shattering before his eyes.

Marisa looked at her husband's blank expression, sipping his breakfast wine as if he hadn't heard a word. She never even imagined that Arelia would want to give all this up to live in a small, filthy village; of course, she was still an ignorant child. Surely peasants such as Cornelius and Camellia would encourage her to claim her share of the family's property once they knew her heritage, and they'd probably come with her, bringing a brood of unruly children. They'd overrun the castle. She had to think quickly.

"Arelia, did you have a special boy in the village?" asked Marisa sweetly.

"I have many friends, Marisa."

"I mean a *special* friend—someone you would like to have a family with?" She smiled sweetly. Edward seemed to be the only one to recognize Marisa's absurdly unnatural attempt at being coy. He suddenly became interested.

Arelia blushed. She had not thought of herself in those terms and was not prepared to discuss it with relative strangers.

"Marisa, Arelia is too young to think of such things at this point. She has just found her father's family. You are assuming too much," Sir Daniel reprimanded, trying to cover his daughter-in-law's boldness.

"But, Father, she is growing into quite a young woman. Surely she has noticed the young men, and I have no doubt they have noticed her."

Arelia spoke up, "Marisa, I was only twelve when the plague overtook us."

Sir Edward understood the direction Marisa was heading. "I am sure there were several young men who noticed you, Arelia." He spoke for the first time, almost as if he had been prodded to do so.

Arelia didn't know what to say. "I had only been in that village a short while, and most of my time was spent helping Cornelius and Camellia."

"You two leave Arelia alone. She is too young to think of such things," dismissed Sir Daniel abruptly. "Let her recover from all she has been through before you go about planning her life for her. She is capable of making her own plans."

Arelia was not sure, but she thought she heard Edward snicker.

Breakfast went quickly and quietly; after his dismissal, Arelia was eager to get back to her room, away from Marisa and her cousin Edward. She would meet with her uncle later and tell him her wishes privately.

Late that afternoon Sarah brought tea and cake. "Would it be proper for me to take a walk, Sarah? I have never seen the ocean and would like to explore a little," Arelia requested.

"Are your legs well enough for a long walk?" Sarah asked with concern in her voice.

"Yes, and I would enjoy the fresh air."

Sarah hesitated.

"Have I said something wrong?"

"Well, my lady, I do not know if Lady Marisa would want you to go to the ocean."

"Lady Marisa? Why would she care?"

Sarah walked with Arelia down a dark hallway to an even longer, outdoor stairway and pointed the way to a path to the ocean. "Do not go far for the sake of your legs and your safety," she cautioned. "May I suggest that for your first time out, you sit on that outcropping of rock at the end of the stairway?"

Arelia was excited about finally being alone without the chance of interruption. She felt she needed time to think about all that had happened and to decide what she should do next. She wished her parents were there to talk with her and to give her some sort of direction. Thoughts about all those evenings when she and her mother had talked about her brothers and sister and their lives returned as she walked down the long stairway. She thought back to their many talks about her friends and some of her problems growing up. Now she had a big problem and found herself without motherly advice. She had enjoyed her conversation with Sir Daniel and was confused by his leaving so soon.

As she came to the end of a long, steep, winding path, the beauty and grandeur of the ocean stopped her. She had never seen such a wide expanse of sky and water. She had never experienced the soft sea spray or the violence of the waves as they crashed upon the rocks.

Up until now, her environment had been somewhat confined within a clearing in the forest where their village was situated. Now there seemed to be no end in sight. The power of the water on the rocks was startling and frightening. Arelia took Sarah's advice and decided not to go to the beach. She climbed up a slight embankment and sat on a rock watching the clouds and waves. Her thoughts returned to her mother and father. Had they seen the ocean together before they married? Had they sat on this exact rock?

Tears began to fall as she realized her aloneness. There was no one to share her fears with or to help her with her decision. Every choice would be her own—right or wrong. There was no one to help her.

Of course, she thought, her uncle was a kind man, much like her father, but he didn't know life in the village; he couldn't understand that Cornelius and Camellia were more like family to her than he was. She couldn't ask his advice because he really didn't know her, and now he seemed to assume that she was leaving with him. What had changed?

Her mother had told her to reflect on the calm and serenity of the trees and flowers, but there were no trees or flowers here, only sand, water, rocks, and clouds. There was something frightening in the expanse of water, endless water. Even the clouds floated forever. Behind her was the massive, dark castle of her family—one she didn't even know. How strange it seemed, compared to the small comfortable hut of her childhood.

My father left this exact castle to find love in a village, she thought as she studied the tall imposing structure.

That was it! She knew. She would leave too. Like her father, she would choose the loving family that waited for her. She would live safely among the tall trees, protected from the outside world. At night she would sit in a small room with a warm fire and tell stories of soldiers, knights, and now of oceans. Her decision was made. She would simply tell her uncle and cousin and Marisa. Her uncle would respect her decision to return to a familiar life, and she didn't care what Marisa and Edward thought.

Marisa will be happy when I leave, she thought. In spite of what Marisa said, her eyes told the truth: Arelia was not a happy discovery for this elusive and frightening woman. She knew that Marisa and her cousin would not shed any tears when she left.

Uncle Daniel was different. Leaving would be painful for both of them. Leaving him would be like leaving her family all over again. Uncle Daniel was really her only connection to her father and their family's history. But like her father, she would also leave, and, hopefully, she would be able to spend time with Sir Daniel before then.

Her life would be different now. She wouldn't be the same little girl when she went back to the village. She had seen the ocean and worn fine dresses. She had learned of her father's heritage. She would never be the same again.

From a distance Arelia heard a roar, a pounding. Her own heart echoed in response as she scrambled up the embankment, hiding behind a large boulder. In the distance she could see dozens of men on horseback racing along the beach. She was frozen in fear. *What does this mean?*

As they came closer, the pounding became louder. The ground literally seemed to shake from the thunderous power of the horses' hoofs. She could see that the men were soldiers, shouting and challenging, racing toward an imaginary finish line. They laughed and cheered as they reached the large outcropping of rocks. Their arms flew up in victory, having finished the race.

Several men rode their horses into the water and others dismounted and let their horses graze on the low grass growing between the rocks along the sand. Arelia's tension was relieved as she watched them having fun. She forgot her own worries for a while and wondered what it would be like to splash playfully in the waves.

As she watched them, she thought she recognized one of the younger men as the soldier who had killed the wolf and carried her to the pallet. He was at too far a distance to know for sure. She thought that whoever the soldier was, he was very brave and handsome. She thanked God that he had come when he did, or she would never have a chance to see Cornelius and Camellia and baby Cornelius again, and she would have never met her uncle.

The soldiers stayed for some time and then started back in the direction from which they came. Some raced back again; others walked, holding the horses' reins. Still others rode bareback, dashing their horses in and out of the waves. Arelia thought that it would be fun to ride a horse into the waves.

After the men left her sight, she realized she had been gone for a long time, and that it was approaching dinnertime. Since she had made her decision to leave, she was excited and confident about talking to her uncle. She would tell him and Edward and Marisa her decision at dinner.

CHAPTER 10

 Sarah was waiting nervously when Arelia returned to her room. "Are you all right, Sarah?" Arelia asked.

"You were gone a very long time," Sarah replied.

"I had never seen the ocean before. Thank you for pointing the way."

"You must hurry to be in time for dinner. Lady Marisa does not like to be kept waiting."

Arelia hadn't seen her upset before and was worried that Sarah would get in trouble if she were late. "I will tell Marisa that I went to the ocean, Sarah. It will be all right."

"No! Do not mention the ocean. She would not want you to walk with your wounds. Do not mention it, please"

"Sarah, my legs are fine with all your herbal baths. Marisa need not be concerned."

"You should not mention the ocean, my lady. She would want you to stay in your room."

"As you say, Sarah. Do not worry. I will not mention it," said Arelia, trying to comfort her. She smiled to herself. *My lady? My father's castle language again.*

As usual, dinner was overly elaborate, with much more food than necessary. Arelia realized that the dresses that were too large before were beginning to fit a little better.

She tried not to stare at Marisa in her heart-shaped headdress that framed

87

her perfectly painted porcelain face. She had never seen or imagined such a display. Sarah had pulled back Arelia's long, straight hair and tied it in a ribbon, but a headdress seemed strange to her.

"Arelia, you look flush. Are you not feeling well?"

"No, Uncle, I am fine. I stood at the window today for some time and watched the ocean. You know I had never seen the ocean before. I must have gotten some sun." Arelia didn't know why Marisa would care if she had walked to the ocean but did as Sarah suggested.

"You must really miss the tranquility of the forest," suggested Marisa temptingly.

"Yes, I do, and I miss my friends in the village. I decided today to go back to the village." Arelia looked at her uncle, waiting for his reaction.

A deep frown clinched his face and pinched his brow. "I was hoping you would consent to return to your grandfather's estate with me."

"Sir," Marisa cut in, "that is very inconsiderate and selfish of you. Arelia disappeared without notice. She should go back to her village, at least for a visit. Everyone should know that she is alive. Besides, she can visit us in a year or two if she decides to stay for a while. She may even have a family by then with more little nieces and nephews to love."

Daniel ignored Marisa's interruption. He didn't want to interfere with Arelia's wishes, mainly because he realized she, like her father, would eventually return to the village on her own. "Arelia, I will be here several more days. I would like to spend as much time with my new niece as possible. If you feel well enough, I will escort you to the beach tomorrow. We can take a picnic. Have you ever ridden a horse?"

"Father, should Arelia ride a horse with her legs in bandages?" Edward interrupted.

Arelia wanted to tell him she had seen the soldiers riding in the waves and wanted to ride also. "I do not ride well, Uncle, but I would love to spend a day at the ocean with you."

Again, dinner couldn't be over soon enough for Arelia. She was tired from her walk and eager to go to bed. As always, Sarah was there to help her undress and bathe her legs.

"The wounds are healing nicely. These bandages are no longer necessary.

Fresh air will do them good now," said Sarah as she bathed Arelia's legs in water steeped with healing herbs.

"Sarah, why did you not want Marisa to know I walked to the ocean?"

"Lady Marisa wants to know all that goes on in her house. She may not care that you went out, but it is better if you ask before you go out again."

"Tomorrow, my uncle and I are going to the beach for the day. We are going to bring a picnic." Her face lit with joy.

"Your uncle and Lady Ruth enjoyed days at the beach. She has a number of dresses suited for the occasion. I will bring one in the morning. You will have a wonderful time. Your uncle is a very kind man, and we are all very sad that he is leaving. Nothing will be the same after he is gone."

"I will be sad, too, Sarah, but I am also leaving. I am going back to my village!"

Lady Marisa's lady-in-waiting Bethany had told Sarah that, although she pretended to be pleased, Marisa was extremely upset that Arelia was here. Sarah was not surprised that Arelia was leaving. "That seems to make you very happy, my lady."

"Yes. I will leave about the same time as my uncle. Although you are so wonderful to me, and I am so happy to find my uncle, I do not feel that I really belong here," offered Arelia.

Sarah seemed surprised. "But this is your family. Where else would you belong if not with them?

"Oh, I am sorry, my lady. That is really not for me to say."

Arelia laughed. "It is all right, Sarah. I have much the same confusion myself."

Their day at the beach was one of the best days of Arelia's life. Sir Daniel arrived early to escort her from her room to the beach, retelling adventures with his brother when they were young. He seemed to grow younger with every story.

They seemed childlike themselves, collecting shells and throwing stale bread to the seagulls, running as they went. They walked along the waves, racing to avoid the cold, salty water and then watched sand crabs scurry back into the tide or burrow into the sand. Uncle Daniel laughed as Arelia felt how cold the water was for the first time. He showed her how to dig for creatures that hid in the sand. He stood back in amusement as she laughed at tiny crabs digging and burrowing to avoid her intrusion and imagined what his daughter would have been like. He wished that his brother was there to enjoy his daughter with him. *How wonderful would it be for both of us to be here with our daughters?*

One of the men from the stable brought two horses, which they rode slowly for some distance as they enjoyed the ocean breeze and the roar of the waves. Arelia wondered if the old man who brought the horses was Sarah's husband.

"Uncle, how long will you be gone before I see you again?" Arelia asked.

"I wish I could tell you it will be only a short time, but I know that is not so. The trip is long and exhausting, and I have many matters to handle with my father's estate. I do not anticipate coming back before a year."

"A whole year!?"

"Yes, child. That is one reason why I want you to go with me."

"How far away will you be?"

"From here, it is just one day by horse or two by wagon. I will ride ahead with four soldiers, and the carts will follow behind. One day in the saddle is plenty for me. You could probably tolerate one day on a horse."

Arelia's mind was made up. She avoided his unspoken request by looking out to the distant horizon.

"Well, it looks like you will have time to consider your decision over our picnic."

"Oh, yes, the picnic. But we forgot the basket."

Uncle Daniel smiled. "Let us head back."

It was only a short distance until Arelia saw something surprising once again. At the base of the long stairs from the castle sat a table and chairs with a butler and two maids, waiting to "serve" the picnic.

Arelia stopped her horse. "Is this a *picnic* in your world?" She laughed, shaking her head in disbelief. "Is there anything you do here that you consider simple enough to do for yourself?"

The kitchen had prepared the usual feast. Not much was said as they ate while Uncle Daniel allowed Arelia time to make her decision.

"Will you visit me in the village, Uncle?" she asked, breaking the anticipatory silence.

They looked into each other's eyes, speaking the unspoken. Arelia looked away from the disappointment in her uncle's face.

"Arelia, if that is where you decide to stay, you must prepare a bed for me." He forced a smile. "I will visit you there in a year's time!" He reached for her hand. She extended her hand to him and smiled as he squeezed it lovingly. "You are definitely my brother's daughter!" he laughed.

She was happy to know that she wouldn't lose her uncle. She and Camellia would prepare a place for him in their small hut when he visited. Knowing they would see each other again would make their parting much easier.

They spent the next day together enjoying a long, early morning walk on the beach. Although a table and chairs unnaturally sat at the bottom of the stairway, a simple picnic basket, with no servants, invited them to a less formal midday meal. Arelia enjoyed the simplicity and privacy of their meal together, as did Sir Daniel.

"Arelia, you spoke of your father's fairytales and said you recognize them to be true. Is there anything missing, or is it as he told?"

She hesitated to reply because she, in fact, was very curious. "Yes, there is a difference I have noticed."

Her uncle smiled. "It is most likely that my brother exaggerated in his storytelling."

"Oh, yes, Uncle. He may have exaggerated greatly." She laughed. "He spoke of many people, a steward, a head butler, a constable, a cellarer, maids, cooks and gardeners, archers, farriers, woodsmen, pages and squires. He told us about jousts, hunts, and archery contests."

"Ahh, yes, I see." He paused to gather his thoughts. "He did not exaggerate. When your father was here, we had all of that; Faircastle was a grand estate."

"You are saying that his stories are true?"

Daniel laughed. "Yes, they are true, and it is good for me to remember. Thank you for the reminder." He began his own stories of grander times, exactly as her father had told. They laughed over the brothers being chased out of the wine cellar by the cellarer, the garden by the gardener, and the kitchen for late night snacks by the head cook. He described archery wins and jousting failures, exciting hunts for fox and wild boar, and grand ballroom feasts.

Without even thinking, Arelia asked the obvious. "What happened?"

Her question brought a dark shadow to his eyes. "Oh, so much, Arelia. My brother left; my mother died; I lost my Ruth and my baby daughter, even before I met her." More memories washed over him but, now, of unhappy times. Arelia felt his loss as she remembered her own family.

"After Edward was born, Lady Ruth and I had many occasions with lords and ladies to spend days feasting on the best the land provides, dancing, long walks and rides along the beach, and, yes, jousting, hunts, and archery contests. It was an amazing time, and then I lost her. I fell into grief." He sighed.

"After a few years without any events, our steward and butler came to me and asked for permission to move on to another estate. It was only fair; there was really nothing for them to do here. Once they left, others followed. I wished them well, as they were all very talented in their positions and deserved a better place. At the height of Faircastle, we employed about sixty; now, we have fewer than twenty. I even took over visiting tenants and keeping record of the taxes and rents. It gave me something to fill my time."

Arelia was curious. "Where did Marisa and Edward celebrate their nuptials?"

Daniel smiled and shook his head. "Here—it was an ordeal. Marisa and Edward had been promised since childhood, and nothing was to stand in the way of that union. The arrangement was to better the Fairchild name and increase the holdings of the Pearce estate, as Marisa's mother was from the Fairchild bloodline. Ruth understood it all. I personally had little interest in the alliance.

"Lady Pearce and Marisa arrived six weeks ahead of the festivities with a staff of about forty. They took over Faircastle—the gardens, the stable, the kitchen and larder, housekeeping, the wine cellar—nothing was left untouched. I feared that I would lose the few loyal staff who had chosen to remain. Fortunately, they did remain loyal, but they developed no affection for Marisa nor her family. It was not a good time, and little has changed since."

"Did Marisa arrange to have festivities after she became Lady Fairchild?"

"Not since then, but I hear she has great plans. I had turned over the books of rents and taxes to Edward shortly before they married. It was a normal transition, but I suspect Marisa has her eye on the finances and in the books and is satisfied with that for now. I do not have the heart to question Edward about it. He has enough of his own concerns.

"Oh, dear, Arelia, I fear I have shared much more than you need to know. For now, let us enjoy the remainder of our time together."

After the picnic, Sir Daniel showed Arelia through the massive castle, from the summer kitchen, which shocked the servants, to the library and to his own massive room and parlor.

"I have one more room to show you in order to finish our tour of Faircastle for today." He seemed excited, as they continued down the hall. He opened the door to a room not far from his own. It was smaller with two beds, sparsely furnished. "This is the room your father and I shared as boys."

Arelia laughed. "He had a story about a boy in the castle. Now I understand. *He* was the boy! Uncle, how can I ever thank you?" She walked slowly around the room remembering her father's boyhood stories.

"Arelia," Uncle Daniel interrupted, "I saved one room from the tour for our last day together. There is something very special I want to show you. We will begin tomorrow after breakfast."

As wonderful as their time had been riding along the beach and touring the castle, their last day together was the most surprising and connected another link in the chain of her history.

"Arelia, I saved this room for our last day together because there is something very special that I want you to see." He had piqued her curiosity as they made their way up the stairs to the middle hall of the castle, not too far from his bedroom and parlor.

"What is this?"

"It is our chapel, where Fr. Martin offered Mass for us, but that is not all that I want to show you. Come in." As he opened the heavy door, Sir Daniel pointed to a table near the altar.

Arelia looked over to a small metal cage bolted down with a very large book locked inside. "What is *this*?"

He laughed. "This is where I believe your father developed his love of Scripture. This is our family Bible."

She was obviously confused. "How can anyone read it all locked up?"

He let out a hearty laugh. "Oh!" He reached behind the tabernacle and pulled a key out. "It was not always locked up. Your Father was probably the one who came here to read it most often, in fact, so much so that my parents thought he would become a priest. I suspect my mother was quick to arrange a marriage for him to ensure heirs and grandchildren. Once he came back from meeting your mother, he frequented the chapel and spent many long hours visiting with Fr. Martin."

He unlocked the enclosure and gently lifted the enormous book out and rested it on the table. "When we were just boys, we went with our mother and father to an abbey in London called Westminster. It was a trip we rarely made to a place beyond imagination. Fr. Martin came along with us, and we were invited to stay at an abbey where we saw a complete Bible just like this. My parents had heard that there were Bibles with the entire Scripture, but they had never seen one until then. Fr. Martin had copied the four Gospels, but that was all we had here at the time. My father decided then and there that we would have a complete copy of all the scriptures at Faircastle. Needless to say, Fr. Martin was elated and set about arranging it.

"A year later, my brother and I went with Father and Fr. Martin to a Benedictine monastery outside London to secure the purchase. The monks there had a large scriptorium where they sat day and night copying the sacred words. We discovered that these men had given their entire lives to pray and copy sacred Scripture."

He opened the book to reveal the pages. Arelia gasped. "I have never seen anything so beautiful."

Sir Daniel smiled. "Yes, and this is simple compared to some of the copies." He slowly turned the pages as Arelia took in the beautiful script, copied with a few first letters beginning in gold, silver, and purple; occasionally a beautifully drawn picture would grace the page.

"This copy has only a few drawings and colored letters. Years later, I saw the king's copy at the Cathedral in London, with jewels embossed on the cover. Of course, my father did not want anything like that nor could he have afforded it."

"How much would something like this cost, and where would they find all this paper? I remember that Father had trouble getting paper and had to wait for vendors to come from London to bring him a few precious sheets at a time in order to copy his Psalter."

"That is right. In fact, I was surprised to see that Edward had copied a Psalter. He must have paid dearly for such a large amount of parchment. The psalms had to be very precious to him."

He paused for a second or two with a wrinkled brow and then laughed a hearty laugh, startling Arelia. "What makes you laugh?"

He wiped his eyes and took a deep breath. "Edward *Davidson* makes me laugh!"

"I do not understand—my father?"

He explained through a broad smile. "Edward was always very clever and somewhat precocious. We never really knew what he would come up with next. I believe it was his love of Scripture, and especially the psalms, which guided him and, in some ways, calmed his mischievous disposition."

"Yes, he read a few verses to us every evening, and then we discussed them, after which we prayed the Our Father and the Angelic Salutation before getting into bed. It calmed us all for bedtime.

"There were times when I knew he was upset, and he would pick up his Psalter and read until he calmed down. I think that is why I know that being the father of a family can be hard.

"Uncle, I still do not know what you find funny."

"Davidson."

"Our surname?"

"Arelia, do you know who wrote the Psalms?"

"Yes, King David." She smiled, beginning to make the connection.

"My dear, my brother and your father Edward was a fair child who became a son of King David's writings. He became Edward Davidson." He smiled.

"Oh, Uncle!" She hugged him. "I truly am your niece!"

"Yes, I think we can confirm that now. Speaking of now, let us have tea in my parlor and return after a visit. Then I will answer your question about the cost of this most valuable book."

Arelia and Sir Daniel returned to the chapel after sharing more stories about Edward Davidson, with the agreement that Arelia could use either surname until she was comfortable with being known as a Fairchild. Sir Daniel hoped that she would be comfortable with the change soon.

They continued their conversation from where they had left off.

"The monks did not accept payment for their work but only for the parchment, pens, and ink. My father saw how elaborate some of the books got to be and requested only a simple copy with minimal embellishment, both to save time and money. It was over a year before the copy was ready. Edward and I suspected that Father also made a generous contribution to the monastery since they would not accept payment for their work."

"I can see why you keep it locked up."

"It was not always so, but years after this became my house, we heard that Bibles were being stolen, and Lady Ruth insisted that we lock it safely away. Fr. Martin carried the key, and so we always had access."

"Sit here," he said leading her to a comfortable chair near the altar. "I would like to read to you some of my favorite passages. Without our priest, we do not have the Eucharist, but we still have the Word of God." He carefully turned through the many pages, "Oh, yes, here it is.

"I am sure I know the answer to this, but do you know the Ten Commandments?"

"Yes, of course, we memorized them."

"Let me read this to you from the Gospel of St. John. Jesus told his apostles this shortly before he was arrested. *My children, I will be with you only a little while longer. You will look for me, and as I told the Jews, 'Where I go you cannot come,' so now I say it to you. I give you a new Commandment: love one another. As I have loved you, so you also should love one another. This is how all will know that you are my disciples, if you have love for one another."*

"My Father quoted that to us often."

"I thought that he probably did. He brought me right to this very place before he left us and told me that reading *that verse* is why he had to leave. He felt that if he stayed for an arranged marriage, he would not truly love. He said he had found true love with Margaret and did not believe that he would ever find it with anyone else. He wanted to have children for love, not to maintain or to expand property.

"Arelia," he said taking her hand. "You are a result of that love. Do not ever forget his words as he learned from Jesus and put them into practice in his own life." She stood and hugged her uncle.

"I feel compelled to say one more thing. I am not sure why except that your father said it to me, and Jesus said it to us, and that is that we are also commanded to love our enemies, not just our neighbors."

"Uncle, I do not have any enemies."

He laughed. "That is exactly what I said to my brother. He slapped me on the back with a big grin and told me that if I were to have an arranged marriage, I probably would one day. We had a good laugh over that, but he was right. It was Jesus's new commandment and his reminding me of it in a letter that saved my marriage and turned it to one of love.

"I do not know that you will ever have enemies, and I pray you will not, but if you love both your neighbor and your enemies, life will be easier for you."

"Uncle, thank you for sharing this with me. I feel I know my father better now because of you."

"I believe if Jesus said this to his disciples before He left them and your father said it to me, I should say it to you. With your love of Scripture, one day I want this Bible to be for you and your family."

He called her to the book and encouraged her to read the Gospels aloud as they enjoyed the day, taking turns sitting in the chair listening and standing to read.

Arelia listened as her uncle read the words of Jesus at the Last Supper. As he returned to his seat to ponder the verses, Arelia's eyes rested on the altar in front of the tabernacle. "Oh, Uncle." She sighed. "Do you miss having Mass and receiving the Holy Eucharist?"

He looked toward the tabernacle. "More than I ever thought I would." They sat quietly, and then he added, "Oh, dear Arelia, how many of us have taken the blessed gift of God for granted?" Tears filled their eyes as holy longing filled their hearts and souls.

Arelia spoke first. "I worry that we have lost all our priests and may never have Communion again."

"Yes, child, I suspect we have lost many priests, but God made us a promise that the gates of hell would not prevail against the Church. We must trust that promise.

"I have sat in this same spot so many times since Fr. Martin left to minister to the people, and I have gazed at the tabernacle, wishing for a miracle, wishing that Jesus would show His face. Once, two passages came to mind as I sat in this chair, 'I will be with you until the end of the era,' and 'I will not leave you orphans.' I was lost in those words for some time, and then I heard the most remarkable words in my mind. They pierced my heart and soul."

Arelia's eyes grew wide with anticipation. "What did you hear?"

His face lit with joy. "In my mind, as clear as if I had heard it in this chapel, I heard, 'I did not come to you in this blessed Sacrament only for your sake but for mine also. I have loved you in the flesh, and I could not bear to leave you alone. I have sent my Mind to you with My Holy Spirit, and I have sent My Body to you in the appearance of bread, hidden in the Holy Eucharist; therefore, I remain with you in Body, Mind, and Spirit always. I love you so much; you are never alone.'"

Tears overwhelmed Arelia; she could not speak. Sir Daniel remembered the flood of love that had consumed him at those words. "Arelia, what I think the Holy Spirit is saying is that when Jesus comes to us Incarnate in Holy Communion, truly in the flesh, it is a real, intimate relationship. Jesus and we are really together as much as you and I are sitting together right now."

She gasped. "Oh my! That must be why I miss Communion so much.

"Uncle, thank you for this time. I never could have imagined being this happy ever again. I thought my life was over when I left our village. I am not alone, am I?" she smiled.

"No, child, I guess we are never really alone. That is a good reminder for me. I miss my Ruth so much, and I will miss you, but we will always be together, in spirit, in this time and this place."

As dusk came and dinner drew near, he placed the Bible back in its cage and locked the door. "Now you know where the key is. You are free to come in here and read at any time. I encourage you to do so. Somehow, I believe it will connect you even more closely to your father."

She saw her cousin and Marisa only at dinner each evening. Conversation was kept to the activities of the day. Everyone retired early for the next day's adventure, not caring to risk another confrontation. Marisa was strangely quiet, which was a relief and yet unnerving at the same time.

As the day for her uncle's departure came near, Arelia had mixed feelings. She would miss him deeply, but she was also closer to going home herself. Her uncle made his feelings clear—he didn't want to leave Arelia, and he was not looking forward to the long trip. Again, he assured her that he would visit her village in a year's time.

Horses and carts were packed with clothes and furniture from his room and provisions for the trip. Many of the people who had served him at Faircastle were going with him to his new estate at Fairfield. Soldiers and knights were saddled for escort. All-in-all, the group made up a long and impressive caravan, more impressive than anything Arelia could ever have imagined. It was another of her father's stories come to life.

Before her uncle mounted his horse, he pulled Arelia aside. "Arelia, I know my son will take good care of you but keep this in case you need it." With that, he dropped a small heavy bag in her hands. "Put it away quickly now and keep it in a safe place. My father gave my brother a similar bag when he left with the knights; I want you to have the same."

Without looking into the bag, Arelia placed it deep into her dress pocket, hugged her uncle, and kissed him gently on the cheek. "Do not worry about me, Uncle, I have been through hard times and have always made it through with God's grace. I will see you again. Thank you for all your love and for sharing my family's history. I will add the last several weeks to my best memories. I will also leave soon and expect to see you at this time next year in my village."

He didn't hide his tears as he hugged her firmly. "Be very careful, Arelia. I love you." With that, he mounted his horse and joined the long caravan away from the castle.

Arelia ran up the long staircase to the surrounding wall and watched the horses and carts move slowly out of sight. Excitement filled her as she thought of her own trip back to the village. She was sure that Cousin Edward would loan her a horse with an escort. She wasn't sure how far she had come from the village but felt it was only a couple of days on horseback at most. She would talk to her cousin immediately about having someone help her find her way home.

Marisa and her husband sat in their adjoining parlor after Sir Daniel's departure. "Arelia will ask to leave now, Marisa."

"Yes, dear, and we will let her," Marisa said deviously, "and *I* will escort her."

"You! Why you?"

"I want to meet Cornelius and Camellia. I will be the best one to judge if they will give us any trouble in the future."

"Marisa, they will not know about my father's affection for Arelia, and besides, she is a girl. There would be no reason for them to expect her to have an inheritance."

"That may be true, Edward, but I want to see for myself."

100

At dinner, Arelia wanted to tell her cousin and Marisa that she was ready to leave, but she dreaded their reactions. "Now that my uncle has left, I do not want to impose on you any longer. I will be returning to my village as quickly as is convenient. I may need to borrow a horse and an escort in order to find my way."

"Arelia, your cousin and I have discussed that. We knew you would be eager to leave, and so we have made a few plans ourselves. I would like to join you on the trip. I look forward to meeting your friends and seeing the village that you have talked so much about. I will return when I know you are comfortable and settled with your friends," Marisa explained.

Arelia was taken aback by this. She had no idea Marisa would undertake such a journey and the thought of it was overwhelming. "Marisa, I cannot put you through so much trouble."

"Do not be ridiculous. I would never rest if I did not know that you were properly settled. I will enjoy the countryside. It will give us time to get to know each other better, and besides, a proper lady cannot go without a chaperone," explained Marisa sweetly.

Arelia already knew Marisa as well as she wanted to, and what she knew, she didn't like, and she sure didn't need a chaperone. Even spending one day with her would be too much. She was looking forward to a quick and simple trip home.

"Do not worry about anything, child. I will make arrangements for the provisions for our trip. We will leave in three days."

Although this was not what Arelia wanted, she would make any concessions necessary to get home. "I look forward to the trip also," agreed Arelia lightly.

CHAPTER 11

Arelia awoke excited about her day. This was the day she had awaited for weeks, and now she would finally have the opportunity to see Camellia, Cornelius, and baby Cornelius again.

She hadn't really thought about clothes but was relieved when Sarah walked in with her cloak. "My lady, I have washed your cloak." She laughed. "I had to empty the pocket. You seemed to have a little forest in there, or maybe it was your dining table," she said lightheartedly. "Seeing it, I am happy the men found you. I do not think you would have enjoyed too many more meals of nuts and berries." She held out her hand. "This is yours. Be sure to tuck it away safely."

Arelia studied the palm of her hand nestling a gold coin. "Why are you giving that to me?"

"Why, because it is yours, my lady; it was in the bottom of your pocket."

"But that cannot be. I have never seen it before."

"Well, take it. It sure did not come from me. Someone wants you to have it. I will put it back in your pocket. Do not forget it is there."

She took the cloak and observed, "Do you have the dress also?"

"The dress?"

"Yes, the dress I came in. I cannot go back dressed like I have been dressed here."

"Oh my, no! Your dress was ruined with the hem and sleeve ripped to shreds, and the bodice and under skirt soaked in blood. It was burned."

Arelia's eyes were wide with shock. "What will I wear?"

"These, my lady." She showed a dark grey dress with a light blue tunic.

"Oh no," she said shaking her head. "This will never do. No one in the village wears anything like this." The wrinkled brow showed her distress. "Does your daughter have anything I can wear? Are we the same size?"

Sarah was speechless. "That is impossible. Sir Daniel said that you must wear Lady Ruth's dresses. Laura has altered them for you. Her clothes have been in trunks since her death."

Arelia turned pale and fell into her chair with a thud. "This cannot be."

Arelia pictured waking into the village, dressed in such a dress. *Will they recognize me? Will they see Marisa and think I look like her?*

"Please, do you have a dress I could wear which is more like your own?"

"No, my lady, Sir Daniel wants you to have Lady Ruth's dresses. We have nothing else prepared for you now."

Sarah helped her dress quickly in the heavy riding dress. While Arelia ate hard rolls and had tea in her room, Sarah left quietly, saying that she had a lot to do to get ready for the trip. Wanting to make up for her lack of cooperation and appreciation, Arelia hoped she would see her again to thank her and wish her well. She gathered her few things, realizing that Sarah was probably preparing food for her and Marisa. She would meet her in the courtyard for a proper goodbye.

The plan was to meet Marisa at first light, and so she hurried to beat the sun. Slipping the familiar amulet around her neck and tucking it into her dress, she then wrapped her father's Psalter in a small lap blanket from Sarah and then picked up the small, heavy bag her uncle had given her, also dropping the new coin inside. It clinked against the dozen gold and silver coins her uncle had given her. Maybe the coin in my pocket was from the bag my grandfather gave my father when he left with the knights. It gave her a warm feeling that all these years later, her father was still providing for her. Now she had coins of her own from both her father and her uncle. She was not sure of their value, but she knew they were precious, because they were a gift from the two men she loved the most. She hurriedly pushed the bag into her pocket, as she was eager to get on her horse and leave.

As her parents had taught, she knelt at the side of her bed to say the Pater Noster before beginning a big task and crossed herself with the Sign of the Cross, focusing on the words, "In the name of the Father, and of the Son, and of the Holy Ghost. Amen. Our Father, who art in heaven, hallowed be Thy name . . . " The small prayer given directly by Jesus gave her confidence for the journey and provided her the feeling that her family in heaven was watching over her, along with Jesus and her Guardian Angel.

She didn't feel any regret hurrying down the long hallway for the last time. Stopping at the end of the stairs into the courtyard, she stood stunned. Before her was a caravan similar to her uncle's but even more extravagant. Sarah and Bethany, Marisa's lady-in-waiting, were seated in a cart with three large trunks. Two more carts were loaded behind them, and a dozen butlers, soldiers, and knights were mounted in full regalia for the trip. At the front of the caravan sat an elegant carriage intended for Marisa and Arelia, along with two flagmen displaying the family banner.

Arelia wanted to leap onto a horse and ride out quickly without looking back. She could not believe the commotion before her. *Why is this necessary?* She wanted to scream.

Perfectly coifed and impeccably dressed, Marisa appeared from the dark castle hallway to begin the journey. She seemed excited and pleased with the same production that appalled Arelia. Edward followed close behind to say goodbye, and the procession began.

Marisa and Arelia sat quietly in the carriage, bumping and jolting with every hole and rock on the road. *This is going to be a very, very long trip.* Neither woman even pretended it necessary to share small talk. The ride was silent.

At noonday, the caravan stopped, and hard bread, dried beef, and cheese were served, with tea and wine passed only to the ladies. Arelia tried to help Sarah and Bethany but was sharply corrected as Marisa called her away from the work.

Back in the carriage after the embarrassing rebuke, Arelia unwrapped her father's book to soak in some of its consoling words.

Her eye rested on the last few verses of Psalm 136.

V 23 The Lord remembered us in our low estate,
for his mercy endures forever;

24 Freed us from our foes,
for his mercy endures forever;

25 And gives bread to all flesh,
for his mercy endures forever.

VI 26 Praise the God of heaven,
for his mercy endures forever.

"Is that a *book*?!" Marisa interrupted, incredulous.

Arelia lifted her eyes in disgust, expecting what was to come.

"How is it you have a book? They are very costly and most difficult to come by. Where would *you* have gotten it, and what is it?"

Arelia tried to relax her jaw enough to speak but managed only through clenched teeth. "It is my father's Psalter. He copied it himself."

"And you can read?" The insults continued.

Although young and having been taught to respect adults, Arelia did not even look up from the page. "Yes."

"I am very confused. *You* have a valuable book *and* you can read?"

Silence

"Arelia, I am speaking to you."

She took a deep breath and attempted with respectful and expected etiquette. "My father is a *Fairchild*, as is my uncle and your husband, my cousin. I also am a Fairchild by birth, by blood." She looked Marisa in the eye, hoping she would catch the implications of *bloodline*.

"Father had a deep love of Scripture and copied these sacred words from the Psalter that Fr. Jerome had for our village. Our teacher also used a copy of the Gospels to teach us to read and write and memorize. I am from a village, but I am not ignorant nor were any of us. I have heard the words and stories of Scripture all my life, as I assume you have. My mother and father and Fr. Jerome have taught me well." She continued to read, ignoring any response Marisa might have, ignoring her stern glare.

After several minutes, Marisa interrupted once again, "And can you also cipher?"

"I know my numbers and can add to and take away, if that is your question."

Once again, Arelia announced, "My father is a Fairchild. I was raised as a Fairchild."

Marisa snickered and then straightened her back and squared her shoulders, as if to make an important announcement, "I also am a Fairchild, both by blood *and* marriage. The only difference between us, Arelia, is that my grandmother and mother carried forth my Fairchild bloodline." She repeated sharply, for effect, "I also am a Fairchild."

Arelia smiled with an unfamiliar feeling of smug pride. "Yes, Marisa, you are right, and I hope you can birth a long line of daughters, like yourself, who can carry on the true Fairchild name. Oh, and of course, the Pearce name also."

Marisa clenched her jaw and locked Arelia into a frightening glare, sending a chill down Arelia's spine. Arelia turned away, focusing on the passing view, refusing to cry. She saw a strange life of new, unforeseeable events: months of the plague, becoming orphaned, rummaging in the forest, staying in a monastery, living in a family of strangers, being attacked by wolves and saved by a soldier, finding her lost family, riding horses and having a picnic along the beach, and, now, witnessing the face of pure hate.

Arelia immediately sensed her own unfamiliar, hate-filled thoughts, and then, oddly, remorse. She resolved to repair the relationship with her uncle's daughter-in-law and cousin's wife, not for Marisa but for her new family.

She was interrupted again. Somehow a smile managed to distort Marisa's face, "Arelia, I also wish you a long line of daughters." A chuckle ended her words as she also turned toward the passing view.

While turning to a page of Psalms, Arelia thought, *If the Black Death did not defeat me, Marisa, neither will you!*

Truly wanting to reconcile would be difficult.

They stopped again around dusk so that the soldiers could set up tents for the ladies before dark.

Just as in the castle, Sarah was there to help Arelia undress and prepare for bed. "Sarah, why did you not tell me you were coming?"

Sarah looked confused. "I told you I had a lot to prepare for the trip. I thought you knew I would go with you to help you dress and fix your hair."

Arelia shook her heads in distress. "Oh no, Sarah. I have done that for myself my whole life. I will do it for myself now that I am not at the castle."

Sarah turned away, appearing hurt that Arelia no longer wanted her help. She slept uncomfortably on the ground next to Arelia's cot. Arelia could not sleep for worry about the older woman sleeping on the cold ground. She got up during the night and covered her with two of her many blankets.

Sarah was up before the sun, making tea and laying out Arelia's clothes. "Sarah, what is in the trunks in your cart?" Arelia asked as she looked at the arrangement piled into the carts.

"One trunk of your clothes and one trunk for Lady Marisa, my lady. Remember my daughter Laura has altered all of dear Sir Daniel's wife's clothes to fit you."

Arelia's eyes grew as large as the silver coins her uncle had given her. "Sarah, all of that! I cannot wear those dresses in the village. I am a common woman. My old clothes will be waiting for me. I cook and garden; I wash clothes and hang them; I feed chickens and milk goats. I cannot stay dressed like this." She held out the soft cloth of her tunic.

In spite of the fact that Sarah had seen Arelia when she was brought into the castle, she seemed surprised to hear that Arelia considered herself common. She had seen the amulet as she helped her and knew its significance. She was confused by Arelia's attitude but did not respond because of her position as Arelia's servant. Sarah felt she didn't even know the girl she had nursed back to health; her words were unfamiliar coming from a Fairchild. It seemed that Arelia herself did not recognize *her own* position.

The second day passed just as the first. Arelia and Marisa spoke occasionally of the scenery, but neither seemed interested in passing time with the other until Marisa interrupted the tense silence. "So, you went to church?"

Arelia was too stunned to answer such an ignorant question. "Marisa, did you ever step outside the castle? Do you not know about anyone or anything other than what is in your little life?"

"My little life! Your life will never be such as mine. You have no idea all that I have experienced."

In spite of her previous lessons in proper comportment, this put Arelia in the mood to persist in revealing Marisa's ignorance and self-centeredness. "You know what I miss most about all the Black Death has taken, other than my family?"

"I cannot begin to imagine." Marisa looked out the window with feigned boredom, working to regain her composure.

"Priests."

"Priests?! Are you serious? Priests?!" She laughed aloud.

"Yes, *priests*, Marisa! Fr. Jerome had drawings of the great churches of England and Italy. We would read beautiful verses from the Psalms and talk about people of different times and places, the times and places of Jesus Himself.

"He would read from the Gospels and relate all the beautiful stories of the early Church and of Jesus and the Apostles. It was so interesting to know that our lives are not all that exists in the world."

"I would not be too sure of that." Marisa grumbled.

"Do you not miss things of the Church since your priest has not returned?" Arelia's curiosity was now sincere as she recalled her experiences with Fr. Jerome in their small village.

"What sort of things? I do not even know what you are talking about."

Arelia thought for a while. The list seemed long to her because her family and community's traditions were entwined so intimately with the Church.

"Well, what about weddings and baptisms and the Mass?"

Marisa's blank stare answered without any words she might have spoken.

"Marisa, were you married by a priest at Mass?"

"Oh, of course, do not be ridiculous! Everyone was invited. We had royalty from all parts of the world. No one would ever doubt that I am Lady Fairchild!"

"But, I mean, you did have a Mass with a priest, correct?"

Marisa snickered as if Arelia was addled. "You cannot get married without a priest, can you?"

"That is what I am talking about, and what about the Mass?" Arelia pressed.

"What about the Mass? What do you mean?"

"I mean, do you miss it?"

"What is there to miss? An old man staring at the wall speaking a language I do not know and then telling us what we can and cannot do; no, there is nothing there to miss."

Arelia sat back and just stared at this woman who looked so perfect but seemed to have little of value inside. "What about Communion?" she ventured, almost in a whisper.

"Communion?"

"Yes, Marisa, *Communion*, the Eucharist, the Body and Blood of Jesus!"

Her ridiculing laugh startled Arelia. "Oh, dear, simpleminded Arelia, you believe the entire story? Poor dear."

This ended the conversation with Marisa, showing once again that they had nothing in common, bringing to mind her parents' pride as each of their children had received First Communion and the joyful celebration of the entire village afterwards. That truly was one of the many things that she missed about not having a priest—Communion.

She boldly studied Marisa as she had turned to look out the window, apparently bored with the conversation. To everyone's view, Marisa would probably be considered beautiful but definitely not to her. Her own mother came to mind, a woman who never had new or beautiful clothes or perfect hair or painted lips but a goodness and kindness that shined through her eyes and floated on her words, a woman of true beauty. Everything about Marisa seemed just the opposite, ugly, false, harsh, not a trace of true beauty. She wondered if her mother's beauty stemmed from her belief in God, her faith, and love of family and friends. Arelia knew the kind of beauty she wanted in her own life, and it had nothing to do with piled hair, painted lips, and fashionable clothes.

Arelia expected to arrive at the village during the second day. "The soldiers traveled with you for three days after they found you. You must not have been aware of the journey because of the potion," Marisa explained.

Halfway through the third day, a soldier approached the carriage. "We will be there shortly, my lady." Arelia could not wait to see her friends but didn't want to be carried to the village in the pretentious carriage. "Marisa, could I mount a horse to ride into the village or even walk?"

"Do not be absurd, Arelia. Why in the world would you? You say you are a Fairchild. You need to act like one," she replied with a smirk.

Arelia sat quietly. *Tomorrow, when the caravan leaves, it will no longer matter. I will remain in the village with Cornelius and the family and can be myself again.* Arelia was beginning to feel the relief of finally being home. Her roots were soaking in the familiar surroundings.

As they approached the village, children began calling to each other, "Soldiers!" "Knights!" They came running to the caravan. Women came out of their huts, and men began walking in from the field. Everyone was curious about the elaborate procession.

The flagmen and carriage stopped in the center of the village. A soldier walked over to the carriage and opened the door with a formal flair. Arelia nearly jumped out, avoiding his helping hand. The crowd stared, initially not recognizing the beautiful young woman.

"Camellia!" Arelia called out excitedly.

"Arelia? Can it be you?" Camellia rushed to hug her.

Marisa watched, pleased, as the villagers rushed around Arelia. *She will stay and be out of our family*, she thought.

After all the questions and excitement from the crowd of curious on-lookers, Camellia and Cornelius ushered Arelia into their hut. Soldiers began setting up their tents under the trees just outside the village square.

Sarah watched Arelia in amazement. It appeared that Arelia really was a common woman, just as she had said. Sarah had never been out of the castle proper except to go to Fairchild Manor with Lord Daniel and Lady Ruth to visit Sir Daniel's father. Much like Arelia, Sarah had been raised from birth in one area. She had no direct knowledge of entire villages of common people with no apparent rulers living among them; she had heard of tenants but had never witnessed them. She found this very interesting, strange, and oddly comfortable.

She and Bethany began preparing tea and an evening meal, while the soldiers set up their tents. Bethany arranged a pile of pillows and tapestries taken from the coach for Marisa to settle onto under a tree.

Several of the villagers walked over and offered Sarah and Bethany eggs and potatoes. The peasant women were curious about what had happened to Arelia and didn't want to wait for the news from Camellia. They immediately asked their questions of Sarah and Bethany and were surprised at the answers. "So, our little Arelia is really royalty?" "How long will she visit?" "Why is she here?" "How do we address her now?"

Arelia was so happy to see Camellia, Cornelius, and the baby that she barely noticed the older woman by the fireplace. Camellia introduced the woman as her grandmother. "Arelia, you remember, I lost most of my family in the plague. Grandmother is staying with us to help with the babies.

"Oh yes, and I forgot, I will have another baby in about six months." She patted her tummy affectionately. "But there is plenty of time for all that. You must tell us everything that has happened. Look at your dress! Who are these people?"

Arelia related her story, from the dog attack and being rescued by the soldiers to finding Uncle Daniel, Marisa, and Cousin Edward.

"Who is Marisa?"

"She is my cousin's wife, who has ridden with me here."

"Oh no! I have left Marisa outside without even introducing her." Remembering her manners, Arelia ran outside to find Marisa resting in her tent. Camellia followed behind slowly but stayed away from the caravan. "Marisa, will you join us in the hut? I will put tea on."

"Thank you, Arelia. That is very kind, but Bethany is preparing tea now. I think I will rest here and join you later, after you have had time to visit your friends." Marisa was all too pleased that Arelia was happy to be home. She wanted to encourage the reunion and be done with her.

"If you do not mind, then, I will go back to Camellia's hut and return for you later. Please feel free to join us at any time."

Arelia walked back into the small hut with Camellia, relieved to leave Marisa behind. As she entered the tiny hut, she noticed how dark and stuffy the tiny houses were.

"Where is baby Cornelius?" asked Arelia.

"Look, he is sleeping right there on the cot. No amount of noise will wake him when he is tired. He will be awake soon, and you can play with him. But now you have more to explain. Are you royalty? Why are you dressed like that?"

"Camellia, I am the same as ever. I am still a villager, but it does appear that my history is connected to the family of Fairchild who lives in a castle along the ocean."

"You mean you have been in a castle wearing beautiful clothes and eating fine food all this time when we thought you dead?" exclaimed Camellia in real amazement.

"Yes, but I am still Arelia. The same girl you met in the woods, and I am home now."

Camellia looked carefully at Arelia. She didn't see the same frightened girl she had met on the path. She saw a beautiful, well-dressed, confident young woman. "Arelia, you are not the same girl we first met. You are beautiful," she said in awe.

"I may *look* different to you, Camellia, but *I am the same*," Arelia defended, fighting back tears.

With a knock at the door came the first of a long line of visitors. Everyone wanted news directly from Arelia, who quickly tired of telling the same story and begged leave of her audience. "I am very tired from my day. Please excuse me to rest for a short while."

"Certainly, my lady," came the immediate response from one of the villagers.

"I am *not* a lady," responded Arelia. "*I am just like you*," she pleaded.

"That is not the story we hear tell, Arelia."

She left the small hut for the peace of the tent, which Sarah had already prepared for her. Sarah helped her remove her heavy riding boots and recline on her sleeping mat. Arelia was confused. She hadn't expected the reception she had received. Everyone treated her strangely, even Camellia. *Of course, when the caravan leaves, they will see that I am the same.* She wasn't sure that she believed her own thoughts; even she wasn't sure who she was.

Arelia sent Sarah to get her old dress from Camellia, thinking that if she dressed the same as the villagers, they would treat her the same as before. She would rest and then change to help Camellia with their evening meal. Everyone would see the same young girl this evening.

When Sarah returned with the dress, Arelia was not as eager to change into it as she had expected. The fabric was so coarse. She had forgotten how stiff and scratchy the cloth was. She chose to wait until morning to change.

"Camellia, may I come in?" Arelia asked after her rest.

"Why, of course, Arelia. Grandmother will get you tea," Camellia responded.

"No, please. I have come to fix dinner for you." She forced a smile.

"Arelia, you have had a long journey. I know you are tired. Grandmother will help me. Please relax and have tea. I want you to enjoy your visit."

Visit! This is not a visit. I have returned home. She felt ill-at-ease. No one treated her the same. No one even looked at her the same as before. She was a stranger in her own village.

Cornelius walked in carrying Little Cornelius in one arm and a bucket of water in the other. Arelia jumped up to hold Little Cornelius, but he wouldn't go to her. He held tight to his father's neck and turned away from Arelia. She couldn't believe his reaction.

"I am sorry; he does not remember you. You have changed so much in the time you have been gone. You do not even look the same," Camellia consoled. "I hardly know you myself, my lady." She smiled and jokingly turned away with a slight curtsy.

"It has been only a few weeks, Camellia."

"Oh, it has been much longer than that. We combed the woods for a couple of weeks before we gave up. Gilbert had found fabric from the hem of your dress. It was blood soaked. We realized that you had been carried off by wolves. We even had a prayer service for you."

Arelia didn't even try to argue. Pain gripped her stomach as she choked down the lump in her throat.

"Besides, Arelia, look at yourself. You could have been gone for years for as much as you have changed."

She ate a polite and quiet dinner with the family. She was their guest now. Camellia's grandmother tended the baby and cleared the dishes so Arelia, Camellia, and Cornelius could talk. It didn't go without Arelia's notice that Camellia had used the best of what she had to entertain her guest.

After dinner, Arelia excused herself and returned to her tent for an early evening. Once Sarah had covered her on her sleeping mat, the tears began to fall. "Father, I know there is a place for me," she whispered prayerfully as she fell asleep.

When morning came, Arelia hesitantly entered the village. Marisa was already up and visiting with the villagers, knowing that the fancy dress and formal caravan had set Arelia apart from them in their minds. She was no longer a commoner, but royalty to them. Marisa knew this unexpected development would change her plans, but she wasn't sure how as of yet.

When Marisa saw Arelia, she knew that Arelia had had the same realization. She was no longer happy and excited as she spoke to people. The children she once played with were standing at a distance, watching. Even Gilbert and his sister, who had explored caves with her just a couple of months earlier, stood at a distance. They watched but did not speak to her. She did not wear her common dress; she had tried, but it no longer fit. She was wearing one of the fine dresses Sarah had packed, although she had intended to send the trunks of dresses back with the caravan. Now she didn't know what to do. With all the good food, fresh ocean air, and rest at the castle, she had grown more than she realized, and now, Lady Ruth's dresses fit perfectly. Oddly, circumstances required her to accept the new wardrobe.

Arelia walked into Camellia's hut as her grandmother was preparing breakfast. Sarah had already provided for Arelia, and she was not hungry, but she had tea with Cornelius and the two women.

"Arelia," said Camellia, "Cornelius and I are so relieved that you are alive and doing so well. Imagine, royalty!"

"Camellia," corrected Arelia, trying not to sound angry. "I am *not* royalty. My father left all of that to marry my mother. I told you all of that last night." Her tone was harsh even to her own ears.

"I know what you said," Camellia said, "but now you have found your real family. Cornelius and I are grateful that you came to visit. We feel honored."

"Honored? Camellia, it is just *me*—Arelia."

Cornelius laughed. "It is not just you anymore. It is Arelia of the House of Fairchild."

"Look at you, Arelia," corrected Camellia. "How else can we think of you, with your perfect hair and dress?"

Perfect! That's exactly what she had thought of Marisa. She certainly didn't see herself that way and didn't want to.

"I would have worn my dress that you gave me, but it no longer fit," said Arelia.

"I should think not," said Cornelius. "I saw all the food the women prepare for you and the soldiers. Nothing would fit after a few days eating like that!"

he laughed. Arelia felt ashamed and embarrassed. She hadn't meant to find a wealthy, caring uncle who would give her fine clothes and food.

"How long have you been here?" Arelia addressed Camellia's grandmother, hoping to change the subject.

"About two weeks," she answered politely. "I was living with one of my sisters and her husband in the village that Camellia left. When I heard about the new baby, I wanted to come to help Camellia and Cornelius. We are awfully crowded, but Cornelius wants me to stay."

Arelia felt sick. Was it the small, musty room or the realization that she could no longer stay with them? She was not needed and maybe not even welcome. *How could things change so quickly?*

Bethany came to the door of the hut. "Arelia, Marisa would like to speak with you, please." Arelia walked out to speak with Marisa, oddly welcoming the excuse to leave the room.

"I wanted to inform you that we will be leaving shortly after our noon meal. Sarah and Bethany are packing now."

"Marisa, would it be possible for me to travel back with you? There seems to be no room for me here as Camellia's grandmother lives with them now. I could ask other families if they need help and have room for me, if you wish."

"Do not be silly. Of course, you can travel with us." Marisa had determined that she would prefer Arelia stay within sight so she could control her activity and know where she was at all times. She was very pleased that Arelia had come to the decision herself and that she would not have to persuade her to leave.

"I would like to spend a little more time with Camellia, and then I will be ready to leave as soon as you wish."

Walking back into the hut, Arelia questioned, "Camellia, would you have time for a short walk with me?"

As they walked into the woods, Arelia was overwhelmed with many feelings. She fondly remembered long walks with her family, but she also felt fear from the life-changing wolf attack.

"Camellia, I am going to leave soon, and I have something for you. You must accept my gift." Arelia reached into her pocket, opened the small, dark bag, and pulled out one gold and one silver coin.

Camellia's eyes opened widely. "Arelia!" she exclaimed. "I cannot accept these from you."

"Camellia, I want to thank you for taking me in and providing me with such a loving home. Save these coins for an emergency. You will have two children soon, and your needs will increase."

Camellia looked at the coins with tears in her eyes. "Thank you, Arelia. I will hide these away and hope I never need them. Cornelius and I are forever indebted to you."

"No, Camellia, this is in gratitude for all you and Cornelius have done for me. You owe me nothing."

The two young women hugged warmly. Without even a glance back, Arelia walked to the caravan to prepare for the long journey home.

It was hard for Sir Daniel to believe that he had been at Fairfield for over two weeks based on the little that had been done since they arrived. It wasn't just the shadow of death that gave the house an icy chill; the walls themselves held the long-winter's cold but no logs for a fire. It didn't feel like a home.

He was disheartened as he walked through the house on the first day when he and his butler, Roland, arrived ahead of the other servants. He had never experienced such a chill nor an eerie sense of foreboding at what he saw. The dust covers over the furniture, spider webs dangling from the ceiling, a thick layer of dust over the floors and tables, and sunlight shut out by heavy draperies hinted that life would never be allowed to return to Fairfield. He had no idea if any of his father's house servants had survived or where to find them if they had. Someone had prepared the house for vacancy, but who?

Sensing Sir Daniel's mood, Roland immediately ushered him into the yard, which was no better, if not worse. The once beautifully landscaped gardens were two feet thick in weeds with grass almost knee high, hiding winding brick pathways that led to the pond and flower gardens. Every direction he turned spoke of desolation and neglect. His royal upbringing had not prepared him for such an ugly reality. His dream of walking with Arelia through flower gardens and sitting by the pond with swans gliding gracefully by evaporated in the bright light of harsh reality.

One of the soldiers carried a chair out for him to sit at the front entryway, out of the dark, dusty house. Everything around him shouted that his wife and daughter, and his mother, father, and brother were gone to him forever. For the first time in his life, he felt the desolation of being alone in the world. His chest tightened as tears began to fall. Even thoughts of having found Arelia did not console him. Roland watched from a distance, not knowing what to do except to work quickly. He hadn't seen Sir Daniel in this state since he had lost Lady Ruth and his little daughter in childbirth.

Oh, Arelia, how I have failed you, my brother's child! I have also failed him. This is the life you had been living before we found you. How could I be so blind?! I should have taken you to your friends myself, and yet, I believed coming here was more important. He was washed in tears. *Who is there to protect you? You have suffered enough, and I have added to your pain. I am so sorry, child. I have abandoned you.* His elbows fell to his knees as he dropped his face into his hands and sobbed. *And now, we are both alone. My dear God, please forgive me and please help her.*

A little ray of hope returned to Sir Daniel when the caravan of people arrived with supplies late the next day. No one even tried to hide their shock at the disorder and the work ahead of them. Roland instructed them to leave the wagon of supplies and to take out only what could be used for sleeping outside. Soldiers quickly replenished the supply of firewood, and so they prepared the evening meal outside and slept under the stars for four nights. The first order of the day was to clean Sir Daniel's areas so he could get comfortably settled inside.

Servants burned plague-ridden, straw-filled mattresses. Rugs and tapestries were taken out, beaten, and hung in the sun. Draperies were shaken, windows opened, and spiderwebs, which hung like icicles from the ceilings, were taken down in any way possible. Maids stirred up clouds of dust, sweeping floors and dusting tables and shelves; sweeping and dusting many times before the job was done.

On the fifth day, Sir Daniel had a clean bedroom and office, a parlor with a warm fire, and a familiar cup of tea; hope returned for everyone. Roland wanted nothing more than to return a smile to his lord's eyes.

"Roland."

"Yes, sire."

"You and the staff have brought this place from dust and devastation to life and calm. It is taking on its original purpose and intent."

"Thank you, sire."

"There is only one thing missing which you cannot replace."

"Lord Daniel, we can locate whatever you need."

"No, Roland. What is missing is *family*. I have lost my family . . . my mother and father, my brother, my baby sister, and sadly, my son is no longer familiar to me." Roland recognized a depth of grief he had never seen in his lord before. He fought back his own tears for this man whom he considered a heartfelt friend.

"Sire, you do have family—there is your niece, Arelia, your brother's daughter."

"Oh, Roland, if only that were true. I have deserted her. She is back with the young family who found a place for her in their home. I will see her in a year's time, but she may be married by then with her own family."

"Sire, you will always be her uncle, and she will always be a Fairchild."

"Yes, that is true. Maybe she will bring her family here one day. We certainly have room for them." He smiled.

CHAPTER 12

Being alone because she had lost her family through no fault of her own was a common pain experienced by everyone she met, but now, she felt a fathomless void which she would never have thought possible. The fairytale image of her father's life had become a threat. It didn't live up to the childhood fantasy played out in her head, listening to her father's stories, sitting around the fire in a loving home. Now the stone walls were real, the table was filled with wasteful abundance, and she feared the people could not be trusted. It was hard to imagine that Marisa was one of her closest relatives and that she would be her family now. She leaned her head against the wall of the carriage and pretended to sleep, not wanting to answer any of Marisa's questions, to make idle chatter, or even to feel Marisa's stare as she studied her.

Her mind raced behind her closed eyelids. *How much time has passed since my family died? How many people have I lost?* She longed to be with her uncle but knew it could be a year or more before she saw him again. Even he could not fill her loneliness now. She considered asking Marisa and Edward if she could go to Fairfield to be with her uncle but knew that Marisa would be less than agreeable. She was at their mercy for everything now.

Her eyes burned with tears she refused to shed—tears Marisa would love to see. Arelia wasn't sure why she distrusted Marisa as much as she did. Marisa had always been extremely kind to her. Here she was, escorting her on this long, uncomfortable journey. She had certainly gone out of her way to make Arelia comfortable and provide her with everything she needed. Maybe her mother's advice wasn't intended for someone like Marisa, she thought. *Maybe women of royalty only appear insincere because they are so beautiful.*

She observed that Camellia had treated her differently because of her appearance, but Arelia knew that she was the same person Camellia had taken into their home. *Maybe my appearance confused Camellia as much as Marisa's appearance confuses me.*

Strangely enough, Arelia felt some relief in the thought of getting back within the heavy stone walls of the castle with Sarah. It was the only home she had now. If only her uncle were there to walk on the beach, enjoy the ocean with her, and read Scripture with her in the little chapel. *What will I do now? I cannot sit in my room alone all day, every day.*

I will ask Marisa if I can do some cooking and weaving with the women. I will enjoy both the work and their company. She fell asleep picturing herself walking along the beach, watching the horses and soldiers playing in the waves.

As she slept, Marisa studied Arelia carefully. She knew Edward would be surprised and concerned to see her return, and she was thankful that she had several days to formulate a plan of action.

She hadn't noticed how attractive Arelia was before now, and she decided that no suitors would be allowed to visit. Her soft smile, dark doe-like eyes, porcelain skin, and dark silky hair would certainly turn heads and hearts. It was of extreme importance that she and Edward produce the first male heir and that Arelia never even marry. She became anxious hoping that her father-in-law was not arranging suitors for Arelia. Somehow she must keep him from seeing Arelia favorably.

The three days' ride was tedious, and nights were sleepless. Neither Arelia nor Marisa even attempted to make small talk. In her boredom and despair on day two, Arelia opened the Psalter, even though she wanted no criticism about her ability to read or to own a book. Turning the pages, she stopped at Psalm 16.

I   1   Keep me safe, O God;
           in you I take refuge.
     2   I say to the LORD,
           you are my Lord,
           you are my only good.
     3   As for the holy ones who are in the land,
           they are noble,
           in whom is all my delight.

4 They multiply their sorrows
  who court other gods.
  Blood libations to them I will not pour out,
  nor will I take their names upon my lips.

5 LORD, my allotted portion and my cup,
  you have made my destiny secure.

6 Pleasant places were measured out for me;
  fair to me indeed is my inheritance.

II 7 I bless the LORD who counsels me;
  even at night my heart exhorts me.

8 I keep the LORD always before me;
  with him at my right hand, I shall never be shaken.

9 Therefore my heart is glad, my soul rejoices;
  my body also dwells secure,

10 For you will not abandon my soul to Sheol,
  nor let your devout one see the pit.

11 You will show me the path to life,
  abounding joy in your presence,
  the delights at your right hand forever.

Arelia read the words again and thought of Marisa. "They multiply their sorrows who court other gods." *I do not know that Marisa courts other gods, but I know for certain that she does not, in any way, see God as I do.*

She wondered about another verse. "Pleasant places were measured out for me; fair to me indeed is my inheritance." *My cousin has an inheritance, but girls do not have inheritances. Why did Uncle think the amulet was so important? How do I get back to him?*

She glanced up only to catch Marisa studying her intently; it sent a chill through her bones. She looked back to the psalm in order to avoid her glare.

"I bless the LORD who counsels me; even at night my heart exhorts me. I keep the LORD always before me; with him at my right hand, I shall never be shaken. Therefore, my heart is glad; my soul rejoices; my body also dwells secure, for you will not abandon my soul to Sheol, nor let your devout one see the pit. You will show me the path to life, abounding joy in your presence, the delights at your right hand forever."

I do call to You at night, Oh Lord. Do you hear me? I feel lost right now. I do not know where to go. Every time I think I have found my place, I am wrong. I do not know where to go or what to do. You know. Please lead me. Where is my hope? Jesus, I still trust You.

Arelia closed the book and rested her head against the side of the carriage, wishing she could sleep to blot out the jumble of thoughts bouncing around in her mind.

Marisa suddenly interrupted the quiet. "This Church you seem to love so much encouraged my brother, Thomas, to leave us." She motioned toward the Psalter.

"Your brother?" Arelia glanced up with interest.

"Yes, my brother left to become a priest."

"Marisa." She sighed. "He was not kidnapped. He had a higher calling."

"Higher calling?! Higher than loyalty to my father's name? He was our only heir."

Arelia was speechless. If Sir Daniel had not explained bloodline, Arelia would have thought Marisa was insane. Perhaps she was. She offered, "And so, you have taken up his charge."

"Yes, proudly, and I will not only retain my father's property, I will enlarge it with Edward and my alliance and with the alliances of my children."

Arelia turned her eyes back to her book. There was nothing left to say.

All the while, Marisa was busy devising a plan to keep Arelia from her uncle and possible suitors. The carriage was filled with tension which neither woman wanted to acknowledge nor cared to remedy. Arelia wished that she could ride with Sarah in the wagon and let Bethany ride with Marisa. It made her smile to think that Bethany probably would not want to trade places, and they would argue over who had to ride comfortably in the carriage. *Maybe we should put Marisa in the cart and the three of us can visit in comfort.* She smiled at the image. *Sleep, Lord. Please let me sleep.*

Marisa noticed the smile cross her face and knew that Arelia was devising a plan to recover her father's inheritance. *You can smile for now and plan all you want, but believe me, the heir to the Fairchild fortune will be mine,* she thought.

Arriving at the castle late the third day was a relief to everyone in the party. Arelia immediately went to her room for the evening.

She requested that Sarah bring a light evening meal to her room, as she had no desire to see her cousin over dinner. She had to have time to rest and think. There was a lot that she needed to know. Maybe she could run away.

"Sarah, tell me again, how is it that my uncle has gone to another castle? Why does he not stay here?" Arelia asked as Sarah put her things away.

"Sir Daniel is going to live in his father's manor house."

"Yes, I understand that, but I do not understand why."

"When your uncle's father, Sir John Fairchild—oh, that would be your grandfather. When he was dubbed a knight and given this property, he built this small castle,"—she smiled—"the place you call a castle, for his family—his wife and two young sons, your uncle and father. The boys were mere children when Sir John built Faircastle for his sons and their families, hoping for a large family with many heirs. That is when I came here—from the beginning of Faircastle. Your father left unexpectedly, leaving only Sir Daniel here. He broke his parents' hearts.

"Unfortunately, Sir Daniel had only the one son Edward, whom he named after his brother. It is rumored that this house haunts him with memories of Lady Ruth and his baby daughter.

"After the plague, Sir Daniel sent a troop to inquire about his father's health and found that he had been taken. That is when your uncle decided to leave. He had planned to leave before you were brought to us. I am not sure if . . . . Never you mind. That is enough for now."

"Is my uncle a knight as his father was?"

"Yes, he was knighted even before he married."

"And my cousin Edward?"

"No." She stifled a chuckle by clearing her throat. "Sir Edward had no interest in things of warriors. Sir Daniel tried to coax him to no avail. He is appointed lord of this land now that Sir Daniel is gone.

"Lady Arelia, you must get your rest. There is really nothing else that I can tell you. I have already said too much."

As Sarah blew out the candle, Arelia snuggled under the covers, happy to be sleeping in a comfortable bed again.

As Marisa changed into her night gown and robe, she was eager to speak to her husband about all that had taken place. She had much to plan before she could rest. "It seems Arelia will be living with us, but we must keep her from becoming part of the family," she declared as she walked into his bedroom unannounced. On seeing her, he got out of bed, grabbed his robe, and walked into their adjoining parlor. She followed without skipping a beat.

"She has gotten quite attractive now that she has rested and filled out. I do not want your father arranging anyone for her to marry. Those common people doted over her as if she were royalty."

"She *is* royalty," he nearly whispered.

"Their simple-mindedness was frightening. She may be more of a threat than we first realized. I think she may have a plan of her own."

Edward poured a large brandy and settled into his high-back chair. "Marisa, Father loves her as the daughter he lost. I am sure he intends to provide for her," Edward said angrily. He was angry as much at Marisa's insensitivity to his family as at Arelia for the trouble she was causing between himself and his overbearing wife. The week apart from her had been something of a relief. He had cherished the quiet. Hearing her now in her conniving state was irritating him.

"I have thought a great deal about this, Edward."

"I am sure you have."

"Do not agitate me! She must discredit herself in your father's eyes. He would never believe anything *we* told him about her. He is blind where she is concerned. Your father will not return for at least a year. We have plenty of time."

Edward drained his goblet, stood, and excused himself to go to bed heavy-hearted. Surprisingly, Marisa followed and climbed into his bed rather than going to her own room as usual. She continued to talk incessantly about how to ruin his only cousin as she arranged the pillows. Weariness from the trip finally won out, and she slipped into restful sleep with deep slow breaths.

Flames reflected off the full decanter of brandy on the table next to his hearthside chair, calling him. He eased himself out of bed, not wanting to awaken Marisa, who was breathing softly beside him. He reached for the familiar goblet, drained it, and filled it again before sitting heavily in his chair. "Be a man for once in your life," was the constant chorus she sang to him over and over. *What would it take to be a man in her eyes?* he thought. Having never been interested in hunting or war, he often questioned his own manhood; her chant was nothing more than a reflection of his own self-doubt. *One more glass of wine and then to bed.*

He slept fitfully with a dream that never seemed to end. Marisa, in a sing-song voice, "Be a man. . . Be a man. . . Be a man," over and over. Arelia stepping out of a golden coach holding three baby boys; Marisa coming at her with a sickle; his father, or maybe Marisa, yelling, *Be a man.* Arelia standing at a gravesite; Marisa leaving in Arelia's golden coach with what appeared to be a *real man*, laughing hysterically; him, choking Arelia around the neck and Marisa laughing and waving from her carriage window. It was a jumble of images, more real than a dream and more horrifying. He couldn't awaken himself to escape the constant barrage of horrific scenes continuing one after another.

Days slowed to a crawl for Arelia with hours of unfamiliar, life-draining idle time.

"What is it, my lady?" Sarah asked one afternoon when she brought Arelia's tea.

"What is what?"

"You, my lady. Your smile is gone. You do not even talk. Are you feeling ill?"

"I do not think that I can continue to sit in this room day after day with nothing to do. I feel like a prisoner."

"Oh, dear, you are not a prisoner. Have you spoken to Lady Marisa of your concern?"

"No. I am not sure that she would care. We only occasionally see each other at dinner and do not talk much, if at all."

Sarah busied herself tidying up the room to give herself time to think. "What do you enjoy doing?"

"My mother and I had a spindle and loom at home; sometimes we would make thread and weave. We spent long hours talking about any and everything. I cooked, fed the chickens, cleaned, washed clothes, swept, worked in the garden, carried water, went for walks with my brothers and sisters, played kick ball. Every day was busy, and I slept well at night."

Sarah tried to hide her surprise. She said with a chuckle, "Well then, it is easy to see why you are bored here! I am afraid that you may find little to do here, but please speak with Lady Marisa. She may have an idea for you."

Marisa had a loom sent to Arelia's room to help her pass the time but would not allow her in the kitchen with the servants. She did allow her to go to the library as long as Sarah escorted her there, waited, and then escorted her back. Arelia felt isolated from everyone around her. She saw servants from a distance, carrying things to and fro, but had no contact with any of them, except Sarah. She would engage Sarah in conversation as long as she could just for human contact, but there was really little to talk about.

She had nothing in common with Marisa and Edward, and she had no desire to spend time with them anyway. She wanted to be in the kitchen or courtyard with other women, but Marisa would never allow it. On the one rare occasion, she did speak with a maid in the dining room, but the girl was so noticeably uncomfortable that she never tried again. She felt isolated, painfully alone, almost invisible.

One day, when Sarah opened her bedroom to bring breakfast, Arelia saw that a man wearing long chain mail and a helmet and holding a spear and battle axe was standing in the hallway outside her door. "Sarah, who is that man outside my door?!"

"He is one of Lady Marisa's housecarls."

"A what?"

"One of her soldiers there to protect you."

"From what?"

"Intruders."

"From where?"

"Sir Edward has raised the levy on peasants to make up for losses from the sickness. Many of the villages have too few people to meet the tax, so there is concern that they will attack."

"That seems terribly cruel. I know our village would not be able to pay more than before the sickness. We had so few people left." Sarah's expression showed that she agreed, but she didn't respond.

"The . . . what is it?"

"Housecarl."

"The housecarl gives me the impression that he is keeping me *in* rather than keeping others out."

"Do not worry about him, my lady. Others are posted at all the doors leading to the outside, and we have a full military posted outside."

Arelia was hoping to meet Sarah's daughter, whom she had seen once in the hallway, but she needed to get out of her room in order to do so. Sarah said that her name was Laura, and that she was only one year older than Arelia. Laura was the one who had altered all the beautiful dresses that her uncle had left for her, and so Arelia knew that they had something in common; they could both sew. Arelia and her mother had sewn all of the family's clothing when she lived in the village. In fact, sewing was one of Arelia's favorite pastimes. She would love to learn how to make one of Lady Ruth's beautiful dresses which Laura had altered. She had never stitched fine fabric and wondered about the thread used to stitch it. Unfortunately, it didn't seem this would ever happen as she was not allowed any contact with anyone. She didn't know if this was Marisa's doing or if the servants were like Camellia and the other women in the village, and they had judged her to be too good for them.

Her only pleasurable time was spent walking along the ocean, watching the waves, and looking at all the unusual shells. Marisa had finally conceded to letting her walk outside at Edward's request. "What harm could there be?" he'd asked. Once a week, she was allowed out, but Sarah was required to check that she was back in her room within a relatively short time. She would have stayed out all day if she had the chance.

She thought how much Marcus, John, Daniel, and Prudence would love to have seen the vast expanse of never-ending water. She wished that they'd had the same opportunity to meet Uncle Daniel, remembering the wonderful days she had with him, digging for sand crabs and shells. Sometimes she pretended he was walking along beside her, and she talked to him about her family.

Occasionally, soldiers would race down the beach while she was walking. As amusing as it was, she watched from behind large boulders on the sea wall. Once, she almost came forward and spoke to the young soldier she recognized from the wolf attack, but she felt it was improper. They seemed to have so much fun racing their horses and splashing in the waves. They reminded her of children playing in the rain. She wished she could be as free to have fun and friends as they were.

To have a friend—that was what Arelia missed most. She enjoyed the ocean, but she knew she would enjoy it more if she could share it with someone. There was so much to talk about, and no one to talk to. Occasionally, Sarah would sit and talk politely, but then when she left, Arelia was alone again with only her thoughts and her Psalter.

Another Psalm, which she had memorized, came to mind.

God is our refuge and our strength, an ever-present help in distress.
Thus we do not fear, though earth be shaken and mountains quake to the
  depths of the sea,
Though waters rage and foam and mountains totter at its surging.
The Lord of hosts is with us;
Our stronghold is the God of Jacob.

Psalm 45, 2-4

Weeks passed into months. Then at dinner one evening, Marisa made a change. "Arelia, how would you like a room on the other side of the house, more directly facing the trees? Edward said he has seen you walking on the beach watching the soldiers. I know you enjoy the beach, but you would have a more familiar view facing trees."

"Yes, Marisa, I would really like that," she replied, relieved at the chance for a change. She knew the servants were on the other side of the castle and was hoping to have an opportunity to meet them, especially Laura.

"You will not be as near us but closer to Sarah. It will be good for her to not walk so far. There is a door directly to the ocean just through the courtyard."

"Thank you." Arelia caught a glimpse of light though the darkness.

"Good, I will have your things moved today. You seem to enjoy watching the soldiers. Would you like to meet one?" asked Marisa sweetly.

"I never thought of meeting one of the men, Marisa. I just enjoy watching them have fun. They remind me of my brothers but older."

"Yes, they can be entertaining." Marisa glanced at her husband. "Edward said that Captain Hardgrave would like to meet you and that he would arrange it." Edward nodded absentmindedly.

Arelia didn't want to be impolite, but she would have much preferred to meet Laura. "If that is your wish, but I do not think that I have anything in common with soldiers," she relented. She spoke out boldly, wanting to take advantage of Marisa's generosity. "I had also would like to meet Laura. We are about the same age, and we can sew together. My mother and I made all of our clothes together. I would like to attempt to make one of the beautiful dresses that Laura sews. We may even be able to make something beautiful for you."

"We will see." Marisa smiled sweetly.

Arelia loved her new room facing the trees. Although the breeze, which blew gently through the large, open window was too cool in the early morning, it carried a fresh scent of the forest that she loved. She was especially excited to see that many of the servants lived in the rooms below hers.

Bethany surprised Arelia by walking in with tea the first day she was in her new room. "It is nice to see you, Bethany, but I hope Sarah is not ill," said Arelia.

"Sarah is well, Arelia, but she works on the other end of the house. It is easier for me to serve you now."

"I thought my move here was to make the walk closer for Sarah."

"Well, there has been a change."

Arelia hoped she would still see Sarah, as they sometimes talked about Laura and all that she did. Bethany poured a cup of strong, dark tea. Arelia became very sleepy as Bethany straightened her bed and idly suggested that the move must have made her very tired. With the soothing sound of rustling leaves, the crackle of the fire and the soft sent of the forest, Arelia soon lay peacefully on her bed. Through drooping eyelids, she imagined her mother coming into the room.

"Mother!" Arelia said drowsily.

"Yes, Arelia, how are you, child?"

"Mother, I miss you desperately. I am so alone."

"Arelia, you are never alone. Your father and I love you very much. We will always love you. We will see you again, dear." The beautiful vision faded as quickly as it came.

"Please, Mother, do not leave me." Arelia cried herself to sleep.

"Arelia, wake up!"

"Mother?" Arelia asked.

"No, child, it is I—Sarah. You have slept the morning away. Are you ill?" Sarah asked lovingly.

"I do not feel very well, but I slept soundly and had a beautiful dream about my mother," Arelia answered. "Will you be with me today?"

"No, I have work to do on the other side of the house. Lady Marisa said Bethany is to care for you from now on. I wanted to tell you goodbye, but I will find time to come over when I am not too busy. You must not sleep so late. It is not healthy for you."

"I know, Sarah. It must be the cool air and familiar sound of the trees that made me so drowsy. I am going to miss you," Arelia said, reaching for her hand and squeezing it gently, fighting back tears.

Sarah seemed embarrassed by Arelia's show of affection. "Now, you get out of bed. Bethany will be in soon. Take care, child," she said as she quickly left the room.

Even after hours of deep sleep, Arelia didn't feel like getting out of bed. As she stood, she was mildly dizzy and sat on the edge of the bed for balance. *I have not felt this groggy since my legs were wounded.* She trembled as she walked to the window, taking in the treetops and fondly remembering the beautiful image of her mother in her dream.

The next several days passed uneventfully as usual, but her energy never returned. Then, late one afternoon, Bethany came in. "You remember that Lady Marisa told you that Captain Hardgrave wanted to meet you?" she questioned.

"Yes," Arelia responded.

"Well, he will meet you this evening."

"Will I join him with Edward and Marisa at dinner?" Arelia questioned.

"No, he will meet you here," Bethany stated emphatically.

"In my bedroom!" Arelia shouted in shock.

"Yes," Bethany said as she left the room without even acknowledging Arelia's response.

Arelia was confused. *This is very improper. Why would he come to my bedroom?*

Later, Bethany brought a cold dinner to her with a cup of strong tea. Arelia finished her meal nervously, expecting the captain to come in at any time. To her relief, Bethany came in. "Let me help you prepare for bed. You seem sleepy," Bethany offered.

Arelia answered, "I am very tired. Thank you for your help, Bethany. I feel a little dizzy." Bethany helped her with her gown and put her into bed. Arelia closed her eyes, relieved that there would be no visitor after all.

Just as the door shut behind Bethany, it opened again. A soldier stood in the doorway surveying the room. Arelia froze, startled.

"You must be Arelia," said the soldier.

"Yes, sir." Her response was confused and frightened.

"I am Captain Hardgrave."

Arelia watched, groggily confused and increasingly concerned. "Sir, if you will wait outside, I will dress for our meeting. Will Bethany return while you are here?"

"No, no, there is no need for that," he said as he approached her bed.

Arelia started to get up and was overcome with a wave of dizziness. She sat hard on the side of the bed.

The soldier walked to her and felt her long, straight hair, "You really *are* lovely," he said lustfully. He bent and kissed her neck.

"Sir, I must leave. Please excuse me," Arelia said in a daze, trying to stand.

"No, you will stay with me tonight," he said as he pushed her back onto the bed.

Her head was spinning. She screamed over and over to deaf ears. The terror turned into lifeless sleep.

She heard the bedroom door close, waking to soreness that was unfamiliar. Opening her eyes slowly, her vision was blurred. She lay there for some time as horrifying visions flashed through her mind. To her shock, she realized she was naked between the sheets, and her gown was tossed carelessly on the floor. She must have fallen asleep, too frightened to move. Light shining through the window indicated it was late morning. She lay numb with an emptiness and despair deeper than ever before. *What has happened to me?*

Experiencing an unfamiliar depth of pain both physically and emotionally, Arelia felt dirty inside and out. The word *rape* never came to mind. Nothing in her young life prepared her to even imagine such a cruel reality. Despair and sadness were familiar, but now mingled with hopelessness, she faced an indescribable feeling of loss. Now, everything had been taken from her.

"I must get to the ocean, to the fresh air," she said aloud. As she got out of bed, she saw several spots of blood on the white sheets. "It is not my time now."

Bethany must have come in. There is a basin of fresh water on the table and a pot of hot tea. Arelia was embarrassed to think that Bethany would have seen her in that state.

Arelia freshened herself with the cloth and warm water that Bethany had generously left for her. She washed away the strange smear of blood between her legs and then put on a dress that was laid out for her. In a daze, she made her way down the stairs to the beach. She sat on a rock overlooking the ocean and wept.

CHAPTER 13

No one seemed to care. Maybe no one noticed. *Why am I so alone? Have I become invisible? Does no one else see this man who enters my room at night and leaves me bruised in the morning? Why have I become so groggy that sometimes I cannot stand? Why do I no longer see Marisa, Edward, and Sarah?* The questions turned over and over in her mind with no answers.

Sometime in her foggy consciousness, she thought that other soldiers came to her bed. She began to lose track of time, a prisoner in her own room. Bethany set her basin out in the morning and brought her meals and strong tea day after day. Even walks along the ocean ended.

"The tea! It must be the tea that causes my sleepiness," Arelia finally realized. That evening, when Bethany left, Arelia poured the tea out of the window and left the empty cup on the tray. After emptying the cup for two days, she was nervous and edgy, unable to sleep. Her skin itched, and her mind was scattered. No soldier came to her room.

When Bethany came into her room early the next morning to bring her water basin, Arelia was pacing the floor. "How is it that you are not asleep, Arelia? Did you not have a late night?" she asked.

"Yes, but I awoke early. I would like to go to the beach." Arelia requested furiously scratching her arms.

"That is not wise. You have been so dizzy. I do not think that you are well. Let me get you some tea," answered Bethany. "You seem so nervous."

"I do not care for tea, Bethany." Arelia shouted. "I would like to see my cousin."

"As you will," Bethany said, leaving the room.

Arelia waited expectantly for her cousin, knowing how shocked he would be at her situation. Now that her mind was not so clouded by the tea, she would be able to escape this nightmare. She was afraid but even more desperate to escape.

"Arelia, you requested to see me?" Edward asked as he opened the door without knocking. He seemed angry.

She ran toward him and impulsively grabbed his straight, stiff body. "You have to help me. Bethany is putting a potion in my tea, and the soldiers are coming to lie with me in my bed!" Her plea fell on deaf ears.

"Do you have all the food you need?" he asked coldly, ignoring her panic.

"Yes, but you do not know what is happening," she continued.

"Do you have a comfortable room?" he continued, ignoring her urgency.

"I do not want the tea, and I do not want to be with the soldiers," she shouted in his face. "Captain Hardgrave is an evil man."

He raised the back of his hand and struck her hard across the face. She fell to the floor. He grabbed her hair and dragged her to her bed. "You are very ungrateful," he shouted. "Marisa provides all your needs. This is my house! You can repay me by making my men happy. You know what you are supposed to do. You do not need the tea any longer."

"Your father would not allow it!" she shouted. She was stunned at her own angry response.

"This is Marisa's home . . . and *mine*," he shouted, "not *yours* or *his*!" He stormed out of the room and fell against the wall, *Am I a man now, Marisa? Is that what a man would do?* He choked on his tears as he hurried down the hallway to his only friend, the decanter that beckoned.

Arelia crawled between the sheets, pulling them over her head, and sobbed herself to sleep. She awoke late during the night. Her jaw was too sore to move, and one eye was swollen shut. She turned over and went back to sleep.

Bethany came in early. "You have really made a mess of yourself. No one will have you now! When was your last blood flow?"

"I have not had blood in my new room. I feel very bloated," Arelia answered.

"You must tell me when you feel this fullness. You could become very sick. I will give you a potion to start your flow," Bethany said casually.

She returned shortly with a thick, bitter-tasting drink. "Drink this quickly. It will make you well." She stood and watched as Arelia drank the nasty liquid.

Hours later, Arelia was cramping violently. Her flow started, but it was heavy with dark, thick patches and solid, bloody clumps. The pains continued for hours. Arelia was doubled over on the floor with no one to help and no one to care.

In spite of ghastly pain and a bruised face, the next several days were a relief because no soldiers came to her. She remembered, months earlier, lying in the leafy cradle, after she'd left her family's village and her family's bones, comforted by the rustle of falling leaves and tiny animals rummaging for nuts and berries. She had lain there oddly comfortable, finally away from the horror of the Black Death that had wreaked havoc on their lives. Now, here she was again, not away from the terror of her existence but free from brutal intrusion for a few days. It was an odd comfort and consolation.

The evening of the third night was interrupted as the door opened slowly. Fear gripped Arelia as a familiar soldier stepped into her room. This was not one of the men of her nightmares but a friendly face.

"Excuse me," he said politely.

"What do you want?" Arelia asked cautiously, hiding her bruised face.

"I was sent to you," he said almost apologetically.

Arelia walked to the bed submissively, wanting to avoid another beating. "Come in."

The young soldier walked over to a chair by the window with long confident strides and said before sitting down, "My captain sent me." He explained and then studied her quietly. "Please forgive me for asking, but what has happened to your face?"

Arelia was unnerved by the unexpected concern. "I fell."

"Sometimes I see you at the beach, although I have not seen you in a while," he continued. "Did you fall on a rock?"

"No, I fell on the stairs," she lied.

"I am sorry. It looks very painful. Could I get you a damp rag?" he asked with concern.

Arelia said, ignoring his kindness, "You are familiar to me."

"We have met, but you would not remember. You were not well at the time," he said.

"Did we meet here in my room?" she questioned nervously.

"No, in the forest; you had been attacked by wolves and wild dogs. I carried you to the camp and then brought you here, but you had been given a pain potion, and so you probably do not remember," he explained.

"Of course, I remember. I have seen you from a distance on the beach. I just cannot see you clearly in this light."

Arelia became increasing self-conscious that she was in bed and gestured toward her chair. "May I inconvenience you to hand me my housecoat, please?"

Stephen lifted the dressing gown from the back of the chair and held it out for her. He stood, looking out the window with his back to her while she slipped into the warm robe. Only after she said "Thank you" did he turn around and move her chair to the fire for her. After she was seated, he placed two more logs on the dying embers and stoked it into a warm blaze.

Feeling strangely comfortable, the two young people continued to talk for hours. He related his part in saving her from the wild animals and filled in lost memories of the trip to the castle. His asked about her childhood and shared stories about his own family, which were interesting and amazingly familiar. He had grown up in a village of tenant farmers, two days' distance from the castle, to the opposite of her village.

"When my father was alive, he would tell us stories about knights and kings. Are you a knight?"

Stephen laughed. "No, but one day I would like to be."

"What are you then, a housecarl?"

"Yes, I have been a housecarl."

"Like the man who used to stand outside my door?"

"I do not know who was outside your door, but I suppose so."

"So, what do you do?"

"Right now, I survey the property for intruders. We suspect that with Sir Daniel's leaving, we may have to defend the property from attack either from the tenants or from enemy armies."

"Why would enemies attack?"

"It is common knowledge throughout the kingdom that Sir Edward is not versed in military affairs. His weakness could cost him his land."

"But it is Sir Daniel's land, is it not?"

"Yes, and actually, it started as Sir John's property, but with Sir John's death and Sir Daniel's departure, the estate is at risk."

"So when did you come to Faircastle?"

"I was summoned from our village about three years ago when they needed extra troops for Sir Edward's wedding festivities. People came from all over the kingdom, and Sir Daniel wanted to ensure their safety. I guess my skill with a longbow caught Captain Hardgrave's attention because he hired me as a housecarl."

"And you decided to stay?"

"Yes." He laughed. "But I cannot stay *here* all night. I really must leave. You need your sleep. I hope you are well soon," he said as he stood to leave.

"Wait," said Arelia. "I do not even know your name."

"Stephen."

"Will you come back, Stephen?" she asked the young man, smiling for the first time in a very long time.

"I would like to, but my captain must suggest it. I am to become an officer. Only officers are allowed to spend time with you. I think this was a token to get me to consider the privileges of being an officer. I have expressed a desire to return to my village. Captain Hardgrave wants me to reconsider."

Like a prize at the fair, Arelia thought and looked down, embarrassed.

Stephen realized his blunder. "That is to say that it is a privilege to spend time with you. We do not have an opportunity to spend time with ladies, and I certainly do not have a chance to talk to anyone about anything that means anything to me personally. My parents and sister and I used to talk around the dinner table every night. I have missed that most of all."

Stephen closed the door behind him, knowing that Arelia's bruises were probably not as she said. Curiosity had led him to accept the captain's offer, but intuition told him all he needed to know based on the rumors and snickers of officers returning from late-night visits.

Arelia looked at the closed door and smiled a deep, self-satisfied smile as she pictured the man who had so magically brought light to her dark cell. His coal-black, wavy hair falling gracefully to his shoulders actuated the subterranean blue of his deep-set eyes, long lashes, and dark brows. Although the shadowy light from the fire concealed his build, Arelia pictured his broad shoulders and narrow waist as he raced through the waves along the beach with his wet shirt clinging to his muscular arms and back. He had walked in with the same long, confident stride that carried him along the beach, and yet, this man, this strong, sure man, did not intrude on her, even though she was given to him as a toy to be used at his whim.

Aside from the looks of him, he was a young man who missed his family and valued their company. He was a man who was officer material, strong and capable. He was a man who respected her dignity as a lady when he was sent to a whore. He was a man who had fought wolves and wild dogs in order to save her life at his own risk. He was a man who ignored rumors in order to see the truth for himself. He was a man who was her friend.

That night, Arelia dreamt that she was walking along the beach with a man. Sometimes he was her father, sometimes her uncle, and sometimes Stephen. It was comfortable but confusing, as she was not really sure who he was. As they were walking, someone called her name. She looked to see her mother calling from the top of the sea wall. She followed the path to their house, which was a large hut with many rooms. Her family was sitting around a large, heavy dining table in a big room made of huge stone blocks. The fire made the room warm and provided a soft glow. She sat at the table listening to her loving family, studying each of their faces. Waves of happiness washed over her as each face imprinted itself in her mind, as if renewing a long-lost relationship.

She awakened refreshed. The edginess from not having the tea had worn off as she lay in bed wrapped in the peace of her dream. As a little girl, her mother had taught her that when you die you go to heaven, a peaceful place where you will be with your family forever. Arelia looked forward to that day. Her mother had said that God lived there, and He took care of all your needs.

Even in the terror that had become her life, she thought of God. When she was younger, her mother often told her that you could recognize God in nature and in the people you love. Lately, Arelia had not had much of a chance to enjoy nature nor to be with anyone she loved. She stayed quietly in bed thinking about God and trying to *feel* what it would be like to be taken care of by an invisible force—someone or something that was with you all the time.

She reviewed her evening with Stephen, the care in his voice and gesture, the similar stories of growing up with a loving family in a village, his sense of humor, and his polite acceptance of her condition. She hoped that he had no idea of her situation with the officers and prayed he never found out. Fear pierced her temporary sense of contentment, but she conquered those threatening thoughts and brought back the wave of peace by imagining that he would return, and that God would give her peaceful times with him. Hope was renewed.

She repeated words which she had memorized from Psalm 16, "You will show me the path to life, abounding joy in your presence, the delights at your right hand forever."

The air was cold, but the sun was beginning to rise. She longed for a walk along the ocean. If she dressed quickly, Bethany would not see her before she brought her basin of water. Arelia threw her clothes on, tucked her pillows under the heavy covers, and ran down the stairway, across the courtyard to the beach. The air was fresh and cold. She welcomed the cold spray that hit her bruised face.

"Mother. Father. I know you are preparing a home for me with you. Nothing anyone does to me here can take that from me," she said aloud. "If you are already with God in heaven, I am happy for you. I look forward to joining you there. Dear God, be with us all."

She sat on her familiar rock, watching the constant waves dashing against the shore. *Is God here?*

Why did Stephen come to me? He was a soldier, but he did not act like one. He seemed more like a villager. God had to have had His hand in that. She prayed to her Heavenly Father that Stephen would come again for another opportunity to talk. The last good conversation she had had before talking with Stephen was with her uncle, many months before. "Dear Father in Heaven, I think that you must have sent Stephen to me. Thank you. If you were the one who arranged it, can you do it again, please? I promise to try to think of You more often."

As the sun rose higher, the rays warmed her cold body and bruised face. It had been so long since she had felt the welcomed heat, except through the window of her prison-like room. She knew she would sneak out again to feel their healing rays and listen to the comforting sound of the waves. She no longer had flowers and long walks to comfort her, but she would not give up the sun and the ocean. She watched waves gently breaking on the sand and then receding back into the deeper waters. Her time with Stephen had allowed her to recede into deeper waters, resting in the consolation that life free from fear and terror still existed and was possible within the cold, hard walls of her prison.

She remembered a conversation she had had with her mother after her grandfather died when she was a very little girl. "What happens to you when you die? Where do you go?" she asked.

"Arelia, I do not know exactly where heaven is, but I know there is a part of you that does not die and goes to God in heaven. The part of you that thinks and feels goes to a beautiful, restful home where you have everything you need. There is only love there, with no sickness or cold."

"Where is it, Mother?" she questioned with sweet innocence.

"I do not really know, but it is called Heaven, and there is a loving Father who takes care of us all. His name is God."

"God!" Arelia said at the time. "I hope heaven is true."

Arelia thought about her own father and uncle and how loving they had been. She knew God was like them. The psalms spoke of God who is strong yet gentle; can anger yet is compassionate; obscure but familiar. She had not seen her cousin since she changed rooms, except that one time, but she knew she did not want God to be like him or any of the soldiers that came to her room, except Stephen.

Reluctantly, she rose to go back to her room before Bethany realized she was gone, being careful not to meet anyone in the courtyard or dark stairway. She got to the bottom of the stairwell and listened for footsteps. Halfway up the first flight, she heard a door close and footsteps approaching. She could not turn back, so she continued quickly up the stairs, holding her head down, her heart pounding, hardly able to catch a breath.

"Oh, hello," a young voice said. Arelia looked up to see Sarah's daughter, whom she had seen in the courtyard. "You must be Arelia," she continued. "I am Laura, Sarah's daughter."

Shocked with relief, she burst into nervous chatter. "Yes, I have seen you in the courtyards. I wanted to meet you. I did not know where your room was. Is it here? Your mother told me you sewed all my dresses."

"I did. There were so many of them." She laughed. "Mother said that you know how to sew, too." Laura tried to slow the conversation.

"I do, but I have never sewn such beautiful fabric. I come from a village, and our fabric is coarse and colorless," explained Arelia.

"Arelia! Go to your room!" shouted Bethany.

Laura looked startled. Arelia cast her eyes down and ran up the stairs, frightened at what would happen to her now. She slammed the door behind her and fell onto her bed.

Bethany threw the door open. "What were you doing? Why were you on the stairs?" she demanded.

"I was only talking to Laura. We are very much alike," she explained, her heart pounding.

"You are nothing alike. Laura is not a whore. She does not lie with soldiers night and day," Bethany insulted.

Arelia hid her head from Bethany's insults. Tears burned her eyes. Bethany slammed the door behind her.

Arelia's tears turned to deep restless sleep. She dreamed Laura and Stephen were riding horses in and out of the waves on the beach. Laura fell from her horse, and Stephen jumped off his to help her. When he bent over to lift her, it was no longer Laura but Arelia. Arelia awoke crying out, "Stephen!"

She lay there shaking. "What is happening to me?" she asked out loud. Her mother's concept of death came back to her. "A part of you that thinks and feels goes to a beautiful, restful home." *If the part of me that thinks and feels is separated from my body at death, can I separate that part from my body and stay alive?*

As she lay there, she thought about her body, bruised and beaten. She realized that while she had been on the seawall overlooking the ocean, she was not aware of her pain. *Would it be possible to distract myself from my pain with my thoughts and feelings—the part that is not my body—the part that is not bruised?* She closed her eyes and pictured the ocean. She imagined the sound of the waves and feel of the spray. Peace filled her as her body let go of its tension. She was consciously aware that she was feeling peaceful and wanted to hang on to it. She was also aware that her physical pain was almost unnoticeable.

Arelia's day was spent quietly, experimenting with her thoughts, reading psalms to guide her thoughts to beautiful places.

> IV 11 Let the heavens be glad and the earth rejoice;
> let the sea and what fills it resound;
> 12 let the plains be joyful and all that is in them.
> Then let all the trees of the forest rejoice
> 13 before the LORD who comes,
> who comes to govern the earth,
> To govern the world with justice
> and the peoples with faithfulness.
>
> Psalm 96: 11-13

She amused herself by realizing that she was doing something very important that no one was aware of nor could stop. She had never had reason to make this discovery before, but now she experimented and worked hard to control what she thought and felt. Since she no longer seemed to have control over her body, she reasoned, what she *could* control was her mind.

She experimented with remembering childhood memories. This seemed easy enough until her cousin or Bethany's face would flash through her mind, or she would see the pile of burning bodies. She would fight to bring back the peaceful feeling but was not always successful. Tears often interrupted her failed attempt at mentally detaching by bringing about loving thoughts.

Other than carrying in a tray for her meals, Bethany didn't come to her room. Arelia pretended to be asleep each time she heard the door creak open. She'd stand at the window or sit on the floor by the hearth until time for the next meal and then hide under the covers until Bethany brought another tray. She longed to have Sarah as her maid, knowing that Sarah would never allow any of this to happen to her. Sarah had treated her as she was sure she treated Laura.

Arelia could not understand how anyone could treat another person as she was being treated. Her mother and father had always taken each other into account and reminded her and her brothers and sister to be mindful of other people. She could not defend herself physically against the abuse, but she knew she could now guard her thoughts and feelings. No one could see or control her thoughts and feelings except herself, she reasoned. Her father had told stories about brave people who had been mistreated by soldiers and knights and how they had bravely lived through horrible abuse. She was determined to become one of those people. She would live through this, if at all possible.

That night, the captain came to her. He appeared to be older than her father, about the age of her uncle, and he was always angry. Each of the men who came was different in some way, but he was by far the most forceful and cruel. He seemed to expect her to read his mind and not only know what would please him but want to provide it. He seemed angry from the minute he walked through the door until he left. Arelia knew to submit without hesitation in order to avoid his cruel blows. He was the most frightening of the men. Aside from her cousin, she had never known such abuse. She compared them to the plague, showing up unannounced and devastating her body to the point of destruction.

Seeing him walk through the doorway drenched Arelia in a panic. Her thoughts were filled with previous abuses. She felt nauseous and weak at the sight of him. She wanted to flee, but instead, fighting back her tears, she listened carefully to the orders he barked, and she performed. He fell quickly to sleep after completing the vile, self-satisfying act.

Arelia looked at his face and realized she was experiencing true hatred for another human being for the first time. *I could kill him. He could not stop me. He is asleep.* There was sick satisfaction in that thought. Of course, she realized that if she did kill him, she would suffer the same fate at her cousin's cruel hand.

My thoughts! She remembered. She walked barefooted across the cold floor to the window, wrapping the same housecoat around her shoulders that Stephen had so respectfully handed her just the night before. She clutched it around her face and imagined that he had just left her room. The full moon was glancing off the trees, casting shadows and light as the wind bounced off the leaves. *How odd that there is so much beauty out there at the same time I am faced with such ugliness in here.*

She remembered telling her father once after days of rain that she was tired of looking at the gray sky. Her father corrected, "The sky is always blue; only the clouds are gray." For the first time, she understood what he meant. She realized the captain was a very dark, menacing cloud in her life, and it would be up to her to protect her own blue sky.

"Father, thank you. I will always try to see my blue sky," she said aloud. She no longer felt the horrible rage and hatred she had just experienced. She turned slowly to the man in her bed. "Take what you will of my body, but you will never have all of me." She was startled to suddenly realize that he was a weak and pathetic man to take advantage of a child. In fact, she was the stronger of the two.

Arelia took her pillow from the bed and one of her many blankets to make a bed on the floor in the light of the moon. She thanked God for the moon's soft, comforting light and fell asleep peacefully in the knowledge of who she was and comfort in who she was becoming.

CHAPTER 14

Arelia had to continually fight for peace of mind. With men showing up at night and the threat of Bethany checking on her unexpectedly, she was afraid to leave her room. A walk along the coastline was a rare occasion. Each time the door opened, she hoped Stephen would walk through, but he had not returned. She felt a void which she struggled to fill. Just as she had fought to save her family from death's door, she was determined to do what she could to save her own life.

Now that she had learned to mentally pull herself away from her physical situation, she could see how different each man was. She was thankful that she had had a loving father and uncle so that she didn't think all men were evil. She knew Stephen was a good man, and there were others like him. It dawned on her one day that only the evil men were attracted to her room. The good men like her father would never have visited, and if they did, they would not harm her. *I must remember to ask Stephen why he came to my room.*

Arelia had learned to engage the intruders in conversation if she could, not for their sake but for her own. After her only visit with Stephen, she would start a conversation with a man she felt might respond, because she was starved for company and news of what was happening outside of her room. On one occasion, one of the men started talking about his wife and children, thanked Arelia for the visit, and left. Arelia was surprised and pleased that he had forgotten the purpose of his visit or changed his mind. Generally, she found some men less forceful if they spoke, even briefly. One man had begun to cry after a conversation about his family, from whom he was separated, and fell asleep without even touching Arelia.

It dawned on her that many of these men were as lonely as she was, even though they were always among other men. *Don't these men ever talk to each other?* She remembered her father and other men in the gardens talking about their crops and livestock. She didn't remember that they ever talked about anything else. At night, she would hear her mother and father talking about their children and what had happened during the day. It was only on rare occasions that her father talked about what he thought or felt, unless her mother pushed him.

She began to wonder if Stephen was one of those who would talk and then never come back because he was a good man. He seemed to enjoy being with her, and she really had thought that she would see him again. With each man who walked through the door, she watched for his face, but she had not seen him since that night.

Each man who arrived at her door was different in his approach: one might appear shy and embarrassed, another angry and violent, and again another detached and self-absorbed. Most all were self-absorbed; most, but certainly not Stephen. Arelia learned to desensitize herself against expected, violent abuse and to respond appropriately so as not to incur even more violence. She learned that if she cooperated rather than resisted, she would not get hurt or, at least, not hurt as badly.

Bethany had brought the dark bitter tea again to start her blood several times. Each time the horrible pain continued for hours after, bringing her to her knees. She would often vomit the vile liquid and still be plagued with cramps and the flow of thick, splotchy blood.

As painful as it was for her, she submitted to this treatment, only because she received several days alone without any soldiers. When the pains were not too great, she would rise in the middle of the night and steal away to the coastline, uninterrupted.

One night as she was walking down the seawall guided by the light of full moon, she saw a man walking along the beach. She started to turn back in fright but didn't want to sacrifice even one minute of her chance to enjoy the ocean. He was at a distance with his back to her, so she quickly made her way to her favorite outcropping of rocks partially hidden from view of the ocean. Just as she sat down behind the rocks, he turned and looked in her direction. She crouched in fear, frozen as he turned to approach. She wasn't sure if he was intentionally coming toward her on the path or just headed in that direction in order to return from where he had come. She didn't look, fearing he would see her.

She wondered if it was her cousin going back to the castle or the captain going back to the camp. She had never seen either of them on her walks before; it could be one of the servants or a soldier. She heard steps on the rock path and froze, unable to breathe, hoping to go unnoticed.

"What are you doing there?" The voice startled her, and she jumped and let out a little scream. Arelia was genuinely frightened when she looked up from her crouched position but then visibly relieved to see Stephen's confused expression. "I was afraid you were my cousin," she explained, still crouched behind the rock.

"Afraid? Why?"

"He does not like for me to leave my room," she responded, trying to fight back tears and to control her hands from shaking. "He gets very angry."

Sorrow filled him as he looked at the girl cowering as a frightened animal having been whipped too often. He offered his hand. "Here, let me help you up." He extended his warm hand to her.

"I do not understand why you would hide from your family," he coaxed again, wanting to keep her hand in his, encouraging her to be truthful with him.

She slowly withdrew her hand. "My cousin gets very angry," she repeated. Stephen remembered the fading bruises that had covered her face the last time he had seen her and decided not to continue his questioning but, instead, to reassure her.

"You do not need to be frightened," he said. "Would you like to walk with me? No one will see us at this time of night."

"Yes, for a short time." The last time she had walked with someone along the beach was with her uncle. Stephen possessed the same sort of kindness and concern. She was comfortable with him. Small wispy clouds floated across the moon on a soft and constant breeze, blowing away the tension and fear that led her behind the rock. All worry faded as they ambled in the moonlight near gently lapping waves.

They walked briefly without speaking, simply taking in the beauty of the evening. "Stephen, why did you come to me in my room when you did?" she asked hesitantly, finally able to ask the question.

"My captain offered me the opportunity. He said that I was good officer material and that I needed to become a man. I was not ready to prove myself in the way he meant, but I had heard so much talk about you that I wanted to meet you. I could not believe that the girl in the room was the same girl we saved from the wolves. I wanted to see for myself," he explained.

"What did you think when you saw me?" She was embarrassed to ask but needed to know.

"Even though I did not know you, I was surprised to see you, knowing that you were a Fairchild, but I was glad to see you again and to get to visit." He continued after a nervous pause. "Arelia, why *are* you that girl?" He stopped and turned to her with such great concern; warmth and tenderness filled his deep-blue eyes.

"I cannot say," she said. Her voice cracked, trying not to cry. "I found my father's family, or rather, they found me. I do not understand what has happened to me. I know if my uncle were here, I would not be trapped in that room." She couldn't stop the tears any longer. "I am sorry. I am so confused." She turned to walk away.

He gently took her shoulders and turned her to him, lifting her chin so she would look at him. "Who is keeping you in the room?" he asked.

"I guess my cousin is." She looked away and started walking. "When a soldier complains about me, he beats me. I do not know why he hates me. I am family; I am his only cousin. Bethany, Marisa's maid, must tell him everything. Sarah helped me before Bethany, but I never see her anymore. She would not let this happen to me."

She wanted to change the subject. "Stephen, why are you walking the beach?" She wiped her eyes with the back of her hand.

He didn't want to make her more uncomfortable than she was. "Sleep escapes me tonight." He looked out over the waves, seeming to be lost in his thoughts. "Captain Hardgrave is grooming me to be an officer. It is quite an honor, which would require more responsibility and allow more comforts. I have been in training for several months, but I am not sure this is what I want. Some of the officers are good people, but they are more interested in their own power and position than in the men. I do not know what will happen to me if I accept the position. I have seen men change, and I do not like what I see."

"You could never be unfair or cruel, Stephen. You are a good man. I do not think becoming an officer could change that."

He laughed. "And you think you know me that well."

Arelia just smiled. "Would you be able to come to my room if you were an officer?"

He looked at her and returned the smile. "That is why I cannot sleep tonight, Arelia. I do not want to pass up an opportunity to be able to visit with you. If I do not become an officer, I may never see you again."

Arelia's face lit up at his compliment. "I would like to visit with you often."

They held their words as he escorted her back to the castle along the rocky coastline. Arelia cherished what he had said. She had thought he hadn't been back to see her because she *was* the girl in the room, but thinking about seeing her had kept him awake. She was excited to have a real friend who didn't shun her because she was *that* girl.

Stephen was considering taking the officer's position primarily for the opportunity to spend time with Arelia. Of course, it meant he would have to associate with other officers and listen to fanciful stories they told about this frightened girl. As it was now, he did not fraternize with officers, so he never heard the stories firsthand that he feared would be told around the campfire. He wasn't sure he could handle it. There was no way he could tell Arelia of the boasts each time a man returned from a visit with her, and he could never tell her how much it upset him. He would never let her know how the men shared the most intimate secrets of the room, which he assumed untrue and exaggerated to satisfy their egos. Maybe there was another way he could see her.

As they reached the steps leading up to the seawall, Stephen put his hands gently on her shoulders, once again turning her slowly to face him in the soft glow of moonlight, and then he hugged her gently. He quickly became aware of immediate tension. "Arelia, seeing you tonight is a gift. I will find a way to see you again. I promise. You need never be afraid of me."

"Thank you, Stephen," was all she could say as she choked back tears.

Reaching the long stairway up to her room, she paused to listen for any motion, not wanting to risk being discovered as she had been the last time.

Making it back without notice, she stood at her window and watched the clouds float overhead; wind continued to blow gently, and she could hear waves on the shore. Warm feelings rested in her heart as she crawled between cold sheets and replayed the scene with Stephen in her mind. "I *must* see you again," she said aloud.

Because of her blood flow, she knew from past experiences that she would have one more day uninterrupted. She would go out once more, hoping to see him one last time before the parade of soldiers began again.

CHAPTER 15

Arelia slept a good part of the day to make up for lost sleep from her walk on the beach with Stephen. All she could think about was seeing him again. Reason suggested that if he didn't accept the officer's position, she might never see him again, but if he did, he might be unhappy. For selfish reasons, she wanted him to be an officer.

Bethany had almost ignored her for the past several days, as she always did when Arelia had no visitors. She would simply bring her a water basin and bread and cheese and then not return until the next day. Because Bethany had already been in earlier, Arelia knew she would be safe to walk along the ocean one more night.

The moon was rising high in the night sky, and she could still hear servants on the stairway. There must have been some festivity with all the commotion. Arelia knew that Bethany would be sure to inform her of what she had missed; she seemed to take delight in increasing Arelia's loneliness and feelings of being excluded.

Hours passed before Arelia felt safe enough to venture down the long stairway, but it was worth the wait when strong wind from the ocean pressed against her face, twisting her long, dark hair into a frenzy. She could see lightning in the distance as the wind grew stronger, indicating that a building storm was heading their way. Still, she didn't want to give up her last night of freedom. She was intent on staying on the seawall as long as possible before the rain came. Lightning fascinated her—such power and beauty. She wondered if her father had ever sat on this exact rock, watching approaching storms, and she wished she'd had one more chance to be with him in the comfort of their family's hut, nestled near a warm fire, drinking in loving conversations. Oddly, her thoughts didn't make her as lonely as they once had because she had a friend now, someone who cared about her.

As horrible as her existence was, she was thankful to have food and a place to sleep, no longer wandering along a wooded path looking for a village. The fright she experienced now was different from what she had experienced then: hearing animals at night, hunger pangs with no relief, and sleeping out in the rain and cold. She remembered a night, much like this, one when the wind blew through the trees with a howl, and lightning lit the night. The rain had started to fall, and she couldn't find cover. She had finally hidden under a fallen branch but was still soaked through and cold. That night, her tears fell as heavily as the rain. She had no sense of hope—only despair. Strangely enough, she realized that tonight was different. She looked forward to the rain, knowing she would have a comfortable, warm bed to sleep in when she got back to her room; she had Stephen as a friend, and food brought in for her every day. Since she had learned to control her thoughts, she could block out much of the nightly abuse. Learning to appreciate and concentrate on the good had greatly relieved her stress and even helped her recognize things to be grateful for, even in her desperate situation.

A large drop of rain hit her in the face, interrupting her peaceful thoughts. "Oh, no," she said, as she began to run up to the castle. The rain pelted her, drenching her from head to toe. She ran up the stairs, forgetting to listen for noise.

Her cold, wet clothes left her shivering as she quickly changed into her nightgown, throwing her wet dress on a chair by the window to dry and then snuggling beneath the heavy covers of her big bed to get warm. Within minutes, she had fallen asleep within the warmth of her blanket, thankful to have another night alone.

Bethany awakened her late in the morning when she brought her basin of water. She was unusually friendly and happy. "There was a lot of excitement last night," she began excitedly, "dancing and fine food, lots of visitors and, of course, the announcement."

Arelia didn't give her the satisfaction of asking, *What announcement?*

Bethany continued, "Sir Edward and Lady Marisa were *so* loving towards each other. Everyone is so excited. I had been thinking something was going to happen."

Arelia had never seen Bethany so animated but refused to respond.

"Her dress was lovely," she rambled on. "There was music and so much wine. Sir Edward was elated when he made the announcement! Oh, too bad you were not there." She made a pout, very unbecoming of an arrogant old woman.

"I did not know about any festivities," Arelia said, immediately disappointed in herself for responding.

"Oh dear, too bad," Bethany said condescendingly. "And imagine, we will have a little one shortly, an heir. It will be such an event!"

"Marisa?" Arelia questioned, genuinely curious now.

"Of course, Lady Marisa. Who else, you stupid girl?!" rebuked Bethany with a sneer.

Arelia lay back in her bed. *Imagine Marisa a mother.* She couldn't make a connection between motherhood and Marisa.

"Arelia, why is your dress wet?" demanded Bethany.

Arelia was taken aback and speechless. "What?" she asked stalling for time.

"Your dress is wet," she said holding it up.

"Oh dear," Arelia covered. "I should have put it away from the window with the hard rain. How foolish of me."

Bethany picked up her dress and noticed the sandy hemline. She didn't say another thing to the girl, knowing she was lying. "I will bring your food up shortly. Dress yourself," Bethany ordered as she quickly left the room.

I must be more careful.

Arelia's meal was a treat, with bread, cheese, and meat left from the evening festivities, and even a piece of roasted potato. She realized with dread that all this attention from Bethany meant her visitors would begin again.

She ate her meal, concentrating on the treat before her while preparing her mind for the day. "I am thankful for this good food and comfortable room," she reminded herself. "I am thankful that I am not wandering in the forest and that I have warm blankets, a bed, and a warm fire. I am thankful that Stephen is my friend." She felt peaceful, even knowing what was in store for her. Gratitude and psalms were the only antidote for her miserable existence.

She was giving thanks and reaching for her father's Psalter when the door opened. It startled her as she was not expecting anyone so soon. Surprise turned to dread as Edward walked into the room.

She covered her fear, as she had so many times with the entrance of so many men. "Hello, Cousin. I understand you and Marisa have wonderful news. Thank you for coming to tell me." She forced a weak, unconvincing smile.

Edward ignored her and walked to her dress and picked it up. "Your dress is wet, Arelia."

"Yes, sir," she admitted, hesitantly.

"Can you explain this to me?" he asked, coldly.

"I was foolish, sire, and left it too near the window when it rained last night."

He grabbed her by the hair and pushed her face to the floor into the hem of her dress. "And how is it that the hem is so dirty? Is this sand from the beach?" he demanded.

Arelia braced herself against his cruel hand as hot tears threatened to fall. "Sire, I sat on the seawall late last night and got caught in the rain," she confessed.

"Who was with you, Arelia?"

"No one, sire. I was alone."

"You have lied to me before. Should I believe you now?" he said releasing her hair as she fell into a heap.

"Yes, sire, please forgive me. I really was alone," she said contritely.

He slapped her. "Is that the truth or another lie from a little tramp?"

Arelia's anger rose, but she knew she would never win against him. "It is the truth."

He slapped her again, causing her lip to bleed. "You will not lie again, will you?"

She wanted to slap him back. Lowering her eyes and cowering as a frightened animal, she replied, "No, sire."

Mercifully, he turned and walked toward the door. "Bethany will inform me how you are doing. I trust there will be no more lies between us."

Arelia pulled herself onto to her hands and knees, staring at the closed door; her tears began to fall. *This is my family?* She wanted to shout but only crawled to her bed, crying hopelessly.

"Are you all right?" a soft voice asked.

Arelia jumped with fright. "Laura?" she asked, relieved to see the young woman's face. "What are you doing here?"

"I heard Sir Fairchild yelling and hid until I saw him leave your room. I have heard him before. Are you all right?"

"Laura, you should not be here. It is not safe," Arelia said, protectively, getting under the blanket and covering her face.

"Arelia, my mother is very worried about you. She is not allowed to visit, but no one has told *me* not to. Mother knows something is wrong but does not know what she can do about it," Laura replied. "Bethany is at the other end of the house. She will not return for some time," Laura continued as she went to the basin to dampen a cloth for Arelia's bloody, swollen lip, not even flinching at the wound.

Arelia watched her in amazement. All this time, Arelia had heard her on the stairwell and wanted to talk to her. Now she was here as a friend, and Arelia didn't know what to say.

"I am sorry he is so cruel to you," Laura said sincerely as she handed her the damp rag.

"How is your mother?" Arelia asked, changing the subject.

"She is fine. Since Bethany spends her time with you, Mother must tend to Marisa. She really misses you, Arelia," Laura explained.

"Please do not tell her what happened to me, Laura. She does not need to worry, and there is nothing she can do."

"It will be our secret," Laura agreed, but her expression said something else.

Laura went around the room straightening while Arelia watched. Neither of the girls spoke, but Arelia was comforted and amazed by her presence.

"Laura, thank you for coming, but it is not safe for you to be here."

"I know. People talk so badly of you, but Mother seems to love you. I needed to talk to you for myself. I cannot stay long or come often. I guess I should leave now."

Laura's comment seemed so casual but startling to Arelia. "People talk badly of me?"

"I am sorry I said that," said Laura, looking away.

"Is that true?" asked Arelia.

"Yes, but they only talk of what they hear. They do not know you. I think many of the women know the truth but would rather tell stories," explained Laura, trying to relieve the hurt of her comment. "I must leave," she said, walking toward the door. "I will try to see you again." She seemed to be fighting back tears herself.

Arelia added Laura's bravery to her list of things she was thankful for and sincerely hoped that no one had seen her to report that she had visited. *I hope I see you again, too.*

The sky grew as dark Arelia's fear. She expected a soldier to walk through the door. Time passed with no visitor, allowing her to lay in bed counting her blessings, with Laura's visit first on her list. She fell asleep imagining that she and Laura were sewing with her mother and Laura's mother, Sarah, by the fire in their cottage in a village far, far away.

"Arelia," a man's voice awakened her. She screamed as a strong hand muffled her mouth, sending a sharp pain through her torn lip.

"It is me, Stephen," this voice reassured as he slowly removed his hand and put a log on the fire.

Arelia sat up. "Stephen!"

"Yes."

"How is it that you are here?" Arelia asked, surprised.

"I overheard the captain telling one of the men that you were sick, and he must wait to see you another time. I was worried."

He couldn't see the swollen lip in the dark. Arelia felt her eyes welling up from his kindness as she pulled the blanket up to dab them and to cover her battered lip.

"Thank you for coming, Stephen. You are my second kind visitor today."

"Second?" he questioned.

"Yes, one of the girls visited. She is Sarah's daughter. You remember me telling you about Sarah?"

"Yes, she is very kind to you. Does her daughter come often?" he asked pleased.

"Oh, no, this was her first visit."

"Now you have a new friend," he said happily.

Arelia didn't respond, knowing that Laura wouldn't be allowed to visit on a regular basis and could only sneak an occasional, rare, and risky visit. She actually wasn't persuaded that she would ever see her again but thought Stephen probably knew that for himself. "Yes, a new friend," she said wistfully.

The door opened slowly with a creak. Stephen quickly dropped to the floor, quietly, rolling under the bed as candlelight entered the room. Bethany walked over to the bed and cast the light on Arelia's face to peruse her swollen lip. Suspiciously, she walked over and looked behind the table and chair, behind the dressing screen and armoire, and then turned toward the door but stopped one last time to survey the room before leaving.

Stephen's military instincts had come into play. He feared that one of the officers was there for his pleasure, and he would be trapped under Arelia's bed, unable to leave or make himself known for fear of her safety. Relieved to see Bethany's skirt sweeping across the cold stone floor, he listened breathlessly until her footsteps faded down the stairs and then eased himself out from under the bed.

"I am going to leave now, but I will see you again," he said as he added one more log to the fire, jabbing dying embers to spark new flames.

No longer able to contain her excitement at seeing him, Arelia sat up on the edge of the bed. "Are you an officer?" she asked hopefully.

"I will be soon," he confirmed with a grin.

Arelia smiled with a big sigh. "Thank you."

He turned from the fireplace just as the new log caught fire and cast a light into the room. "Oh my God! What has happened to you?" His voice softened as he walked toward her.

She turned away. "Oh, please do not make me say it. I cannot bear to talk about it."

He gently stroked her hair away from her face. "Oh, dear Arelia . . . ."

"Stephen," Arelia asked hesitantly, "Laura said people speak badly about me."

Stephen interrupted, "Arelia, I know you. I am the one who brought you from the woods. I have seen your bruises. Do not worry about what I hear or about what others say. Those who really know you would never believe any of what they hear. It only makes me angry because I know it is not true. I know what the truth is. I see it for myself! I see it now."

"Then you *have* heard bad things."

"People talk, but I do not listen."

"Thank you," she said, gently touching his strong hand which caressed her face.

He leaned and kissed her softly on the forehead. "Go to sleep. I will see you again."

Arelia felt she had been in a dream. Laura's and Stephen's kindness were more than she could have hoped for. She wondered why Stephen cared so much for her when he knew what she had become.

Stephen leaned against the closed door in the hallway, fighting an impulse to burst into Sir Edward's room and kill him.

Weeks passed, with soldiers as her only visitors. She heard Laura on the stairs several times but never saw her. There was no sign of Stephen. Each time the door opened, she anticipated him but was disappointed. She managed her days by controlling her thoughts and acknowledging things to appreciate through prayer. God often seemed as far from her and unreachable as Laura and Stephen, but she fought for her sanity through her connection with her family within her father's Psalter.

Psalm 57

I 2   Have mercy on me, God,
        have mercy on me.
        In you I seek shelter.
        In the shadow of your wings I seek shelter
        till harm pass by.

   3   I call to God Most High,
        to God who provides for me.

   4   May God send help from heaven to save me,
        shame those who trample upon me.

> May God send fidelity and mercy.
>
> 5   I must lie down in the midst of lions
> hungry for human prey.
> Their teeth are spears and arrows;
> their tongue, a sharpened sword.
>
> 6   Be exalted over the heavens, God;
> may your glory appear above all the earth.
>
> II 7   They have set a trap for my feet;
> my soul is bowed down;
> They have dug a pit before me.
> May they fall into it themselves!
>
> 8   My heart is steadfast, God,
> my heart is steadfast.
> I will sing and chant praise.
>
> 9   Awake, my soul;
> awake, lyre and harp!
> I will wake the dawn.

She wished that she knew the way to the little chapel where she and Sir Daniel had shared their last day together. She wanted to read the words of Jesus, and she needed to feel the unbroken bond with her uncle.

Months passed slowly, and then, finally, Stephen walked through the door in full officer's uniform. He wore chainmail to his knees, holding his helmet and surcoat on one arm and carrying his large metal shield on the other. "Stephen!" Arelia jumped up and ran to him. "You look wonderful."

"I was informally commissioned today. I wanted you to see me in this. It may be the only time I have the opportunity to show you, although your uncle will commission me formally when he comes."

"My uncle is coming!" Arelia exclaimed. "When?"

"When Lady Marisa has her baby. He is due to arrive in three or four months," Stephen beamed.

"Stephen, it is still light, and you have come through my door!" Arelia's heart beat in fear, her face blanched in terror.

Stephen quickly placed his shield against the hearth, and helmet and surcoat on the bed and then, taking her hands into his, said, "The captain has awarded me the entire night with you, as I am now an officer."

Arelia squealed with delight. "This is a dream come true, an answered prayer!" He impulsively took her into his arms just as the door opened.

Bethany walked in, without a knock, as usual. "Oh, excuse me, sir. It is early, and I thought that Arelia was alone," she humbly apologized.

"No matter. I have not eaten since midday. I would like tea and a meal, if you would." Not even letting go of Arelia, Stephen responded in a deep, commanding yet unfamiliar voice. "Bring a man's portion and enough for the girl."

"Yes, sir, I will send something immediately." Bethany hurried out the door.

Arelia stared wide-eyed. "I cannot believe that."

"So you think I am learning how to be a very good officer?" Stephen laughed.

Arelia nodded in agreement. "You must tell me everything," Arelia pleaded.

Stephen related the entire experience of his training and commissioning while he took off his heavy chainmail, stoked the fire, and then paced proudly, back and forth, as he spoke, making himself at home. Arelia sat near the fire, appreciating every word. He was leaning comfortably on a large chair only in his trousers and undershirt when a knock interrupted them. Bethany walked in carrying a tray with tea and wine and even a flower on the tray. Laura walked in behind her carrying a tray with fruit, cheese, meat boiled in herbs, and fresh bread. Being very careful not to appear familiar, Laura fought back a smile at Arelia's shocked expression. She also tried not to stare at the dark, handsome officer with deep blue eyes but did notice that the mood in the room was comfortable and not the least bit strained. In fact, Arelia seemed to glow. Laura hoped that Bethany was too distracted by the officer to notice.

Bethany said, "Sir, I hope this is satisfactory."

"Yes, thank you. I will stay the night and do not wish to be disturbed again." Arelia covered a gasp with a cough at Stephen's comment and Laura's shocked expression.

"Yes, sir, I understand. Come, girl," was Bethany's reply as she hurried out the door. Laura waved at Arelia just before shutting the door behind her.

Arelia laughed joyfully. "I have never seen Bethany take an order. You do that quite well."

"I only mimic other officers." Stephen smiled. "That must have been your friend Laura."

The room took on a soft glow as the sun dropped slowly behind the trees. Arelia added to the warmth by lighting the lantern while Stephen lit a roaring fire in the large stone fireplace. They talked pleasantly over their sumptuous meal as if they were the only two people in the world.

"Arelia, we can walk on the beach tonight in the open and unafraid. Would you like that?" Stephen asked.

"Oh my, this *is* a dream," responded Arelia, not even hiding a sigh and a giggle.

Stephen led her casually down the long stairs, passing servants along the way. Several women looked away from Arelia but openly appreciated the handsome, young officer now in his long surcoat. Stephen's eyes were only for Arelia. Laura was with the women. As she passed Arelia, she grabbed her hand and winked with the knowledge that they were friends, and she knew that Arelia was safe and happy tonight. Arelia smiled at being with both her friends at the same time, even if for only a second.

"Stephen, tell me what you know about my uncle's visit." She began the conversation on the seawall.

"I do not know anything, except that he is coming when the baby is born. There will be a formal ceremony to introduce the new heir. Marisa is expecting a boy, but there are rumors that the women servants say she is carrying a girl."

"There will be a celebration if it is a girl also." Arelia smiled. "Families celebrate all new babies. Please tell me my uncle will come for either!"

"Yes, there will be a celebration for a girl, too, but not as big, it seems. The big celebration will be for an heir. Your uncle is planning to be here no matter what."

"Oh, yes, I forgot. It is all about breeding." She smirked. "I just do not understand."

"Nor do I."

The two young people walked away from the castle until Arelia needed a rest before climbing onto a rock outcropping. Stephen climbed up first and stretched to grab Arelia's hand, steadying her steps until she was settled on the rock. He was careful to sit close but not too close. They sat quietly watching whitecaps illuminated by a half moon. The sound of the waves and the wind brought a sort of peace seldom known to either of them. Their feelings moved beyond friendship with an unspoken understanding.

"Arelia," Stephen began, watching the rhythm of continuous waves gently lapping on the shore. "It hurts me and makes me so angry to see how you are treated. I do not understand how this is happening to you. I know that I have to help you, and I want to help, but I do not know exactly how at this time." He took her hand. "I became an officer mainly for you. If we never have another night after this, it is already worth it." He looked into her dark, watery eyes as tears glistened on her cheek. He wiped away her tears with the tips of his fingers and then lifted her hand to his lips.

Confused but not wanting to let go of her hand, he asked, "Have I frightened or offended you?"

"No, oh, Stephen, no; it has been so long since I have been happy. In fact, I do not know that I have ever been this happy. I guess my tears are tears of joy, and I do not want this time to end." She began to sob. "I feel safe for the first time since my uncle left."

Stephen held her as her tears flowed. He was so conflicted, confused, and angry, at the same time, overwhelmed with concern for this young woman he held not only in his arms but now in his heart. He had been given the opportunity to spend time with her by becoming an officer, but now he must determine how to free her from bondage.

CHAPTER 16

Two things got Arelia out of bed each morning and kept her going each day. The first was the chance that Stephen would visit, and the second was that her uncle was coming. In the three months since Stephen's commissioning, he had only been able to visit twice. The first time he was allowed only a couple of hours in the evening, and the second time he was allowed the entire night. Both times had been worth the wait, realizing not only a growing affection but also recognizing an awareness of common values, common dreams, and common memories. They'd both come from loving families, nurtured and caring relationships, and they grew up in welcoming and safe villages. They both had a desire to have children and to create a loving home for themselves and their families.

Since Arelia was not sure when Stephen would come again, she began keeping herself very clean and attractive. Night after night, she was disappointed, but she maintained her hopeful attitude, which had previously been rewarded by his two visits. Her demeanor was evident to Bethany, who stopped bringing Arelia the strong, mind-altering tea. Arelia was easier to care for when in her right mind, and Bethany could leave her to wash and dress herself, something she felt was too lowly for her position. Arelia was clear-minded and hopeful, often even smiling at Bethany. Bethany suspected the change had something to do with the handsome young officer but would never give Arelia the satisfaction of suggesting that she saw a developing relationship, an observation that she did not keep from Marisa.

The last night Stephen visited, he had told her goodbye as he was going out on a mission. She had no idea what that meant and didn't realize that he could be wounded or killed in battle until he had been gone several days. Occasionally, other officers had talked about battles and soldiers who had died, but she had never related those stories to Stephen. She had not prayed for anyone but herself in a long time, but now she began to pray daily and sometimes hourly for Stephen. Our Fathers became a constant mental prayer coupled with long pleading appeals for his safe return. One late night when no soldier entered her room, she waited till the moon was high in the sky and no noise could be heard in the hallway. She wanted to sit in the chapel as she had with her uncle and read from the large Bible. The only problem was that she had never gone there from her room on the servants' side and was confused about how to get there.

She gathered her mother's large cloak around her, leaving her shoes under her bed, not wanting to make any unnecessary noise. The door creaked as it always did, but this time it sounded like thunder, igniting her heart to pound against her ribs. Up or down; which stairway should she take? Down to the courtyard, past the kitchen and larder to her old room as a starting point, or up to unfamiliar hallways? Fear and anticipation cut her breath short. Up; she wanted no part of being anywhere close to Edward's and Marisa's rooms.

Cold stone chilled her feet, and fear chilled her bones. Every creak and groan of the old castle that had become familiar to her ears now stopped her in her tracks as her eyes darted down dim passages and stairways, looking for the right path. Coming to yet another unfamiliar flight of steps brought her to a stop with the realization that if she found the chapel, she may not be able to find her way back, and she might be discovered in the light of day, wandering aimlessly through the halls. The result of that would be devastating. She fought the urge to sit on the steps and cry, wanting to call out for help, but she knew no one was there to respond kindly to her. With a deep sigh, she wiped the trail of tears coursing down her cheeks and headed back downstairs to her room.

Finally, settled under her covers, she remembered Sir Daniel saying that they would always be together, bound by their time with the Word of God, both in Scripture and in the Holy Eucharist.

Our Father who art in heaven . . .

Oddly, she awoke in excited anticipation of seeing her uncle, and her spirits were good. It was not easy to ignore the circumstances of her daily life, but she had become adept at controlling her thoughts and attitudes. Even though Edward could come into her room at any time, she knew he could never get into her mind unless she allowed it. In fact, although she had not found the chapel, she had walked the halls undetected and returned safely. She felt a new sense of courage.

Knowing that her uncle would never allow the abuse her cousin allowed to continue and that the violence would stop as soon as he arrived, she had new energy and hope. She practiced their reunion over and over in her mind. This time, she decided that when he left, she would leave with him and talk him into taking Stephen with them. The only reason she had not left with him before was because of her injuries and her plans to return to a normal life with Camellia and Cornelius. With that option gone, she was free to leave with the man who would love and care for her as her own father had. She had the love and concern of both her uncle and Stephen on her side.

Late one afternoon, weeks after the announcement, Arelia had ventured down the stairs to steal a glimpse of the ocean and had seen Marisa walking across the courtyard, from a distance. She had quickly ducked down, peeking over the low stairway wall, and she could see that Marisa was very obviously with child. Seeing her as big as she was reminded Arelia of her mother when she had carried Prudence and John. Even with Marisa's appearance, Arelia couldn't imagine her as a mother.

Fortunately, she and Edward had not crossed paths; she had no desire to be a victim of his hand again. He and many of the soldiers were all in the same category in Arelia's mind—devoid of all human emotion and concern, no better than the wild animals that prowled about the earth for their next taste of flesh.

As the birth date drew nearer, excitement spread throughout the castle like spring flowers across a valley. Late one night, Laura sneaked into Arelia's room. Laura found her sleeping soundly. "Arelia . . . Arelia."

"Mother?" Arelia answered in her sleep.

"No, Arelia, it is me, Laura."

"Laura?" she repeated, trying to wake up.

"Arelia, Mother said to tell you that your uncle will arrive in two or three weeks and that you are not to drink the tea that Bethany brings."

"Do not drink tea?" asked Arelia, confused.

"Yes, Mother said it is very important. Please remember," emphasized Laura. "I must leave now. Sleep well."

Laura was gone as quickly and silently as she had come. Arelia fell back asleep repeating, "Do not drink the tea."

When she awoke, Arelia remembered Laura's visit as a dream, confused about whether it was Laura or her mother who had come to her with the warning. *How strange dreams are that Sarah would send Laura to tell me not to have tea. Bethany has not tainted my tea in months. Sarah and Laura would not know that.* She laughed at its insignificance.

When Bethany came in with her water basin, she boldly commented, "I understand my uncle will be here soon."

"I am not aware of that. Where did you hear such nonsense?" defended Bethany.

"Some of the soldiers have spoken of his visit."

"The soldiers carry rumors. You should not listen to them. Why would your uncle make such a long journey?"

"For the birth of his grandchild," Arelia stated, smugly.

"His grandchild? Nonsense! He will not come unless it is a boy, Sir Edward's heir. How silly of you! We will not know if he is coming until we know for sure if it is a boy or a girl. Get dressed and put away your silly notions. You know nothing of royalty."

Surely Stephen knows the truth. Bethany would not hesitate to lie.

Bethany went straight to Marisa. "Lady Marisa, Arelia knows about Sir Daniel's visit. She was talking about his heir."

"I was afraid of this," Marisa said, disturbed, patting her large girth. She sat silently for some time. "Bethany, you must do as I say and work only with me. We must discredit Arelia in my father-in-law's eyes. Either that or we must keep them completely apart.

"How is Arelia these days?" Marisa's question was sinister.

"Actually, she appears remarkably well. She keeps herself clean and nicely dressed. Sometimes, I hear her singing. I discontinued the potion in her tea as she seems cooperative."

"How interesting," observed Marisa. "So, she may enjoy the variety of men and their private time with her."

Bethany looked thoughtfully, "I had not considered that, my lady, but she does seem to enjoy the company of the young officer I told you about."

"Oh, yes, I remember now."

"Well, we will take advantage of that. Give her weak dosages of potion in her tea to prepare her for her uncle's visit. Begin very slowly tomorrow and then increase the potion slightly each day. I do not want her to be aware of the drug," explained Marisa.

"I understand," said Bethany, smiling.

The next afternoon, Bethany entered Arelia's room cheerfully carrying an unexpected teapot and two little cakes.

"What is the occasion for cake, Bethany?" questioned Arelia.

"I thought you would enjoy a traditional tea today. I realized I have overlooked your sweets for some time. I apologize," said Bethany, sweetly.

I apologize! You can apologize for not bringing sweets and say nothing of holding me in slavery for men to abuse me! Arelia sat quietly, watching Bethany suspiciously.

"Bethany, you have never brought me sweets since I have been in this room."

"Here, drink your tea while it is still warm, my lady. I confess, Sarah insisted you have the sweets. The cakes are from her," Bethany tempted.

My lady, what is she doing? "Thank you, Bethany. This is really a very nice treat. Please tell Sarah thank you." Arelia dipped a corner of the cake into her tea, relishing the sweet flavor. Bethany smiled with approval as she enjoyed teatime.

Arelia was very relaxed with the surprise treat from Sarah and with images of leaving with Uncle Daniel and Officer Stephen.

She felt strangely relaxed and calm. Watching the trees below and feeling a cool breeze on her face increased her feeling of peace and contentment. Sea gulls shrieked messages to each other as they headed toward white-capped waves. She wished Stephen were back or that her uncle had arrived.

As she stood at the window, the door opened and yet another soldier entered. Her evening had begun.

The next afternoon, Bethany arrived with tea and cake again. She generously poured Arelia's cup. "Sarah said she will send you a treat every day until you have tea with your uncle."

"My uncle? I thought you said that we do not know when he is coming."

"Oh, not exactly when, but Marisa is sure she will have a boy, and so we are confident that he will be here soon."

"There is something strange about this tea, Bethany. It has an unusual aroma."

"Oh?" responded Bethany innocently. "Cook has a new blend of herbs she's trying. Most everyone is enjoying the flavor."

Arelia sipped her tea, analyzing the taste. "It isn't bad. Actually, it does have an interesting flavor."

A soldier was loosening her blouse. "What are you doing?" she demanded confused just waking from a deep sleep.

"Oh." He laughed. "Are we going to play today?"

Arelia was frightened in her confusion. She couldn't think. The soldier slapped her into submission; afterward, he fell asleep, having gotten what he came for.

She awoke with a great deal of pain that became worse as she saw the grotesque man sleeping in her bed. She began to cry, realizing how confused she had become. "What's happening?" she asked aloud. As she lay there, she remembered the other times she had felt the same. The first was in the forest after the dog attack when she drank the potion for pain. The next horrible and all too vivid memory was when she was moved to her new room. *The tea! Laura! She warned me*, she recalled. *It was not a dream.*

When Bethany arrived with her tea the next afternoon, there were dresses draped over the table but Arelia was in bed. "Hello, Bethany. How nice of you to bring my tea, and I have cake again. Sit it there. I will enjoy it later after I nap."

Bethany watched Arelia suspiciously, wondering the cause for her good mood. "You are very happy today," she observed curiously. "You are sorting through your dresses?"

"Yes, I guess the excitement of Marisa's baby is rubbing off. I am excited to see my uncle. I want to look my best. I am very excited for Lady Marisa and my cousin."

"We all are," said Bethany dryly. "I will pour your tea."

"Thank you. You are so kind," said Arelia, sweetly.

Bethany poured the tea and left with a curious look on her face. Arelia walked to the window and poured out the potion.

"You will never take my mind again," she vowed.

Arelia enjoyed sorting through her clothes. She had forgotten how lovely the dresses were. She didn't have any occasion to wear them. Today, she took them out and pretended that she and her friends were dressing for a beautiful ball—a ball for her uncle. She was deciding which dress each of her friends from the past would like when Bethany walked in.

Bethany seemed surprised when she saw Arelia. "What are you doing?" she asked.

"I told you. I am airing my dresses and deciding what to wear."

"I came in to get your tea pot. How do you feel?" Bethany asked, studying Arelia carefully.

The tea! she thought.

"I was full of energy earlier, but now I am getting very sleepy. I wanted to finish my dresses before I lay down, but I think I will not be able to."

"I hope your tea was not cold," Bethany pried.

Arelia caught the clue. "It was my fault, Bethany. I have just drunk it. I was too busy. My, I really am getting sleepy. Would you help me move these dresses from the bed?" asked Arelia, appearing drowsy.

"I will be happy to," said Bethany, smiling.

She heard Bethany take the tray and leave the room. "Why do they want me drugged? I haven't resisted the men?" she asked aloud. She knew that she had made a very big mistake and would need to learn to think as Bethany if she were to fool her. Marisa and Bethany's ways were not her way, but she would need to be more careful to beat them at their own game.

That night, no soldier came to her room, and the next day was the same, with the tea tossed out the window and no visitors. This time, Arelia pretended to drink from the cup for Bethany's benefit. She let it sit until she heard Bethany go down the stairway for fear she would return and catch her throwing it out the window.

Arelia knew the intruders would begin again. Each day she went through the same routine with Bethany, pretending to drink the tea and discarding it through the window. *How long will we play this game?* She decided to just stay in bed, rather than risk appearing too alert.

She was lying on her bed when Stephen walked into her room after a brief knock. He was smiling from ear to ear. "Hello, my lady." His greeting was casual and cheerful, as if he had never been away.

Arelia rushed to him for a big hug. "You are finally back," she exclaimed.

"Yes, I have won you for the entire night. My mission was a success, and time with you is my prize." He lifted her and spun her in the air.

Arelia took his hand and pulled him to the bed with dresses still on the table and chairs. "Tell me everything," she pleaded, hoping for a story like the ones her father used to tell.

"I will not tell you everything. Not all of being a soldier is good or adventurous. All you need to know is that my men fought their first battle with me as their leader, and we overcame our enemies," he quickly explained.

"Enemies? Whose enemies?" Arelia questioned.

"Your family's enemies, especially your cousin's. Sir Edward changed many boundaries when your uncle left. This upset long-time landholders, and they are fighting to recover their land. Our job is to turn them back and prove his strength," he explained. "They were beginning to withhold their goods and taxes because they think that Sir Edward is unfair. Captain Hardgrave thinks that we will have more battles as long as Edward is making the rules. The people loved Sir Daniel because he was fair. Sir Edward has raised the taxes and divided their land into smaller portions. Our job is to defend his decision."

"Is that right?" she pried.

"Arelia, my job is not to decide right and wrong. I do not know the real issues. I only do my job," he defended. "And how have things been with you?" he said, wanting to change the subject.

"Stephen, something strange is happening," she began. The door creaked slightly. Arelia fell back against her pillow pretending to sleep. Stephen knew to play along.

The door opened a little more, and Bethany looked around it. "Excuse me, sir. I did not know the captain sent you. I must apologize. You can see the girl has not been well. I do not think that she is up for a visit this evening. She may sleep through the night."

Catching the hint, Stephen said, "No mind. I sleep on the hard ground night after night. I will welcome a warm bed, even without company." He winked.

"Shall I bring you a tray to make amends for your evening?"

"Yes, please do—and bring plenty. I have not had a good meal since what you generously provided at my last visit." He laughed in an unfamiliar, for-mal-officer tone.

"I will return shortly, sir." Bethany smiled as she left the room.

"What was that all about?" Stephen asked when the door closed.

"That is what I am trying to tell you. For some reason, Bethany is giving me a potion to put me into a deep sleep again. I do not know why. She stopped the potion when I corrected my attitude and started taking care of myself."

"She plays evil games. We will play a little game with her when she re-turns." He laughed. "Promise not to be offended by anything that I say. Just stay quiet."

"What are you going to do?" Arelia begged to be a part of it.

"I am going to play the officer."

172

CHAPTER 17

Later, when Bethany returned, Arelia appeared to be sleeping, and the young officer had made himself comfortable by removing his undershirt, boots, and stockings. He was lounging bare-chested on the big bed with Arelia sleeping, apparently unaware, by his side.

"You made it back quickly," he said as he jumped up from the bed. "I hear they call you Bethany," he said as he took the tray from her. "Let me carry that for you."

She was taken by his kindness. "Yes, sir, my name is Bethany."

"How lovely," he responded, feigning sincerity. "A name as beautiful as the woman, and might I ask, a mature, experienced woman?"

"Sir?" Bethany asked with a puzzled expression on her face.

"You pretend not to know how the men talk about you—how many of them who come here only hoping to catch a glimpse of you—a mature woman, not a child."

"No, sir, I do not know."

"How could you not know that real men do not want a child? They would rather have a *real* woman like you," he teased.

"Sire!" Bethany blushed and nearly giggled. It was all Arelia could do not to open her eyes to watch the charade. She couldn't believe her ears.

"When you see the men, you must smile their way. Let them know the value of a *true* woman," he coaxed.

Bethany smiled sheepishly. *I wish Arelia could see this*, he thought.

"And poor me," Stephen continued, "I am barely a man. At some time in my life, I will experience a woman like you, but now I must content myself with this girl. Now, leave me alone with my thoughts of you, but promise to make the others happy with an occasional smile and a little attention." He reached over and kissed Bethany's wrinkled, splotchy hand.

"For you, sir, I will. Can I bring you anything else now? We have cake in the kitchen. I can bring it right up for you." Bethany smiled sweetly.

Stephen patted his strong, muscular stomach, "I cannot afford to have cake." Bethany's eyes grew large at the attention to his uncovered physique. She blushed when she realized that she was staring.

"No, I will sleep late tomorrow. I have been in the field, and I do not want to be disturbed until noon. You may bring me a little piece of cake then. Thank you, lovely lady, for your concern."

Bethany left the room feeling flattered but also confused and disgruntled. She hurried to the kitchen to put away a huge piece of cake for the chivalrous and handsome young officer.

When the door closed, Arelia jumped up and tossed a pillow, catching Stephen on the back of his head as he was putting his undershirt back on. "You are awful! That poor, ignorant woman."

Stephen jumped on the bed and gently returned the blow with the pillow. "Oh, she loved it and believed every word. It serves her right. I would like to do more to her for what she has done to you. Now she will embarrass herself in front of the men. It is a small injustice and not much of a payback. But now, we have until noon tomorrow for just the two of us and lots of food to eat tonight."

Arelia leaned forward and kissed him on the cheek. "All right, I forgive you. You are not all bad. In fact, you *are* the only light in my life."

Stephen put his arm around her waist and pulled her to him. He laid her back against her pillow and kissed her tenderly. "You give me good reason." He looked deep into her eyes. She did not resist or look away and caught her breath at the intensity of his stare. He kissed her again, feeling a passion that was unfamiliar to him. With all the strength he could muster, he turned away from her and got out of bed. Now he understood the desire the men talked about, but he did not want to be like other men. He wanted it to be right, not just self-gratifying. He did not want her to think of him as just another soldier here for the evening. He would never do that to her; she was too important to him for that.

He walked over to the table. "Now come and eat. She brought enough food for ten men." He laughed as he picked up a piece of cheese.

Arelia bounded out of bed. She would have liked for Stephen to stay in bed longer to enjoy his embrace. "We cannot walk on the beach tonight. Bethany thinks that I am sleeping."

"We can get some sleep and walk before sunrise. That would seem normal. Besides, I really am tired."

They talked for hours about any and everything. "Arelia, I really am tired. I would like to just hold you while I sleep, if you do not mind." His request was cautious and gentle.

"I would like that, too."

Stephen pulled back the covers as Arelia took off her heavy shawl. She slid under the covers as Stephen tucked her in. "I am used to sleeping in a tent. It might get a little warm for me under all these covers, but I do not want you to be cold without them. Besides, it would not be right for us to sleep too closely. I think this is close enough," he said as he lay at her side on top of the pile of blankets. He could not trust himself under the blankets with her warmth so near.

As she pulled her arms from under the covers, she could hardly wait to feel the strength of his arms cradling her and holding her through the night. There would be no fear tonight. He kissed her on the forehead as she nestled in the crook of his arm. "I will see you shortly. Do not go anywhere without me," he teased.

She rested her arm over his and stroked the firm muscular skin of his forearm. She had never felt a man's arm around her like this before, except for her father's as she sat on his lap as a little girl, listening to stories by the fire. She lay there listening to the rhythm of his breath as it deepened into sleep. There had been so many nights as a child when she had been reassured by her father's breathing as he fell asleep across the room in their little hut. If she awoke frightened, she would quickly fall back to sleep to the constant rhythm of his breath. Now, she was completely at peace lying in the cradle of Stephen's arm. She wondered if her mother had ever experienced the same peace.

She awoke to the sound of thunder. Stephen was already up and standing by the window. The fire was blazing, making the room warm and cozy.

"Good morning," she said.

He turned toward her, smiling. "Good morning, beautiful lady!" He walked to the bed, leaned over, and kissed her deeply.

For the first time in her life, she returned the kiss, welcoming him and enjoying the taste of him. The only thoughts in her mind were of him—his touch, his smile, his willingness to listen and to love her. They enjoyed the long, lingering kiss until Stephen realized that he had to restrain himself. It wasn't easy, and it was getting harder to pull away.

"How about a walk in the rain?" he suggested.

"It is too cold," she protested.

"You are no fun. Where is your sense of adventure?" he teased.

"I have spent some very hard times in cold rain. It does not sound fun to me," she said seriously. "When you are wet and cold and lost, it is no fun. I have had my share of cold, rainy adventures."

"Oh, I forgot. But next time I come, we will go to the beach. One day I will even bring my horse, and we can ride through the waves together."

Arelia smiled at the thought of it. "I have seen you ride into the waves before. That does look like a *safe* adventure." She laughed. "But it cannot be raining," she added.

Arelia carried a plate of fruit and cheese to bed. They ate leisurely as the thunder rumbled and lightning lit the early morning sky.

There was a quiet knock at the door. Stephen jumped out of bed and put on his shirt. Arelia was startled to see Laura when she opened the door. "What are you doing here? It is not safe for you." She grabbed her arm and pulled her into the room.

"Relax. Bethany sent me to see if the officer was still here. Lady Marisa is becoming more demanding, and she could not get away. Poor Bethany—Lady Marisa complains continually and will hardly let Bethany out of her sight."

Laura turned to Stephen and looked embarrassed at the intimacy of the warm fire and rumpled bed covers. "Bethany asked me to give you a message, sir. She said that she enjoyed the conversation and asked if you would stay until she could bring your midday meal and piece of cake—whatever that means."

Stephen laughed. "Tell her that I will wait, at her request."

Arelia looked at him disapprovingly. "You flatter her too much."

"It is what a gentleman would do." He smiled.

Laura pulled Arelia aside and whispered, "Are you happy? Is this as good as it seems?"

Stephen walked to the window to let them talk.

"Is he special to you, Arelia?" Laura was intrigued.

"Yes, but do not breathe a word of it." Arelia was emphatic. "My cousin would not approve."

Laura smiled. "I am happy for you. No one will hear a word of it from me." Laura squeezed her hand and hurried out the door.

"Is that the same girl that we saw on the stairs?"

"Yes, her name is Laura."

"So, she is your friend."

"Yes, she is. I dreamed about her recently; at least I thought I did. She warned me not to drink Bethany's tea weeks ago in the middle of the night. She had come to warn me that Sarah said not to drink the tea! It was confusing, and I drank the tea for a while. Bethany still thinks I am drinking it."

"Laura is a good friend to risk her own safety."

"You are a good friend, too."

"Yes, but I am the lucky friend, because I get to spend time with you." He smiled an impish, little-boy smile.

Several hours later Bethany walked in carrying a huge tray and wearing a smile just as wide. Arelia hardly recognized her. "I brought you a tray, sir," she said sweetly, completely ignoring Arelia.

"Thank you, Bethany. This looks just wonderful—and look at this cake! You have made my visit most pleasant."

Indeed, she has made it more entertaining, Arelia thought.

Bethany poured a goblet of wine for Stephen and spread a clean cloth over the table and then laid out fresh bread, the huge piece of cake, cheese, meat, and potatoes. "This is a feast," he exclaimed.

"A meal fit for a king," Bethany added. "I must take my leave. Lady Marisa is close to her time and out of sorts. Sir, thank you for your conversation last night. I will take your recommendation, although I do not want to be attached to a man," Bethany said as she walked toward the door.

"Goodbye, Bethany," Arelia said. Bethany looked startled for a split second, as though she was unaware that Arelia was in the room. She walked out the door without responding.

Arelia sat thinking about how much Bethany had changed after Stephen's short visit with her. Even her appearance was different. "Stephen, how do you think that Marisa treats Bethany?"

"Like a pathetic slave," he answered without even thinking.

"Do you think that she is ever kind to her or considerate of her feelings?"

"Marisa does not have a kind bone in her body. I have heard stories about her that you would not believe. They say that she was cruel even as a child."

"What do you think would happen to Bethany if she disobeyed Marisa's orders?" Arelia continued to probe as she pieced her thoughts together.

"She would throw her out like those before her, like a dog."

"Like those before her?"

Stephen took a drink of wine and wiped his mouth. "People say that when Marisa was a little girl, she had her parents discard her maids like trash. Those they kept usually ran away during the night. She was very spoiled and hateful."

Arelia sat quietly with her own thoughts for a long time. "Bethany was so good to you because she thought that you were genuinely being nice to her."

"I know you feel badly about how I led her on, but she is cruel to you," he defended.

"She and I are the same, you know," Arelia said sadly.

"You are nothing alike. Do not even think it."

"Stephen, look at us. We have the same fear. I know what it is like to be hungry and cold and frightened. I know what it is like to be completely alone. My greatest fear is that I will be cast out and be hungry and alone again. That is why I stay in this room and do things that I hate and would never do otherwise.

"I remember the old women in the village who lost their husbands and had no sons to care for them. They ended up as servants to someone or died trying to survive. I do not want that to happen to me." She began to cry.

"Arelia," he said as he put his arm around her, "that will never happen to you. You are not an old woman."

"I am not an old woman, but I have no family, and I have already been cast aside. I am no different from Bethany. We have the same fears and look how we live."

"I would never let that happen," Stephen stated firmly, almost angrily.

"It is happening."

She saw that her words hurt him. He was ashamed that he hadn't already taken her away.

Arelia studied his face for a long time as he wiped away her tears. "I believe you, Stephen. But the point is that my fears have made me a prisoner in this room as much as if I were chained to this bed. You called Bethany a slave, but what am I? What have Bethany's fears caused her to do?" Arelia covered her face and cried, not just for herself but for Bethany and all the women like her who submitted to their fears and compromised their values and ideals.

Stephen was confused by her tears but knew that her fears were well founded. There were many occasions when a troop of soldiers on a mission would come across a woman who was alone and homeless. It was common practice for the men to lure her into the camp with the promise of a meal and then take turns raping her, only to leave her more wounded and frightened than before. He had never seen an officer stop it—most officers were as involved as the men were if they hadn't started it themselves.

He gently stroked her long hair, letting her cry out her grief. He remembered his mother crying at the table when his baby brother died. Her tears seemed to go on forever. His father simply stroked her hair and patted her hand, not knowing what else to do. Stephen identified with his father now. He had no solution.

"Arelia, I hate to leave you like this, but my time is long gone."

Looking up through dark, tear-filled eyes, she said, "I know. Thank you for all you are to me. It gives me strength, just knowing that you are my friend." She hugged him firmly, trying to stop the tidal wave of tears.

He leaned down and kissed her warm, soft lips, wishing that he could be with her forever. "I will be back as soon as possible. Please take care of yourself." He opened the door and stood in the open doorway to get one more look at the woman he knew he loved.

Arelia lay on her bed and surrendered to her tears. Months of grief washed over her—thoughts, both good and bad, flashed like lightning through her mind. Tears flowed for all the women who suffered as she was suffering now and would suffer in the future. "Will I ever find a place, a safe place for me,"—she sobbed—"a place away from here?"

CHAPTER 18

Excitement mounted as the birth date drew near. Although Arelia was not part of the festivities, she could hear increased activity on the stairwell. She smelled the aroma of meats smoking in the courtyard day and night, in preparation for the lengthy celebration.

Marisa announced to the kitchen staff that Sir Daniel was due to arrive in two weeks, and everyone knew she and Edward would put on a grand show to impress his father. Arelia could hardly bear to wait for his company. She felt the excitement of the upcoming celebration, not for the baby but for the chance to see her uncle again.

Each day Bethany brought the tea, sometimes twice a day. Arelia was having a harder time trying to fool her now that she understood her better and empathized with her situation. She felt sorry for her and even thought about confronting or confiding in her.

Bethany was beginning to suspect that Arelia was not drinking the tea but had not been able to prove it. One day, she prepared the tea for Arelia and left out the powerfully depressing potion. "Arelia, here is your tea. I hope you enjoy it."

"Thank you, Bethany," Arelia said as she poured herself a cup. Bethany left the room.

She returned an hour later to find Arelia getting very sleepy as before. When Arelia crawled into her bed and appeared to fall into a deep sleep, Bethany knew then that Arelia had not even tasted the tea. Not having the potion after taking such large doses over an extended time would have caused itching and nervousness as it had before.

You foolish girl, thought Bethany. *No one can stop Lady Marisa. She'll have her way at your expense, and no one will stop her. You are an ignorant fool not to accept the merciful drug to cover the forthcoming pain.*

"Lady Marisa," Bethany volunteered, "I suspect Arelia is only pretending to drink her tea and discarding it out the window. Your plan will not be successful if she is, but I cannot force her to drink."

"Thank you for the information, Bethany. I will handle this," said Marisa. Bethany regretted that she was forced to protect herself at Arelia's expense, but she wasn't willing to sacrifice her own wellbeing for the sake of an orphan girl.

When Marisa knocked firmly on the door, Arelia was hoping it was Laura, as her friend always knocked, fearing embarrassment from what she might see. Arelia ran to the door and threw it open happily. She stopped cold at the unexpected sight of Marisa.

"Lady Marisa." She gasped, frozen in shock and fear.

"May I come in?" Marisa asked sweetly.

"I am sorry, of course, please come in," stammered Arelia, startled. "Please sit down and make yourself comfortable. You appear ready to have the child any minute," she said, as she consciously tried to regain her composure.

"Yes, the day is soon," she agreed as she looked around the room before sitting.

"As I am sure you know by now, Edward's father will be here soon. We know he will be especially excited to see you. Edward and I would like you to join us for dinner tomorrow evening to plan his stay. Would you be so gracious as to join us?" Marisa asked.

Arelia's mother's warning came back. *Be careful, her mouth says one thing; her eyes and heart say something else.*

"I will be delighted to join you. I will be ready. Just send someone for me when it is time," replied Arelia politely.

"That will be good. I will see you tomorrow." Marisa smiled sweetly as she walked toward the door. Only the glint in her eyes suggested ill intentions.

What is her plan? Arelia asked herself. *Sometimes, I wish I had an evil mind in order to protect myself from her. Marisa must know that her father-in-law would not stand for their abusive treatment of me, and they are afraid he will find out. They must want to win my favor to avoid my telling him.*

I do not want him to know either. How could he still love me knowing how I live? Her thoughts turned sadly to the hopelessness of the life she had come to live.

The next afternoon, Arelia chose her favorite dress for dinner with Marisa and her cousin. She had not been to the dining room since she was moved to the servants' side of the house. She was very nervous and self-conscious when the maid came for her. *I will not threaten them so as to cause any suspicion. I want time with my uncle so he will take me back with him. Maybe that is their desire, too.*

Edward and Marisa greeted her warmly when she entered the room. Marisa was wearing a bright yellow dress with a deep orange surcoat and a headdress shaped like a butterfly. With her huge belly, she looked like a flower in full bloom with a butterfly resting in the sunlight. Arelia tried not to stare or laugh.

The reception was similar to their first meeting and just as superficial. Conversation was light and meaningless. Edward seemed almost lifeless as Marisa chattered about nothing.

"Cousin Edward, when will your father arrive?" inquired Arelia.

"We expect him within the next two weeks, Arelia. I know he is most eager to see you." His flat, detached tone was less than eager.

"I am eager to see him, too, sire."

I bet you are, thought Marisa, *but you will not have the opportunity to steal our estate.*

After dinner, Marisa offered, "Arelia, would you like a touch of tea or brandy to complement your meal?"

Arelia had heard her father mention brandy in his stories. He told about the fine ladies and gentlemen sipping it leisurely after a fine meal.

"I have never tried brandy, but I would like to try some, if you please. My father spoke of it."

"Edward, may I pour brandy for you also?"

"Yes, please."

Dismissing the servant, Marisa walked to the side table and poured three glasses of brandy, slipping a thick, dark liquid into Arelia's silver goblet.

"Here you are, Arelia. Sip this slowly, so you do not choke. The flavor is very strong. Some say you must develop a taste for it," instructed Marisa.

"Thank you," said Arelia as she took her first small sip. "You are right. This is very strong. My father talked about brandy and its soothing effect. It has a very unusual flavor. I think it is bittersweet."

"Yes, you should feel quite relaxed soon. It is a good drink before bedtime," offered Marisa condescendingly.

Arelia sipped the strong drink and grew more and more relaxed. Soon, she was having difficulty focusing on her dinner companions and understanding the garbled talk. Within minutes, Arelia slumped over in her chair.

"Our work is done," said Marisa, smiling with self-satisfaction. "Bethany will keep her groggy until your father sees her in the arms of one of your soldiers." She laughed maliciously. "This is going to be easier than I thought."

Edward smiled at his wife's cunning. "You always seem to know the best thing to do," he complimented.

"We must protect our interest," she said, patting her swollen stomach.

Bethany watched the manservant carry Arelia out of the room. "What has happened to Arelia?" she asked with true concern.

"Too much wine and brandy. Come, help me put her to bed," he answered.

Bethany had become a main source of information for all the servants. She not only tended Marisa but also Arelia. The women were entertained by Marisa's conniving and appalled by Arelia's shocking lifestyle. They did not know the truth of Arelia's imprisonment, and Bethany had no intention of telling, or they would know her part in it. Bethany always reported what she observed and enjoyed being the focus of everyone's attention. It wasn't unusual for her to stretch the truth, although she conveniently left information out about her own involvement in Arelia's situation.

Her only regret was that she had lost Sarah as a friend. She and Sarah had basically grown up together on the estate. Bethany had attended Edward's mother until her death, and Sarah had tended more to sewing, cooking, and cleaning. Bethany was assigned Lady Marisa's maid at her arrival at Faircastle. Bethany answered every trite need or desire, while Sarah stitched Marisa's elegant new wardrobe. The women had become partners in maintaining the all-too-demanding woman.

When Arelia was brought in, the balance of the sewing had gone to Laura, and Sarah's service went to Arelia. Bethany missed her close association with her friend and was jealous when Sarah's new charge was modest and pleasant while she was still saddled with Marisa. Now that Arelia was Bethany's concern, Sarah did not like the direction the young girl's life had taken. Her displeasure showed in her attitude toward Bethany, although she never spoke of it. Sarah was convinced that Arelia's circumstances were determined by Marisa but was meted out at Bethany's hand.

Bethany became aware of Marisa's strange concern over Arelia early on but followed all orders from Marisa, fearing that she would be sent to the scullery or washroom, if not put out on the street. Bethany had no family to care for her, and she knew her existence was at Marisa's mercy.

Now, watching Arelia being carried down the maze-like hallways, Bethany realized her life would soon become more complicated. Marisa had a plan that was sure to involve her, whether she agreed with it or not. Even Bethany had hoped that Sir Daniel would put an end to the madness.

When they reached the room, Bethany loosened Arelia's tight corset, removed her shoes, and tucked her in under the heavy covers. Laura came hurriedly into the room.

"Is she sick?"

"No," Bethany lied, "just too much to drink at dinner, but she will feel very sick tomorrow."

"I have never seen anyone like this unless they were going to die," said Laura, studying her unconscious friend.

"Shut your mouth and go away, girl. You have work to do. Let me be about mine," demanded Bethany.

Laura ran to the door looking back briefly. "Should I get help?" she asked.

"Of course not! Let the girl sleep. I am here to help her," Bethany answered angrily.

Bethany looked at the sleeping young woman, *so innocent*. She wouldn't allow herself any tender feelings. "This is my work, Arelia. You have yours, and I have mine," she said aloud. She then turned and returned to Marisa's room to help her prepare for bed.

"You saw the girl?" Marisa asked. Bethany nodded yes in response but did not speak.

"Was she sleeping soundly?" Again, Bethany only nodded. "Bethany, listen to me carefully. You must keep her that way until my uncle leaves."

"But she will die without food, my lady," replied Bethany, sincerely concerned for Arelia's fate.

"Oh, you fool! Of course, she would die. I do not mean to keep her unconscious, I mean drugged. She would not drink her tea, so I had to take over. Now you can do your work more easily. Allow her to be groggy and spoon-feed her soup with enough potion in it to keep her confused. When Sir Daniel leaves, we will let her come back to herself."

Bethany was both horrified and relieved. For a brief moment, she had thought Marisa wanted her to kill the child.

"Bethany, you must schedule a steady flow of soldiers to her bed while my father-in-law is here. Let her be awake enough to have visitors but not to get out of bed," instructed Marisa.

"My lady, this will take a good deal of time. I fear I will neglect you in your last critical days."

"I thought of that too. I have instructed Sarah and her daughter to assist me while Sir Daniel is here. I will want you to come every morning with my basin for an accounting of Arelia, and then you will be free until evening to tend to her," Marisa explained. "Bethany, I hope you have listened carefully. Have you understood my instructions?"

"Yes, my lady," Bethany said, looking at the floor.

"Well, I certainly hope you understand. I will need tremendous help with the baby soon, and I would like you to be available for that. It would be unfortunate if you had to spend long hours washing floors, especially at your age."

"Lady Marisa, I assure you I understand your instructions," Bethany reaffirmed.

"Very well. You have never disappointed me before. I know you will do as you are told."

Bethany left the room, sick to her stomach. Marisa had always been manipulative and spoiled but never this evil. She would follow her plan, giving the least amount of potion possible to keep Arelia disoriented. She knew Arelia would have to go through withdrawal again after Sir Daniel left. This would be a painful and frightening process. She had seen men with serious wounds sedated for long amounts of time who screamed in agony from being without drugs. Bethany dreaded the next several weeks but knew it had to be done in order to keep Marisa happy.

She checked on Arelia before first light the next day. She was still unconscious.

"What are you doing?" a frightened voice demanded.

Bethany turned toward the voice, startled. "Who is there?" she demanded.

"It is I, Laura," she said approaching the bed. "I am so worried about Arelia; she has not moved even one time all night."

"You were here all night?" asked Bethany, surprised.

"Most of it. I could not sleep worrying about her. She will not die, will she?"

"You foolish girl! Tend to your own matters. This does not concern you," screamed Bethany.

"What is wrong, Bethany? She is going to die. I know it!" Laura cried in a panic.

"What would it matter if she did? Look how she lives," said Bethany exasperated.

"Do not say that. She will leave here one day. Stephen will take her away."

Bethany slapped her hard. "Shut up. You are too stupid to understand! Do not say that outside of this room if Arelia is your friend."

Laura stood stunned, touching her reddened face.

Bethany touched her arm and sat on the bed, exhausted. "Child, you do not understand the ways in this house now, and you do not need to know. I will not let Arelia die. That is why I am here now. Her life will not be easy. Neither you nor I can help her now."

Laura looked at her and Arelia sadly. "I do not understand," said Laura, confused and tearful.

"Neither do I, Laura, but I know my job, and I must do it. *I must do it.* I want you to bring Arelia a basin every morning and wash her. After that, feed her a bowl of soup. I must tend to Marisa at breakfast; then I will tend to Arelia after that."

"At least the soldiers will not bother her," said Laura innocently.

"Laura, the soldiers will start again. You and I will tend to her without question. Do you understand?" asked Bethany.

"No, but I will help her as long as you need me. You promise she will not die?" repeated Laura.

"We will do our best. You go get a basin of water and wash her face. I will prepare soup for when she awakens," instructed Bethany.

This is going to be harder than I thought, said Bethany to herself. She turned toward the unconscious girl. *How has this happened?* She remembered the day Arelia was brought into the castle walls with all the talk about her amulet and heritage.

Sir Daniel was obviously elated to have found his brother's daughter. Everyone was so happy to see life in him for the first time since his wife had passed away. Arelia had brought that spark back to him. *Now look what his son has done to her,* thought Bethany.

She rose to report to Marisa. "Stephen," moaned Arelia in her sleep.

"Even Stephen cannot help you now, child," answered Bethany as she left the room.

CHAPTER 19

The expected day of Sir Daniel's arrival came with unbridled excitement. A horseman rode in before dawn to alert the family that he would arrive shortly after noon.

Everyone was busy with preparing food and cleaning rooms. Marisa made sure that everything would be perfect for his arrival, and he would find no cause for criticism. She wanted no doubts about her worthiness as mistress of the manor and mother of Edward's heir.

Bethany was very careful to keep Arelia on the brink of confusion without pushing her into sleep. It had taken several days to judge the correct potion for the desired effect, but she had finally found the proper dose in order to keep her in her bed while still lucid.

No soldiers had visited, but Bethany arranged that they would begin the day of Sir Daniel's arrival. Marisa had spoken to the captain and Bethany in order to coordinate the schedule, lest there be any mistakes. Much to Marisa's relief, the captain confirmed that several officers would be out on patrol with their troops while Sir Daniel was at the estate in order to avoid any uncomfortable confrontations from peasants or neighboring landholders during his stay. Tension had been mounting in some of the villages, and she feared that they might take advantage of Sir Daniel's visit and stir up trouble to make Edward look bad.

Bethany did not want Marisa to suspect Stephen and Arelia's association, so she was very careful when asking the captain, "I understand you have several troops out. Will there be enough officers to fill the schedule? Who are the able-bodied men defending us?" she asked casually. She had hoped that she covered her relief when Stephen's name was mentioned as one of the officers out on patrol. Even though she wasn't absolutely sure herself, she could never let Marisa get even a hint of Arelia's involvement with the young officer.

The party arrived with fanfare. Trumpeters and jesters contracted for celebrating the baby's arrival were performing in full force. All the servants were out to greet visitors and help with supplies and baggage. Stable men and servants helped the riders dismount and led their horses away for food and water.

To Sir Daniel, only one person was notably missing: *Arelia.* His eyes searched the crowd from one end to the other looking for her. There were his son and Marisa, much larger than he had expected, and beloved Sarah and her daughter, Laura. Many of the servants were familiar, but he did not see the one face he had anticipated the most.

"Hello, Father," greeted Edward. "How was your trip? Have you seen Marisa?"

"Yes, she is ripe." He smiled in response. "Where is Arelia?"

"I am sorry, Father. She took ill. We feared her sickness would spread, so she stayed in bed. She will see you in a few days," Edward said as he escorted his father to Marisa. With memory of the ravages of the plague, it seemed a very reasonable response.

"Hello, Father," Marisa said warmly. "You must be exhausted. Your old room has been prepared for your stay. I know you will be comfortable there."

"Thank you. I would like to rest until morning, if you do not mind. A comfortable bed is in order for this old man." He smiled as he patted his stiff, aching back.

"But, Father, we've prepared festivities in your honor this evening. Please join us," interrupted Marisa.

"All right, I will rest now and join you at dark," he acquiesced.

Roland escorted Sir Daniel to his room and helped him prepare for a rest, concerned about his master—and friend's—wellbeing. Sir Daniel's bones ached from the long trip, yet all he wanted to do was to see Arelia and then sleep. As sleep quickly overcame him, he dreamed that Arelia was hot with a fever one minute and then lying in a coffin the next. He awoke startled. "Roland," he called. "I must see my niece at once. Talk to Lady Marisa. I demand to see her immediately."

Marisa was thrown off by her father-in-law's insistence. He was not a forceful man, and so she knew she had to give in to his request. She had expected to stall him, but her plans had to change. "Tell your Master that I will arrange a visit in one hour."

Marisa hurried down the hallway in search of Bethany—as quickly as her rotund figure would allow. She didn't want to have her father-in-law find Arelia with a soldier yet.

"Bethany," Marisa called as she ran into Arelia's room. Bethany was startled, as she had never known Marisa to go to the servant side of the manor. "We must prepare Arelia for a visit from Sir Daniel. When did you give her the last potion?"

"She has had nothing since morning." Her expression reflected her concern about Marisa's next request. "I fear she has had too much already."

"Nonsense, she is not dead, is she?" Marisa asked condescendingly. "Clean her up and dampen her face with a cold cloth. I do not want her to appear unconscious. That would cause too much concern. I will be back shortly."

"Yes, my lady."

Marisa stormed out of the room while Bethany changed Arelia's bedclothes. Arelia's eyes began to flutter from all the jostling about. At the touch of the cold compress, she began to mutter. Bethany ignored her, not wanting to form any attachment to the child. "Why do I have to handle you? This should not be my chore," she complained.

Shortly after Bethany had arranged Arelia among her pillows, there was a knock at the door. She knew it would be Sir Daniel and Roland because Marisa would never knock.

"May we come in, Bethany?" asked Roland politely.

"Of course."

Sir Daniel walked slowly to the large bed, taking in the picture of the small woman bundled in the warm covers. "How long has she been ill, Bethany?" he asked.

Bethany was taken aback. She had not discussed any of this with Marisa and did not know what to say. "I am not sure, sire. I have only been called in this morning."

"I am happy that Marisa has sacrificed your service to her in order to care for Arelia. I will relax knowing you are here with her, using your knowledge of healing herbs," he complimented.

"Thank you, sire," she said, feeling ashamed of her true role.

There was a soft knock at the door, and then it opened slowly, hesitantly. "Father, I was hoping to prepare you for your first visit with Arelia. She has been this way for several days but did stir some today. Is that right, Bethany?"

Casting her eyes toward the floor, Bethany responded. "Yes, my lady," supporting Marisa's lie.

"I have been checking on her regularly, and she does appear better," Marisa lied.

"I cannot imagine that she could have been worse," Sir Daniel observed with sad concern.

"I called Bethany in to care for her because of her knowledge of herbs. I know Arelia will be well cared for in her capable hands," Marisa said, sweetly. She walked to the window, pretending to fight back tears. "Father, she has been well and happy with us. I fear you will blame *me* for her poor health."

"Do not be ridiculous, Marisa. You could not make the child ill. Though, I do wonder why her room is here with the servants."

Marisa caught her breath and pretended a weak smile. She shook her head slowly and replied with her well-rehearsed lines, "After you left, she was very sad. She was caught between being a villager and part of her new royal family. Edward and I could see her difficulty in adjusting to her new life and allowed Sarah's daughter Laura to sew with her for entertainment. The girls struck up such a friendship that Arelia requested to have a room closer to Laura. You can imagine my reaction. I was not raised such a way as that. Sarah and Bethany convinced me that, for *Arelia's* happiness, I should give in and let her have her way—at least for a while.

"Everything was fine, at least until . . . ," she stopped abruptly and turned away.

"Until what?" Sir Daniel insisted.

Marisa slowly turned toward him with actual tears. Bethany was curious to hear what she would say. Taking his hand gently, she said, fighting back tears, "Father I cannot bear to tell you this now. Edward and I will speak to you privately, later, when I can control my sadness."

"Marisa, you must tell me," he insisted.

"No, Father, I do not want to ruin the festivities of the evening," she said, forcing a smile.

"Stephen," Arelia called weakly.

"What did she say?" Sir Daniel asked.

"Stephen, sire," repeated Marisa, very distinctly.

"And who is Stephen? We did not have a servant named Stephen," he searched his memory.

Marisa looked down shaking her head. "Stephen is a young soldier."

"A soldier? Is he the young man who saved her from the wild dogs?" Sir Daniel asked, remembering the fateful event.

"Yes, unfortunately, he is. Father, you still have a short time to rest for the evening. I will stay with Arelia a while and then see you at dinner. I will have time to rest and prepare for the evening." She hugged him gently then walked toward the bed and gently rested her hand on Arelia's pale forehead as if to check for a fever.

Sir Daniel took one last questioning look at Arelia, "Marisa, you should not expose yourself and your baby to an infection."

"Sir, how can I consider myself with this poor girl in this condition? I will not stay much longer. I know she is in good hands with Bethany."

Daniel encouraged her to get some rest, too, and then left with Roland.

Shortly after the door closed, Marisa turned from the bed laughing, "The old fool! That was better than I had planned! You have done well, Bethany. I will expect your report in the morning."

The evening was filled with food, laughter, and entertainment for Marisa and nightmares for Arelia. Bethany watched as Arelia tossed and called for her parents and Stephen. She called other names that Bethany did not know and did not want to know. With each fitful turn, the sword of guilt drove more deeply into her heart.

She knew Arelia would regain some consciousness in the morning; she would have to alert Laura to give her the tea that she would prepare before she reported to Marisa. She was not at all comfortable with the arrangement but did not know how to change the course of events against Marisa's will.

She spent the evening thinking of different ways to sway Marisa from her single-minded course. She would need to approach her carefully, as she did not know why Marisa was so set against the girl. Nothing Arelia had done since she arrived seemed inappropriate until Sir Edward and Marisa had moved her to the servant's quarters and sent the first soldier to her room. Bethany and all of the servants had been amazed and saddened by that turn of events. They all realized that, although Arelia was part of the royal family, she was more a commoner like each of them. Some of them even remembered Arelia's father as a boy. Many had predicted that the servants would receive better treatment with Arelia's influence until this happened. Now everyone talked badly about her rather than carry any hope that she could make their lives better.

Now Bethany realized that with everything that was happening, Arelia was too young and innocent to be a match for Marisa. She knew she was the only one to distract Marisa from Arelia's abuse. If only she knew what motivated her vicious plans in the first place; certainly this girl posed no threat to her son's inheritance.

She stood at Marisa's door with a pitcher of water and a basin, dreading their impending conversation. She knocked weakly, hoping that Marisa was sleeping in from her celebration the night before.

"Come in," came Marisa's strong response. "Bethany, I am glad it is you. How is our plan coming along?"

Bethany cringed at her wording. "I am following your plan as you requested. Arelia is beginning to awaken, my lady," replied Bethany, hesitantly.

"You are not allowing her to awaken too much, I take it," said Marisa, forcefully. "She will not leave her room in a stupor?"

"No, my lady, Laura is with her now," she answered, trying to hide her aggravation. "My lady, I take it you want Arelia out of your way," Bethany continued, cautiously.

"You *are* perceptive," said Marisa, sarcastically.

"And you want Sir Daniel to see that she is very ill," she continued bravely.

"And . . .? What is your point?" demanded Marisa impatiently.

"If Sir Daniel is concerned about her health, he could take her back with him to care for her," Bethany finished boldly.

"You idiot!" Marisa screamed. "We will disgrace Arelia so that does not happen! Why do you think I am wasting my energy on her?"

Bethany was taken aback. She stood speechless.

Marisa studied the older woman thoughtfully through pinched eyes as she tapped her finger on her chin. "Bethany, maybe you are not the servant to help me with this," she observed.

"I am very capable and have proven myself trustworthy, my lady," Bethany defended.

"Yes, capable and trustworthy, but too nosy and prying," Marisa contended.

"Please forgive me, Lady Marisa. I know this is none of my concern, but I do not understand the intent of your actions."

To Bethany's surprise, Marisa laughed loudly. "Understand my actions! And why is it that *my* servant thinks *she* should understand *my* actions? Have I requested your advice?"

"No, my lady," Bethany said, guarded and frightened. "I may be able to better serve you if I understand the results you are striving for."

"And make no mistake, Bethany, I will *never* consult with you on my plans," Marisa said angrily as she stood and walked toward the door. "You, my maid, will follow my instructions without asking questions, or someone else will. There are many jobs in this house and only a few as pleasant as yours."

Marisa opened the door and then walked toward her basin, dismissing Bethany. As Bethany reached the doorway, she turned and said with conviction, "I will not offer advice nor ask questions again. Your instructions will be followed as you wish." She closed the door behind her.

Stunned and humiliated, Bethany stood in the hallway reviewing what had happened. Unfamiliar tears welled up in burning eyes. Everything had run smoothly until Arelia had been brought to Faircastle. Since that day, Marisa had been in a foul mood. Sir Edward was not much better, and Bethany no longer had the honor of serving Marisa exclusively. Bethany wished she had never laid eyes on the young troublemaker. Rage began to brew against Marisa . . . or Arelia . . . or both.

CHAPTER 20

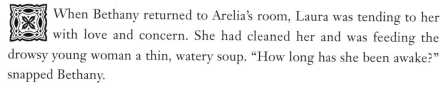 When Bethany returned to Arelia's room, Laura was tending to her with love and concern. She had cleaned her and was feeding the drowsy young woman a thin, watery soup. "How long has she been awake?" snapped Bethany.

"She came to as I was freshening her," answered Laura coldly.

Bethany left the room to prepare a mild potion to keep the girl sedated. *You will cause me no more trouble*, Bethany resolved.

Laura was confused by Bethany's reaction. The night before, Bethany had almost seemed warm toward Arelia. Today, she was not the least relieved to see her awake. "Arelia, do you know who I am?" Laura asked, hoping that Arelia would respond.

Arelia stared at Laura confused. She looked around the room and then touched Laura's hand without speaking. Tears clouded Laura's eyes as she asked, "What has happened to you?" Arelia laid her head back against the pillow and closed her eyes.

When Bethany returned, Laura was looking out the window, and Arelia was sound asleep. "Bethany, I will stay with Arelia for a while longer. I can sew here."

"That will be fine, Laura. I will return shortly to bring her tea."

Laura busied herself the remainder of the morning by sewing small delicate gowns for the new baby. "Mother," Arelia called weakly.

Laura hurried to the bed. "Arelia, it is Laura."

"Laura?" Arelia responded in a fog of confusion. Laura hugged her excitedly. "Yes!"

"What happened to me, Laura? I feel so sick and weak."

"You had too much wine at the festivities, and you never recovered. You have been asleep for a long time," explained Laura.

"Too much wine?"

"Yes," continued Laura. "You had dinner with Lady Marisa and Sir Edward, and you drank too much. One of the waiters carried you to your room."

Arelia lay quietly, thinking. "Yes, I had never drunk brandy before. It does not take much to make you sleep. I want to sleep again, now," Arelia said rolling away from Laura and closing her eyes.

Laura was so relieved. Arelia would be well now. *Bethany was mistaken in believing that she would have many difficult weeks ahead. Obviously, Arelia will be well now,* Laura thought.

She continued with her sewing, happy that Arelia was well and happy to be making gowns for the new baby. Her mother would also be relieved to hear the good news. She concentrated on the delicate stitches, straining her eyes to fashion tiny flowers and leaves. One day, she hoped to meet someone and have a child of her own. She knew that Arelia loved Stephen, and one day she would leave and become a mother. She did not understand why Arelia was trapped here now.

Dusk was coming. Except for a few bites of hard bread and cheese, Laura had not even had a break. She stretched and walked over to the window, feeling the cold breeze rush across her face. "Laura," a firm voice called.

"Yes, Bethany, I did not notice that you came in."

"Has the girl awakened?"

"Yes, we spoke earlier. Then she fell back asleep."

"Did she make sense?" Bethany questioned.

"Yes, briefly, but she could not stay awake," said Laura as she gathered her sewing.

"Tomorrow, I will not be in until mid-morning. You should return at dawn to tend to her," Bethany instructed.

"Yes, madam," Laura said as she left the room.

"Arelia," said Bethany, trying to awaken Arelia. She stirred but did not awaken.

Bethany set about preparing a sleeping mat for herself. She could not risk Arelia leaving her room. She would sleep lightly in tune to Arelia's breath and movement. Sleep came gradually for the older woman. It was difficult to find a comfortable position for her old bones on the cold, hard floor.

"Mother," Arelia called, waking Bethany from her light sleep.

"Yes, Arelia," Bethany replied from light unsettled sleep.

Arelia pushed back the covers and tried to get out of bed. She sat back hard on the side of the straw mattress to keep from falling. "I am very weak and dizzy," she said in a weak, frightened voice.

"You are not well enough to be out of bed, child. Let me get you some tea," offered Bethany.

"Bethany?" questioned Arelia in sudden disappointment.

"Yes."

"Oh!" was Arelia's response as she looked slowly around the room, allowing her eyes time to adjust to the streams of moonlight pouring through the window. "Have I been ill?"

"Yes, very ill, and you still are," explained Bethany. "I am tending to you."

"I must pass my water. Can you help me?" asked Arelia, trying to stand on wobbly legs, teetering like a baby doe.

Bethany took her arm and helped her to the chamber pot. "Your weakness is part of your sickness. I have tea here to help you get stronger."

"Was Laura here, or did I dream it?"

"Yes, Laura stays with you while I help Lady Marisa. She is nearly ready to deliver."

Bethany helped Arelia get back into the tall bed. "Let me get your tea. I know you are thirsty," offered Bethany.

"You are so kind to stay with me, Bethany. I know Lady Marisa needs you now," said Arelia appreciatively.

Bethany ignored her as she poured her tea that was now cold. "Thank you," said Arelia as she drank the tea thirstily. "May I have another cup?"

"Let's see how that does before you have more. You have not had much in your stomach. You do not want to get any more sick than you are," Bethany stalled. "Let me straighten your bed covers so you will be more comfortable."

"Who will help Marisa deliver the baby if you are with me?"

"The ladies will summon me. Sarah is with Marisa now," answered Bethany.

"Oh, Sarah," said Arelia softly. "She was like my mother. I miss her."

Bethany felt a tinge of jealousy. "She is busy now," Bethany cut off Arelia's comments, not wanting to hear more of the beloved Sarah.

197

"Bethany, how can I feel sleepy again?" Arelia asked as she closed her eyes.

Bethany did not even bother to reply. "Sarah! I have been with you for weeks, and you still ask about Sarah," Bethany said in a huff. "Now I can sleep soundly. I do not have to worry about you anymore tonight."

Bethany left Arelia's room early the next morning as Arelia slept, knowing that Laura would be in to care for her. She was proud to report to Marisa that Arelia had awakened and had been sedated at her hands. Marisa was obviously pleased with the news. "Leave her awake enough to start the visitors today," instructed Marisa.

"The soldiers?" asked Bethany in surprise. "Today?"

"Yes, Bethany, the *soldiers*—who else? Do you understand?" Marisa said with strong emphasis.

"But, Sir Daniel . . ."

"Shut up!"

"Yes, my lady, of course."

"Good. Then Edward will instruct the captain to begin today at dusk."

"I will have her ready, my lady," said Bethany.

"You may leave, Bethany, but be prepared to come quickly if I send for you. I feel my time is near." Marisa seemed frightened and vulnerable as she made the request. "You may leave," she said, regaining her composure.

The soldiers? What will Sir Daniel think? Bethany thought as she returned to the nearby room, which Marisa had arranged for her when she had become her maid. Marisa had hoped to cut down on gossip between the servants, and she wanted to keep her maid within calling distance.

It had been a while since Bethany had been given time alone in her small, closet-like cell. She had thought that Arelia would have been given a reprieve from the never-ending parade of abusive soldiers, and now she realized it would not end. She sat on her small hard bed, put her head in her hands, and cried. She was exhausted, with no relief in sight.

Bethany remembered walking into the dark courtyard as a child so long ago and being brutally raped by a drunken soldier who had wandered into the courtyard late at night. Her mother had sent her to get tea from the kitchen for father who wasn't feeling well. Bethany did not return for some time, and when her brother found her in the courtyard, the deed was done, and the soldier was nowhere to be found. No one seemed to care; in fact, nothing was ever said or done to find the soldier who had assaulted her.

Although Bethany was nearly a woman at the time, she no longer had an interest in any of the young men that her parents chose for her. She developed a cold, hard exterior and frightened away every young man who came to call. No amount of pleading or threatening from her parents could sway her attitude. Now, years later, Bethany was alone as a result of her experience, the memories still vivid in her scarred mind, frighteningly real.

"Arelia, I am so sorry." She cried, confusing the girl's pain with her own.

A loud knock startled her. "Yes!" she answered, wiping away her tears.

"Lady Marisa needs you now. Her water has burst!" Bethany jumped to her feet. So many babies she'd birthed but none of her own. Her mother had wisely taught her midwifery and the healing power of herbs in order to give her value as a woman without a husband or son. Her advice had saved Bethany from the scullery and washroom as her talents were needed and proven time and again, adding value to her for the royal family.

Bethany ran down the hall, knowing Lady Marisa would be panicking with her first child. She found that vain women seemed to have the hardest time because they focused on themselves and their discomfort rather than on the reward at the end of the pain. "We are in for a long spell," she told the young girl that had sent for her. "Summon Sarah immediately," she ordered.

As she neared Marisa's room, she could hear her premature screams.

"This is going to be a very long day for us all."

When she opened the door, the tearful Marisa pleaded, "Help me, Bethany. What is happening?"

"Lady Marisa, all is well. This is normal. Let me get you into nightclothes and into bed. The girls are gathering clean cloths and water. When Sarah comes, I will prepare a soothing tea for you," Bethany reassured.

Marisa seemed to calm down under Bethany's care. Sarah hurried into the room. "Let me help you with your bedclothes, my lady. I have birthed a few myself. You are safe with Bethany, and I will not leave your side until the baby arrives."

Marisa took Sarah's hand, and the tension seemed to leave her face. "Sarah, Bethany, you will not let me die, will you?"

"Of course not, my lady, but you must cooperate. Babies are birthed all the time. That is how we all got here." Sarah smiled warmly.

Bethany left the room to get tea. *How ironic*, she thought, *that I now prepare a tonic to help Lady Marisa. Arelia suffers at her hand and mine, yet I will spare her pain.* Bethany knew that without the tonic, Marisa would scream for hours and possibly harm the baby through her hysteria. Her mother had taught her the fine balance between healing and killing.

The kitchen was buzzing with activity. Large pots of water were being filled, the fire was flaming, and rags were being torn to soak up blood. Bethany requested a pot of water for tea as she approached her herb cupboard. There were dozens of jars with different herbs for different purposes. Many people thought she was magic with her healing talents, but she knew that healing came through the wondrous leaves, flowers, and roots. Her mother had worked with her for years, sharing all her secrets. Up until now, Bethany had not shared her knowledge with anyone. Laura had gone with her once to collect herbs, but Bethany had not wanted to continue with her at the risk of losing her own value to the family.

Now, she stood at her cabinet, mixing a soothing blend, ready to brew for Marisa. She measured carefully, knowing from experience that too much could ultimately harm the baby. She dropped the finely ground leaves into the steaming water and returned to Marisa's room. Marisa was much calmer now with Sarah at her side. Edward was holding her hand and stroking her brow. She reveled in his attention. "I will leave you now, dear Marisa, in the hands of Bethany and Sarah. I will rejoice to see our son," he said proudly.

Turning to Bethany, he said, "I will be in my room with my father and Roland. Please let us know any news."

Bethany poured Marisa a small amount of tea. "This will calm you, my lady. We may have a long wait. You should sleep if you can." Marisa drank the tea slowly and winced with pain. "Bethany, will this stop the pain? I do not want to be uncomfortable. You must stop it?"

"As long as the pain is light, you will not feel it, and you will sleep. As the baby comes nearer, the pain will awaken you. You must allow yourself to sleep now," explained Bethany.

In a short time, Marisa was sleeping peacefully. "Sarah, I will report to Sir

Daniel, and then I must check on Arelia. She will probably awaken around dusk, but I will be back before then," Bethany said.

Bethany knocked on Sir Edward's door where Sir Daniel and Roland waited with him. "Sire, Marisa is sleeping peacefully with Sarah at her side."

"Thank you, Bethany. May I have a word with you outside?" Sir Edward requested, ushering her to the door.

Once the door closed behind them, he began in a quiet voice, just above a whisper, "Marisa has given you a job with Arelia. Is that correct?"

"Yes, sire. I am going to check on her now." Bethany copied his hushed tone.

"Good. Just because Marisa is birthing, I *do not* want you to neglect your duties there. I am sure Marisa has helped you understand the importance of your job with Arelia." He stood too close as he spoke.

"Yes, sire. I understand." *I understand too well*, she thought.

"Good. Then you will not disappoint us. If you do well, Marisa said you may have some time to tend the baby." He smiled menacingly, the unspoken threat showing in his eyes.

Bethany could not leave his presence quickly enough. It was a relief to enter Arelia's quiet room. Laura sat by the window still sewing baby clothes. "Marisa is in labor, Laura," Bethany announced.

Laura jumped up from her chair. "How exciting. A new baby to care for."

"How is Arelia?" She glanced over at the girl.

"She woke earlier and ate two bowls of soup. She tried to stand—but was too weak. We talked for a while, and then she asked for tea. There was less than half a cup. Shall I make more?" Laura asked innocently.

"No, child, I will prepare it. Do not give her more than a half cup, or it will make her sick," responded Bethany. "Go now, and I will sit with her. Do not come back until mid-morning. You must prepare the baby's wardrobe," instructed Bethany.

Bethany did not want Laura to know that the soldiers' visits would begin this evening. Bethany busied herself around Arelia's room, stoked the fire, and then sat on the edge of Arelia's bed and cried. When the tears started to pour, she couldn't seem to stop them. She was exhausted and caught in a trap with no way out. She had always followed Marisa's commands before but never to the point of endangering someone's life or ruining their future.

"Bethany, what is it?" Arelia awoke surprised to see Bethany crying.

"Oh, Arelia. I thought you were sleeping. I am very tired, but I am all right," Bethany explained. She tried to cover her tears, but her red eyes gave her away.

Arelia struggled to sit up. "Why are you crying?" Arelia persisted.

"Arelia, I am worried about you and me. We are trapped here, you and I," Bethany tried to regain her composure.

"Bethany, I do not understand how or why this is happening. Can you not leave the room either?!" Confusion and fear shadowed expression.

"It has gone on too long for me. I cannot explain. I do not understand myself," said Bethany sadly. She realized how low the sun was getting. She needed to get back to Marisa and did not want to be with Arelia when the soldier came in. "Arelia, Marisa is in labor. I will be with her until the baby comes. You must stay in your room."

"I cannot even stand without help. There is no chance that I will leave. Will Laura come to help me?" Arelia slurred her words innocently. "I am thankful that you can leave." Her innocence touched Bethany's heart.

"Someone will be in," Bethany answered as she left the room.

Bethany dreaded the long night with Marisa. She hoped that the tea was allowing her to sleep through the initial pains for Marisa's sake and for all those who tended her. The hallway outside her room was quiet. The room was dark, except for one candle on her night table. Marisa was fast asleep. Sarah had made a sleeping mat on the floor next to her bed and was also asleep. A young girl from the kitchen was in a chair, resting her head on Marisa's large dressing table. Bethany walked over to her. "Helen," she said, shaking her shoulder.

Helen's head shot up. "What is it?" she asked, startled.

"How long has Marisa been asleep?"

"She was whimpering not long ago, and Sarah gave her more tea. She has been asleep again for a short time."

Bethany walked over to the bed and laid her hand on Marisa's large, swollen belly. She waited for the tightness for some time and was satisfied that the pains were still slight and intermediate.

Returning to the girl, she said, "I will be in my room. Come to me the minute Lady Marisa awakens." Bethany was relieved to have even a short time to go back to her room, and she hoped for a full night's sleep.

Arelia was still drowsy but not really sleepy. She was trying to remember what had happened since her dinner with her cousin and Marisa. Everything was a fog. She could not remember going back to her room from the dining area and had no idea how many days she had slept. She wondered when her uncle would arrive.

Her bedroom door creaked open. "Laura?" she questioned. There was no answer. The door closed quietly, shutting out the little light from the hallway. An all-too-familiar form moved toward the bed. "No!" Arelia moaned in dread. Her long night had begun.

Sir Daniel returned to his room, knowing the length of the wait ahead of them. Edward had fallen asleep in his chair by the fire. Roland covered him with a blanket and kept the logs burning.

The house held a sense of expectancy, yet everyone slept—everyone except Arelia.

CHAPTER 21

 Bethany was awakened by a loud knock on her door. "Come quickly. Lady Marisa needs you *now*."

Having slept in her clothes, Bethany ran down the hallway, keeping up with the girl. Marisa's cries could be heard all the way down the long hall. *The pain must be great*, thought Bethany.

"Bethany, give me a tonic. I cannot tolerate this *pain*. *No* estate is worth *this*," she cried. Bethany poured her another cup of warm tea.

"Lady Marisa, I can give you more tea, but nothing will completely remove the pain without harming the baby. You must be strong for your reward. Sarah will stay with you while I prepare your potion."

Bethany ran down the hall to prepare the soothing tea. She would make two mixtures: one for now and a stronger one for the stronger pains and soon for delivery. "Send a large teapot with hot water to Lady Marisa's room. Make sure her fire stays lit," she ordered the kitchen help. The house had come alive with excitement and activity. The time was finally here.

Bethany returned to Marisa's room to find Edward standing nervously outside her door. "Bethany, what is the screaming about?" His voice was tense and demanding.

"Lady Marisa is in labor pains. She does not understand it is normal, and she is very frightened."

"Then I *order* you to stop the pain!" Edward screeched.

"Sir Edward, the pain cannot be stopped completely, or we will harm the baby. I have a tea here to help her, but she may still scream. I am afraid it is her nature," explained Bethany. "You should sit with your father in his room. I will send someone when there is news."

Bethany walked in to another one of Marisa's agonizing screeches. "Help me, Bethany. I order it!"

"Lady Marisa, you must try to relax. Sarah and I are here with you. I have a tea to help," said Bethany patiently.

"Relax! *You* have never had the pain of childbirth, you idiot. How can *you* tell *me* to relax?"

Sarah took the cup from Bethany. "Here, Lady Marisa, drink this. Bethany knows how to help you." Sarah squeezed Bethany's arm apologetically.

Bethany walked to the fire to warm her hands. *Your fate is in my hands, Lady Marisa. You should think again before being so cruel to me.* She went back to her room, unable to tolerate any more.

Marisa was quiet between contractions, but the screams were getting closer together along with the contractions. "Bethany," alerted Sarah, "I think she is going quickly now. It is almost time."

Bethany approached the bed and could see a dark patch of hair about the size of a small coin showing through the birth opening. "Yes," she agreed. "She is moving more quickly than I thought, but it is still too early."

Bethany poured a half-cup of the stronger tea. "Drink this, my lady."

Marisa took the cup and dropped it as she screamed with yet another pain. "I need to push."

"Not yet, my lady," Sarah and Bethany both cautioned. "You will tear yourself."

Marisa's screams continued. Bethany poured more tea. "Drink this quickly," she instructed Marisa.

Marisa drank it down. "Give me more."

"In a short time, not now."

Marisa closed her eyes. "I want to sleep. I do *not* want to do this anymore!" Sarah smiled knowingly.

Another scream, then another. "Please, give me a potion and let me sleep, Bethany, *please!*"

"Here is one more swallow, Marisa," Bethany condescended.

Bethany checked the vaginal opening several more times before determining it was wide enough to push the baby through. "Lady Marisa, when you feel the pain this time, do not scream but push."

"Gladly," said Marisa. "Now!" she screamed.

Bethany gently moved the tissue away from the baby's head, turned the first tiny, delicate shoulder, then the other, and pulled out a very small baby boy. "You have a boy, Lady Marisa," said Bethany.

Sarah and Bethany looked at each other curiously. "This baby is too small for the size of her belly, Bethany," Sarah said.

Bethany felt Marisa's still swollen womb. "Lady Marisa, you are not through. There is still more."

"No, Bethany. That is enough. I have our heir."

Sarah laughed. She understood Marisa's exhaustion and pain. "My lady, the pain will not stop until you have another baby."

Marisa lay exhausted. "I have had enough. I do not *need* another one." Bethany looked at her in disbelief. *What does* need *have to do with this?*

Bethany quickly cut the first cord and cleared the bed for the next birth. The pains began again. "Push, Marisa, it is almost over." One strong push delivered a speckled, blood-coated little girl.

Bethany held her up. "You have a new sister, young Master Fairchild. Lady Marisa, you delivered an entire family at one time." Sarah and Bethany laughed.

Sarah turned to Helen. "Run downstairs and deliver the news. Gather more clothes to wrap these babies. On the way back give Sir Edward the news. That will give us time to prepare Lady Marisa and the babies for their father."

The two women set about stripping the bed and discarding the bloody sheets. They each took a baby, cleaned them, and wrapped them in warm blankets. Bethany emptied one of the drawers from Marisa's chest in which to lay the little girl, while the little boy lay in the cradle by the warm fire.

Bethany suggested to Sarah, "We will need to find another wet-nurse for the baby girl."

Marisa was shaking and cold from delivery. Sarah took a bed warmer and placed it at her feet with extra blankets to warm her. "Marisa, you have two beautiful babies. Sir Edward will be very proud."

"Is my son well?" Marisa questioned.

"Yes, he is well and so is your beautiful daughter," replied Sarah.

"Where *is* Sir Edward?" asked Marisa.

"Here I am," said Edward as he walked through the door with Helen. "I understand I have a son."

"Yes, and a beautiful daughter," interjected Sarah.

"Let me see the boy." He walked to the fire and saw the tiny baby. "Is he too small?"

"He is small, all right, but we will fatten him up. Your daughter is a little bigger," said Bethany, carrying over the baby girl.

"She looks strange," he commented absently, looking only at his prized son.

Bethany carried the tiny child to the rocking chair by the fire and began to rock her slowly, humming a soft tune.

Edward sat on the side of Marisa's bed. "You are a good wife, Marisa. You have given me a legacy on your first attempt. I am proud of you."

"May I come in?" interrupted Sir Daniel.

"Of course, Father. Marisa has given me a legacy," said the proud new father.

Sir Daniel approached Marisa's bed and took her hand warmly. "You have done a fine job, Marisa. I understand you have given me *two* beautiful grand-children."

He walked over to the babies and the two proud midwives. "Take care of these children. It is too painful to lose a child. They are both very small. Are they in danger?"

"They do not seem to be, sire," said Bethany. "Their color is good, and their cries are strong, as I am sure you have already heard."

"Yes, and happily so, I might add. I never heard my daughter's cry," he said sadly. "And Marisa, is she well? She appears wan."

"She just needs rest, sire," reassured Sarah.

"May I hold this precious little girl, Bethany?"

"Of course, sire. Sit here by the fire."

Sir Daniel took his precious granddaughter, cradling her carefully in the crook of his arm, while tears trickled gently down his cheek. "She is *wonderful*," he said wistfully.

"Sire, I must leave for a short time. Sarah will stay with the babies and Marisa until I return," said Bethany.

Bethany returned to her small room, exhausted from the hectic morning. She lay on her bed reviewing the miraculous process. It didn't seem to matter how many babies she birthed; she was always overcome with the miracle. It never became commonplace. This was the first time she had delivered twins. The confusion of delivering such a small baby had quickly turned to amazement when the little girl showed her face. She had once delivered stillborn twins to the shock of the expectant mother and father. Marisa and Edward's attitudes had somehow managed to turn even this most joyous occasion sour. Thankfully, Sir Daniel appreciated the little sister that tagged along with *The Heir*.

Marisa's reaction to the infants was not surprising. No one expected such a cruel, self-serving woman to care about anyone but herself. *She seems to view life as through a mirror, seeing no one but herself*, she thought. Thankfully, Sarah had intuitively arranged for a wet nurse, knowing Marisa would be disgusted with the common practice of breastfeeding. Bethany hoped one woman could handle the demand of two small babies who needed continuous feeding to fatten up. The little girl appeared hardier than the boy. Judging from Marisa's comments and lack of interest, Bethany felt the little girl would definitely need to be stronger to withstand the life before her.

Her thoughts turned to Arelia. Here was a young woman who could be a wonderful mother but would never have an opportunity under Marisa's control and Bethany's own hand. *Where is the justice in this?*

Bethany wanted to sleep to block out all that was happening in her life, but she knew she had too much to do. Marisa would demand continuous attention. She would probably resent not being the main attraction and would be more demanding in order to draw attention away from the babies and back to herself. Then there was Arelia, who needed continuous observation to keep her sedated. *Why does this all rest on me?* Bethany sighed.

She rose begrudgingly from the comfort of her bed and started down the hallway to Arelia's room. "Bethany," someone called her name. She turned to see Sir Daniel.

"Are you going to Arelia's room?" he asked.

"Yes, sire," she replied nervously.

"I know she is not well and may not even hear you but give her my love."

He hesitated, "If you feel it is all right, I would like to sit with her." Somehow his voice was more pained and lonelier than before.

Bethany recognized his anguish but didn't know what to say in consolation. Personally, she wanted to tell him everything, but she did not want to face Marisa's wrath and lies. She suspected that Edward and Marisa would turn Sir Daniel against her and convince him she was somehow responsible for Arelia's condition.

"I know she would like that if she were well enough. For now, though, it would not be wise. You may pass what she has on to the babies. That could be very serious," she covered.

"Oh yes, the babies. I am so glad you thought of that. I have become somewhat foolish in my old age," he apologized.

"Not at all, sire. It is your love and concern for Arelia that allows you to forget," she consoled.

"Bethany, in the short time I came to know Arelia, I came to love her as my own daughter. She is all I have left of my brother. I can never make up to him for not staying in touch, but I can make sure that Arelia is well cared for. I know that you are the best person for her now."

Bethany looked at the cold, hard floor. Her eyes clouded with tears of guilt and shame. "Sire, I do not deserve your praise or gratitude."

"It is not idle praise, Bethany. I speak only the truth. You are one of the few who has the knowledge of healing."

Bethany turned and hurried down the hall to Arelia's room. Her mind was torn. *You are one of the few who has the knowledge of healing.* How could she continue the course Marisa had plotted and set into place? *Marisa is evil. Arelia should not suffer at her selfish whim.*

Laura was freshening Arelia's sweat-soaked bedclothes when Bethany entered the room. Tears were gently falling down her face. "Bethany, the soldiers have begun again. Look at poor Arelia. She is hardly awake, and they come, one after another. Can you do something?"

"What can I do?" She wanted to scream.

"Tell Marisa that Arelia is too sick for these men. Tell her she must stop it. She is such a witch!" said Laura.

"Laura, be careful! You know we do not tell Lady Marisa anything," Bethany scolded.

"Tell Sir Daniel!" said Laura excited at the thought. "That is it! He will save her."

"Sir Daniel is an old man who has had so much tragedy. I could not bear the thought of telling him. He is so happy about the babies. Knowing about Arelia could kill him," rationalized Bethany, believing it to be true.

Laura continued her work. Arelia was lost somewhere between sleep and wakefulness. She tossed and mumbled. Her eyes opened in a glaze and shut time and again.

I will not give her another potion, declared Bethany silently. *Arelia can tell her uncle herself.*

"Laura, try to feed Arelia some soup today. I will be caring for Marisa and the babies," instructed Bethany.

Bethany was relieved at her decision. She would no longer follow Marisa's destructive authority. *If Marisa wants Arelia drugged, she will have to do it herself.* Bethany smiled at her own rebellion.

She returned to Marisa's room feeling that she had regained control over her life. *After Arelia has had time to withdraw from the heavy potion, she will invite her uncle to take her for a walk on the beach. Surely Arelia will explain her plight, and he will save her from Marisa and his son*, she thought.

"Bethany, where have you been?" Marisa demanded.

"I checked on Arelia, my lady," answered Bethany coyly.

"I have pain. You must fix me a potion. Sarah, those babies are keeping me from resting. Return them to the wet nurse," Marisa declared irritably.

"My lady, I thought you would want them with you between feedings," coached Sarah.

"Why should I have them with me? I do not need to feed them, and they only cry to eat. Take them to that woman," commanded Marisa.

"Bethany, why are you standing there? I told you I am in pain. Do something about it."

"My lady," interrupted Sarah as she prepared the babies, "Sir Edward and Sir Daniel requested to see you and the babies in here at dinner. Can I arrange that your meal be brought in here, and I will bring the babies in for a very short visit?"

"Yes, if we must, but please also arrange that they are quiet when they see their father." Marisa's tone was condescending. She was willing to be impositioned in order to be seen as the mother who had already suffered so much for her precious children.

"My lady, would you like to hold the babies before I leave?" Sarah offered hopefully.

"There is no need for that, Sarah. I will need time for Bethany to prepare me for my dinner guests. I have not been dressed in so long; we will need all of the little time I have."

Sarah placed the two tiny babies in the basket and carried them out of the room.

"Bethany, get my royal blue velvet dress with the white lace. We will need to find my new corset. I do not want to look fat. The babies are delivered, and now I can get back to myself. Bring my brush and royal blue ribbon so you can braid my hair."

Bethany begrudgingly began locating all of Marisa's things. "Bethany," she screamed. "Have you forgotten my potion? How do you expect me to dress when I am in such pain?"

"My lady, you have delivered the babies. You will have pain for several days. Sir Edward and Sir Daniel would not begrudge you your bedclothes for this one evening. Your pain will be less if you are comfortably dressed."

Marisa thought for a moment. "You are right, Bethany. I think my bedclothes *will* be best, but I do want you to braid my hair. I do not want them to underestimate the ordeal I have just been through. Neither of them would make such sacrifices for their name. I guess I should not look *too* good." She laughed. "Good thinking, Bethany, I did not know you had it in you."

Bethany left the room, happy to have escaped the ordeal of the corset for the evening and relieved to escape more of Marisa's insults.

CHAPTER 22

Marisa had time to sleep before dinner. The potion that had relieved her pain left her wrapped in blissful grogginess. She and Bethany had arranged her hair attractively and dressed her in a splendid rose-colored bed jacket that Laura had stitched. By the time she finished dressing, she was alert and ready for the evening.

When the gentlemen entered the room, they were obviously surprised at how beautiful and rested Marisa looked. "Father, would you believe this beautiful woman has given me my legacy today?" complimented Edward.

"Marisa, you are lovely," agreed Sir Daniel. "To think you delivered my two grandchildren today."

Marisa smiled weakly. "Thank you, kind sirs. I know your compliments are contrived. I did not even have time to prepare myself. My pain and my tending to the babies has kept me occupied."

Bethany felt sick thinking about the number of times she had had to redo Marisa's hair to get it perfect, and the number of housecoats she had tried for the perfect effect—and to use the babies that she had sent from the room, short of an hour after their birth, as an excuse!

Sarah knocked softly on the door and then walked in with the little basket. "There are my little darlings now," said Marisa reaching out her arms warmly. "Bring them to me, Sarah. It has been too long since I have seen my precious angels."

Sarah appeared mildly surprised but brought the babies to the bed. "Tonight, kind sirs, we will name these wonderful little bundles. Here, Sarah, lay them here next to me."

"Gentlemen, I hope you do not mind if I am selfish with my prize. I went through a lot of time and suffering and do not feel that I need to share just yet."

"Of course, Marisa. Any child would be blessed to have such a loving mother. We will have plenty of time to enjoy them later, they are your babies now," replied Edward proudly, glancing at his father.

Sarah and Bethany looked at each other in disbelief as they prepared a small table for dinner. The kitchen girls had begun to bring in the meal. "Sir Edward and Sir Daniel, would you like to eat here at the table?" offered Bethany. "Lady Marisa, will you join them?"

"Bethany, if you ever had a child, much less *two*, you would know that is an offer I cannot accept," Marisa replied with a sickly smile.

"Ladies, take the babies near the fire, and I will try to eat in bed. Bring the table here close to me," Marisa requested weakly.

The women carried the heavy, dark wooden table to her bedside, and the happy family began their festive meal. They talked about their future with the new heir and the future of their estates. Marisa even went so far as to project possible families for potential marital bonds for their children. Both men made light of her foresight, which offended her sensitivities.

"You two laugh, but now that we have a daughter, this is an opportunity to increase our estate. She could produce the first heir for some noble family," she said emphatically.

"I have thought quite a bit about my estate as of late," said Sir Daniel. "The two of you seem content with what you have, and my father's property is some distance from here. I was thinking of taking Arelia back with me and arranging a marriage as Marisa suggests."

Marisa was shocked. She did not expect her father-in-law to approach the subject at the dinner honoring his new, and only, heir.

"Father, this is very sudden and seems a little hasty," said Marisa coolly. "There is something you need to know before you make that a firm decision."

Sarah and Bethany looked at each other nervously, fearing what she would say next. Edward sat quietly, not knowing what his shrewd wife had fabricated.

"Remember when you visited Arelia's room the other night, and you asked why she was in a room near the servants?" she prompted.

"Yes, you said she and Laura requested that she have a room near Laura's, and that Sarah and Bethany convinced you it would be the right thing to do for her," he reviewed thoughtfully.

"That is right. I agreed that it would be but for only a short time." Marisa looked away, appearing too choked up to continue.

"Please, Marisa, go on," pleaded Sir Daniel. "Is she very ill?"

"Bethany," Marisa waved her hand in Bethany's direction to stall for effect, "my pains are increasing. Do you have my tea?"

"Yes, my lady." Bethany poured her tea and handed it to her.

"I am sorry, Father. It pains me as much as the horrendous pains of childbirth to tell you this. In fact, I do not know which is greater," she said tearfully, as she slowly took a sip of her tea.

"Please, Marisa, continue," Sir Daniel insisted.

"Laura is such a lovely young woman," Marisa said, looking at Sarah sweetly. "We were so happy that the two girls were such friends. One night they went to the kitchen to get some water for tea when Arelia came across the wine. She commented that her mother loved to drink wine, and she drank with her on occasion. Laura, of course, was surprised at this and said nothing in response. The next morning, Arelia was taken ill. With a brief investigation, Laura discovered Arelia had gotten into the wine and brandy. She, of course, reported it to her mother, who shared this information with me. Arelia started making reference to the handsome young soldier who had saved her life and who soon began coming to her room at night. On more than one occasion, Bethany found her clothes wet and sandy from the beach. We suspected she was meeting the soldier called Stephen. You may recall she called his name the night you were in her room."

"Marisa, stop," Sir Daniel pleaded. He rose from the table and walked to the window. Edward patted Marisa's hand lovingly. He was concerned about his father but wanted to provide amply for his new family. As always, he trusted Marisa's judgment better than his own.

"Bethany," continued Marisa, "you have seen Arelia unconscious with wine and brandy, have you not?"

"Yes, but—"

Marisa interrupted, "And you have seen soldiers in her room?"

Sir Daniel turned and asked, "At whose bidding?"

"Mine, Father," interjected Marisa. "Please forgive me, but I asked Bethany to watch her when I suspected her immoral behavior. Since then, the flow of soldiers has been continuous. You witnessed her drunkenness the other night," she reminded.

"Drunkenness? I thought she was ill," he responded in surprise.

"Ill in spirit only. Edward and I wanted to protect you. We tried to keep her from drinking before your visit, but somehow she found wine, probably from one of her many soldiers."

"Lady Marisa," interrupted Sarah. "I am not aware of this. Laura hasn't told me any of it."

Sir Daniel walked to Sarah and touched her arm. "You know nothing of this?" he asked the woman who had been with his family since she was young.

Marisa cut off her answer. "Father, Sarah, please forgive me. Laura and Bethany and I have erred by thinking we could help the poor child. I requested that Arelia's behavior be covered for and kept secret. Sarah, I know how much you cared for Arelia, and I could not bear that you be hurt by her behavior," Marisa apologized.

Sarah sat in the rocking chair putting her head in her hands and cried.

"Marisa, I cannot believe this. I must talk to Arelia myself!" Sir Daniel said as he headed for the door.

"Sire, wait," shouted Bethany. "You can see her tomorrow." Bethany grabbed his arm, surprising them both.

He looked at her hand on his arm with wrinkled brow as she pulled away, embarrassed at her forwardness.

"Bethany, you cannot protect her any longer. Let him talk to her. He must see if she is worthy of his estate," shouted Marisa through tears of malice.

Sir Daniel turned with such great heaviness of heart, fighting back tears of anger and confusion, grief and despair, falling from the joyful expectation of seeing the babies for the first time to learning this about Arelia. It was nearly more than he could grasp.

Marisa, oblivious to his pain, or because she was satisfied with it, requested demurely, "Now, Bethany, my pain is so great. Fix me something to sleep." She smiled, pitifully. "And make it strong. I do not want to feel anything tonight. I have been through so much today."

Bethany poured another cup of tea. Taking the tea, Marisa continued, "Bethany, would you please get Roland to help Father back to his room."

"Sarah, take these babies out. I will prepare for bed. Oh, and Bethany, get me something to sleep." Marisa skillfully orchestrated the production.

A minute later, Bethany returned with Roland, who escorted Sir Daniel to his room.

Bethany helped Sarah prepare the babies in the basket, and the two women left the room to bring the babies to their wet-nurses.

"You were wonderful!" exclaimed Edward. "You never cease to amaze me. You, my dear, are my estate."

"Thank you, but our job is not done. Bethany is getting soft. Catch up with her and remind her of her place. Did you see her grab your father!?"

Bethany carried the basket for Sarah who was too distraught. She so badly wanted to confess her part in Arelia's situation to her friend but could hardly bear to think of it. She knew she would set it right by discontinuing Arelia's potion. *Time will heal everything; just a little more time. Once she goes through withdrawal, she will confide in her uncle, and he will not turn her away*, she thought.

"Bethany," Edward called from behind her. "I would like to talk to you. Sarah, keep the babies until noon tomorrow. Marisa will need her rest." Bethany waited as Sarah took the basket.

"Bethany, Lady Marisa and I are so grateful for your assistance. We would like to thank you by giving you the privilege of being in charge of the babies. You and Sarah will work closely together. I know you are getting older and caring for Marisa may be too tedious now, but you and Sarah together will share the burden of the babies. Laura may also be called in to help." He waited for a response, but none came.

"Be on your way now. Lady Marisa will need your help tonight," Edward said, smiling warmly into her cold stare.

Bethany turned without response and went to her herb cupboard. She prepared a stout tea to allow Marisa to sleep soundly with no pain.

Bethany returned to Marisa's room with tea. She watched her lady snuggle between the warm covers with an icy cold stare. "Here is your tea, my lady."

"Thank you, Bethany. I assume your master spoke to you. I know you will be pleased with your new position after Sir Daniel leaves. Bethany, I am speaking to you," said Marisa in a huff as her maid handed her the strong tranquilizing tea just as she had ordered and turned away from her.

"Yes, my lady," answered Bethany coldly.

"May I assume you do not approve of my story?" questioned Marisa as she downed the cup of strong tea.

Bethany did not respond.

"Let me remind you that I do not care about *your* opinion. *My* job is to protect my children's estate. That is a *mother's* job," Marisa continued.

Again, Bethany was silent. Marisa fluffed her pillows and pulled the heavy warm cover up to her shoulders. "I do not care if you will not speak now, I am too tired anyway, but we will continue this conversation tomorrow. Your approval or disapproval means nothing to me as long as you do exactly as I say.

"Is this strong enough to help me sleep?"

"It should be," was Bethany's withdrawn response.

"Then give me two cups. I want to sleep soundly," insisted Marisa. "Leave the rest on the table."

"As you will," agreed Bethany, pouring a second cup near to spilling. "Good night, my lady."

Marisa drank her tea quickly and snuggled between the covers. Bethany walked to the dressing table, poured another cup, and then snuffed out the light.

After hours of tossing and turning, Sir Daniel hurried down the hallway to Arelia's room. He hesitated at her door, having second thoughts about interrupting her sleep. He thought he heard her voice, so he knocked softly before walking in. He froze at the sight hinted at in the moonlit room.

A man turned quickly and sat up in the darkness. "What do you want? This is my night. Come back tomorrow."

"Arelia," said her uncle hesitantly.

"I said she is mine tonight, old man. You can have her tomorrow. Get out so I can finish."

Sir Daniel walked out the doorway and fell against the wall. "Oh, my dear God!"

CHAPTER 23

Bethany checked on Arelia at mid-morning and could see that she was starting to go through withdrawal. Her eyes were frightened and flighty. She was scratching at her arms nervously and doubling over from stomach pains.

Laura stood over her, crying. "Is she dying?"

"No, Laura, but I will prepare her a mild tea. She is getting well, but we must stay close and watch her carefully. Stay with her until I return," said Bethany.

"What can I do for her?"

"Just dampen her face and keep her covered as best you can."

Bethany had seen withdrawals many times among the soldiers she had been called on to help. She knew it was a painful process that might last days or even weeks. On occasion, men had died during this cleansing, but she would help Arelia back to good health.

The kitchen was buzzing with the normal morning chores. Sarah came in briefly for cheese and fruit and started to leave without speaking. "Sarah," called Bethany. "Are you all right?"

"No, I am very confused. I have not talked to Laura today," she said distantly.

"Sarah, I promise things will get better," reassured Bethany.

"You cannot make such a promise to me," Sarah said as she angrily walked away from her friend.

Bethany prepared a very mild brew of healing tea for Arelia and returned to Arelia's room. "Arelia, sit up," Bethany coaxed her gently. Arelia continued to thrash in bed, not seeming to hear.

"Laura, get in her bed. We must pull her up." The two women struggled to sit Arelia up. Laura held her while Bethany forced the medicinal brew down her throat. Tears filled Laura's eyes as she held her friend.

"Good job, Laura. This will give her some relief," assured Bethany.

There was an urgent knock on the door. "Bethany," called Sarah as the door flew open. "Come with me quickly."

The two women hurried down the hall. "What is it, Sarah?"

"You will see." Sarah rushed toward Marisa's room. "Follow me." Bethany could hardly keep up.

"Look," she said as they hurried into Marisa's room.

Bethany looked at Marisa's ashen face with dried blood caked down the side of her mouth, staining her pillow. Her lips were blue.

"I cannot awaken her," declared Sarah in a panic.

Bethany looked at her calmly. "That is because she is dead."

Sarah stood paralyzed with fear. "Dead? How did this happen?"

"She insisted on two cups of tea," exclaimed Bethany casually. "Maybe she drank even more," she said as she checked the teapot.

Sarah froze at the implications of Bethany's statement. She walked over to the softly flickering fire and sat in the rocking chair, questioning what this would mean. Neither woman spoke for some time.

"Bethany, I will get a basin. We will change the bed dressing and clean Marisa's body. Everyone will suspect that she was not strong enough to survive the birth of two babies."

The women immediately set about their jobs. "I will send for Sir Edward. This time the story will be mine," said Sarah.

Once the room was set, Sarah summoned Helen to send for Sir Edward.

Within minutes, he hurried into the room. "Sarah, did you send for me?"

"Yes, sire. I am sorry to inform you that Lady Marisa has hemorrhaged and expired during the night. She had been complaining about her pain, as you recall, and she said herself, the birth was horrendous. Bethany fixed the soothing tea as she requested, but because she was so upset after last evening, she refused to drink it. Bethany found the pot and her cup this morning."

Edward walked over to his wife's bed and stared dumbly. "This cannot be! What will I do? Where were you when this happened? How could it happen?"

"I had left the room only briefly to get clean water for her basin and a little to eat. She was sleeping soundly when I left but must have hemorrhaged while I was gone."

"We will care for her, sire. You should go back to your room. We will send for your father," Bethany added with feigned compassion.

"This is how my mother died, but she took my sister with her at birth. Where is my son? Is he all right? What will I do?"

"Sire, Bethany and I will care for Lady Marisa now and for both your son and daughter. You must go to your room," coaxed Sarah sadly. "Helen, help Sir Edward to his room."

He turned and walked blindly through the door. Sarah walked over to Bethany, still sitting in the chair. "Bethany, were the things that Marisa said about Arelia true?"

"No, Sarah, Arelia has been trapped by Marisa. There is no escape for her." Although Bethany only confirmed her suspicions, Sarah was dumfounded.

"Do you think Sir Daniel believed her lies?" continued Sarah.

"He does not want to, but Lady Marisa was very convincing." Bethany said it with such detachment that it chilled Sarah to the bone.

"I am worried, Bethany. I did not want to believe her either, but I did. Even though I knew better, the things she said sounded so sensible," explained Sarah. "What I do not understand is why Arelia did nothing to stop her."

Bethany lowered her eyes and began to cry. She could not admit her part in Arelia's tragic life.

"Bethany, I do not need to know right now. I know this has been hard for you. Maybe now that Marisa is gone, Arelia can take her rightful place in the family."

"I pray you are right, Sarah." Bethany wiped her tears on her apron, but anguish remained in her eyes.

Sarah and Bethany went together to tell Sir Daniel the news of Marisa's death and ask him to join his son in his room. "At least she did not take the babies with her," he said sadly. "The two of you must keep those babies alive. They are all we have left of our family." He moaned with tears brimming over.

"Sire, you still have your brother's daughter," reminded Bethany.

"Arelia is not part of my family. I went to talk to her last night and saw more than I wanted. At least Marisa saved me from further shaming the family with that girl," he said angrily.

Sarah interrupted, "Sire, Arelia was under evil influence. If you took her with you, she would return to the lovely young woman you first knew."

"She will not go with me. That was my original intention but no longer. You are right about evil, but I cannot erase her mother's influence or cure the power of alcohol over her disposition. She was bred to such a life. My poor brother. How he must have suffered with such a woman. My parents were right all along." He left the room, leaving Sarah and Bethany behind, stunned and bewildered.

"Bethany, this is not right. We cannot let this lie continue," Sarah said emphatically.

"Sarah, be calm. We must think through this very carefully. We cannot expose Lady Marisa at her death. Sir Daniel would not believe us anyway, and Sir Edward would never forgive us. We would be sent to the scullery or worse, into the forest. We must move very cautiously. If not, we may never see the babies again. They need us now more than ever."

Sir Daniel joined Edward in his bedroom, recognizing his deep shock and grief. "Son, I am so sorry about Marisa. I have also suffered such a loss. I understand your pain and know I cannot erase it, but it will be necessary for you to focus on your children now; it is what Marisa would have wanted." Watching his grief-stricken son renewed memories of his own loss.

"Son," he said after sitting quietly for some time, "I will leave directly after the burial. I had intended to stay, but there is nothing left for me now, and I have many things to tend to at home. I will have my servants prepare to leave."

"I understand, Father. I do not want you to relive the pain you experienced when you lost Mother any longer than necessary. I had no idea your grief was so great. Now I understand.

"When will you return?"

"I will plan to return for the first birthday of my new grandchildren. I would think that will be a festive occasion," he said with a soft smile.

"Father, thank you for understanding. Next year at this time, things will be very different."

The following day was busy with preparation for the funeral service and burial. Horses were groomed and saddles oiled for the funeral procession. The coffin was washed and draped. Riders had been sent out immediately after Marisa's death to spread the word to nearby neighbors for an afternoon service two days later. Only those who lived within a day's ride were expected to attend; they couldn't hold the body too long, and besides, people were still numb from the death of so many friends and loved ones; few people remained.

Hoping for a traditional Christian burial, Edward sent for a priest, but so many had died with the plague that he didn't know if one could be found. Even now, some monasteries were becoming overgrown with weeds and underbrush, with rotting bodies of the remaining monks no one was there to care for. Before the plague, Sir Daniel had always had a priest in residence. At the first word of the pestilence, Fr. Martin had left to bring Extreme Unction, the last rites of the Church, to neighboring tenants but had never returned. The chapel on the top floor sat empty, gathering dust and spider webs, and was seldom attended, except for quiet, individual prayer, something Arelia wished for since her time there with Sir Daniel. Before he left a year ago, Sir Daniel often went to pray for his family, especially for Arelia, but to Marisa religion was a matter of convenience, for appearance's sake only. She had little tolerance for talk about God, and having a priest in residence had been a constant annoyance to her with reminders about what she should and shouldn't do, with instructions on right and wrong. No one was going to tell her what to do—not even God. So, apparently, there would be no priest to send her along to eternity's door.

The kitchen staff buzzed with preparations for extra food for the guests: bread and pastries to bake, fish and meats to smoke, and vegetables to peel and boil. Maids opened and dusted the many closed and sparsely furnished rooms that might be filled overnight. All the preparations that had been made for a birth celebration were quickly turned into preparation for a funeral.

Marisa's mother had been taken by the scourge, her father having passed earlier. Marisa's sister had sent word that she was not up for travel, not stating that the event was of no consequence to her since neither of Marisa's children benefited her estate. There had been no love between them in life, and so her death was of no significance now. No one had heard from her brother, who had become a priest, and most assumed he was dead.

The stables accommodated horses and carriages from guests already arriving. In spite of the occasion, the house took on an almost festive air with the hustle and bustle of the few attending, both the curious and respectful.

Faircastle rarely received guests since Daniel's wife had passed, and so those attending were curious about changes made since Lady Marisa's arrival. The last gathering had been Marisa and Edward's wedding, which some declared an *event* by most standards. They would be painfully disappointed by the lack of luxury and elegance under Marisa's reign. Other than her own personal wardrobe, she had little interest in design and furnishings; she was too busy studying landholdings and making suggestions to Edward as to how to squeeze additional payments from tenants.

Edward had summoned the captain to prepare the troops for their part as honor guard in the funeral service. He had mentioned that his father would be leaving the day after the burial, and normal operations would resume. The captain had sent riders to locate the troops out on detail and had them prepare to return immediately. They would be dressed in full regalia with banners flying, as appropriate to the occasion.

The servants' attitudes were surprisingly light for the amount of work required for the occasion. Sir Daniel's wife had been a dear woman who took sincere interest in everyone's lives, including the servants. She had an uncanny knack for remembering everyone's birthdays and did not let the day go by without recognition. Marisa, on the other hand, cared only about herself and looked at the staff as a whole in light of how they could make her life more pleasant. So, rather than grief, most servants were relieved by her death; a weight had been lifted. Their lives had changed drastically when she took control of the estate; now, hopefully, it would change for the better. Servants presented an appropriate facade around the guests and Fairchild men, which was quickly left behind when they returned to the kitchen and courtyard. In fact, the idea that they were obviously pretending grief made the entire situation humorous to some of them. They winked and smiled knowingly at each other as they changed from one expression to the other. Bethany and Sarah were well aware of the pretense from the servants and were afraid Sir Edward and the guests were also conscious of the ruse.

Sarah spent her time preparing the babies and had no desire to be involved with any other preparation. She intended to limit their presentation time, but she knew everyone would want to view the new heirs out of curiosity. Fear of letting something slip about Marisa's untimely death kept her away from the staff and Sir Daniel. Her distress was construed as grief over Marisa's passing as she had attended to her personally. Sir Daniel had even offered his condolences on seeing her apparent sorrow and obvious concern for the now-motherless children.

Bethany and Laura spent their morning dressing Marisa and preparing her hair and makeup. Bethany had dressed Sir Daniel's wife's body and the bodies of others who had died over the years. Laura had never had the experience and was fighting back strong waves of nausea. She pretended to be as unaffected as Bethany but spent much of the time with the ocean breeze blowing over her face at the window, pretending to check the weather for the burial service. She was not at all prepared for rubbing oils and perfumes over the hard, cold, dead body, although Bethany somehow seemed to detach herself from the experience and could have been basting a chicken for her casual regard for the process.

When Sir Daniel saw that only seven guests had arrived, he invited Bethany and Sarah to be part of the funeral party. Both women were surprised and flattered to be included. Bethany wondered at his lack of decorum and thought how humiliated Marisa would be to have servants included in her funeral procession, especially the one who had provided the tranquilizing tea. It gave her a sense of deep satisfaction that she hoped did not show.

As time for the procession neared, the few guests began gathering in the great hall. No musicians could be found to hire, and so the room was strangely quiet except for the wailers that Edward had arranged for from the staff. Their mournful lament that echoed off the massive stone walls had little to do with Marisa's passing but rather was for appearances, and out of fear of facing their own mortality and the spirit of death that had passed over them without harm just months before.

The service and procession were a show that would have made Marisa cringe. The right people were represented and performing appropriately; there were just so few of them. Guests questioned Sarah and Bethany's identities and made cruel comments about the inappropriateness of their inclusion. Daniel and Edward seemed unaware of their evident faux pas.

No priest had been found, and so Sir Daniel read Psalm 23 from the ornate Bible that had been gathering dust upstairs in the neglected chapel. His voice cracked several times as he remembered the same words read at his beloved's ceremony, wishing he could turn back the clock fifteen years and hold her again. Many were moved by his obvious sadness over the passing of his one and only daughter-in-law. He thanked the guests for attending, using the plague as an excuse for the small number of mourners. Oddly, little was said about Marisa herself; baby Edward started to cry and drowned out Daniel's words, which was a relief to him and everyone else. Laura made a hasty retreat, drawing attention to the babies. Shortly after, everyone gathered outside for the short ride to the family cemetery. It appeared that the weather would hold for the outdoor ceremony; gusts of wind blew from the coastline as gulls shrieked in the distance. Women pulled their black veils and heavy woolen coats tight to keep out the wind and the chill of death.

No funeral dirge accompanied the wagon carrying the coffin to the family's burial site. The cadence of creaking wooden wheels and the shuffle of horses' hooves through the rutted pathway was the only music to accompany Marisa to the deep pit.

What a farce, thought Bethany. *When I die, I want sincere grief, not pretending and apathy. How sad that a woman, through her selfishness, could create such a nightmare for so many.*

Other than the hired wailers, Edward was the only one who shed a tear. Bethany wondered if Marisa would have led her life differently if she could have foreseen the indifference, and even relief, felt at her passing.

Irony escaped everyone but Bethany that this woman who, so manipulated having the first heir to the Fairchild estate, was no longer alive to see it.

226

Bethany had prepared a weak tea that she and Laura had forced down Arelia earlier in the day. One of the girls from the scullery was summoned by Bethany to care for her until Laura returned. All of the servants were aware of Arelia's plight, but their responses to her had been very different since she was housed in the servants' area.

Many of the older women shunned even the sight of her and spoke of her as an evil girl who deserved every punishment she got. The older men completely avoided making any comments and were quick to avoid even listening to the ladies talk about her. They knew the truth and wanted no part of it, maybe feeling guilty for not helping the girl. The younger girls from the scullery tried to catch glimpses of her and then gossiped continually, sharing every imaginable story about her mysterious life. Some of the younger men hoped to catch her eye and made up stories about their own escapades. Many thought that she was possessed by evil spirits that could jump from one body to the next, and only a soldier was strong enough to stop the assault and final possession.

Poor Arelia was totally unaware of Marisa's death and of all the formalities taking place in her own house. She was consumed with the pains of withdrawal and was incoherent. Fortunately, the last soldier to visit had been repulsed by her stench and erratic behavior and reported her condition to the captain. He had immediately suspended all future visits, and with Marisa's death, he did not intend to resume them for some time.

The captain had dealt with Marisa previously and wondered how Edward would handle all the decisions that lie ahead. He had no personal regrets over Marisa's death except that he had hoped for a liaison with her in the future. He knew that she would eventually tire of her weak, sniveling husband, and he had every intention of filling her needs after Edward failed to satisfy her insatiable desire for attention. He was attracted to her strong focus and single-mindedness of purpose, but now that she was dead, he looked forward to regaining some of the control he had lost under her domination. Edward was clearly left groping down a dark lane with no sense of direction. The captain saw an opportunity for even more control with Marisa's death, especially if Edward took to his brandy.

Edward retired to his room soon after the interment, leaving Sir Daniel the hard task of hosting the visitors. Having heard rumors about a long-lost niece, several of the guests asked about Arelia, noting the absence of an unfamiliar young woman. His response was short and direct, not welcoming any further questions. "Arelia is no longer with us." Sarah overheard his response but knew there was no way she could rectify it. Others assumed she was taken in the plague and did not push for obvious, familiar, and grotesque details.

When Laura returned to Arelia's room late in the afternoon, she found her crying uncontrollably. "Arelia, what is it?" she asked in panic.

Arelia stopped, startled for a minute, and looked at her with a blank, vacant expression. She didn't seem to recognize Laura and simply stared at her for a long time.

"Laura?" Arelia finally asked surprised, patting the bed next to her. Laura sat on the side of the bed. Arelia gently lay her head on Laura's lap. Laura was taken aback and held her, not knowing what to do. When she fell asleep, Laura laid Arelia back on her pillow and took up her sewing, keeping close watch on her.

As the night went on, Arelia began to mumble in her sleep. Her forehead broke out in a sweat, and she began to shiver. Laura covered her with blankets and wiped her face with a cool rag.

"Arelia, please do not die. I do not know what to do for you. Please, please, God, save her. How could this have happened?"

Bethany overheard Laura's concern as she came into the room. "Bethany, what is happening? Is she dying?"

"No, child. You are doing well. I will prepare a weak tea. Give her only one sip. No more. The cup must last the entire night. Tomorrow, we will give her soup. She will be well soon."

The funeral guests and Sir Daniel left the next morning for the long ride back to their estates. Sir Daniel bid Sarah and Bethany goodbye without mention of Arelia. "Take care of my precious grandchildren. I will return next year for their birthday."

"Sire, shall we take you to see Arelia before you leave?" asked Bethany. "She is getting better now."

Anger flashed in Sir Daniel's tired eyes, "I have seen all of Arelia that I ever intend to see. She is not the girl I thought she was."

Sarah bravely interrupted, "Lady Marisa was not speaking clearly, sire."

"Sarah, I have seen with my own eyes more than Marisa could ever have described." He held up his hand to stop any further interruption. Shaking his head, he said, "I will listen to no more." With that he climbed into his carriage. The women stood in dismay watching the procession leave the estate, wondering about Arelia's fate under Sir Edward's hand.

The house seemed unusually quiet after all the activity. The only sounds were the babies' cries . . . and Arelia's.

CHAPTER 24

With horses trudging single file over paths overgrown from lack of use, their return seemed to take forever. Stephen wanted to charge ahead at breakneck speed, but the other soldiers were apparently in no hurry. News of Marisa's death had reached them. Although he'd been away for only weeks, it seemed like years to him. He wondered how Arelia's visit had gone with her uncle, and how Marisa's death would affect her situation. With Sir Daniel back at Faircastle, he expected to find her free and happy, under his loving care. Having never seen her in a normal, healthy situation, his imagination was filled with what their relationship could be if she were happy and healthy.

His only thought on returning to camp was of Arelia. "Captain," he called across the camp. Catching his attention, he ran over to him. "Sir, I want to be first to visit the girl, Arelia."

"There will be no visitors. The girl has gone mad," said the captain as he walked off casually.

"Wait, sir. What do you mean, *gone mad*?"

"I mean, the men say she has gone mad. She has lost her mind. No one is visiting. No one wants to," explained the captain.

Confusion flooded every recess of his mind. He wanted to run to her, but he knew he must restrain himself until dark and then leave the camp unnoticed. Each minute seemed like hours as the sun dipped slowly behind the trees.

He was known for walking along the beach at night, so it was not unusual for him to leave the camp and return hours later. Finally, when camp had quieted and most of the men were sleeping, with only a few settled around the fire, he headed casually toward the beach. They didn't pay much attention as he walked past the blazing campfire. "It's going to be cold along the water tonight," one of the men commented.

"It will feel good after being away from the water for so long," he responded casually.

Walking along the ocean was refreshing, but bone-chilling. *How has Arelia gone mad? What could it mean?*

As soon as he was out of sight, he began to run toward the castle on the cliff, climbing the crag in full stride, only stopping when he reached the stairwell that led to Arelia's room. Stilling his breath, he listened carefully for any noise before proceeding unnoticed up the cold, dark stairway. It was good to know that he would not interrupt any soldier when he opened the door. Slowly, cautiously, he peered around the door and noticed a candle flickering on a table.

"Who is there?" called a woman's voice.

"Arelia?" he asked through the slightly opened door.

"No, it is I, Laura. Is that you, Stephen?" she asked as she hurried to the door. Seeing him standing in the hallway, she grabbed his arm and pulled him into the room. "Come in quickly."

"What is wrong? How is Arelia?" he asked frantically.

"She seems to be better. How do you know about her?"

"The captain told me she had gone mad. She looks the same." He knelt against the bed and lovingly stroked Arelia's hair. "What happened?"

"I cannot say, Stephen. Marisa said she had too much wine and brandy, but she became very sick after that and was unconscious for a long time. She is finally beginning to sleep restfully." Laura explained the situation which made no sense to her.

"Where is Bethany? Does she know?"

"Bethany has me give her soup and tea, which is making her better. I think Bethany has saved her life with her mixtures of herbal teas."

Stephen gently moved Arelia's arm and sat on the edge of the bed watching her sleep. "She has gone through so much, Laura. She does not deserve any of this." He took her limp hand and held it gently on his lap. "Laura, get some sleep. I will stay with her."

"Stephen, Arelia called your name many times. She would want you to be with her more than anyone," she smiled, not even acknowledging the impropriety of his staying overnight. *Who would think anything of it with Arelia?*

"She has to be all right. I missed her so much while I was away. Somehow, I have to get her away from here."

Laura smiled from ear to ear. "I have been waiting for you to say that!"

"By the way, what did her uncle say? Why is she still here and not with him?" Stephen asked the obvious question with pinched brow, the tone of his voice between anger and frustration.

"I do not know. She was sick the whole time he was here, and they never talked. He left right after Marisa's funeral. I do not think Arelia even knew he was here," Laura explained.

He shook his head and rubbed his forehead. "That does not make any sense. She is going to be heartbroken. All she talked about was seeing him again. I do not understand what happened," he said. "Something is very wrong."

He lifted Arelia's hand and held it to his lips, looking at her with such grief. "Laura, thank you. You had better get some sleep. I will stay until just before sunrise."

"Goodnight, Stephen." Before she walked to the door, she briefly rested her hand on his shoulder. "I am glad you are back. You are just the medicine she needs right now," she said, quietly closing the door behind her.

Stephen sat watching Arelia sleep, thinking about what he would do to get her away from the estate. Although an avalanche of ideas crashed through his mind, he wanted their departure to be smooth and permanent, without any threat from Edward. Safety had to be the paramount consideration; she had suffered enough.

Arelia began to mumble in her sleep. He leaned close but couldn't understand what she was saying. He was finally relieved from the stress of his trip and the anxiety over seeing Arelia as he watched her sleep, and stroked the palm of her soft hand. He removed his heavy boots and jacket and climbed in bed next to her, feeling her warmth through heavy blankets. He slid his arm slowly under her head, and then lay back, relishing the comfort of finally holding her. He felt the same desire he had felt before and wanted to do more than hold her in his arms.

"I will not have you in this bed, Arelia. One day, far from here, we will love each other without any harm or selfish desire as husband and wife. We will love each other at the right time and in the right place with hearts and minds joined in mutual affection and sincere commitment."

Stephen slept totally satisfied with Arelia sleeping peacefully at his side.

"Stephen! Stephen! Is it really you, or am I dreaming?" Arelia whispered excitedly as she shook his shoulder, waking him from a sound sleep. The room was dark but for the moon and she wasn't sure of who she saw. "What are you doing here?"

Stephen opened his eyes slowly and smiled at the beautiful face that greeted him. "So I surprised you?" he said coyly.

"Surprised? Of course, I am surprised. How did you get here?" she laughed.

"I have been here for days, and you slept through it the whole time," he teased.

"You have not! Have you?" she asked, propped up on one elbow, not really sure whether he was teasing her or not, acknowledging the fog that had nearly drowned her. "Something strange happened to me. I have had horrible dreams and could not wake up. I know Laura has been with me, but I am so confused about what has been happening. I am not even sure if you are real," she stammered.

Stephen laughed. "I am real. Everything is all right now, but Laura says you have been very sick. Bethany and Laura nursed you back to health," Stephen explained.

"Bethany," she said pensively. "Bethany made me well?"

"That is what Laura told me," he explained.

She lay back against her pillow. "I had horrible dreams about Bethany," she said, remembering parts of the nightmare she had gone through.

Stephen scooped her up in his arms, hugging her gently. "You are fine now. We will walk on the beach together soon."

"The beach . . . I have missed it so much," she smiled at the thought of long moonlit walks. "My uncle! Where is my uncle?" Arelia asked, beginning to remember some of what had happened.

"Arelia . . .," he started slowly. "Your uncle left. He has gone back to his estate."

Arelia sat up in a start, dizzy with the sudden move. Catching herself she cried "No, that is impossible! I did not get to see him. He would never leave without seeing me. How could he?"

"I do not know. Laura said he left the day after the funeral."

"The funeral?" Arelia asked sitting up cross legged. "What funeral?"

Stephen didn't know what to say. He'd gone too far not to explain. He hadn't realized how much she'd missed during her illness. "Arelia, Marisa died the day after she had the babies," he explained as he got out of bed to stoke the fire.

"Marisa's dead! How is that possible? I just had dinner with her and my cousin."

"You got sick at the dinner. Since then a lot has happened. Marisa had twins, a boy and a girl."

"Twins, how wonderful! How can it be that I did not know any this? How long has it been since the babies were born?" she asked as she eased herself carefully to side of the bed, feeling confused and frightened.

"Over a week . . . Marisa died the day after they were born, and your uncle left the morning after the funeral."

Her weak, unstable legs carried her to the window where she stood staring blindly at the vast expanse before her, holding the ledge tightly. "How has all of this happened? Why did my uncle leave? Stephen, my uncle was supposed to stay a long time. He must have been worried that I was sick. How could he leave me?" she asked with tears streaming down her face, stunned by the news.

Stephen walked to her and held her in his arms while the tears flowed. "I cannot say. It does not make any sense."

Laura knocked softly on the door and then stepped in quietly. "I see you are up. How is she, Stephen?"

"Not good, Laura. I just told her about Marisa, and she realized that her uncle left without talking to her."

"Arelia," said Laura stroking her shoulder. "Your uncle visited the first day he was here, but you were so sick. He could not take you with him."

"If he knew I was sick, how could he leave? I do not understand." She cried. "How could he leave without me?"

"Stephen, it is almost sunup. You should leave. I will stay until Bethany comes," Laura reminded.

The pain showed in Stephen's face. "I cannot just leave her."

"You must leave now, or Arelia could be in trouble," Laura pressed for her safety.

"You are right. Arelia, I will come back as soon as I can. You need to rest and eat. You are very thin. Laura, take care of her." He pulled on his boots and tunic and hurried down the stairs into the pre-morning light.

When Stephen returned to the camp, the men were just rising to begin the day. Fortunately, no one seemed to notice that he had been out overnight. The walk back along the water with the cool, crisp morning air did little to clear his thoughts. Plan after plan rushed into his mind only to be replaced by another as futile sounding as the one before.

He first thought that he would kidnap her, suspecting that Sir Edward wouldn't even try to find her; or he could ask for her hand, knowing that her cousin would probably give her away to be rid of her. Whatever he decided, he just knew he had to get her out as quickly as possible. He wasn't sure where the threat came from, but imagining Edward's condition without Marisa gave him a renewed sense of urgency.

Even with the hope that Stephen brought, a black cloud of despair threatened Arelia's tenuous sense of sanity. It was difficult enough to understand how she had lost several critical weeks of her life, and now she had to struggle for control over her thoughts and attitudes. She couldn't understand what had happened; from believing that her uncle would save her from the horror of her life, only to find he was gone without even seeing her, evidently not concerned about her at all.

"Laura, how could he have left? You must be mistaken." Arelia cried. "He would not have left without seeing me."

"He did see you the first day he was here, but you were sick," Laura repeated, not knowing what to say.

"I know, but he *would never* leave if he knew how ill I was. He must still be

235

here." Arelia hurried toward the door, racing past Laura, through the court-yard, and down the long dark hallway into the family's wing, bursting into Marisa's room. She staggered, out of breath and startled by what she saw. Laura hurried along quietly behind her, praying no one was awake yet.

The room was dark and cold. There was no fire in the hearth, and candles were not lit. The air was still. Arelia froze, only now accepting that Marisa was really dead. She walked slowly into the room, looking at the neatly made bed and the empty water basin. She fell on the floor in a flood of tears. "It must be true." She cried.

Bethany heard crying from her room and came to investigate. She couldn't believe her eyes, seeing Arelia lying on the floor with Laura kneeling helplessly by her side. "What are you doing here, Arelia? Get up," she said with startled concern.

"Oh, Bethany! What has happened?" Arelia cried desperately, grasping at the hem of the older woman's dress. "Please tell me my uncle is still here."

"I am sorry, Arelia," Bethany said as she knelt next to her. "I am so sorry." Bethany fought to control her own tears. She also had thought that Sir Daniel would free Arelia once Marisa was gone. She had no idea that he would witness Arelia with one of the soldiers after Marisa's slanderous lies. If only she had stopped Marisa sooner! "Let me take you back to your room. You should rest."

Arelia hardly had the strength to move. There was no reason to. She wanted to lie there and sleep forever.

"Arelia, please get up. You cannot stay here. Laura is worried about you," Bethany pleaded.

"Why, Bethany? What have I to move for? For the soldiers? For you? For my prison cell?"

Laura knelt at her side and brushed long streaks of tear-dampened hair from her face.

With a deep sigh, Bethany pushed her weary, aged frame up and walked to the window. *Somehow I will make it right*, she thought. "Arelia, get up for Stephen."

Arelia lay there without moving. "Please, Arelia," pleaded Bethany. "Let me help you to your room."

Arelia struggled to her feet with Laura and Bethany's help. "I do not think that I can make it to my room. I am so weak. What is wrong with me?"

"You have been very sick. I will fix you some soup, and then you can sleep," Bethany said as she helped her take one step after another down the upstairs hallway back to her room.

"Yes, sleep until a soldier walks through the door; then I begin my nightmare," Arelia said sardonically.

"No! I will stop the soldiers as long as I can. Tomorrow Laura will walk with you on the beach. Would you like that?" Bethany offered.

"Bethany, are you sure? With Laura?" Arelia asked brightening somewhat, seeing Laura smile in agreement.

"Yes, I will arrange it."

Once she returned to her room, Laura encouraged her to eat a bowl of soup and hard bread. She helped her into clean nightclothes, although it was still morning, and tucked her into bed. Arelia slept peacefully and comfortably for the first time in weeks.

She awakened during the night to a cold, empty room with a dwindling fire and cheese and bread on the table. No one was with her, no soldier and no helper. Oddly, she was content to be alone. After stoking logs into orange and yellow flickering flames, she wrapped a heavy blanket around her thin shoulders and carried the plate of cheese and bread to sit near the fire.

How my life has changed. She remembered sitting cozily at the foot of her mother's rocking chair with little Prudence sleeping peacefully on her lap and listening to her father and brothers gathered around the long trestle table with a drone of conversation floating weightlessly in the cool night air. The fire was the same, and the chill from the floor flowed through the blanket, but now, again, she was alone.

Yes, tonight she was alone and, for the first time, was relieved that no one was there. Those who were in her life now couldn't provide long-lasting peace and comfort; it was fleeting with each visit, taken away as the door closed behind them until the next chance visit. Maybe it was better to be alone. She loved Laura and Stephen, but they were only visitors who had to get permission to see her or to steal small tidbits of time at great risk. They didn't have permission to have a true, ongoing friendship, and besides, a friendship with her was a threat. Bethany confused her, and Sarah no longer seemed a part of her life since she never saw her even for a minute. Sarah was a mystery to her.

She didn't understand why she had left her and why Bethany had taken over. It seemed everything had changed for the worse.

Breath of life . . . The words floated through her mind. "Breath of life?" she spoke aloud, remembering the words from the Book of Genesis, which she had heard at school in the story of Adam and Eve. She walked over and picked up her father's Psalter, letting the pages fall where they may. Her eyes rested on the words of Psalm 139.

II 13 You formed my inmost being;
        you knit me in my mother's womb.

    14 I praise you, because I am wonderfully made;
        wonderful are your works!
        My very self you know.

    15 My bones are not hidden from you,
        When I was being made in secret,
        fashioned in the depths of the earth.

    16 Your eyes saw me unformed;
        in your book all are written down;
        my days were shaped, before one came to be.

Truly, her room was a cold, isolated prison cell and she the prisoner with permission to do nothing, except to stay alive—and to control her vulnerable, self-guarded thoughts. She was a slave at her own cousin's hands, and the men he allowed to abuse her.

"Lord, You know me. I will trust You one more day. Tomorrow, I will walk on the beach," she said aloud, fighting back tears. "I will walk with a friend."

CHAPTER 25

Thanks to Bethany's unexpected care, over the next several days Arelia regained her strength. As promised, she and Laura walked each day. Going to the beach stimulated her appetite and brought color back to her washed out complexion. The first day she made it only to the stoop at the end of the stairwell before she needed to rest, but the coastal breeze and warmth of the sun on her face breathed new life into her. By the fourth day, she and Laura walked to the same outcropping where she and Stephen had had many long talks about "the old days." To have the peace and freedom to walk with a friend without threat of attack, in the light of day, went a long way in bringing light back to her sad eyes.

As Bethany had promised, no soldiers had crossed her doorstep, but she did wish to see Stephen. Bethany had only been in once or twice. She was surprisingly pleasant with each visit and seemed genuinely concerned about Arelia's well-being.

Even though her uncle had left without her, the shackles of her cell had been loosened since Marisa's death. As she wondered what other changes had been made, she remembered that Stephen had said that Marisa had had twins. *Imagine, twins*, she thought; that would be a huge change in the household. For a minute she felt sorry for the babies, motherless at birth, but then decided, with some guilt, that they were better with no mother than with a mother like Marisa who used them only as pawns to gain property.

"Laura," Arelia asked, "who is caring for the babies?"

"Oh, it is so exciting. Mother and Bethany are in charge. They have two wet nurses, but Mother and Bethany do everything else."

"So that is why I rarely see Bethany now?" Arelia asked.

"Yes. Have you noticed how much nicer Bethany is now that she is caring for the twins? She has especially attached herself to the little girl. Mother says she is the best 'grandmother' a baby could have."

The girls laughed at the thought of Bethany as a grandmother, preoccupied with a baby. The absurdity of it was strangely funny and incomprehensible.

"I have to say, Bethany does seem like a different person. I no longer know what to expect from her," said Arelia.

"Mother said it is like having the old Bethany back from before Marisa moved here," explained Laura.

"Marisa! Laura, I have never met someone so evil. It is hard to imagine that she is gone forever. How is my cousin?" Arelia asked for the first time, thinking about Edward.

"I have not seen him. Mother said he stays in his room all day and night. Occasionally, he calls someone in, and of course, they bring his meals to him, but he has not left his room since the funeral. He has not even asked to see the babies, his own children."

"How strange. I do not know him very well, but I know he must be better off without Marisa."

"We all are," Laura agreed.

Later that evening, Laura returned to Arelia's room. "I have a surprise for you," she announced. No sooner had she said it than Stephen walked through the door. Arelia jumped up and ran to him.

Stephen picked her up, laughing. "You look wonderful. I have watched you and Laura walking on the beach, so I knew you were recovering."

"How is it that you get to visit?" she asked. She pushed away from Stephen, appearing frightened. "Laura, the visits are not beginning, are they?"

"No, Arelia," Laura said, taking her hand. "I caught Stephen sneaking up the stairs. In fact, I think I scared him to death." She laughed.

"Yes, all this sneaking around is going to make an old man out of me. So far, my soldier training has paid off. Arelia, I have to talk to you about something important."

Laura took the hint and begged her leave.

"Oh no, Stephen, you are not leaving again, are you?"

"Maybe," he answered.

"How long will you be gone?" she asked, already missing him.

"That depends on you," was his curious response.

"Me? What do I have to do with it?" she asked confused.

"It depends on whether or not you go with me," he explained, smiling at her confused expression.

"Go with you! Where? How?"

Stephen laughed as she stumbled over her words. "Arelia, I want to take you away from here. My family lives in a distant village. They would love you as much as I do, and I know they will help us settle," he explained.

"Stephen, we cannot just walk out of here. You do not know what you are talking about." As much as things had changed, Arelia feared that her life was still not her own to choose to leave if she pleased.

"I think we have two options. That is why I want to talk to you. One way of leaving is to just walk out of here like you say. Just grab your heavy boots and cloak and leave in the middle of the night. The other way would be to get permission for your hand and leave with your cousin's best wishes."

"My hand?" she asked.

"Yes, Arelia. I would not just steal you away. I want to marry you," he said, looking into her wide, surprised eyes.

"Marry *me*?" she repeated.

"Yes, I want you to be my wife," he emphasized.

"Your *wife*?"

Stephen laughed heartily. "You keep repeating everything I say. Tell me what you think."

Arelia walked to the chair and sat down. "I do not know what to say. This is such a surprise."

"Are you really surprised? Do you not miss me when I am away?" he asked.

"Of course, I do, and I think about you all the time, but . . ."

"But what?" he asked. Now he was confused.

Arelia turned from him and walked to the window.

"But what?" he asked impatiently, his confidence weakening.

"Stephen, you know who I am and what I am. How could you want me to marry you?" she asked sadly.

"You are right. I do know you. I know who you are, and I also know who you have been forced to become. That is exactly why I must get you away from here. Arelia, please do not refuse me." It had never crossed his mind that she would not agree to leave with him. He was becoming concerned.

"You do want to leave?" he asked.

"Yes, of course. But what will happen?"

"I do not know what will happen if we leave, but I do know what will happen if we stay. I cannot stand to think of it," he replied.

"Where would we go?" she questioned.

Stephen took her firmly by the shoulders. "Arelia, look at me and answer only 'yes' or 'no.' Do you want to leave this place?"

"Of course, I do," she replied.

"That is all I need to know for right now. I do not know how or when, but I do know we will leave. Do not worry now. We will think of the best way," he assured. "I cannot stay any longer. I have duty tonight, but I could not wait a minute longer to talk to you. Arelia, I love you," he said as he wrapped his arms around her.

"Stephen, I am afraid."

He kissed her gently on the forehead. "We cannot let fear keep you a prisoner here any longer. Trust me to help you." His expression was strong and reassuring.

"What will happen if something happens to you?" she asked tearfully.

He put his finger over her lips. "What will happen if you do not leave? Please trust me," he repeated. "I can take care of myself."

"I want to trust you," she said, lying her head against his chest. "I am so afraid of what could happen to you."

"One kiss, then I must leave." Arelia kissed him but did not want him to leave.

"Do not worry. I will be back, and then we will decide how we will leave *together*. Remember, I love you," he said as he hurried out the door.

Arelia heard him run down the stairs, wishing she were with him. Her door creaked open slowly, startling her.

"Is he gone?" asked Laura. "What did he want?"

Arelia looked concerned. "It did not take you long to get here. Were you waiting outside the door?"

"Of course not. What did he want?" Laura insisted.

"Laura, if I tell you, you cannot mention it, not even to your mother. Can you swear?"

"Of course, Arelia. Tell me," Laura insisted.

"He wants me to leave with him," Arelia whispered.

Laura squealed with excitement. "I knew it," she said, clapping her hands together.

"He wants me to marry him," Arelia continued.

Laura's eyes grew wide. "Marry him. Oh, Arelia how wonderful! It will be a wonderful occasion." She hugged Arelia roughly.

"Laura, settle down. There will be no *occasion*. You know who I am," reminded Arelia.

Laura lost her smile and looked worried. "Oh, dear. This will not be easy, will it?"

"No," said Arelia fretfully. "He says to trust him, but I am so afraid."

"All right, Lady Arelia," Laura said jokingly. "He will find a way. He is an officer, after all, right?"

"You sound like him," Arelia teased.

"He is right, you know. You worry too much. I will think good thoughts and say a prayer for you tonight, too," said Laura lovingly.

"Good thoughts and prayers," Arelia repeated. "I had forgotten about good thoughts. That is what has kept me hopeful, but I have been so disappointed before. I cannot stand to be disappointed again. Mother always said that prayers work. I will hang on to good thoughts, too, and prayers," she said with little enthusiasm.

"Listen to you," reprimanded Laura. "Which makes you happier and helps you sleep better, good thoughts or bad thoughts?"

"Good thoughts," answered Arelia sheepishly.

"Then why would you ever choose the bad ones?" said Laura, smiling.

"It is not that simple, Laura," replied Arelia.

"It is *simple* but not *easy*, Arelia." She took Arelia's hand and looked into her eyes, wanting to both encourage her and thank her for Arelia's inspiration.

243

"I have watched you do it over and over to my amazement. You have shown me that no one can influence your thoughts without your permission. So think what you will. *You* taught me that. Do not give anyone permission to destroy the good that has just happened to you this evening.

"If I were you, I would go to sleep with good thoughts about leaving with Stephen," Laura winked impishly. "Oh my, Arelia, Stephen proposed marriage tonight!"

Arelia's eyes twinkled with sudden realization. "Oh my gosh, you are right! Then good thoughts it is until tomorrow."

After Arelia dressed for bed and settled under the covers, she wrestled with her thoughts, fighting fear against faith, grief against hope, anger against love, despair against trust, and surrender against courage. Her tossing and restlessness got her out of bed to light the lantern, straining to search the Psalms.

Psalm 86

I 1 Incline your ear, LORD, and answer me,
    for I am poor and oppressed.

  2 Preserve my life, for I am devoted;
    save your servant who trusts in you.
    You are my God;

  3 be gracious to me, Lord;
    to you I call all the day.

  4 Gladden the soul of your servant;
    to you, Lord, I lift up my soul.

  5 Lord, you are good and forgiving,
    most merciful to all who call on you.

  6 LORD, hear my prayer;
    listen to my cry for help.

  7 On the day of my distress I call to you,
    for you will answer me.

II 8 None among the gods can equal you, O Lord;
    nor can their deeds compare to yours.

She read and reread the words her father had copied from words composed before the birth of Jesus, words that spoke to her personally even now. Peace filled her. She turned down the wick of the lantern, but before she got into bed, she knelt and prayed, "My dearest and only Lord Jesus, you are God above all others. Help me to remember that You are my only God, Savior of my body, mind, and soul. Thank you for sending Stephen to do what I cannot do for myself. Help me to trust him as I know you sent him to save me from the wolves. He brought me to safety then; help him bring me to safety now. My Lord, I trust You. Protect my thoughts of You, of Stephen, and my hope in escaping this place. I love you. Amen."

CHAPTER 26

While Stephen was on night duty, he spent most of the time weighing his two most obvious options. First, he could kidnap Arelia, leaving Edward with one of two ways to respond. If they ran, Sir Edward could hunt them down and kill him for kidnapping her and drag her back to Faircastle, or they may have to stay in hiding forever; or, seeing Arelia's condition as it stood, Edward may be happy to be done with her and ignore the entire situation, which, because of pride, was probably unlikely.

And option number two: If he asked for her hand, Edward would be forced to express his concerns about the relationship and face the issue. This would open up an honest discussion without risk to Arelia. Edward would have nothing to lose by allowing them to marry now that he had an heir, and Arelia would be released to have a family and a normal life. Asking for her hand was the more honorable and less risky thing to do.

His decision was made. He would talk to the captain and ask him to schedule a meeting for him with Sir Edward.

Early that morning, Stephen went to the captain's tent in order to follow through with his plan. "Captain, I would like to speak with you," he requested.

"Come in." He stood to greet him. "Go ahead, Stephen. Have your say."

"Sir, I need a meeting with Sir Edward," Stephen stated firmly.

"Sir Edward? Are you displeased with your treatment here?"

"No, sir. I am treated well," Stephen stated flatly.

"Then what is it? You cannot interrupt him just for a visit," the captain said derisively. "You report to me, and if you have a complaint, you speak to me."

"It is a personal matter," Stephen continued, trying to stay calm but not liking the direction the conversation was going.

"Personal? *You* have a personal matter that concerns Sir Edward. This is very interesting. Why do you think he would be concerned about anything personal to you?" pushed the captain. "I cannot allow you to take his time for just any reason. His wife has just died, if you recall."

"Yes, sir, I realize that, but I also have a serious situation that needs to be handled."

"Do you want my job, soldier?" the captain demanded with a spark of anger.

"No, sir. Not at all," defended Stephen.

"Then what is it, boy?" the captain asked even more forcefully.

"I want to ask for his cousin's hand, sir," he blurted it out with some relief.

The captain sat silently for some time. "His cousin?" he asked, appearing confused. "And which cousin is this?"

"The girl, Arelia, sir," Stephen answered.

"Arelia." The captain laughed wholeheartedly, obviously ridiculing his plan. "John, this young officer wants to marry the whore," he shouted to an officer standing outside the tent.

Stephen was shocked and angry at his response but knew to restrain himself for fear of losing any privileges.

"So, you want the whore to yourself, huh, boy?" asked the officer as he stepped inside the tent.

"She is not a whore, sir," Stephen defended, trying not to show his growing anger.

"Oh? And what do you think we do during our visits, sing ballads?" The two men laughed even more loudly.

"I know. The boy cannot perform, so he wants to make it legal."

"What is the matter, boy?" teased the captain, leaning toward him with a sneer. "You are not a man yet?"

Stephen was growing angrier by the minute but didn't want to work against himself. "Sir, may I talk to Sir Edward? This concerns only him and me!"

"You bet you can talk to him. He can use a good laugh by now. I will request your meeting today." The captain and soldier walked off, laughing and shaking their heads.

All day long, Stephen was the laughingstock of the camp. Not one officer passed without getting a jab in. "Will we call your new wife 'Madam Whore?'"

247

"I understand you are putting the officers out of business!" "I get her first on the wedding night." "I hope the captain can schedule you." "What will we call the son of 'Lady Whore' and an Officer?" "What is his inheritance?"

Stephen fought hard to ignore the men and maintain his focus. Keeping Arelia and her escape from these men in mind gave him the fuel he needed in order to follow through with his plan and confirmed his intentions.

"Stephen," called Captain Hardgrave. "Sir Edward will see you before lunch tomorrow in his parlor. He is very curious about the reason for your visit, but I could not bring myself to tell him." The captain walked away, laughing boisterously. "He should hear the joke firsthand," he roared.

Stephen awoke before dawn and practiced what he would say to Sir Edward. Nothing sounded right. He was concerned that he wouldn't be taken seriously and knew he would have to be forceful and strong without getting angry. Captain Hardgrave had prepared him for what he would not have expected.

As the hour approached, he started the long walk along the water's edge. The men laughed and made insulting remarks as they saw him leave. Stephen was thankful for the quiet walk along the beach to prepare his thoughts. So oblivious was he to the crashing waves and screeching gulls, he could have been in a tunnel. He walked slowly, considering and practicing every word. Once he arrived at the castle, he was immediately escorted to Sir Edward's parlor. He tried to cover his surprise at how very old and drawn Edward had become in such a short time. Marisa's death had clearly taken its toll.

"Good morning, sire. Thank you for this meeting. I know this is not a good time for you. I am so sorry about your wife," began Stephen.

"Thank you, boy, sit down. This is my first day out of my room since Lady Marisa's death. It is all very odd and uncomfortable," Sir Edward said absently.

"Yes, sire. I am sure it is." Stephen didn't know what to say or how to begin his request. He had not expected Sir Edward to be in such grief. They sat quietly in tense, deafening silence. Stephen sat back in the chair with a rigidly straight back, searching for the right words to begin. He cleared his throat, but no words came to mind.

"What is it you want from me?" asked Edward bluntly.

Stephen was startled by the question and responded just as bluntly. "I want Arelia's hand in marriage, sire."

"Arelia, the young whore?!" returned Edward.

"No, sire, Arelia, your *cousin*. I would like your cousin's hand in marriage," Stephen repeated. He was surprisingly thankful for the men's insults as they had unsuspectingly hardened him for Edward's response, although he would never have suspected Edward would refer to his own family with such disrespect.

"I see . . . . You know she is my relative?" stated Edward accusingly.

"I am the one who saved her from the dogs in the woods and brought her here," explained Stephen. "Yes, she is your cousin."

"I see," he said again, studying Stephen carefully, with Marisa's warning echoing through his muddled mind. "And what is it you want from me?" he asked again.

"Sire, all I want is permission for Arelia's hand," Stephen stated firmly.

"And her dowry?" asked Edward.

"I understand that she is an orphan, sire," answered Stephen.

"Do you think that I am her guardian?" Edward asked.

"I have not thought about it, sire." Stephen paused. "I do not believe that you are."

"But you are asking me for her hand. What property do you think she has?" Edward pressured.

"None, sire. Her family is dead," repeated Stephen.

"My father has disowned her, you know."

Stephen was surprised by that comment. Arelia didn't remember seeing Sir Daniel on his short visit. She didn't know what had happened.

"I see I have surprised you. What did you expect from my father? Money? Property?"

"Nothing, sire, all I want is Arelia's hand. I will provide for her," explained Stephen.

"As a soldier? Do you intend to live here in the house with us?" Sir Edward asked suspiciously.

"No, sire. I will take Arelia to live in my family's village," Stephen assured. "They are your tenants."

"And you will leave your young wife and be a soldier here?" Sir Edward questioned intently.

"Sire, I would like to resign my commission and remain in the village with my family."

Sir Edward laughed. "And I suppose you will tell your parents all about your new wife and her family. Will they love the young whore as much as you do?"

Stephen was speechless. He didn't understand how Sir Edward had come to do this to Arelia and how he could be so hateful.

"You know, Stephen, Arelia has lived this life now and has been given fine things. I do not think she will be satisfied with such a simple life. Maybe she would not be satisfied with just one man either." He leaned forward and laughed maliciously. "Have you thought of that?"

"No, sire, but I know that Arelia longs to get back to life in a village," explained Stephen.

"Oh, and how do you know?" Edward's sinister look pierced Stephen's composure.

"She has told me, sire."

"It sounds like you have spent some time getting to know my cousin," Edward probed.

"Yes, sire. We have had many conversations."

"On your *scheduled* visits?" Edward asked.

"Yes, sire," Stephen answered simply, not knowing where he was leading.

"And what happens if I say no to you?" asked Edward. "You know, of course, I *can* say no." Stephen appeared to have said something very funny as Fairchild laughed deeply. "Please forgive me, but I understand many young men fall in love with their first conquest."

Stephen was seething. "May I have her hand, sire?" he asked firmly.

"And if I say no?" Edward repeated.

"I do not anticipate that," said Stephen flatly.

"You do not seem to understand that Arelia provides a great service for my men. She would be missed by many. She is very valuable to me." He smiled cruelly.

"And she is valuable to me, also. It is unusual for a family member to be in such a position as Arelia, is it not, sire?" Stephen asked, watching Edward grow defensive and angry.

"Do not tell me about my family. I can make any sort of arrangement for her that I like. Besides, this was Arelia's choice," Edward shouted.

"Can it then be her choice to leave?" asked Stephen, knowing he had him.

Sir Edward's eyes were burning, and his jaw was clinched. "You are very bold and stupid. Arelia would never leave," he said.

"But if she requested to leave with me, she could?" Stephen pushed.

Edward glared at Stephen and then said with a big smile, "Yes, she may leave, but only if it is her choice. And now *you* may leave."

Stephen stood confidently and said, "I will respect her decision as I know you will."

"I will call for you tomorrow or the next day, and we will ask her together. Then we will both respect her decision." Edward seemed confident but not as confident as Stephen.

Later that afternoon, Arelia was startled by her cousin when he walked into her room without knocking. Like Stephen, she was surprised to see him looking so old.

"Arelia, I understand you wish to leave my care!" he began directly. "What are your plans?"

"I am sorry, sire. I do not understand your question," she answered hesitantly, defensively backing toward the window.

"The young officer Stephen has requested your hand," he clarified.

Arelia turned away, smiling. *So Stephen talked to Sir Edward. Maybe I will leave.*

"Well, Arelia. What do you think? How have you persuaded this man to speak for you?" Edward coaxed.

From his accusatory tone, Arelia knew to proceed cautiously. "He has spoken of such, sire, but I have not answered him."

"So, this is his idea?"

"Yes, sire."

"Have you considered his proposal?" he continued.

Arelia didn't know how to answer. She sensed a trap. "Sire, I have not answered. I do not know if the answer is mine to give." She fought to hide her trembling voice.

"Stephen seems to think, as an orphan, you can answer for yourself. I came to help you make your decision. Sit down," he requested politely.

Although still cautious, Arelia sat at the table and was somewhat taken aback by his sudden change of tone. "Thank you, sire."

"What kind of wife do you think a whore would make?" he asked cruelly.

Arelia's eyes burned, but she didn't speak for fear of crying.

"Of course, you would not stay here. He says he would take you to his family's village. I guess he could tell them you were one of the servants in the house. He would have no need to describe your services here," he said smirking.

Arelia's eyes welled up with tears.

"I understand you and your parents were very close," he continued. "Your father enjoyed telling stories, and your mother taught you to sew. Parents are wonderful people. What stories would you share with your children?" He seemed to delight in his cruelty.

"Have you thought of these things?" he asked.

Arelia looked down, avoiding contact with the storm building behind his dark blue eyes. "No, sire."

"You really should consider these things. My warriors go to many villages. You may see them again. I know Stephen would enjoy seeing his old friends. You could entertain them in your own home and then introduce them to Stephen's family." He laughed heartily.

Her resistance broke as Arelia stood to strike him. He grabbed her wrist. "You really are an idiot," he mocked. "Stephen wants your estate, not you. Who would want a whore to sire his children with?" He released her arm and walked to the window.

"Stephen knows I do not have an estate," Arelia insisted. "He has never spoken of such."

"Does he? He seemed surprised that my father has disowned you!" he said dryly.

"Your father? I have not seen him. Is he back?" asked Arelia in surprise.

"No, and he is not coming back. You have disgraced him," said Edward, glaring.

"But I never saw him," she defended.

"Oh, but he saw you . . . you and one of your soldiers." Again, he laughed at his own cruelty.

Arelia sat in stunned silence. Edward walked up behind her and grabbed her hair, turning her to look him in the eye. "Do not think you and Stephen can run to my father. He knows the whore you are and wants no part of you. Who would? You will ruin Stephen's life. He said he would resign his commission for you. What happens after his family disowns him as you have been disowned? Will you starve again, and, this time, bring him and your children with you? You are an idiot," he said, releasing her hair with a jerk.

"Sire, he loves me," Arelia said weakly.

"Loves you?" he mocked. "He loves what he thinks you possess. Do you love him?"

"Yes, sire. I think that I do," she answered hesitantly, nearly too frightened to breathe.

"And you still wish to ruin his life?" he asked with a smirk.

Arelia shook her head, too numb to even cry.

"You are a long way from village life, Arelia. You will eventually disgrace Stephen, as you have disgraced my father." He walked to the door and turned toward her. "Your place is here, Arelia." He walked out closing the door solidly behind him.

"My place is here," she repeated numbly.

The next morning, the door opened again to reveal Sir Edward. Arelia looked at him through swollen, red-rimmed eyes. "Good morning," he greeted lightly. "I see you have considered our conversation. Have you made a decision?"

"Yes, sire."

"And?"

"I have my place here," she said sadly.

"Good. We will have visitors momentarily who want to hear your decision," he said. "You may be smarter than I originally thought." He smiled.

As if on cue, there was a knock at the door. Captain Hardgrave walked through with Stephen following confidently behind. Arelia could not look at him and kept her eyes cast toward the floor. She remained in her chair by the fire, too weary to move.

"Well, Stephen. I think you have a question for Arelia, do you not?" goaded Edward.

Stephen was surprised at his directness but was most concerned about Arelia's demeanor. "Are you all right, Arelia?" Stephen asked, taking her hand gently and kneeling at her side. Arelia let him take her hand but couldn't bear to look at him.

"Officer, you have a question," commanded Sir Edward. "Ask it!"

Stephen cast a challenging glare at him. The captain, alerted, came to attention. "Arelia, look at me," Stephen persuaded lovingly.

Arelia's swollen, tear-filled eyes met his. Stephen jumped to his feet. "What have you done to her?" he demanded angrily.

Edward glared. "Ask your question, soldier!"

Stephen knelt at Arelia's side. "Arelia, I do not know what has happened here, but you do know that I love you." Arelia was silent, unable to meet his probing eyes. "Arelia, will you be my wife?" She could not speak.

"Arelia, answer the soldier," commanded Edward.

"My place is here," she answered weakly.

"I do not think I heard you," Stephen said in disbelief. "What are you saying?" he pleaded.

"You have your answer, soldier," sneered Edward. "Now get out!"

Stephen lunged at him. Captain Hardgrave drew his sword and stood staunchly between them.

"You do not want to do this," the captain said strongly, wishing for a fight.

Stephen shook with anger. "What have you done to her?"

Arelia rose slowly from the chair and took his arm. "Stephen, please, this is my decision," she said facing him squarely. "Do not cause yourself any harm. This is best."

"Best for whom, Arelia?" he begged. She could not speak.

"Officer," interrupted Edward. "You have your answer. Now get out!"

"Sir, I cannot go without Arelia," he said, standing his ground.

The captain grabbed Stephen's arm. Arelia stood at the window, her back to the room. Stephen shook his arm loose and stood directly in front of Edward. "You have done something here. This is not Arelia's decision."

Sir Edward smiled coldly. "You have heard her answer as well as I. Your love must only go one way," he said as to mock him.

Arelia's heart was breaking. She couldn't bear to see Stephen's hurt, but she knew it was better for him to be hurt now than disgraced before his family later.

"Arelia," Stephen pleaded. She did not move. The captain shoved Stephen toward the door.

"Captain," said Edward. "You should stay with Arelia. I am certain she would enjoy the company." He laughed maliciously.

Stephen lunged toward him, and the captain held his sword to Stephen's throat, "You can walk out or be carried out," Captain Hardgrave threatened.

"Stephen, I beseech you. It is what I have decided!" Arelia implored, fearing for his life.

Stephen stood, unable to understand what was happening. He also feared for her life if he pursued his cause. All too often he had witnessed the results of Edward's anger on her delicate face, and he knew the captain's murderous actions should not be tested. There was nothing left to say; he would have to find another way, and he couldn't do it if he were dead.

He walked out, slamming the door. "Good job, Captain," Edward Fairchild said. "Arelia will repay you for me." Both men laughed. "You will need to watch him carefully. It would be good to send him out on detail soon."

The men continued talking as Arelia imagined Stephen walking down the beach. "Arelia, you have made a wise decision. You will be happier now that it is your decision to stay," interrupted Edward smugly. "Captain, enjoy your stay. You have earned it." He winked and left the room.

"You have decided well," said the captain, walking toward Arelia. She watched him through tear-blurred eyes, hating everything about him. He took her shoulders and turned her to face him.

Stephen looked over the water, with tears of anger burning his eyes. He ran down the beach, blindly racing to blot out the image of what was ahead for Arelia.

Captain Hardgrave laid his belt and sheath on the table. "Here, help me get these boots off, and then we will really enjoy the afternoon together." Arelia followed his orders, repulsed by who he was and all he stood for. She resigned herself to his advance as she had always done, trying to find something good to focus on. There was no good. Tears flowed as a heavy shroud of darkness settled over her.

CHAPTER 27

Stephen saddled a horse from the camp and took off along the beach until he came to the massive outcropping where he and Arelia had spent stolen minutes together talking about family and friends, fears, and dreams. No matter how hard he tried, he couldn't understand what motivated Arelia to come to her decision. He knew that she cared for him and that she wanted to leave her hell. "Why has she chosen to stay?" he asked aloud. She had been threatened. It was not her decision. His dream for Arelia had been like a bird gliding freely on currents of wind, rising and falling with occasional gusts; but now it was shattered, shot out of the air, falling lifeless into unfathomable depths.

And at this moment, she is suffering the consequences of her decision. Poor Arelia. What have they done to her? The afternoon quickly turned to evening as he sat watching the ocean, determined to free her but, once again, not knowing how. He prayed for clarity of thought, mesmerized by the rhythm of the waves. *Lord Fairchild would never have allowed this—Lord Daniel Fairchild, that is. This seems to have begun when he left Faircastle in Sir Edward's hands. We have quelled dissension in certain villages because of Sir Edward Fairchild, and all the while, Arelia was suffering here. Arelia is suffering at the hands of Sir Edward Fairchild.*

When he arrived back at camp, the usual fires were burning, and men were settling into their tedious evening routine. He spotted the captain laughing and talking to a group of officers, and he knew that he was the butt of every fireside joke.

"Stephen," the captain shouted. "I hope you enjoyed your afternoon as much as we did." The men laughed uproariously. Stephen turned away, seething with anger and hatred, yet knowing he had not given up and confident that both Hardgrave and Fairchild had underestimated his blind determination.

Sensing renewed conviction, Hardgrave walked up quickly behind him. "Do not be foolish. You have heard Arelia's decision firsthand, and you know she is not interested in your proposal. You can only hurt yourself now. There is nothing you can do for her; she does not want you. She wants more." Stephen walked away without comment. "Stephen," the captain shouted. "I am watching every move you make."

The next several weeks were torturous as he watched officers parade to the castle, each laughing and making insulting comments when they left camp. Obviously, Edward Fairchild had found himself remiss in allowing Arelia's brief taste of freedom, but now Stephen believed the renewed visits were meant as a strong, clear message from Edward to him, as well as Arelia, and the message was, *I have all the power*. Strangely, the captain seemed to become bored with the situation, and as time passed, he stopped his grandstanding completely.

After watching men leave night after night, Stephen finally had enough. "Sir, I have not had time with the girl. I would like my chance, too."

Captain Hardgrave shook his head. "Stephen, Fairchild and I have agreed that you will never visit again. Arelia does not want to see you, and Fairchild does not want you to see her."

"Captain, I do a good job here. I deserve my reward, just like the other men," he persisted.

"It is no longer a reward for you," the captain said flatly.

As they sat around the fire the next evening, Stephen watched one of the officers go to the castle and return shortly after. He was whistling and laughing to be sure Stephen noticed. He even went out of his way to pat Stephen on the shoulder. "She is as good as ever." No one else went. He took a mental count of the officers. Everyone was accounted for. Tonight, *he* would see Arelia.

Clouds rolled over a thin sliver of silver moon hanging delicately overhead. After listening for voices or footsteps at the landing of the long narrow stairway, he stole up the stairs to Arelia's room, thankful for the dark and quiet of night. The door creaked when he pushed it open. The sudden noise startled him as he slipped quietly into her room. She was sleeping soundly. He sat for a minute watching her, thinking of the peace and happiness he had felt every time they were together. Tonight was no different; seeing her seemed to erase all that had happened.

"Arelia," he said softly. She didn't move. "Arelia," he repeated, tapping her arm.

"No, please leave me alone." She moaned.

"Arelia, do not be afraid," he said lovingly. He walked to the table to light a candle.

"Stephen?" she whispered.

"Yes."

She jumped out of bed at the sound of his voice and ran into his arms.

"Do we have the night together?"

"No, I am not allowed to see you, but I could not stay away."

"I have been so worried about you," she said.

"Arelia, you have to tell me why you are staying here. I cannot stand to see the men coming up here night after night."

Arelia turned away and pulled a blanket from the bed. He helped wrap it around her shoulders and then lifted her chin to look into his dark eyes. "Stephen, I cannot leave with you."

"Why? It makes no sense," he declared, trying to hold back his anger and frustration. He turned from her and busied himself with the comfortable routine of stoking the fire.

"No, it is the only thing that does make sense," she cried.

He turned to her with clenched jaw. "How? I do not understand you." The fire took hold, and blue flames danced crazily behind him.

"Stephen, you should be with someone like Laura, not someone like me," she insisted.

"Let *me* choose who *I* want to be with," he responded angrily. "Arelia, we were meant to be together."

"How can you say that, Stephen? We can never be together! Have you seen who I am?" she whimpered.

"Arelia," he said, holding her shoulders. "Have *you* seen who you *really* are? You are not the girl those men come to; you are Arelia Fairchild, daughter of Edward and Margaret."

She began to cry. "That girl was killed by wolves. Do you not remember?"

"Do not say that! Can you not see that your cousin is destroying you? Arelia, we can have it back if you leave with me."

"Stephen, I have already said no. It is too late." She cried, burying her head in her hands.

"No. We can leave right now."

The door opened. Fear seized her.

"Are you all right, Arelia?" asked Laura. "I heard you crying. Oh, I am sorry, Stephen. I did not know you were here. I am happy to see you," Laura said warmly.

"I am glad you are here, Laura. You can help me talk to Arelia," said Stephen. "I want her to leave with me."

Laura sat on the bed, wide-eyed. "I have tried to talk to her, but she does not listen to me either," said Laura.

Arelia walked to the window. "I cannot leave. This is my place."

"No," shouted Stephen. "It is not your place. Your place is with me."

"Quiet!" insisted Laura. "You are not safe here."

"I cannot understand. Laura, can you explain what she is doing?"

"Arelia does not want to disgrace you," Laura explained simply.

He stood in stunned silence. "Arelia, . . . is this true? That is why you will not leave with me?" he asked, amazed at the simplicity of her concern.

"Yes, Stephen, I would ruin your life, and you would lose your family, as I lost mine." Arelia cried.

"That is not true. We will leave all this behind, and my family will love you as I do. Laura, talk to her," he pleaded.

"I cannot convince her. I have tried," she said, nodding her head and waving her hand in futility. "Arelia, please listen to Stephen. He is a grown man. He will take care of you, but you have to trust him."

There was a knock at the door. "Laura, are you there?" Laura ran to the door as it opened, blocking the view from the hallway. "Your mother needs you," said the servant.

"Thank you," said Laura as she hurried down the hallway.

"Stephen, you had better leave," Arelia said frightened.

"I will, but I am going to come back, and when I do, I want you to leave with me." He hugged her and then left as quickly as he had come.

At daybreak, with the sun just peeking over the horizon, Laura returned to Arelia's room. She looked exhausted. "What is wrong, Laura? Is your mother all right?"

"Yes, but baby Edward is very ill, and mother needed help." Weariness was interwoven with concern across her wrinkled brow. "Arelia, she wants to talk to you."

"Is she coming here?" Arelia asked.

"No, she wants me to bring you to her. She cannot leave the babies. Get dressed. She wants to see you now."

Arelia dressed quickly, wondering why Sarah needed her. She had not been out of her room for so long that she was almost frightened hurrying down the hall. Images of Edward or Bethany walking out a doorway to the surprise of both hastened her steps. Except for the night she learned that Marisa had died, she had not been on the floor with the family's rooms.

"I am afraid that Edward or Bethany will find I have left my room."

"Do not worry. Mother took care of that."

"What does your mother want?"

"She will tell you." Laura avoided her question.

Seeing Sarah was like being home again. Arelia had forgotten how much she cared for the plump little woman with welcoming eyes and soft smile. At the sight of Arelia, Sarah's expression demonstrated she was equally happy to see her. "Hello, child." They hugged warmly, Arelia never wanted to let go.

"I am so happy to see you, Sarah. I have missed you," Arelia whispered with a sigh of relief to finally be together again. "You look tired," she observed.

"Yes, the baby has been sick for several days. Bethany is doing her best, but he does not seem to be getting well."

"How is the little girl?" Arelia asked.

"She is well, but she has always been the more robust of the two."

"Come sit with me by the fire. We need to talk," Sarah said, sitting to the end of a bench and patting a cushion next to her.

"I understand the young soldier, Stephen, has asked you to leave with him," she said, probing.

"Yes . . . . It seems that Laura has been talking to you."

"We had a long, sleepless night with lots of time to talk." She smiled at Laura. "Why have you refused him?" Sarah asked.

"I am afraid, Sarah," Arelia answered honestly.

"Arelia, we are almost always afraid about any big decision we make. That is normal. What is the *real* reason you refused?" she continued.

"I belong here," said Arelia weakly.

"Nonsense! What is the *real* reason?" Sarah persisted.

"Sarah, I would ruin Stephen's life. I would disgrace him." Tears began to well up.

"And what are you doing to his life by *refusing* him? Men do not take rejection well. I am sure he feels that your decision has already ruined his life." Sarah smiled and patted Arelia's hand. "Child, sometimes we have to take chances. See that little baby? By refusing Stephen, you have refused to have a home and children of your own. Think carefully about what you are doing; not all decisions are final, but this one could be."

Tears streaked Arelia's face. "Sarah, I am so confused. I do not know what to do."

"Arelia, you may get only one more chance. Choose carefully. Love can be worth the risk."

"But can I risk Stephen's life, too?" Arelia asked sincerely.

"He is the one asking you to leave with him, is he not?" Sarah probed. "Let that be his choice, not yours."

"I thought when Marisa died I would be freed from this prison and the men," said Arelia.

"So did we, child," Sarah agreed sadly. "Until Sir Daniel rode away, I was sure that he would bundle you up and carry you out of here. To say we were left disappointed and confused is an understatement."

"We?"

"Yes, Bethany and I."

"Bethany . . . . I have not seen her in weeks. How is she?" She asked to be polite, not out of real concern.

"Bethany was having the time of her life until this sickness. Now she is very worried, because she thought that he would be on the mend by now, but there is no sign of it. She loves the children so much," answered Sarah. "It does not appear to be the plague attacking his little body." She studied Laura as she rocked baby Edward and then turned to Arelia with a deeply consoling look.

"I know she misses you, but she does not know if you would care to see her. She is confident that you are in good hands with Laura." She smiled at Laura and then patted Arelia's leg. "Enough about Bethany. I want to talk about you. Think very carefully about the choice you have made. It may be the only chance you get."

"But I have already said no," reminded Arelia.

"Yes, but Laura told me Stephen returned for you last night."

"He wanted me to leave, but I just could not go with him. He is going to come back again," Arelia said with obvious concern. "I know he will."

"Yes, he will, because he loves you. What will you do then?"

"I cannot say. I need to think. Things are so different when I am here with you. Everything seems much simpler. I could leave with him right now. I could just walk right out of this room and never look back." She smiled. "But things seem so dark in my room. I get very frightened." Her face darkened.

"Arelia, Bethany and Laura and I care for you so much. We want you to be happy. It is not possible for us to save you; only you can save yourself. Child, I wish we could."

Later, as Arelia stood at the window of her cell mesmerized by leaves swaying in the gentle breeze, she thought how her life had become much like those trees—sometimes still and quiet, sometimes touched by strong wind and rain, but always confined. She could hear Sarah's words. *It is not possible for us to save you; only you can save yourself.*

263

The afternoon provided her with time to think and pray, bearing in mind all that Sarah had said, never even having considered that her decision to stay could ruin Stephen's life. Had God not sent him to save her from the wolves and, now, possibly to save her from Edward? Thoughts and prayers turned into a long, peaceful nap as clouds began to build on the horizon, and a soft breeze flowed through the open window.

When Laura brought her dinner, Arelia was at the window, again so lost in her thoughts that she didn't hear her come in. "Please consider all that my mother said," Laura said, interrupting Arelia's reflection. "I would miss you, but I would feel much better knowing you were happy, even if I never saw you again." Laura smiled sweetly as Arelia turned from the window, hoping that her friend would have time to stay and help her sort through her thoughts.

The door flew open with a bang. "Girl, leave us!" commanded Sir Edward as he stormed in with Captain Hardgrave close behind. Laura ran from the room, casting a frightened glance at Arelia.

"Who was here last night?" Edward thundered.

"I do not remember, sire," she answered, wanting to flee with Laura.

"Who was here last night?" he demanded persistently, with his raised hand, waiting for her response.

"Officer Thompson, sire."

He struck her. "And who else?"

"No one, sire," she lied.

"Captain, will you remind the whore of her visitor?"

"Officer Wingate, sire," stated the captain.

Fairchild's powerful blow knocked her to the floor. "Who was here last night?" he shouted.

"Stephen," she cried out. "Officer Wingate, sire"

He kicked her in the ribs. "Get up, you ungrateful wench!"

Arelia's ribs ached as she struggled to pull herself onto the chair.

"You made your decision. You have no room for him in your life. Captain, tell this little wench what will happen to her if she allows Officer Wingate to visit again."

"The man will be tried as a traitor and executed, sire," the captain answered.

"Officer Wingate is pushing me, Arelia, but I have no need for him. I have plenty of good men to replace him since you seem so set on ruining his life," Fairchild said caustically. "He is as dispensable as you are."

"I have honored your decision. Do not change it." She could feel his hot, alcohol-laced breath on her face. "I have an army that will find you and your lover. You will never have any of my estate! Marisa warned me about you. My life was ruined the day you came into this house."

"And mine," she whispered softly.

He grabbed her hair. "Speak up." He pulled her to her feet, shouting in her face. "What is it?"

"Nothing, sire." She cried.

"You repulse me, whore," he shouted, flinging her by her hair.

Arelia fell against the side of the table, cutting a gash into her forehead. Blood poured into her eyes as she lay on the floor, too frightened to move.

Fairchild and the captain stomped out of her room. All was quiet. Arelia lay on the floor, blood mixing with her tears, too hurt and empty to move. *What have I done, Stephen? I will not let this happen to you*, she thought before she lost consciousness.

Laura heard the shouts and screams from her room. All the servants heard, but no one dared to interfere or to help. Only after everyone had gone to bed did Laura find Arelia. She couldn't awaken her. With panic overcoming fear, she ran down the dark, musty hallway unconcerned about the noise of her heavy boots pounding the cold stone floor.

"Bethany," she said in alarm as she threw open the door to Bethany's tiny room. "Wake up! Arelia is hurt, . . . really hurt! Hurry!"

Bethany jumped out of bed, grabbed her shawl, and followed Laura down the passage in stocking feet. She was shocked to see Arelia lying in a pool of blood.

"What happened?"

"Sir Edward and Captain Hardgrave were here. Can you help her?"

Bethany could feel Arelia's weak breath on the palm of her hand. "Help me get her on the bed and then get water and rags quickly," she ordered.

The women worked together to get Arelia's limp and battered body onto the high bed. Laura quickly returned with a pitcher of warm water and began washing blood from Arelia's neck and face, trying not to put pressure on the dark bruises. Bethany left to make a poultice for her wounds and a mild potion for pain. When she returned, Laura helped her change Arelia's bloody clothes and wrap her distended ribs, moving her about like a rag doll.

"I do not understand," said Bethany with rage beginning to boil. "I thought Arelia was through with this abuse when Marisa died. Poor child." She wiped tears from cheeks red with anger.

The sun was rising as the two women finished tending to Arelia's cuts, bruises, and broken bones. Bethany left only briefly to check on the sick baby boy, while Laura stayed and fell asleep, protectively, next to her friend in her big bed. She awoke to Arelia's moans as she tried to turn over.

"Laura?" she moaned.

"Yes," Laura answered. "Sir Edward and the captain were here."

Arelia lay quietly, with the reality of intense pain, as the tears slowly began to flow. "I remember now."

Several days passed, and Arelia stayed in bed, too sore and too despondent to move, tethered by invisible shackles of fear and foreboding. Both eyes turned black, and one was completely swollen shut; her distended jaw was red, black, and greenish-blue. The gash on her forehead had formed a dark, crusty scab that was beginning to heal with Bethany's care. Laura rarely left her side, and Bethany visited every day.

One day, when she and Bethany were alone, Arelia asked, "Bethany, you know all about plants and herbs, is that right?" Her voice was almost too weak to hear.

"Yes," stating the obvious.

"My mother told me that we must be very careful about the wild plants that we eat . . . That some are poison."

"That is right," not liking the direction the conversation was going.

"Bethany," Arelia whispered. "Can you bring me such a plant?"

Bethany couldn't answer. It had seemed so easy with Marisa, but her mother had cautioned her not to use her knowledge to take life. Her mother had told her, "Your knowledge gives you power over people's lives, but it is not your power to have. Never use it to destroy life, only to save it." She thought she had saved Arelia's life.

"Bethany, please," Arelia pleaded with tears flooding swollen eyes.

Bethany sat on the side of Arelia's bed and took her delicate hand, and then, touching her frail face disfigured by a cruel hand, she said. "Arelia, we will think of some other way to help you. That is not the way."

Unintentionally interrupting the moment, Laura cautiously came into Arelia's room. "Guess who I just spoke with."

"Who?"

"Stephen!" she reported. "He was in the courtyard and asked how you were."

"Oh no, Laura. Please tell me you did not tell him."

"Well, yes, of course," Laura answered hesitantly. "He said he wants to come get you. I told him you could not be moved now."

"No. He cannot come back. I have given him my answer. I am not leaving with him." Arelia's voice was weak and frightened.

Laura was shocked. "What do you mean? How can you stay for more of this abuse?"

"Leave me alone. I know what I have to do," Arelia cried in desperation.

Now Laura was angry. "I do not understand you. How can you let them treat you so cruelly—and Stephen?"

"Laura, I either hurt him now, or I hurt him later. He is in less danger if I leave my decision as it is," explained Arelia more calmly now. "I do not *let* this to happen to me. I have to protect him."

"That is it? You think it is that simple?" Laura pursued.

"I know it is not simple, but that is my decision. I want to sleep now." Arelia turned away from Laura and closed her eyes, unable to shut out the pain.

As weeks passed, Arelia slowly regained her strength and began to eat again and to shuffle around the room with Laura's help. Bethany kept the soldiers away during her recovery. Laura casually related that she had spoken to

Stephen again, but she didn't continue the conversation. Arelia didn't even respond.

One bright, sunshiny afternoon, weeks later, Bethany suggested that Arelia sit on the seawall for fresh air and sunlight. Arelia welcomed the chance to enjoy the sun and ocean and made her way down the steep steps. Her ribs were not as sore as she had expected, but she moved cautiously, watching every step for fear of falling. Bethany had certainly taken good care of her, and she didn't want to risk another injury. The scab on her forehead was healing, and the bruises were little more than pale, greenish shadows.

She thought about Bethany's change since Marisa's death. Bethany talked about the babies all the time, and Laura said she sometimes referred to herself as "grandmother." The babies seemed to consume her every waking thought. Fortunately, baby Edward had recovered and was gaining weight and strength. Arelia didn't understand how Bethany had managed to nurse them both back to good health without collapsing herself.

The change in scenery and fresh air seemed to revive Arelia in body, mind, and spirit. She wanted to walk down to the beach but decided to wait a few more days to give her ribs more time to heal. As she sat peacefully soaking up rays of golden sunlight, she heard the thunder of horses' hooves running along the coastline. She remembered her first trip to the beach over a year ago when she had watched the soldiers for the first time; but this time, she didn't hide behind the rocks. She didn't care. *How has this place become so familiar?* she thought.

The men raced, shouting and laughing as always. Many ran their horses into the waves; others jumped into the water themselves. The one man that held her attention continued farther down the beach alone and then ran his horse into the waves.

She had not had the opportunity to watch Stephen so boldly in his own environment. He was a man much like her father but yet something of a boy like her brother. She was as comfortable with him as she had been with her own family. Watching him unnoticed made her feel warm and peaceful. It was reassuring to know that all men were not like her cousin and the captain. She wondered if most men were more like Stephen or more like her cousin.

The village men were mostly like Stephen and her father. She remembered only one man who was extremely cruel to his wife, but no one ever really talked about it. Everyone heard the shouts and screams, and then no one would see his wife for days, or sometimes weeks, at a time. Arelia hadn't understood then what that poor woman was going through until now. *Why did we not help her?*

As she watched him wade his horse deeper into the ocean, she wondered what her life would be like in a village with Stephen at her side. She remembered that he had said he would bring his horse for them to ride together along the beach and wondered what it would feel like to wrap her arms around his waist and hold on to him as they rode into the waves. How would his body feel? Would I feel safe and protected? She imagined his laughter as they would race along the wave's edge with water splashing over them from the horse's hooves. She pictured him, glancing back at her over his shoulder and smiling at the sheer pleasure of being together. She felt the same warmth inside that she had felt the night she fell asleep while cradled in his arms, listening to his deep, peaceful breathing as he slept.

She imagined her brothers as grown men and wondered how her family would have accepted their new wives. She knew that the family would love them as their own. Then sorrow overwhelmed her, knowing that day would never come for her. What would Stephen tell his family about me? What would we do if the soldiers passed through the village? Would Edward track him down and kill him if we ran away? What would happen to me if he were killed?

"I cannot think about this. *None of it* will ever happen," she said aloud, resigned to her fate.

Stephen had gone some distance into the waves. His horse was wading back toward the beach when he spotted Arelia sitting on the seawall watching him. Arelia realized that he had seen her and raised her hand slightly in a wave before she stopped herself and looked away.

How strange, she thought, that they were not allowed to acknowledge each other openly. She knew the punishment they would both suffer. She wanted to stand and wave openly, calling to him, but she had learned, all too hard, that her desires were dangerous to pursue, and she would never risk his safety. Her frustration turned to a deep sadness for all the loved ones she had lost in her life. Now, she would add Stephen to the list.

I will not cry. It is done. My decision is made.

She looked up slowly, unable to keep her eyes off him. He had ridden only in his trousers, wet from the ocean. He was walking his horse slowly along the beach now, stealing glimpses of her occasionally. Arelia had not realized what a strong, solidly built man he was. She wanted to get to know him, but she could never allow herself the pleasure.

As she watched him walk away, she knew he was walking out of her life forever. He stopped his horse as the other riders raced ahead, and he turned to her. Time seemed to stop in that short moment. For Arelia, it was their moment of parting.

Her Angel Sang Out:

10   *You who love the LORD, hate evil,*
        he protects the souls of the faithful,
        rescues them from the hand of the wicked.

11   *Light dawns for the just,*
        and gladness for the honest of heart.

Psalm 97:10-11

CHAPTER 28

Months had passed since Arelia and Stephen had parted. Arelia lay on her bed, too frail from weeks of refusing to eat—too weak to move. Nothing Bethany and Laura tried was to any avail: vapors, poultices, herbal teas, weak broth; it was to no benefit. Nothing could penetrate the stone-hard cocoon she had spun around herself for protection from the fate her cousin had cursed her with. The smell of her own body repulsed her, but she did not care. The soldiers were repulsed too, and they had stopped their continuous, insane ritual. She closed her eyes, wanting to sleep, wanting to stop the memories, wanting to forget.

Deep in the recesses of her mind, she heard a quiet voice and laughter. A vivid memory returned.

"Arelia, take comfort in Mary. She lost her son and her husband, and certainly her mother and father. She understands our pain."

"I am sorry, Mother. Are you talking about our neighbor?"

"Our neighbor?"

"Yes, Mary."

Margaret's confused expression turned to unexpected yet weak laughter. Arelia was stunned and realized that, in fact, her mother had lost her mind.

"Oh my. No dear, Mary, the Mother of Jesus." She smiled.

Arelia laughed at the misunderstanding but mostly from relief that her mother's words made sense after all.

"Arelia, Jesus gave us His mother from the cross. Both Mary and Jesus are always here for us, and they understand everything we are going through. We are in terrible times, but we are never alone. I shudder to think it, but it may get even worse for you, and there is nothing I can do to help you."

"Oh, Mother, it could never get worse."

It could never get worse; it could never get worse, echoed in her mind. She was numb from how much worse it had gotten, now at her own hand, by refusing to eat.

Mother Mary, are you really here for me as Mother said?

There were no words in reply, just a feeling greater than words could express, a feeling of love coming from someone who understood.

Mother Mary, is that you? How can you understand? You never suffered abuse.

With that thought, Arelia received an image of Mary standing nearby as a Roman soldier took the leather whip with metal spiked tips and bore them into her Son's body, shredding his flesh. Arelia could feel Mary's heart breaking with no power to stop the abuse. It was as if the whip was tearing her own flesh. John was standing at Mary's side, holding her to keep her from falling.

Oh, Mother Mary. You do know the pain of physical abuse.

Another image showed itself of Jesus standing before Pontius Pilate with a crown of thorns on His blood-stained head. Mary and John were standing in the crowd as those He had taught and healed shouted, "Crucify him! Crucify him!" He was betrayed by the Tribes of Israel, those He had come to redeem. They disowned Him. They mocked Him. They traded a criminal for a Man Who was without sin. He was a threat; one they could not tolerate.

Oh, Mother Mary, He carried the weight of rejection, hatred, and shame.

Again, the images continued. Jesus, carrying his cross, falling under the weight of it three times. The cross falling onto His bruised and torn body. A soldier pulling a man from the crowd and forcing him to help Jesus carry the cross so Jesus would not die before He was nailed and raised in full view of onlookers. Mary's heart broke that no one would step forward to help Him.

Oh, Mother Mary, He was alone. Was there no one to save Him?

The final image of Mary standing under the cross knowing Jesus's life was at an end. As she raised her eyes to her Son in his last moments, a drop of blood fell, as if in slow motion, from His thorn-pierced scalp. "Father, into your hands I commend my spirit." As His last words reached His mother's ears, His last drop of blood reached her arm.

Oh, Mother Mary, Mother of God, you do understand.

Darkness. Oblivion.

She awakened to the words of the Angelic Salutation floating through her mind.

There seemed to be a light in the distance. It was barely perceptible but bright, growing in size and intensity. Although she felt drawn to the light, she would not go.

"Arelia."

No answer.

"Arelia." A soft, gentle voice called, distant but somehow familiar.

She sat up in her bed, renewed—no longer afraid.

"Arelia."

"Who calls my name?"

"I do."

She watched a soft, billowy glow shimmering near the window. "I cannot see you."

"You do not choose to see. Your eyes have brought you such sadness. You are in the darkness. We understand."

As Arelia continued to watch the light, the glow began to take shape. "Who are you?" she asked as the pink and gold lights glistened.

"I am a messenger."

"For me?"

"Yes. Your family has requested that you have help. Their love is so strong and their faith so deep that they have called in your name."

"I do not understand."

"Nor do you need to understand." The light responded with every color of the rainbow, billowing rhythmic hues. "You are being offered a chance to go back."

"Back to where? To my family?"

"No, Arelia. You cannot be with them now. You are being given the chance to go back to your life."

273

"I do not understand. Go back?"

"You have passed over, Arelia."

Arelia sat quietly, observing. She looked first at the room that was the same as it had been: the window overlooking the trees, a fire with small flickers of orange and blue flame, and oddly, a washtub that Bethany and Laura had tried to coax her into, a heavy table with a cloth-covered bowl . . . all familiar. She looked at her legs, tucked loosely under the covers. She was not prepared for what she saw next. The sight shocked her.

The messenger laughed. "It is always startling at first, Arelia. Do not be afraid."

Arelia saw her hand resting limply on the bed, and then her arm, her shoulder, and her thin, ashen face, lying on the pillow behind her, yet she was sitting up. "Who am I?!"

"You are Arelia."

"Who is she?"

"She is the body of Arelia." Somehow the odd explanation made sense.

"And I have passed over?"

"Yes." The luminous form's answer was loving and comforting with misty white vapor growing in brightness behind it. "And you will now have the opportunity to go back if you choose."

"No, I cannot do that. I will not do that!"

Patiently and calmly the messenger asked a simple, "Why?"

"Look at that body. It is putrid and violated. I will not go back."

"We are not asking you to return to the death form which you have chosen. We are offering you the opportunity for a different choice *before* you chose this for yourself.

"Arelia," the light continued. "You had a chance to go to the Light. It is what you thought you wanted, but you did not go. Can you tell me why?"

"It does not feel right to leave yet. I do not want to stay, yet I do not want to go. I cannot tell you why because I do not know myself."

The colors of the form seemed to pulsate, changing from pink to violet to gold. "Continue."

"I do not know how to continue. I do not know how this life has happened to me."

"You have chosen it."

Arelia stayed amazingly calm at such an outrageous accusation. "I do not want to be disagreeable, but I would not have chosen such a life for myself."

"But have you not?" the light coaxed.

"No, of course not — at least, not that I am aware."

The form was silent. Arelia saw a real-life image of the night that Stephen came hastily to her room and pleaded with her to leave. She watched with a new awareness as she heard the frightened girl in the shadowy scene say, "I cannot leave. This is my place."

The scene disappeared, and the voice from the light repeated, "You have chosen it."

"I chose not to put Stephen at risk. I did not really choose to stay here."

"But by choosing one, you have chosen the other," the light emphasized Arelia's ironic decision. The sound seemed to echo within the walls. *You have chosen. You have chosen. You have chosen.*

"I had to make the choice that I did, or I would have ruined Stephen's life," confidently Arelia defended the choice she had made with love and logic.

"How did the choice that you *did* make affect him?"

Arelia's peaceful feeling waned. "I do not know. I have never seen him again."

When the second scene appeared, Arelia felt a sadness and responsibility which she had never felt before. The images came quickly — Stephen, riding away from the castle, running his horse into the waves, the captain telling Stephen that Sir Daniel needed soldiers to defend his property, and, finally, Stephen lying face up in a field with an arrow through his neck.

"No, this cannot be," Arelia cried.

"Why, Arelia? Why do you think that this is not possible?"

"It cannot be possible because I wanted to protect him."

"And you have that power?" The form grew brighter. "Look closely and tell me honestly if you know of another reason that you refused to leave."

Another scene materialized. There in the forest lay a small, frightened girl, hungry and cold. Arelia relived the origin of her fear and sadness as the memories of her parents' burning bodies blazed in her mind. She could smell the burning flesh and hear the crackle of the flames as they consumed her security. "I was afraid. I did not want to be left again with no food and no place to stay. I was so afraid." Her voice was a whisper, muffled by a flood of emotion and confusion exaggerated by childlike perceptions and fear.

The light pulsated with brilliant golds and lavenders. "That is right, Arelia. You made your choice out of fear. Your fear kept you from trusting the one person who was sent to save you."

Understanding came quickly. She felt overwhelming remorse and grief. She suffered Stephen's broken heart and his disbelief at her decision at the moment she refused him. "I am beginning to understand."

"Of course." The light glowed. "We always understand when we see as others see and feel as others feel."

"Is Stephen being given another chance?" Arelia could feel his hurt, and she did not want his life to end as it did.

"That depends on you. His love for you has not changed. His only choice would be to be with you by saving you from this fate."

"But it is too late!"

The image shone green and blue. "You are separated in body alone. You are joined in love just as you are joined with your family."

"But he is . . . dead. I saw it." Arelia could hardly bear to let the words cross her lips.

"You saw his death as it would be on the course chosen. The image is a different time, later than now, if you continue on the path you have currently taken."

"I do not understand why I am being given another chance."

"You had no choice when the plague struck your family down or when wolves attacked you. You had no choice when Marisa drugged you and sent the first soldier in. You had no choice when Edward attacked you, yet you were faithful through it all and wrestled with evil to preserve your mind and soul. The first real choice you had for yourself was from Stephen through the inspiration of the Holy Spirit. Unfortunately, you both thought you were only fighting against a man and not the evil spirits which overcame Edward and his wife. God has heard your prayers and all the prayers for you. Now, you are being given a chance to make a choice for yourself, but love, not fear, must guide you this time. It is your choice."

276

The messenger extended its luminous hand, and a flood of light emitted another billowing form, pouring forth like a river overflowing its banks. Arelia gasped at its beauty.

"Love." The second image seemed to reverberate as light filled the room rich with color. "Love cannot be separated."

"Who are you?"

"I am your guardian who has been with you from the instant your father planted his seed deep within your mother's womb. We have been together through good times and bad. I have heard your prayers and tried to reach you, but the darkness of the deceiver has blinded you from us."

"My Guardian Angel?"

"Yes."

"My mother told me I had an angel, but I thought it was just a story like my father used to tell."

"And you have seen that your father's stories are also true." A sound between laughter and a deep moan came from the angel. "Yes, the deceiver would have you believe that God Himself did not exist and neither His Angels whom He sent to guide and protect you."

"Why can I see you now?" The form of the Angel, filled with Love, glowed with bright lights uniting and then becoming distinct again, a rhythm.

"Love . . . prayers are heard . . . your prayers, Stephen's, Laura's, Sarah's, and even Bethany's whispers. Your family has stormed heaven with love for you. God's mercy allows you one last time to make this critical decision."

"It is time. You must decide now," the first voice said.

A feeling of joy washed over Arelia. It was strangely warm and familiar. "I choose to live."

"You live always." There was a hint of a smile in the correction.

"I choose to make another choice with my life," Arelia corrected herself.

"We knew you would," the lights assured in unison.

The Angel spoke once again. "When there is understanding, the choice is always sure. But before you leave, there is something you must know. You will remember none of this. When you retake your human form, you take all the limitations it offers: the loss of memory of this meeting and of the peace of being unrestrained by human form. It is not a bad thing. It is a lesson—one that you will have a chance to learn. Human life is about learning lessons of the spirit. It is about learning to love unselfishly."

Her guardian added, "Be assured that I keep the face of our Creator in my sight, and that image is Love. As I guide and protect you, I will not tell you anything new, but I will stir your memory with the love that God and your family and friends have for you. With love is hope and the promise of green pastures. The Holy Spirit prompts us both for your well-being."

"But, if I return without this memory, will I make the wrong choice again?" Arelia expressed deep concern; she did not want to live the horror again.

"You will always have free will. No one, not even the Source, Who is God, will take that from you. You can give your free will away, or you can believe that it has been stolen, but in reality, it is always yours."

"Are you saying that when I go back, I could make the wrong choice again?"

"Yes." The lights became a kaleidoscope of color and form. "You must have faith in yourself and in your Creator. Self is strong and sure. The Creator has given you an Indwelling Spirit to guide you. Ask for help. He will not refuse."

"And you have me," her Guardian added with golden radiance. "And as you have seen before passing over, you have your Mother Mary, who understands it all, just as your earthly mother told you she did. Because you recognized that truth before passing, that reality will remain with you."

Peace overwhelmed her. In fact, she did feel confident and strong.

"There is knowledge that you have that the deceiver has concealed in the darkness of your human trials. I have been sent to you to lighten your awareness so that when you return your life will not be in total darkness. Your spark is rekindled."

"Teach me." Arelia was ready.

"Remind you," the Messenger corrected. "The truth is buried inside under all your misery. The Light has never left you. The spark is *always* there." The word *always* seemed to come to life, echoing off the walls.

Arelia smiled. "Remind me. I am ready."

"There is much to remember."

Both forms floated over the bed. Her Guardian lowered Arelia's head onto the pillow where she returned to the lifeless flesh beneath her. A breeze flowed over her, renewing the Breath of Life. Warm, white light encompassed her. There was not a voice, only awareness. "Your body is a gift from your Creator, made in His image. Cherish it. It is the expression of God within you. God's work is done through the hands and feet and voices of those who are open to His will on earth. Accept help and offer it." Color began to return to her bluish lips and fingertips.

"Free will is your greatest gift as well as your greatest challenge. You are responsible for yourself and for your choices. Your choices, large and small, determine your future. Your thinking determines your choices, so your thinking determines your future." Blood began to surge through her brain and vital organs. As awareness became clear, Arelia could perceive the results of choices she had made—choices based on fear. She became aware of how her fear-filled thoughts led to wrong choices. New hope grew as the seeds of truth cultivated by Angels burrowed deep within her soul.

"Always be grateful." More reminders flooded her being, pushing away the lies she had come to believe. "Even evil teaches; therefore, love your enemies for the lessons they teach. Love always guides you, but you must ask." More remembering. "Love never forces, punishes, or asks for sacrifice. Sacrifice is your gift to give. Love guides and lights the way. Always choose Love." Arelia was washed in peace.

Awareness continued. "Human challenges are lessons. Unlearned lessons are repeated. No choice is permanent. You have free will. Forgiveness is Love. Forgiveness is release. Trust in Forgiveness. Trust in Love; God is Love."

Peace. Awareness. Breath. The voices and luminous images began to grow dimmer, more distant.

"Arelia, you are ready."

PART II
HEALING OF MEMORIES

CHAPTER 29

 Arelia slowly opened her eyes. The room was getting dark with dusk settling into night. The rancid smell of her own filthy body burned her nostrils and turned her stomach.

Somehow she felt strangely rested and excited about something, but she had no idea what it was; she felt that something wonderful was about to happen. As she sat up, hunger drew her to a cloth-covered bowl resting on the heavy wooden table. She lifted the cover to find an apple, a slice of hard bread, and a thick piece of cheese. "Laura," she said lovingly. "Precious Laura . . . you have never given up on me." She felt strangely appreciative but covered the bowl as the smell of her own body wafted around her.

The first thing I will do is wash away this filth, she thought. A basin remained untouched on the table just as Laura had left it, in hopes that Arelia would at least rinse her face. At long last, the clean water invited her. She splashed the cold, refreshing water in her face and gasped at the shock of it. Gooseflesh covered her arms and legs.

As she turned toward the dying embers in the fireplace, she saw the large, metal washtub that Sarah had asked her son Joseph to carry to Arelia's room in hopes of washing her weak, sickly body. *Oh, Sarah, how you and Laura have loved me.* She dipped her hand into the cold water and shivered at the thought of stepping into the tub. "This fire will warm you up," she said to the cold water as she laid three heavy logs on the fire and fanned the flames. Marisa had been the only one to use the tub on a regular basis, but in this case, Arelia felt a real need for a long bath and appreciated the luxury of it.

She opened the large armoire and took out her warm wool robe, thinking how fortunate she was to have a quiet room to herself and a wardrobe of fine clothes. She unfastened her loose-fitting dress a little too easily and realized that she could probably slip out of it without even unfastening the tiny buttons. She was surprised to find that she was not wearing the traditional corset and undergarments, only the loose-fitting gown as a night dress.

As it fell to the floor, she hardly recognized her emaciated body. A flicker of light from the fire danced off her protruding ribs, giving them a frightening, skeleton-like appearance. She ran her hand down her shrunken breasts, her sharp ribs, and her strangely swollen belly. A tear came to her eyes. "Oh, have I hated you so much?"

As she bent to pick up the filthy gown, a pungent odor washed over her. Without even thinking, she gathered up the thick folds of fabric lying at her feet and tossed it into the fire. The room was filled with smoke as flashes of fire lapped at the edges of fabric until bright flames engulfed the heavy woolen threads. The smell of burning animal hair filled the room. Memories of burning bodies washed over her. She sunk to the floor in front of the hot flames hugging her knees to her shrunken frame. "They have loved me so much. I am all that is left to carry on their memories and their name. How my mother would cry to see what I have done to myself." Tears of grief and regret washed over her. "How could I do this to them? They gave me so much. Why have I allowed myself to be treated this way?" For the first time, she relished the tears; she knew they were healing. They were filled not only with grief but also with the knowledge of how much she was loved. She realized that she had lost her family, but now she had Laura and Sarah—and Stephen. "Why have I been so blind?"

Just then, the door opened. "Oh, Arelia," Laura cried at the shock of seeing Arelia naked on the floor. "What has happened to you? The terrible smell of something burning frightened me."

Arelia laughed realizing how she must look. "Everything is fine, Laura," she said as she stood and reached for her robe, slipping it over her thin shoulders.

"How can you say everything is fine when I find you crying and naked in front of the fire?"

"At least I am out of bed and out of that smelly gown. I was just heating water to bathe so I could have a bite to eat without making myself sick with the smell of me."

The shocked look on Laura's face said it all. "What has happened to you?"

284

Tears filled Laura's eyes as she wrapped Arelia's delicate body in a gentle hug. "I have prayed to see you like this, but I did not think it would ever happen." Arelia rested in the comfort of Laura's tender embrace. "Now," said Laura, "you will eat while I heat this water for your bath."

Arelia carried the bowl next to the warm fire and sat before the flames while Laura scooped pots of water to hang on the hook in the fireplace. She watched Laura and remembered how her mother had warmed water for the family every night for cooking and each month or two for their baths. Images of little Prudence splashing in the water made Arelia smile. Laura glanced at her and was surprised to see a contented smile on her face. "Arelia, what is it? You are different."

"I was just remembering my family. My mother would heat water over the fire for us just as you are doing for me now. Maybe I will do that for my family one day."

"Your and Stephen's family?" Laura teased.

"Laura, that thought frightens and excites me. I do not know that I could ever leave with Stephen."

"What do you mean? How could you not? Do not say it again. I just cannot hear it." Laura's voice bordered on anger. "Let me enjoy seeing you out of bed and eating for now. This is an answer to my prayers."

"Laura, I cannot expect you to understand." Laura noted that the tone of Arelia's voice had changed somewhat. She sounded less pitiful, but she still defended her fears.

"I do understand. I understand that you will die or be killed if you stay here. We have had this conversation so many times. I do not want to hear it again. I thought you were different."

Arelia was quiet. She knew Laura was right, but she couldn't stop the fear that nipped at her mind.

"Arelia, how can you turn away from the people who love you? Sir Edward will never let you out of this room, and Sir Daniel will not save you. He believes the lies. You will eventually be killed from one of Edward's beatings or by one of the soldiers. You are the only one who can save yourself!"

The words sounded familiar, and they rang true. "But, Laura, I am so afraid. I do not know if I am strong enough to do this myself."

Laura was tempted to walk out and leave Arelia to her excuses. Instead, she poured the steaming cauldron of water into the tub and tried to calm herself before speaking. She extended her hand to Arelia. "Here, get into this tub and get cleaned up." Arelia let her robe fall to the floor and stepped over the side of the tub, slowly letting her toes test the water. "Get in now," Laura coaxed. Arelia sank deep into the lukewarm water. The familiar pain in her side felt some relief from the warm water. "Take this soap and scrub yourself clean. Get your hair, too. You are a mess." Arelia smiled at Laura's motherly ways.

Laura pulled a chair to the side of the tub as Arelia dunked her head under the water. "Arelia," Laura said sincerely, "I can never understand your fear, but I do have such a fear myself. Each time I open the door, my fear is that I will find you dead. You will have died in the night from your own neglect or at the hands of a night visitor. *Each time*, Arelia."

"Laura, you are so good to watch over me and to never give up on me."

"You forget that you are my friend. Why would I ever give up on you? You are suffering so much. I do not understand why your fear of this place is not enough to drive you *out* of it." Laura's sad eyes questioned.

"I was alone for such a long time after my family died," Arelia explained. "I did not know if I would have food or if I would be food for some wild animal. That is a terrible fear which I do not ever want to live through again."

"You have food here, but it sits on the table uneaten. Look at yourself. You are all bones. Is your life any less fearful here?" Laura's question was sincere, and it rang true.

She had never thought of it like that. She dipped under the water for a few seconds to avoid the stinging reproach. "No, Laura, you are right. I have no hope here. Men attack me almost every night, but I would never starve here. I never actually starved in the woods either, although I was attacked by wolves."

"Yes," Laura said with a twinkle in her eyes, "and Stephen saved you. If you let him, he will save you again."

Arelia smiled. "Yes, he did." Laura instinctively walked over to the bed to straighten the covers and then stoked the fire once more before settling back into her chair.

"Look at yourself now. It looks as if you are starving, and there is food right here. You need something to eat. "Out of that tub now. Dry off. I will choose a dress for you."

Arelia rinsed her dark hair one more time, noting that her once thick hair was thinning, and it seemed to be coming out. She stepped out of the tub to dry in front of the fire while Laura pulled two chairs within its warm glow. Arelia wrapped herself in her robe, warm from the fire while Laura gathered her undergarments and helped her dress. She picked up a brush and began to brush out her hair, noticing the hair was coming out in clumps. She fought back tears at what Arelia had done to herself by refusing to eat.

"Sit down and eat this, *you who are afraid to starve but refuses to eat,*" Laura said to make the point one more time.

Arelia laughed. "I guess it does not make any sense."

"Not to me. None of this makes sense. Eat slowly; you have not eaten in a long time."

Laura had been gone for only a short time as Arelia settled into a deep sleep. She had a vivid dream about her family—sitting around the table at Sunday dinner, picking berries in the woods, helping her father in the field, having prayer time, telling stories in front of the fire. It all ran together. A creak at the door caused her to open her eyes. Her heart pounded in fear. It seemed to be just before dawn, but she didn't have any idea what time. The room seemed lighter than before, but the fire still blazed.

"Arelia," the man's voice called quietly. She lay still and quiet, pretending to sleep, hoping that he would leave. She regretted having washed and wished she still had her body stench to repulse him. He made his way to the bed. "Arelia." She didn't move or open her eyes, hoping he would think her dead. Silence.

She was surprised to hear a chair being dragged to the side of the bed. She heard the man sit. She didn't move and could scarcely breathe. *Can it be Stephen?* She was afraid to open her eyes.

"Arelia," he said as he took her hand. His voice was tense and strained but familiar. She opened her eyes slowly. "Oh God," he cried. "I feared you were dead."

"Stephen." She cried as she sat up to hug him. The pain in her side, from Edward's cruel kick, was intense, but she didn't care.

"Oh my, you certainly are not dead. What is this? Is this a clean dress? Is your hair damp?"

"Yes, I have just bathed." She smiled proudly, standing by her bed for him to get the full view of her. She was embarrassed by his obvious surprise. It pointed out how she had neglected herself so severely.

"What are you doing here?"

"I come every night, but I never wake you. Tonight, with the fire lit, I came in, hoping to be able to talk to you. I have wanted to talk every night," he stammered, "but tonight the fire invited me in." He looked at her lovingly as she sat on the side of the bed, firelight glimmering in her dark eyes. "Arelia, you are different."

"I am clean," she teased.

"No, it is more than that. I come to your room every night that I can manage to sneak away, only to ask you one question, but you have been so close to death that I thought I would never be able to ask."

Arelia knew the question. "What is it?" she invited hesitantly.

He took her hands into his. "I want you to leave with me right now. Can you trust me?" Stephen pleaded. Arelia looked deeply into his questioning eyes but didn't answer. All the old fears returned, but this time, she thought about him—about his concern for her safety and his desire to take care of her. She realized—fully, for the first time—that he loved her.

"Arelia, I know that it will not be easy, but I can promise that I will do everything within my power to love and protect you. You can either take that risk with me or stay in this room forever." A trace of a smile crossed her face. "You do want to leave with me. I can see it." He smiled in excited anticipation.

"Yes, but—"

"If you stay," he interrupted, "you are building a dungeon of fear for yourself. No one, not even I, can break down that wall. Only you can do that. Arelia, you have to trust someone, if not yourself." Familiar words.

"Where will we go?"

Stephen took her question as a yes. "Get your dress and put on your heavy boots. You will see." He handed her the dress Laura had laid out and her mother's boots, which had carried her from another time and place to this very moment. She dressed quickly as he found her cloak. "Do you need to take anything else?" he asked as he draped her cloak around her.

"No. There is nothing for me here."

Stephen cracked the door and listened for any noise in the hallway. "Stephen," came a loud whisper from behind. Their hearts sank as they turned toward the voice. Laura smiled and waved. "I talked to my brother. All is well!"

After a quick hug for Laura, with no chance for a proper goodbye, tears filled Arelia's eyes as they ran down the steep steps into the cold ocean air. As they started down the seawall, she stopped. "Wait! I have to go back," she insisted.

"No, you cannot turn back now. You have come this far."

Arelia looked back at the house, remembering the small, dark bag with coins her uncle had given her and the amulet from her father. "I left something important. My amulet."

"The only important thing is that we leave quickly," Stephen said as he took her hand and ran down the seawall steps. When they reached the sand, Arelia froze in fear.

"Stephen, there are two men with horses."

"Perfect!" Stephen said as he lifted her off her feet, running toward the men. As he set her down, he said, "Arelia, this is Jacob, Sarah's husband, and Joseph, Laura's brother. They manage the stable." Arelia was confused, but she was determined to continue on faith.

"Laura told us this was the night," Jacob said. "Go quickly."

"Do you have the boat?" Stephen asked as Jacob pointed to a boat pulled onto the sand. "I can never thank you enough," Stephen said, hugging Jacob stoutly.

"Be on your way, quickly. We will brush over your tracks."

"Officer Stephen," said Joseph as he took a bag from his horse. "Mother packed this bag for you and Arelia. She said to change your clothes as soon as you reach shore." Stephen laughed and hugged him, too.

"Lady Arelia, Mother and Bethany and Laura said to wish you Godspeed and to tell you that you have decided well. They have put something special in the bag for you."

"Thank you, Joseph. But how did they know?" Arelia asked.

Stephen took her arm. "We do not have time to talk. I will explain everything later."

"There is more in the boat for you," Joseph shouted as they ran toward the boat.

Joseph and Jacob pushed the small boat into the waves as Stephen pulled out two sets of oars. Father and son erased their tracks with branches and then mounted horses they had hidden near the boat. They raced along the coastline, away from the castle, and then disappeared into the woods.

"Here, take these paddles. You are going to get a lesson in rowing tonight."

Arelia was overwhelmed with everything that was happening so quickly. She settled into the bottom of the boat as well as she could with her sore ribs.

"Stephen, where did Jacob and Joseph go on the horses?"

"Down the beach, then into the woods," he answered casually.

"Why?" Arelia asked, more confused than before.

"They are throwing off our route. We are going the opposite direction, but by the time the captain realizes that we are gone, they will see the horse tracks and take off after us into the forest. Jacob is going to report two horses stolen tomorrow. They should be distracted for several days."

"They will look for us in your village." Her words were laced in panic.

"Yes, of course. You will enjoy the plan I have for that. Stop talking now and take a rest. We have a long way to go."

Clouds floated high in the sky and occasionally covered the moon, giving it an eerie feel. The water was black and frightening. Arelia had never been in the ocean but only in the shallow streams near her village. Her emotions were a jumble; she was torn between fear and excitement, between trust and panic. Stars peeked through the clouds at the passing boat while the vast expanse of sky was as broad as the ocean, pointing to some unknown direction her life was so unpredictably taking. There was no turning back as the shackles were opened and left in her cell. She decided to trust Stephen and concentrate on excitement.

"Stephen, how much longer will we paddle?"

"Another two or three hours, and then we will catch a current into shore. Are you rested?"

"Somewhat. Are you?" Arelia smiled, expecting his answer.

"Do not worry, I row often. You can take over for me later." He smiled, knowing he could row all night if necessary for Arelia's escape. They sat quietly with only the cadence of the wooden oars cutting through the water interrupting the silence. Arelia had never seen how bright the stars were over open water.

"Stephen, this is beautiful. I feel more peaceful than frightened now. Thank you."

Stephen smiled broadly. "Do not thank me yet," he said jokingly. "We have a long way to go."

"Stephen, even if we do not get to your village, I want you to know I made the right decision. I feel more peaceful now than I have felt since the plague took my family."

"We will make it to the village. Do not worry about that. I am an officer, you know." Stephen continued his steady rhythm to bring them closer to their goal.

Arelia was sleepy, but she didn't want to sleep and leave Stephen alone. More to the point, she was afraid she would fall out of the boat; her head bobbed, unable to fight off sleep.

"Arelia, lie down and sleep. You are not fully recovered, and you need to be rested for our walk when we get to shore."

She gladly gave in to his suggestion and quickly fell asleep to the rocking motion of the boat. She dreamed she was nestled within a giant cradle in a tree deep in the forest, with wind blowing gently through the branches, rocking her from side to side while the rustle of leaves whispered a soothing lullaby.

Stephen watched her as she slept, hardly able to believe that he was finally getting her away from her cousin. Although he would never let her know it, he was concerned about his family's reaction to his unexpected return and about the story he would tell them. He would have plenty of time to rehearse their account with Arelia while they made their three-day walk to the village.

CHAPTER 30

"Arelia, wake up." Stephen was pulling the boat onto the beach near an outcropping of rocks as the sun peeked over the flat, still sea.

She tried to open her eyes but had no idea where she was or even who she was. She had slept so deeply that she couldn't wake up.

"Lady Arelia," Stephen said shaking her shoulder gently. Arelia opened her eyes to see the sides of the boat and then the familiar smiling face. "We are here. You do not need to row anymore." He grinned at her groggy, confused expression. He laughed and reached out his hands to offer to lift her tired body.

She sat up slowly and broke out in a grin. "You did get me here." She pushed the hair out of her eyes and reached out her hand to accept his assistance.

"We still have a long way to go. You need to help me now." Stephen helped her out of the boat and then took a rope and tied it around the seat.

"You must help me get the boat up these rocks."

Arelia knew by now to save her questions for later. She used all the strength she could muster to help him push and pull the boat to the top of the ten-foot outcropping. Her bruised ribs ached with every move, but she couldn't let Stephen see the pain she felt, knowing that he was risking his own life in order to save hers.

"Now, tear the hem of your dress and your sleeve." Arelia looked at him like he had gone mad. "Here, I will help," he said as he ripped her dress without permission. "Now, give me the ribbon." Arelia pulled the ribbon from the bodice as he said, knowing that she would understand later.

He threw the fabric from her skirt and the ribbon between the rocks and then cut the rope from the seat and pushed the boat over the side. The small wooden boat hit a rock and shattered into pieces. "Looks like a shipwreck to me." He laughed smugly. Arelia laughed, too, when she realized his plan.

He helped her down from the rocks and walked into the trees. Then he opened the bag that Joseph had given them. The first thing he pulled out was a pair of trousers and, next, a shirt.

"Here, put these on." He handed her the clothes.

"You want me to wear this? I think that they are for you." Now she was really confused.

"Just put them on, and put your hair under this cap. If anyone sees us, they will report seeing two village men." Stephen took another pair of trousers and a shirt out of the bag. "No one will report seeing a soldier and a girl," he said smiling. He walked over to the trees as he took off his military garb.

Arelia followed suit by going deeper into the trees for privacy. She was happy to have other clothes as her gown was wet and cold from sleeping in the bottom of the boat.

Stephen changed quickly and found hard bread and cheese wrapped neatly in the other bag. Sarah had even packed dried meat. He walked deeper into the woods to find kindling and a safe place to start a fire. He came through the thick underbrush just as Arelia was putting on her manly shirt. He was startled to see her out of her room and here in the forest with him. Arelia didn't see him as he stepped quickly into the brush and busied himself collecting kindling wood.

When she walked out, he called to her. "Would my lady join me in a picnic?" he teased.

"Yes, kind sir," she answered, playing the part and collecting kindling along the way. She was starving from her past weeks of depression and the strenuous activity in getting to this place. Warmth from the fire cut through the damp morning chill as they enjoyed the treats Sarah had packed, including two small pieces of butter cake. The orange glow of sunrise filtered through the trees, lending a hint of something mystical. Peace settled over her as she watched her rescuer bite off a healthy mouthful of bread.

"We are going to have a very long day," Stephen explained while wiping his mouth with the back of his hand. "It will take us three days to get to the village. I want you to push yourself as hard as you can, but tell me when you need to rest. My family will make us comfortable when we arrive. But until then, we must push hard. Tear another strip from your skirt and leave it on the shoreline away from the rocks and water while I cover the fire."

Arelia tore a strip from her hem and laid it in the underbrush away from the outcropping. Being in the familiar setting of the forest, she felt energetic and excited about the day. She intended to keep an eye open for berries and nuts and hoped that Stephen would be impressed with her ingenuity. This was beginning to feel like a wonderful adventure rather than the frightening escape it actually was.

"Stephen, no matter what happens now, it can never be as bad as what I went through in that house," she said as she met him back at the campsite.

Stephen smiled lovingly and pulled her to him, kissed her gently on her cheek. Arelia hesitated momentarily and then rested her head against his chest.

"Oh, dear," Stephen said. "We cannot get distracted. We have a long way to go. I must be the happiest man in the world today!"

Just as he had promised, the walk was long and tiring. Several times Arelia wanted to stop, but she pushed on, following Stephen's lead as closely as possible. Every muscle in her body ached, but her side was especially painful. They had found a stream and used that as their guide. Arelia prided herself on finding nuts and berries for them to snack on along the way.

"My father taught me to let the squirrels lead me to the nuts."

Arelia began to fall farther and farther behind. Stephen was so intent on his goal that he did not even notice until she called to him. He was surprised to see her sitting on a fallen tree so far behind.

"Am I going to have to carry you?" he called half-jokingly but with genuine concern for her.

"You certainly may, if you would like," came her answer.

Noticing her deep, labored breaths, he sat on the fallen tree next to her to give her time to rest.

"Stephen, you must be exhausted. You have not slept at all since we left."

"I am used to this. When I have night watch, I am not allowed to sleep. Besides, I am too excited to sleep now. We will stop again at dusk and make camp, but we need to keep going as best we can."

"It is nice being with you," Arelia said. "Last time I made a trip looking for a village, I was alone. That seems like another life."

"This will be a better time for you, I promise," he reassured. "At least, this time you have a destination."

"You are the one with the destination." She laughed. "I am just following you."

"And I am glad of that!" He opened the bag of bread and cheese. "You never saw what Laura and the ladies sent for you."

In all the activity, Arelia had forgotten about her surprise. "What is it?" she asked excitedly.

He pulled a small flat box from the bag. "I guess this is it," he said as he handed it to her.

She untied the soft pink ribbon that held it closed and opened the box to find a delicately embroidered lace handkerchief with the Fairchild emblem and the initials "A.W." Her eyes grew wide and teary. Stephen smiled when he saw the initials. Arelia didn't seem to notice.

"Why are you crying?"

"It is my family's emblem as it is on the amulet. This is so sweet. I did not get to tell them goodbye or even to thank them for all they did for me."

"They know you appreciate their help. They just want you to be happy," Stephen consoled.

"How did they know about last night?" Arelia wanted to know every detail.

"When I came to the estate years ago, I helped with the horses, and Jacob was like a father to me. He is Laura's father, you know?"

"Laura's father? I did not realize that in all that was happening."

"Yes, anyway—I had gone to the stable to talk to him about my plan, and he encouraged me to move quickly. It was his idea to take the boat. I was going to ride horses to the village. Fortunately, he was thinking straight and devised the distraction to buy us time. Joseph, you know, Laura's brother, was aware of your situation and sympathetic to your cause. Jacob solicited him to ride the other horse. They must have shared the plan with Laura and Sarah. Jacob told me that they would be ready at any time."

"I never appreciated them as much as I should have. I only concentrated on myself and my situation. Laura was a true friend." Arelia thought back to all the nights that Laura and Bethany had tended her, and then she remembered her last conversation with Sarah.

295

"Stephen, Sarah wanted me to leave with you. I think she was the one who convinced me."

"What? Was it not your love for me that convinced you?" he teased as he held his hands over his heart with a mock pout on his face. Arelia blushed at his comment. "Have I offended you?" he apologized.

"No, but it seems strange to hear it spoken aloud," she explained. Stephen stood up and walked away, considering his words and feelings.

He walked back toward her seriously and knelt on one knee before her.

Looking into her eyes, he asked, "Arelia, I may not have given you a proper choice. I asked you to leave with me in order to save yourself. Marrying you was just assumed on my part. I realize now that leaving and marrying are two different things. Whether or not you marry me now is up to you. I want you away from there, whether you agree to be my wife or not." He took both her hands into his. "Arelia, will you marry me? Will you live with me forever and be the mother of my children?"

Arelia studied his strong, determined yet sensitive face. He had risked his life to free her without any ties. She was overwhelmed with his kindness and love in contrast to the cruelty to which she had been subjected. She put her hand on his cheek.

"Stephen, there is no one in this world I would rather be with than you."

He grabbed her up in a strong hug and spun around. "I was hoping you would say that." He laughed with relief. "We will have plenty of time together. Now, I must get you home."

Arelia pushed herself beyond her limits. She wanted to stop several times but stayed close behind Stephen until dusk.

"We can make camp in these rocks," he said, to Arelia's great relief. Her muscles ached from months of idleness and the little bit of exertion it took to hurry to the boat. She still felt the pain in her ribs from her cousin's abuse. "You look through the bag. I will start a fire." While Stephen gathered wood, Arelia brought water from the stream in a small pan that the ladies had packed;

they seemed to have thought of everything. Stephen dragged two large, leafy branches to the campsite for cover. Arelia sprinkled loose tea leaves into the steaming pan and set out dried meat with hard bread and the berries she had picked.

"We have quite a feast tonight. This is an appropriate meal to celebrate our lives together," he said.

Arelia smiled at his comment and thought how different her life had been just the night before. "Stephen, I thought I would die in that room."

"You would have if you had not made the choice to leave," he confirmed.

Night settled in quickly as the air became very cold. Stephen gathered enough wood to keep the fire going throughout the night while Arelia gathered a pile of leaves and spread her torn dress over them to make a soft, crunchy bed. Stephen smiled as he watched her preparing such a cozy spot. He was not sure if the bed was intended for both of them and didn't want to cause her any concern by asking.

Arelia felt such a tremendous relief as she lay back on the soft bed of leaves. She looked up into the trees so familiar from her childhood.

"Stephen, I am so happy to be back in the forest. Now, this is comfortable to me. I loved the sea but really missed walking through the trees," she told him as he sat by the fire.

Stephen looked up. "I know what you mean. I grew up here too. There's something comforting about being here. The trees seem protective somehow."

"The fire feels good. I will help you keep it through the night."

Stephen smiled, knowing she would be too tired to wake to tend the fire.

"If you would like to join me in this soft bed, you may," she invited.

"Is there room for me?" he asked, trying not to give away his excitement.

"I can make room. It will be warmer that way."

Stephen wished that she had invited him not just for warmth but for comfort. He knew that one day soon they would have the right to be together with no impropriety and no fear of her misunderstanding his true intentions.

Arelia fell asleep quickly, almost before Stephen settled in next to her. Unfortunately, sleep didn't come easily for him. Every sound startled him awake. He hoped Jacob's plan to distract Hardgrave had worked. They were making slow progress because Arelia was in no condition to do more. Considering her recent injuries, he didn't want to push her, because he didn't want her to know how concerned he was about their slow pace.

Although he got up several times to stoke the fire, Arelia never even moved. He kept her covered with her heavy wool cloak, noticing each time how thin and delicate she was.

I hope I haven't made a mistake, he thought. *I must get her to my family quickly so if anything happens, she will be cared for.* He dozed on and off, unable to sleep soundly, staying continually alert.

CHAPTER 31

Laura paced expectantly in the dark stable, waiting with fear and anticipation for news of her friend's escape. Joseph was so excited and proud of his part in the rescue that the details of the adventure came tumbling out as soon as he saw her without need for even one question. He told how Jacob had ridden to just within the tree line and then walked back while Joseph led the horses deeper into the forest and let them go. Jacob heard Joseph's excited report and cautioned them to be quiet, go to bed until morning, and pretend it never happened.

As Laura crept into her dorm-like room, Helen rolled over under the covers and let out a gentle sigh. Laura froze in her steps until she could hear normal, deep, sleep-filled breaths. After settling under a woolen blanket, she realized that no one would be surprised to see her up in the middle of the night as she often was with Arelia. It had become commonplace for her to go in and out of the room.

She also realized it was important to play her part convincingly in order to give Stephen and Arelia plenty of time to escape. When the sun rose, she started her day as normal, bringing a water basin and hard bread to Arelia's room, leaving it on the table as usual, pretending nothing had changed. As an afterthought, she stuffed pillows under the cover of the heavy blanket to make it appear that Arelia was asleep. She stood back and laughed at her own deceptive nature, satisfied that she had added something to the escape plan.

"Godspeed, Arelia," she said aloud.

At sunrise, Jacob reported two missing horses. Captain Hardgrave yelled "Wingate!" when he first heard the news. Soldiers searched the camp, finding no sign of him. As on cue, Joseph ran into the camp to tell the captain that he had found traces of two horses which seemed to have been running down the beach at full speed.

"Have you seen Officer Wingate?"

"Yes, Captain. He told me he had night watch and needed a couple of extra horses. He has done that several times before, but they are always back before sunrise."

Captain Hardgrave turned, nearly knocking Joseph over and roughly pushed him aside.

He stormed into Edward's room without knocking. "Wingate is gone," he shouted.

Edward was immediately aroused from his normal lethargy with a renewed focus. "Captain, come with me."

The two men stormed down the hallway toward Arelia's room as Laura was going to the children's room to talk to her mother. The thunder of boots echoed down the hallway. She jumped to the side as Edward stopped to challenge. "Where is Arelia?"

Laura caught her breath and stammered, "I . . . was in her room earlier to leave her breakfast. . . . She was asleep."

"Come with us." Laura ran to keep up.

The captain threw Arelia's door open, nearly breaking the hinges. Sir Edward ran to her bed and threw back the covers. He picked up one of the pillows and threw it to the floor.

"He took her," he shouted.

Laura gasped and responded with real tears at the violence of the discovery, backing into the doorway in natural fear of becoming Sir Edward's likely scapegoat.

"Summon your mother and Bethany immediately. I will be in my room." He and the captain rumbled back down the hallway as Laura ran to find her mother.

The two women entered the room with genuine anxiety over the situation. "What is it, sire?" Bethany asked innocently.

"Look, you idiot. Where is the girl?"

"She may be at the seawall, sire. She is trying to recover her strength."

"No. She has left with Wingate!" shouted Sir Edward.

"No." Sarah appeared truly shocked. "How could that be?"

"What do you know of this?" he demanded.

"Sire, we know nothing. Arelia has not been well at all. In fact, she appeared to be dying. You and Captain Hardgrave have seen her. She never even left her bed and refused to eat," reminded Bethany.

"We will find her without your help."

"Come, Captain, to the stables."

Sarah and Bethany smiled at each other when the men had left the room. "I hope Jacob's plan has convinced them," laughed Bethany. "Let us check her room."

The silence of the room was ghostly. After seeing her near death for so many weeks, each woman, in her own mind, had anticipated the day when they would remove the dresses from the wardrobe and burn her straw mattress at her inevitable death. Now the room was as they had imagined it would be, but miraculously, she was alive.

Bethany looked through Arelia's few dresses. "She did not take anything but her boots and wool cloak. Those are the only things she came with."

"And her amulet!" Sarah added.

Sarah opened the drawer in her table and pulled out a small dark, heavy bag and the amulet. "She left it!"

"Hide it in your dress, Sarah. We must not let Sir Edward find it." She closed the drawer, and the women returned to care for the babies.

Sir Edward and the captain called Jacob and Joseph to the parlor for an interrogation. "What time did Wingate get the horses?" "Did you see him with the girl?" "Did he have a saddle bag?" "Did you see him leave?" "Which direction did he go?" The questions went on and on and were answered with feigned ignorance.

"Joseph found tracks along the beach." Jacob pointed in the direction of the tracks. "They may be theirs."

"Send Joseph to the camp for ten men. Have them meet us at the beach."

Jacob saddled horses for Sir Edward and Captain Hardgrave, who rode out to locate the tracks before the soldiers arrived. "Sire," the captain shouted over the noise of the wind and slashing waves. "Joseph was right. Look at these tracks. The boy should have ridden in the surf to disguise them. He was not using his training. We will find them now. He should not have allowed the girl to distract him." The captain laughed.

When the other soldiers gathered, Captain Hardgrave gave orders. "Follow the tracks until they end; then one group continue along the beach watching for them. They may have ridden into the surf to cover their trail. Do not return until you find them or until dark."

Soldiers rode away, following the tracks down the beach as Sir Edward and the captain watched, confident that the men would find them.

After dark, one of the soldiers reported that the tracks had turned into the woods. They rode through the woods for several hours but found nothing.

"Tomorrow, you and your men will take provisions and hunt them down. Prepare tonight to leave at dawn."

After dinner, the captain reported the news to Sir Edward.

"Captain, would you say that Officer Wingate is a good soldier?"

"Yes, sire—one of the best."

"Why would he have left tracks for us to follow?"

"He may not have been thinking. With the girl in her condition, he was probably distracted. I had heard she couldn't even walk and was probably unconscious. The boy was blinded by her for some reason. Maybe he tried to go through the underbrush but found it too difficult, especially if she was strapped to a saddle. They could not ride two abreast on the narrow paths."

"Perhaps, but could he have distracted *us* from his real escape route in order to buy time? Do you not think that he had spent some time planning their escape?"

"That is very likely, sire, but riding along the beach would give them a faster start."

"Where do you think he wanted to take her, Captain?"

"Sire, I think most obviously to his family."

"Or mine," Sir Edward, interjected.

"Captain, if *you* had planned the escape, how would you have gone?" The captain thought for only a moment.

"By boat; there would be no tracks. His village and Fairfield are in opposite directions."

"Exactly."

"First thing tomorrow, I will send men on horses *opposite* the tracks and men in boats to search the shoreline."

"Good . . .. I do not want Arelia and Officer Wingate to show up at my father's doorstep."

"At some point, either heading to Fairfield or to his village, they would need horses."

"Yes, but do not lose any time. He may have two horses. Are any other soldiers gone? Maybe he had an accomplice."

"Everyone else is accounted for."

Early the next morning, six men left in two boats in the direction of Fairfield, another six left on horseback into the forest, and another six left in boats opposite the first boats. Captain Hardgrave wasn't as confident as before that the two young people would be found. Stephen had been commissioned at a young age because he had instinctive military skills. The captain knew he would put those skills to work in maneuvering his escape.

Before the sun came up, Arelia stretched and walked into the trees.

"Where are you going?" Stephen asked.

"To take care of private matters. Put water on the fire, please. I will find leaves and berries for tea." She continued to astonish him with her resourcefulness. He kept forgetting that she had been raised as a villager and not in that horrible place.

Stephen was surprised at the pleasantly sweet concoction Arelia brewed. It was perfect with hard bread and nuts.

"I do not know how you did it, but somehow you managed to turn this meal of hard bread into a treat," complimented Stephen.

"Nature is full of surprises," answered Arelia sweetly.

"And so are you" Stephen winked. "We must get started. We have another long day ahead of us."

The pace of the second day was a little faster. Although Arelia was painfully sore, she had rested well and was eager to get to the village to meet Stephen's family.

"Stephen, is your family as nice as you?" she asked as they walked along.

Stephen laughed at her question. "Of course not, I am the nicest."

Arelia hit his arm gently. "I am serious. I am very nervous. What are we going to tell them about me? Who will we say I am?"

"You are Arelia Fairchild and . . ."

"No, Stephen. I am Arelia Davidson."

"Who? Davidson?"

"Oh dear." She sighed, fighting back tears. "It is a very long story for another time. It has to do with my father's Psalter."

"Your father's Psalter?"

"Just remember that my father loved the Psalms, and King David wrote them, and so my father changed his surname to *Davidson* rather than using Fairchild."

He was completely puzzled and caught off guard. "I am completely confused. I thought that Sir Daniel is your uncle and Sir Edward is your cousin!"

"Yes, I have discovered from the amulet that what you say is true. Before the wolf attack, I thought I was Arelia Davidson, and I truly did live with my family in Ravenshire."

"You will need to explain all that to me tonight over a fire. I am very confused, but what I do know is that we must have the same story. I plan to tell them about my saving you from the wolves, taking you back to the estate, and falling in love," he answered simply.

"You do know that I am asking you about what we will tell your family why I was at Faircastle?" She was frustrated and a little angry with his simple answer.

"Yes, I do. We will tell them you sewed and worked in the kitchen, which is where we met."

Arelia smiled. "Can it be that easy?"

"I do not know why not. Do you?" he responded.

"No. Because that is how I thought it would be when Laura and I became friends. I still do not understand what happened after that."

"Did Laura talk to you about what she did for her chores?" Stephen asked.

"Not at first, but after a while she told me stories about almost everyone. I did not know any of them, but I enjoyed her stories."

"Good. Then you can share those stories and maybe some your father told. They will not know any different. That will be your identity. Can you present yourself as though you were in the same position as Laura?"

"What a great idea. That will be easy for me." Arelia giggled with relief. She took Stephen's arm and stopped him.

They sat quietly considering their stories. "Oh dear."

"What is it? That will work, Arelia. Do not be afraid."

"I have one thing that I do not have a story for. They may ask why I am so thin."

Stephen felt a slight panic. Arelia certainly looked sickly. Maybe that could be the reason for his running off with her, but why? He was stumped.

Arelia saw his concern and started to cry. "Please, Arelia, we have time to think of something before we get there. We will come up with a plan." He smiled. Arelia couldn't help but smile back. She wiped her eyes and calmed herself, knowing that she could trust Stephen. Besides, what choice did she have?

"Stephen, I can never repay you for getting me out of that house," she said sincerely.

He smiled warmly. "You are repaying me by trusting me. We will both be rewarded with a family." He winked as she blushed and looked away from his intimate gaze.

Most of the day was spent quietly as they followed the stream, often stepping into the water to conceal their tracks, each lost in their own thoughts.

Arelia interrupted the silence. "Stephen, I traded fear for love." She smiled.

"You made a good trade," he affirmed, returning her smile. "You know my family will love you too. You will have more love than you thought possible." He stopped and hugged her, aware of her very thin frame. He kissed her warmly on her forehead and then rested his head lightly on the top of hers. She felt feather-like, fragile. For the first time, he realized how hard their escape must be on her, and yet she pushed on.

"Keep your eyes open for a place to camp tonight. I think it is going to be colder than last night," Stephen said. "We can stop early."

Searching off the beaten path for a campsite brought painful memories of the Black Death with finds of abandoned camps littered with pull carts and filthily dressed skeletons. They stayed close to the path in order to avoid those grim reminders.

After several hours of a steady pace, Stephen spotted a dark shadow on the side of a small rise. "Stay here. I think I spot a cave." He waded across a shallow stream and threw rocks into the dark shadow from a distance. After no response, he drew his lance, picked up a heavy stick and climbed a gentle incline to the cave. As he crawled into a small, dark opening, disappearing for a few moments, he was swallowed up by the hill but quickly came out smiling.

"I have found a lovely room for the night," he said as he waved, calling her to him.

The thought of sleeping in a cave was a treat for Arelia. Since the wolf attack, she hadn't felt safe in the open, and she needed a good night's sleep. Pain and exhaustion were getting increasingly difficult to hide.

They began their routine as the night before—Arelia gathered leaves to make a bed, and Stephen gathered wood for a fire.

"We can only have a small fire at the opening. We do not want any animals returning to their home to find us sleeping here, but we do not want to get smoked out either. "

Arelia offered to sit up and tend the small fire while Stephen slept. He had basically had two nights with only a few hours of sleep and two days of strenuous activity. After a half-hearted refusal, he lay down on their makeshift bed and fell asleep within seconds.

Arelia watched him, barely able to believe all that had happened in just two short days. She thought about the times she had watched her parents talking late at night in front of a warm fire, wondering how it felt to be a wife and mother. Many nights, she would try to imagine who the man would be, sitting across the fire from her. She sighed, knowing that never in her wildest imagination would she have pictured herself in a cave fending off wild animals to protect her future husband.

She was bone tired, and every bone in her body ached. Her side had begun to cramp with sharp, shooting pains. She didn't want to alarm Stephen, especially since there wasn't a thing he could do. The pains reminded her of the ones she had experienced after drinking Bethany's tea to start her blood.

Time had passed so quickly since the soldiers had brought her to the castle. The seasons had seemed to go by almost without notice, and she couldn't determine how long she had been trapped in that room. It felt like an eternity. She knew it had to be more than a year because Marisa became pregnant and had twins during that time. She estimated that she had been at Faircastle at least a couple of months before her uncle left, and then she went back to her village. It was hard to imagine that she had lost track of time the way she had.

She thought about how Stephen had sacrificed his own life in order to save her and about how thankful she was to be away from Faircastle. Her thoughts went from thanksgiving to concern. In spite of all Stephen's reassurances, she couldn't shake the fear of disgracing him before his family or her fear of being left alone in the world again with no way to provide for herself. Soon her head began to bob with the heaviness of sleep even as the myriad of thoughts swirled through her mind. She caught herself and stood up to replenish the fire before she fell asleep.

"You are a good watchman, Arelia." Stephen sat up, rubbing his eyes and stretching broadly as he watched her stoke the fire. "Have I been asleep long?" he asked with a big yawn.

"It did not seem long, but I was starting to fall asleep myself."

"Come here," he said patting the leafy bed. Arelia accepted his kind offer and was asleep nearly before she closed her eyes. He noted that she had done well gathering sticks and branches for the fire. The new flames made soft willowy images on the walls of the cave. Stephen was no longer able to fight the much-welcomed sleep with Arelia's warm body snuggled within the crook of his arm.

He awoke with the hair on the back of his neck standing on end. His nostrils burned with a strong odor, and his ears discerned a low, gravelly growl.

All his senses were on alert, and fear gripped him when he made out the snout and paw of a brown bear reaching through the opening to drag their food bag away.

"What is it?" asked Arelia in a whisper, waking to his rigid body.

"Do not move," he whispered. Fortunately, the opening to the cave was small. Stephen slowly gathered two hands full of leaves from their bed and threw them on the embers. The dry leaves burst into smoke and flame, setting the bear back on his haunches. Stephen lit the end of a branch into a flame and jabbed through the opening at the bear's face. The animal stood upright on his hind feet, letting out a loud growl, and then turned and ran away.

Every inch of Arelia's body trembled with fear. She could hardly catch her breath as sobs welled up from the pit of her stomach. Stephen was surprised by her strong reaction. He quickly rekindled the fire to a hot blaze and then put his arms around her trembling shoulders, letting her cry out her fear.

"I am sorry, Arelia. I let the fire die out. I slept too soundly."

"Stephen, I told you I would watch the fire. We could have been killed. You saved me from wolves, and you could have been killed by a bear because of me." She sobbed uncontrollably. "I am *no good* for you. You should have left me there."

"Stop it! The fire is burning now. Go back to sleep."

"You would have been better off if the bear had killed me, or even better if the wolves had done me in."

He grabbed her shoulders. Her eyes grew wide at his anger, and the tears stopped in shock.

"Arelia, listen to me." Stephen's voice was louder than she had ever heard. "This is not going to be easy for either of us. We have both taken great risks to get this far, and our battles are far from over. You cannot allow yourself the luxury of feeling sorry for yourself now. I need you to be strong. We have days to go. This can get much harder."

Arelia's tears fell gently as she realized how she had disappointed him.

He wrapped his arms around her. "Listen to me," he continued calmly. "Your fears are not going to go away overnight. You have been through more than most people go through in a lifetime, but you must fight your fear like you did the night we left the estate. Do not give up on me or on yourself.

Please do not ever say you are not good for me. I chose you, did I not?" he asked as he wiped tears from her cheeks. "You are the best thing that ever happened to me." He sighed.

"Yes, but . . . ," she began.

He placed his finger over her lips. His voice softened. "The answer is just 'yes.' I had good cause to choose you. One day you will know that. Until then, remember what you told me. You traded fear for love. Remember?"

"Yes," she answered hesitantly.

"The bear is gone. The fire is blazing, and we are alive and cozy on a soft bed in a warm, cozy cave. That bear would never have fit in here anyway." She smiled, knowing he was right.

"I am glad you chose me. Keep reminding me. I will try harder to prove you right," she said, beginning to feel peaceful but still not confident that he was right.

He laughed. "You do not have to prove anything to me, only to yourself."

He got up and put another log on the fire. "This will last until daybreak. Now, sleep while you can."

As Stephen watched Arelia sleep, he regretted speaking so harshly to her, but he didn't know how to protect and encourage her, all the while sheltering her from the dangers they faced. He needed her vigilance and cooperation, not knowing how much ahead they were of Captain Hardgrave and Sir Edward's soldiers.

CHAPTER 32

 The soldiers returned the evening of day two. Sir Edward was angry and frustrated that there was apparently no sign of the two. He knew that the search would become increasingly difficult as time passed.

The captain was concerned that Sir Edward would turn his anger against him as no sure signs were reported. He had sent out another search party to comb the beach for any clues, but none had been reported. He was growing more desperate to appease Sir Edward, who had made this search his total and immediate focus. It was almost as if the spirit of Marisa drove him.

The captain returned to the servants' quarters and banged on Laura's door.

"I want to talk to you, your mother, and the maid, Bethany, immediately. Meet me in Arelia's room," he commanded.

Laura ran through dark halls, nervous that they had found Arelia and Stephen. Sarah and Bethany quickly left the babies in Helen's care.

"Laura, you are too nervous. Do not speak. Your mother and I will speak for you."

The captain was going through Arelia's things when they entered her room. Sarah was thankful that they had discovered the small bag and amulet before his search.

"Ladies, please sit down." The captain was unusually polite. "How do you feel about Arelia's disappearance?" he began.

Sarah and Laura looked at Bethany, who said, "We are very concerned about her, sir. She had been ill and could not possibly be strong enough to make any sort of trip. She was hardly conscious the last time I saw her; in fact, I had thought her dead."

"But you told me you thought she had gone to the beach. She must have been better," the captain reminded with a suspicious tone.

"Actually, sir, I think I said she was at the seawall if she was strong enough to be out of her room. She would not have been strong enough for a long walk," corrected Bethany.

"And you, Laura?" He came uncomfortably close and lay his hand on her shoulder. "What do you think of all this?"

Laura was so frightened and nervous. She had heard Arelia's screams at the hands of Sir Edward and the captain. She didn't want to say anything that would jeopardize Arelia's escape. She began to cry before she could speak.

"Sir, please forgive Laura," explained her mother. "She became very attached to the girl and fears for her life. She knows how ill she is." The captain drew away from her and turned to Sarah.

"And you, madam. You were also close to the girl. You shared her confidence, did you not?" he asked Sarah.

"Yes, sir. We were very close. That is, until the babies were born. Since that time, I saw Arelia briefly on only one occasion."

The captain was growing frustrated.

"Laura, did Arelia ever talk of leaving?"

Laura was startled by such a straightforward question. "Yes, sir."

Bethany stiffened at her candid response.

"Oh really? Tell me about it," pressed the captain.

Bethany interrupted, "Arelia has talked to all of us about leaving with her uncle. He reminded her so much of her own father and longed to be in his company. Since he had left without her, she had not spoken of leaving. Had she, Laura?"

Laura took the cue. "No, she had not spoken to me about it."

"Laura," addressed the captain, sensing a weakness. "Do you know the soldier, Stephen?"

"Yes, sir. I have seen him in the courtyard," came her honest response.

"Did he visit Arelia?"

"Yes, sir. Many officers came to visit," she answered innocently.

"I am asking if he came at unusual times?"

"Not that I know of. I did not know her schedule, sire. I think you and Bethany made those arrangements." Her response seemed almost too casual.

"Bethany, you are familiar with her schedule, are you not?"

"Yes, sir."

"Did Stephen visit at unscheduled times?"

Bethany stayed calm. "I am sorry I am no help to you. I do not stay on this end of the house, so I was not aware of who went in and out. I only prepared her for the evening. I never stayed. In fact, I do not know who came. You would know better than I."

Captain Hardgrave sensed a challenge and was growing increasingly angry.

"You know Stephen was here!"

"Yes, sir. We know he visited, as did you and other officers. Lady Marisa advised me on how to provide for the men. We just do not know when each man visited," Bethany repeated.

Captain Hardgrave was angry and frustrated about the lack of information. He didn't even know what he was hoping for but thought the women would carelessly provide some insight.

"Sir, I have tended Arelia for some time, and I do not think she could survive this strenuous trip with Stephen. She will need rest and will not be able to push herself."

The captain smiled maliciously. "I appreciate knowing that, Bethany. I am sure that will give Sir Edward some reassurance."

Laura had begun to cry again. After the captain left, she begged Bethany, "Is she really going to die? She finally has a chance of being happy."

Bethany laughed as Sarah wrapped her arms around her daughter. "I am glad I was convincing, Laura. I just wanted to throw him off. They will not search for her if they think she is dead. You know that Stephen will take care of her."

Morning came quickly for Stephen and Arelia. Arelia refused to leave the cave until Stephen checked for bears. Stephen himself was nervous about another attack and checked the area with his knife drawn in one hand and a large stone in the other.

Finally, after reassuring Arelia, they began what Stephen hoped would be their last day of hiking. He had not anticipated such a slow pace. He normally hiked with his men, who were in excellent condition. Occasionally, he would look back and find Arelia lagging far behind or sitting on a stump.

Today, she seemed slower than ever. Once she called out from a tree stump, completely out of breath.

"Arelia, are you all right?"

"Yes, I am just not ready for all this hiking. Before I came to the estate, I could have hiked for days."

"Eat some berries. I will go for water," he offered.

"Please let me come with you. I will rest by the stream," requested Arelia as she followed slowly behind him.

Arelia felt she had hardly regained her breath when Stephen was ready to take off again. She remembered her promise to try and be strong, so she pushed herself to stay up, but she didn't know how much longer she would last. The pains in her side were becoming more continuous, even more intense than before, like the ones she had had each time Bethany would give her the strong brew to start her flow.

Stephen spotted a small grotto in the rocks shortly before dusk and began preparing a place for the night. Arelia didn't gather the leaves this time but just sat and watched him, too tired to move. By the time Stephen had prepared the fire, Arelia had fallen asleep on the cold, damp ground. He covered her with her woolen cloak and her dress, tucked away in the bag, and then fell asleep next to her.

A squirrel running down the tree at dawn surprised itself by jumping on Stephen's leg. Stephen jumped to attention, not seeing his attacker, and Arelia froze in terror. The little squirrel scurried hurriedly up the trunk and peeked out at his intruders from the safety of his hole in the tree.

Arelia laughed at Stephen, lance drawn, defending them from a squirrel. Stephen wasn't amused.

Neither of them could believe they had slept through the night uninterrupted. Although Arelia was more rested, every inch of her body ached. She collected water from the stream to brew tea while Stephen laid out the last few bites of bread and dried meat. He cracked nuts that they had picked up along the way to supplement their breakfast.

"We had better be to the village soon, or we'll go hungry," Stephen commented lightly.

Arelia's stomach tightened. She remembered those terrifying days of fear and hunger before meeting Camellia and Cornelius.

"Is this the last of our food?" Arelia's pained expression gave away her fear.

Stephen drew his lance to make a point. "As long as this mighty hunter is here, we will not be hungry." Arelia laughed but wasn't completely convinced. "I have not wanted to roast meat with the scent, but I think we are far enough in now. I am not exactly sure, but I think we will be at the village before nightfall."

"Do you really think we are that close?" Arelia was excited now.

"Maybe even closer. Tonight you will eat real food and sleep in a real bed," Stephen promised.

"That sounds like heaven."

The thought of being in the village before nightfall made the walk easier for Arelia. She began to imagine the homecoming and the people who would greet them. Memories of being welcomed with Cornelius and Camellia gave her hope.

"Stephen, you have not told me much about your family except from when you were a little boy," Arelia coaxed.

"I have not seen them in almost two years. They are like most other villagers. My father farms and tends livestock, while my mother cooks, sews, and cares for the family. I have two sisters. One is nearly your age, and the other is only eleven. The rest you will have to see for yourself."

"You mentioned an aunt. Does she have a family?"

"No. My uncle died shortly after they married. She is well versed in things of the Church, herbs, and healing potions. She supports herself by healing people with herbs and potions, and she sells fine fabrics she weaves; she never remarried. Some people think she is crazy because her hut is set away from the village and she never wanted to remarry. She just enjoys the quiet of being alone."

Time seemed to pass more quickly than usual. When they stopped for the mid-day break, Stephen took out Arelia's torn dress. "We are very close now. All of this is familiar. You will need to put on your dress."

"But, Stephen, it's badly torn and wrinkled. I couldn't possibly meet your family in that."

He laughed. "I know Arelia, but my family may not understand if you come in dressed like a boy. We will have a big enough story to tell, but I think the dress will be easier to explain."

"What story will we tell about how thin I am? We never talked about it."

He shook out her dress and handed it to her. "Here is the explanation, which is true. They do not need to know how long you were there."

"Oh! How long do we tell them since the wolf attack?"

"Well,"—he thought through wrinkled brow—"what about a little less than a year?"

"Why did you take me?"

Stephen laughed. "I did not *take* you. If I could have taken you, I would have done it the first night I came to you! You chose to leave with me, remember?"

"Yes." She smiled. "I remember."

"All right then. It took months for your leg wounds to heal and that is when they offered you a job, sewing with Laura to make baby clothes."

She smiled. "I would have liked that."

"Unfortunately, you became very ill on and off for months. You had difficulty eating, and then you would be fine. After the babies were born and Marisa died, the head of the household staff decided that you were not strong enough for the job. That is when I decided to bring you to my family to help you heal and to marry. You were very thin when we left, and all the days in the forest have been difficult." He cocked his head and asked, "What do you think?"

"What I think does not matter. You know your parents. What do you think?"

"I think my parents are very loving and that they will want you to get well. I also think that Aunt Miriam will actually get you strong again.

"For now, you need to put that dress on. We do not want to run out of light. I promised you a meal and a bed tonight." Arelia did as Stephen suggested. To the embarrassment of both, he had to help her with the buttons on the back of her dress. His thick, clumsy fingers were little help, and Arelia had to finish the job as best she could. She was painfully aware of the wrinkles and the torn sleeve and hem. It wasn't at all how she imagined meeting Stephen's family.

"Are all the buttons done? I cannot go in only half-buttoned."

Looking at her in total disarray, Stephen could only smile at her concern.

"Oh, you! Give me some time at the stream, and then I will be ready." Arelia splashed cool, clean water on her face and arms to remove days of caked-on dust and dirt, and then she splashed her skirt with a little water, hoping the wrinkles would fall out as it dried. She remembered the frightening state of her hair when she arrived at the monastery and ran her fingers through her hair, picking out leaves and stems, and then worked to untangle knots in her normally silky hair.

Stephen smiled as he watched her nervously preparing to meet his family. "My family has a surprise in store today," he called to her.

"Oh dear, Stephen. How does my hair look?"

"You look fine, Arelia," he reassured. "Look. The ladies put a comb in the bag for you." He offered the comb. "You really look just fine."

"Oh, thank goodness. Those dear ladies thought of everything." Arelia smiled weakly. "Your family is going to think you have lost your senses when they see me," she whined. "I cannot even get this comb through my tangles."

Stephen put his arms around her. "You will have many years to show them your beautiful hair. They will understand when they hear about our trip." He took the comb out of her hand. "Time to get started; I do not want to spend another night in the woods."

When Arelia stood, a sharp pain shot through her side. Stephen had started walking and didn't notice as she fell back against a tree to catch her breath. Tears filled her eyes as she followed him along the stream.

"Mother, Father, this is the place for me. Please help me," she whispered. She walked along, praying the Our Father and the Angelic Salutation.

CHAPTER 33

Stephen finally noticed how far she had fallen behind.

"Are you all right?" Although his words were calm, fear and concern showed in his eyes as he helped her sit down. "You look very pale."

"I am in terrible pain. Let me rest just a minute."

Stephen ran to the stream for water. "Arelia, I know we are close. Would you like me to run up ahead and get a horse?"

"No, I am ready." She felt a warm trickle of blood on her leg and was afraid to be alone and prey for wolves again.

He put his hands under her elbows as she gripped his forearms supporting her weight as she stood. He finally picked her up to carry her, as she seemed to falter with each step. Her body tensed with pain every few minutes. Even stopping frequently for water didn't seem to help. After about an hour, Stephen pointed excitedly. "Look, there is my home."

Thick trees circled a scattering of thatch-roofed cottages. Arelia could make out a clearing with similar huts. Her eyes filled with tears of relief. "You can put me down now." She attempted a smile. "How do I look?" she asked.

Stephen just smiled without answering, smoothing away sweat-soaked hair from her face.

As they came closer, they could hear the familiar sound of children playing and a baby crying in the background. Arelia felt that she was really going home this time.

One of the children shouted, "Look! Who is that?"

All of the children froze as they watched the weary travelers enter the clearing. With rumors of new plague victims, unexpected travelers were unwelcome, especially those on foot. Several of the smaller children took cover in their huts, but some of the older boys recognized Stephen and ran toward them.

Stephen led Arelia toward his parents' hut, feeling the ever-increasing weight of her tired body against his side.

His mother came to the door to see what the children were yelling about. She stood motionless as she realized that it was her son who was helping a disheveled girl.

"Stephen!" she called as she ran to help him. "Jean, get your father quickly." Stephen's little sister ran toward the field. "Get your aunt, too."

They helped Arelia to a cot, and Stephen was gone immediately. She closed her eyes in relief, knowing they had finally reached their destination, not caring what she looked like or even who the woman was staring at her in alarm.

Stephen's father ran through the door and stopped at the cot with a puzzled expression.

"Who is this? Where is Stephen?"

Stephen's mother responded, "Stephen was helping this girl; he did not say who she is. He ran to get Miriam."

"Here, child, drink this water." When Arelia sat up with her help to drink the cool, refreshing liquid, the pain in her side intensified.

"Miriam, thank God you are here." Joan said as her sister-in-law hurried through the door on Stephen's heels.

Miriam studied Arelia's pale and pain-streaked face as she touched her forehead.

"Stephen, can you and your father carry her to my hut? She will need to rest in quiet."

"Should we move her now, Miriam?" Stephen's mother asked.

"Yes, I think she needs quiet, and all my herbs are there."

As Stephen lifted Arelia, Miriam made a quick note of the bloodstains on her petticoats, and quickly covered her with a blanket, lest the others notice. Jean was following closely behind as Stephen's other sister, Martha, came running toward them, past neighbors standing in clusters speculating about the stranger and Stephen's unexpected arrival.

"Jean, you and Martha stay home. I will send for you if I need something." Miriam said.

When Stephen laid Arelia on the cot near the fireplace in Miriam's hut, she said, "Now you go back to your parents. You must have a lot to tell them. The girl will be all right with me. I will call you soon." As she followed him to the door, she asked, "By the way, what is her name?"

"Arelia. Please take care of her, Miriam. We have taken great risks to get here. I have promised to take care of her and make her a part of my family."

Arelia strained to hear as they talked quietly by the door, but she was in too much pain to concentrate. Miriam's hand on Stephen's arm and the way she leaned in as she spoke to him with complete attention showed the love and trust that existed between them. She immediately felt comfortable with Miriam and appreciated the quiet and privacy of her hut. From the little she'd seen, his aunt reminded her of Sarah and of her own mother.

Hoping to understand the blood, Miriam questioned. "You *intend* to marry her, or you *have* married already?"

Stephen smiled. "No, we have not married yet. You must get her well first."

"I will do my best." Miriam opened the door. "Now go. Your parents must have a hundred questions. You will have to answer them for me later."

Stephen left hesitantly but knew Arelia was in the best of hands. Many people thought Miriam had magic powers, but Miriam said the only magic was in patience, love, and God's healing herbs.

"Arelia, I think the first thing you need to do is to put on clean clothes. Let us help you into something comfortable. Can you stand up?"

Arelia nodded weakly.

"Sit up slowly. And rest there a minute before you stand while I fill the basin for you. Promise not to stand until I am here to help you."

Arelia looked around the small hut while Miriam went for water. There was another cot in the corner on the opposite side of the hearth. Both cots were covered with finely woven wool blankets. A large spinning wheel stood before the fire, and behind that, a small loom rested against the wall under a shuttered window. Two small bales of wool, one stacked on top of the other, were propped in the corner behind the door. Half of a wall was covered with shelves containing odd shapes and sizes of wooden and glass jars. From the ceiling above the shelves hung bunches of drying plants and flowers. Arelia recognized many of these as the herbs the women in her village collected. A small table stood to the side of the spinning wheel near the fire. There was a rocking chair near the table and a bench long enough for two or three. Although the hut was simple, it felt peaceful and warm. Arelia had never experienced such tranquility even in her own home with her family.

"Now, young lady," Miriam said as she came through the door. "Let me help you get out of that filthy dress and get you cleaned up. Several boys are going to leave water outside the door for me so you can have a *real* bath later."

Arelia stood slowly but then doubled over in pain. Tears filled her eyes. Miriam watched drops of blood puddle at her feet as she helped her back onto the cot. "Have you had this much blood and pain before, child?"

"Only after drinking the bitter tea," Arelia answered innocently.

"And what purpose was the tea?"

"Bethany said it was to start my life blood."

"I see, . . . and who is Bethany?" continued Miriam, trying not to sound accusatory or overly curious, but she suspected she was dealing with a miscarriage.

Another sharp pain kept Arelia from responding. She pulled her legs to her chest. Water and blood stained the thick layers of her filthy dress and petticoats. "Arelia, lie back and help me get this dress off you. I will give you one of my night dresses and some cloths to soak up the blood."

Arelia lay back against the pillow on the narrow cot, fighting back sobs. Miriam quickly loosened the bodice of her dress and brought a cool, damp cloth to her.

"Here, child. Douse your face and neck with this cool cloth. I will prepare a mild tea for you to help you relax."

Arelia felt yet another sharp pain that lasted for a considerable amount of time. She called out in panic. Miriam came to her and held her delicate, damp hand.

"It will be over soon. I am with you," she consoled.

Another sharp pain came quickly, and then another. Miriam soaked several rags with the thick dark discharge and clumps of bloody tissue. Finally, Arelia lay back and fell asleep. Miriam left her undisturbed while she rekindled the fire and put pots of water to heat from buckets the boys had left outside the door. "Child, let me help you get out of that dress," she said as she gently awoke Arelia from a sound sleep.

There was a knock at the door. "Aunt Miriam," Stephen called as he opened the door just a bit, without walking in, "How is Arelia?"

Miriam caught tension in Arelia's tired face. She quickly covered her with a blanket.

"Pretend to sleep. Do not speak," she prompted. "Yes, Stephen," she greeted him warmly but stood in the doorway.

"Father said to bring the washtub. Do you want me to bring it in? We set jugs of water here."

"Thank you. You may bring the tub in. That is very kind; I was going to send for it. Tell John thank you."

"I want to check on Arelia. How is she?"

"I told you I would send for you. You must let her sleep. She has had quite an experience."

"Yes, I know it was a strain. It has been hours—she must be more rested by now." He stepped into the room, washtub in hand, but stopped when he saw her sleeping. "Is she all right?"

"She *will* be all right. I will talk with you *tomorrow*. You need sleep, too."

"Yes, I am very tired. Mother fed me like a king. All of the neighbors have been over. There has been no time to talk with Mother and Father privately," he explained.

"Then go and let Arelia sleep until morning."

Arelia didn't have to pretend to sleep; it had overtaken her as soon as Miriam pulled the blanket over her.

When the water came to a steam, Miriam filled the washtub with warm water. She sprinkled several different leaves into the water and put two more logs on the fire.

Miriam woke Arelia gently. "Child, can you try again? We need to get you clean; the warm water will be good for you." It was painful for Arelia to cooperate in removing her dress and getting into the tub, but once she was settled into the warm water, she was consumed with a feeling of serenity.

Miriam smiled as she watched strain and tension drain from the young woman's face.

"I have warm soup for you. Would you like to eat in the tub?" Miriam offered.

Arelia had not realized how hungry she was. "That would be wonderful but very unacceptable," she acknowledged. "I have never eaten in the tub before." She managed a slight smile.

"It will be good for you to soak in warm water. I will add more warm water as that cools; then you will sleep well."

Miriam handed Arelia a bowl of steamy potato and turnip soup and then gathered blood-soaked rags along with Arelia's dress and placed them in a basket to be burned in the morning.

"Miriam, I am so sorry to have made so much work for you," Arelia apologized, drinking her soup from a cup.

"Child, I am glad you were here and not in the woods when this happened," reassured Miriam. "You say this has happened before?"

"Yes, several times, but never without Bethany's tea," Arelia explained while taking a bite of potato.

"Who is Bethany?" Miriam asked, trying to piece the puzzle together.

"Bethany cared for me at the estate. She brought my food and water," Arelia answered.

Miriam quietly considered her reply but didn't continue to question her. She hummed while she found a large bar of lye soap and washed the empty soup bowl. Arelia lathered herself, occasionally grabbing the sides of the tub when pain struck. Miriam gently washed her tangled hair and combed out the knots. She poured clean water over her head and then emptied four large pitchers of dirty water from the tub and replaced four more with clean warm water. "The boys were very generous with water," Miriam noted with appreciation.

"Are you ready to sleep now?" Miriam asked as she brought Arelia a clean dry cloth and helped her out of the tub. "Put on this night dress and get into bed. I want you to sleep as long as possible tomorrow." She handed her several torn rags to soak up blood that would continue to drain.

"I have not met Stephen's parents. What must they think? Oh dear, Miriam, what must *you* think?" she asked with obvious concern and embarrassment.

"I think you have been through quite a bit that I will hear about later, but right now, you need plenty of sleep." Miriam removed the bloodstained blanket while Arelia dressed for bed and pulled a clean one from a wooden box under her bed.

Every bone in Arelia's body ached, but even the hard, hay-filled cot was comfortable with the prospect of safe, uninterrupted sleep.

Miriam watched Arelia sleep, knowing that there was much more to the girl than would ever be told. Blood and clotted discharge were not common and were never seen in girls who were not married.

❄

As the sun began to set, the neighbors made their way back to their huts. The excitement of the afternoon gave way to a quiet evening.

Everyone had brought something for the unexpected guests: eggs, cheese, cream, boiled potatoes, shelled nuts, and berries. The table had the appearance of a feast. Stephen had forgotten the generosity of villagers, which was far from the life of a soldier. He realized the only time he had seen so much food as a soldier was at Arelia's table from Bethany.

"All right, son. Now your mother and I want the real story . . . nothing about your horses running off, frightened by wolves. The neighbors might believe it, but I do not. Since when can you not catch a horse in the woods?" Stephen's father stoked the fire and added another thick log. Sparks popped and jumped around the hearth.

Stephen's mother set about storing food from the neighbors. "Girls, go to bed. Tomorrow will come early enough. We will prepare a celebration for Stephen and his friend."

The girls went behind the curtain begrudgingly to prepare for bed. Martha reappeared quickly. "Mother, I am old enough to stay up. I am not a child."

Stephen's mother laughed. "No, but you are still *my* child. Your father and Stephen want to talk in private. We will all have the morning together and, I assume, a long time after that." She glanced over her shoulder for Stephen's reaction, but he wasn't paying attention to woman talk.

"As you wish." Martha kissed Stephen on the cheek. "I am really happy you are home." She was sincerely happy.

"You cannot imagine how happy I am!" Stephen agreed.

"Now, son, I think you have a lot to tell," said Stephen's father as Martha disappeared behind the curtain. "Who is the girl?" His mother listened to the men talk as she cleared the table and put away the food. "Stephen, what is her name?"

"Mother, I told you, Arelia!"

"Her surname?"

"Davidson."

He desperately wanted to tell his father and mother everything about Arelia, but he didn't want to jeopardize her position in the family. He related the incident about the wolves and about bringing Arelia back to the estate. He didn't mention the amulet or Arelia's relationship to the Fairchild family. From their arrival at the estate, he talked about Sarah, Bethany, and Laura, with Arelia as one of the servants working along with Laura.

His father listened intently, feeling that part of the story was missing. "And why did you not ride in on horses? You have risked the girl's life by running away as you did."

"One of the older officers wanted to marry Arelia, and she despised the man. Sir Edward would have forced the arrangement if we had not left when we did."

Is this Sir Edward *Fairchild* you are speaking of?

Stephen nodded. "Yes."

"That is what I feared. Are they looking for you now?" Stephen's father asked the next logical question.

"Yes, sir, I fear they are," Stephen answered simply.

"And are you in danger?"

"Possibly."

"And the girl?"

"Sir Edward will want her back. Now that I am here, I realize I have put you in danger also," Stephen apologized.

"Stephen, answer me seriously. Do you love this girl?" Father asked, looking deeply into Stephen's eyes.

Stephen returned his gaze, strong and confident. "Yes, Father. I want her to be the mother of my children."

Stephen's mother stopped her work and sat next to him at the table. "Son, are you sure of this?" she questioned with great concern.

"Yes, Mother. I am sure," Stephen answered strongly with conviction.

"Well, it seems the boy knows what he wants and is willing to fight for it. Mother, I suggest we need to help him," John announced.

Joan sat quietly for a moment. "Stephen, you have told us only the name Arelia. What is her surname, and where is she from?"

He drew a deep breath, remembering what Arelia had told him. "Mother, I told you Davidson. She is Arelia Davidson from Ravenshire."

"Joan, I want you to sleep now. We have plans to make tomorrow, and I fear we do not have much time." John Wingate lay in bed while one unasked question after another flashed through his mind. "Why did the soldiers bring her to Faircastle rather than to her own village?" "Where are her parents?" "Why would Edward Fairchild care if a servant ran away?" "What will happen with Stephen's commission?" "How could she have gotten so thin and sick in the couple of days it took to get to the village?" "How would a servant girl meet and fall in love with a soldier?"

Joan tossed and sighed under the covers next to him. John wondered if the same questions were keeping Joan awake, but he would never ask.

Sir Edward couldn't rest until he had news of Stephen and Arelia. He surprised the captain by walking into the camp after dark.

"Captain, what news do you have for me?" he barked.

"Sire," the captain responded by jumping to his feet, knocking his cup of whiskey into the fire. The dark liquid burst into flames and sent a stream of steam into the air. "I have not heard from any of the men."

Sir Edward glared at the captain as if he were waiting for another response. The captain stood before his glare, not knowing what to expect from such unlikely behavior. "Sire, I am sure one of the troops will return tomorrow. They have a large area to search."

"I am tired of waiting, Captain. Do you understand the importance of finding Arelia and the officer?" Sir Edward spoke through clenched teeth.

"Yes, sire." The captain wasn't a man to back down. His determination and blind drive had earned his position. But this time he knew he was faced with an obstacle he couldn't easily overcome. In truth, he had lost interest in Arelia, who was probably dead, and Stephen, a lovesick, misguided kid. He would enjoy the hunt, but his passion was exactly that, hunting something that was taken from him—nothing more. He would not be outsmarted by a young officer if it came down to it.

Sir Edward stood a foot in front of the captain. His breath reeked of wine and strong cheese.

"Do you really understand?" he repeated.

"Sire, I understand Arelia's significance. If she is not dead, we will bring her back."

"Dead?" repeated Sir Edward, brought to his senses by a seemingly new idea.

"Yes, sire. The women seem to think Arelia was not well enough to make such a journey."

Sir Edward seemed satisfied with this new information. Sitting down on a stump, staring into the flames, he said, "Have them bring her body to me. My father will want some sort of proof." He snickered. "How odd that she would be done in by her own careless hand." He laughed loudly, as if amused by some private joke. "Marisa would see the humor of it. I think this would satisfy her." He sighed, laughing as he walked away.

Even the captain was put off by Sir Edward's sick reaction.

CHAPTER 34

Havenshire, Norwich County

While everyone in the village slept, Miriam sat at her spinning wheel, spinning a fine, soft thread. Because she spent so much time at her wheel and loom, she spun the most delicate threads and wove the most beautiful cloth. She was known in several of the larger estates for her fine fabrics. Buyers often came to the village in hopes of acquiring large sections of cloth for their ladies.

Miriam found spinning and weaving a time for quiet, contemplative thought. Her fingers wound and twisted the thread without effort. She stretched, pulled, and twisted the fibers, eventually turning out long continuous threads. *The experiences of our lives are like fibers that intertwine to make a story; the time we spend working the fiber and the effort we concentrate on smoothing out the imperfections will determine its quality and beauty. Some fibers knot, causing imperfections; others stretch to a fine soft filament. The thread is made of fine and coarse fibers, but from a distance, they simply appear as a single cord. If we work out the knotted fiber until it is smooth, we will have fine, soft fabric. If we ignore the knots and spin them into thread, the finished fabric will not be as beautiful. If we work through the "knots" in our lives and smooth them out, our lives will be more beautiful. Every knot can be smoothed out with patience and persistence.*

She turned toward the young woman sleeping peacefully on the cot. "Arelia, you are working on coarse, knotted fibers now. If you let me, I will teach you to soften them to make a beautiful fine thread from which you can weave a beautiful cloth."

Miriam walked out into the night to feel the cool, crisp air and the healing power of God. She looked into a clear sky, as the stars seemed to welcome her. "I am woven into a coarse cloth. I need your help. I do not have strength without you."

Morning came quickly to Stephen's family. "Quiet, girls, your brother needs his sleep. Jean, go gather as many eggs as you can. Ask your father to bring in the milk."

"Mother," Martha interrupted her. "What did Stephen say about the girl? Who is she?"

Joan didn't want to take time to explain everything to Martha. Besides, she wasn't sure of the story herself and didn't want any of it repeated in the village. Many questions were left unanswered in her mind, and the information they were given raised more questions than were answered.

"Martha, I do not have time to talk now. Go help your sister gather eggs." Martha knew this was not the time to push for answers.

Joan kept herself as busy as possible to keep from thinking about the girl. *Why was there so much blood on her skirt? Is Stephen having relations with her when they are obviously not married?* She reflected on images of the girl's blood-stained dress but did not really want to know.

"Good morning," Stephen greeted, interrupting his mother's thoughts. "Something smells good in here." His mother smiled slightly over her shoulder but didn't stop her work or even greet him.

"Do I smell fresh bread already?"

"Yes, it is on the hearth," she responded coolly.

"How have you had time to bake bread? It is hardly daylight," he asked.

"Sleep escaped me. Your father is outside. You should talk to him."

Stephen was a little surprised by his mother's cool response. She was normally a very warm, loving person.

"Mother, are you all right?" he asked with sincere concern.

She turned toward him with tears in her eyes. "Stephen, who is this girl you brought home?"

"I told you about her last night," he answered.

"Did you?" she challenged.

"What do you want to know?" he answered defensively. He turned from her and walked to the fire to avoid her challenging stare.

"What should I know?" Her voice was angry and agitated.

"Mother," he responded firmly to her now. "I have told you all you should know."

"All I *should* know!" She started her busywork again. Stephen was surprised at her reaction and was not looking forward to talking to his father.

He walked out into the cool, damp morning as Martha and Jean came in carrying the eggs.

"Put them in the bowl," he heard his mother snap.

His father was talking to a small group of men and waved Stephen over. Stephen braced himself for whatever his father had to offer.

"Hello, Stephen," Mr. Hawthorn greeted warmly. "We are happy that you have come back. I am sorry that your situation is not the best."

"Thank you, sir."

"Stephen, your father tells us that you need our help. We have been discussing a plan," said Mr. Shoemaker, a large, thoughtful, quick-minded man who always seemed to come up with good ideas. He was known as someone who could always find a solution if you were stumped.

At that moment, Stephen noticed the door to Miriam's hut open. She was carrying a basket overfilled with blood-soaked rags. He could see Arelia's dress in the pile. He ran to her. "What is this?" he demanded. Stephen's father was close behind.

Miriam closed the door behind her. "Stephen, Arelia is sleeping soundly. Did she tell you about her pains?"

"Yes, but I could not stop. I needed help. We had to get here quickly," he defended.

"I know, I know. You did the right thing. Arelia lost a large amount of blood last night. She needs plenty of sleep and hot, rich soup to heal. You can help me by not disturbing her, and do not say anything to anyone." She looked over at her brother, John, with the same warning. He understood the need for total secrecy.

Stephen felt all the tension of the trip coming to a peak. He had not expected his mother's cold reaction—and now to think that Arelia could have died because of what he had put her through. His eyes filled with tears.

"Stephen, this is not over for you yet. I know you are tired, but you must finish what you have begun," his father interrupted, putting his hand firmly on his son's shoulder. "Miriam, I think this dress and these rags may be exactly what we need," he continued.

Stephen looked up with a puzzled expression.

"Son, as a soldier, would you continue to search for a dead lady?"

"Of course not!" he replied. Stephen was too tired to follow his father's train of thought. "Is Arelia asleep?" he asked Miriam, reaching for the door.

"Yes, but you can only see her if you do not wake her." Miriam smiled and touched his arm gently to calm him.

"What would you like me to do with these rags?" she asked John, after the door closed behind Stephen.

"I am going to bury them near the burial plot. Mr. Carpenter is making a box today for a coffin. The dress will confirm her death, if necessary."

Stephen stood quietly over Arelia's cot. *How many times have I watched you sleep?* He studied her even breath and ashen complexion. *You will be safe soon.*

Her face was so pale and thin. She seemed so fragile, almost childlike under the heavy blanket; her hair was clean with dark locks laying softly over her shoulders. She looked like an angel. His tears flowed freely. "I hope I have done the right thing," he whispered.

Stephen's father called in a hushed voice from the door, but Stephen was so engrossed by his thoughts that he didn't hear. "Stephen." His father put his arm around his shoulder. "You feel deeply about her?"

"Yes, sir."

"I almost lost your mother in childbirth before you were born. Miriam stopped her bleeding to save her, but we lost the baby. I stood over her just as you are now. I thought my world would end. Son, let me help you and Arelia now."

Stephen rested his head on his father's arm and cried. He was no longer a soldier avoiding the enemy, but a boy turning to his father for help. "I fear I have not done the right thing."

"Of course you do. You may never know. But the job you started is not done yet. You are a soldier in the heat of battle, maybe more now than ever."

"I thought it would be over when we got here," Stephen explained.

"Only the first part is over. Do you still want Arelia as your wife?" his father questioned.

"Yes, I have told you." Stephen's voice was strained, on the verge of anger.

"You saw the basket of blood-soaked rags. Are you sure?"

Stephen set his jaw as if challenged to fight. "I am sure."

"Then you must continue on for her, but the first thing I want you to do is sleep. You are too exhausted to help now."

"Father, I cannot sleep. What would you have me do?"

John smiled at his son's revived energy. "Mr. Shoemaker has a plan that will work. We will explain as we go; but first, go with Mr. Hawthorn to investigate the caves on the cliff. Choose one for you and Arelia to live in for several days. I will work with the men on our plan here."

As they walked into the clearing, Stephen expressed his concern. "Mother is very cold toward me. I never expected that. I thought she would help Arelia and love her as I do."

"You have a lot to learn about women, son. Do not worry. Your mother has imagined that you would come home to wed Madeline. She has spent many hours in the garden with Madeline's mother planning your life. You have plenty of other things to be concerned about now. I will take care of your mother. You know, that will be the hardest job." He winked at Stephen. "You thought Sir Edward would be your strongest opponent." He laughed and slapped Stephen good-naturedly on the back.

Stephen and Mr. Hawthorn set off immediately to find a hiding place.

"We should find a place some distance away," Mr. Hawthorn suggested. "You will need to keep enough supplies with you for several days. We will send some of the boys to replenish your water and supplies, if necessary, and tell you when it is safe to return."

After hiking and investigating every cave, they discovered a cave that appeared shallow at first glance but expanded into a large room through a second, narrow opening.

While they explored the dark opening, Stephen related his experience with the bear during his last stay in a cave. Although Stephen failed to see the humor in nearly losing his life, the older man laughed until he cried.

They experimented with camouflaging the interior opening of the seemingly shallow cave. They brought in large stones which they stacked at the opening, but those seemed to attract attention. They brought in brush but realized that would be unnatural and even more obvious. Not knowing how much time they had, they finally decided that they needed to go back for Arelia and that Stephen could experiment with the camouflage during their extended stay. There wasn't much time.

Mr. Hawthorn suggested that they return to the village before dark and bring several men back with supplies the next morning. Stephen was beginning to feel comfortable with his decision to return home. He had forgotten the security of having the support of common men in village life. As a soldier, he had never felt that support. Although all of the soldiers basically had the same goal, instructions came from higher up—from men who made decisions without consulting those who would implement them. The foot soldiers only followed directions but were never part of planning: Their motivations came from fear of punishment, not from a desire to be truly helpful or from comradeship.

On returning to the village, Stephen went directly to Miriam's hut where Arelia had just wakened from nearly twenty hours of sleep. She was dressed in one of Miriam's dresses—more suited to the women of the village. She was sitting at the table while Miriam combed her long, straight hair. Her face lit up in a warm, loving smile when Stephen came in. He stood silently and took in the beauty before him.

"Do you not have anything to say, or are you just going to stand there?" Arelia smiled.

"You are so beautiful," he responded.

Arelia smiled, actually feeling beautiful, but didn't know how to respond.

Miriam set down the comb and settled at her spinning wheel, watching the two young people, remembering feelings from twenty years earlier. All her doubts and concerns about Arelia's suitability from the night before vanished.

"Stephen, will you join us for supper?" Miriam asked.

"Yes, I would love to. What can I do to help?"

Miriam laughed. "I can tell you have been away. Not many men offer to help with supper. A soldier's life is very different, I see?"

"It is a different life that I do not want to live again," he responded seriously.

"Arelia, stir the potatoes and carrots on the fire. I will brew tea," she instructed.

Stephen watched Arelia at the large hearth in her simple village dress. Before now, he had not understood how truly beautiful she was. From the first time he saw her, she was struggling for survival, first physically, and then emotionally and spiritually. He had never seen her in a normal setting, doing normal things. Again he thought, *I have done the right thing.*

Arelia smiled over her shoulder, aware of his gaze. "What have you done today?" she asked.

"I found a place for us to hide."

Fear and concern crossed her face. "Hide?"

"Yes," he answered. "Sir Edward's soldiers will probably come for us."

Arelia sat hard on the bench, eyes wide with fear. "How long must we hide? When will they come?"

"I do not know for sure. We may need to hide for weeks," he answered hesitantly, realizing he had blurted it out too quickly.

Arelia looked down, fighting back tears. *I will not cry. I am strong.* She raised her eyes confidently. "Did you find a safe place?"

Stephen was pleased with her quick recovery. "Yes, a very safe place."

Miriam was concerned but did not interrupt.

He placed his hand over hers. "We will gather supplies tomorrow. Some of the men are scouting for soldiers. We will probably need to leave tomorrow but not later than the next day."

Arelia's heart sank, but she said in an even tone, "So we will have one more restful day before we begin. I will enjoy that."

She looked warmly toward Miriam. "Miriam, you have been so kind. I will miss you."

Miriam laughed. "You will not be gone that long. We will be busy here convincing the soldiers to never look for you again."

Stephen was surprised. "How do you know that?"

"You have forgotten how the men in this village work. Your father was here last night. I have Arelia's things prepared." She pointed to a box near the door.

The next hour was spent over a delicious, finely seasoned meal of fresh, warm bread, eggs, and hot, steamy vegetables. Miriam brought Stephen up to date on the events and lives of people in the village. Both Stephen and Arelia appreciated that she didn't ask about their lives before coming home.

"There is one thing I do not understand. You seem to have escaped Black Death. How?" Stephen was curious to know.

"Only by the grace of God. Looking back, it seems we were the last to fall. We had only twelve deaths before the first hard freeze. Twelve is too many, but we heard of entire villages being wiped out. No one knows for sure, but some say something in the ice stopped the death. We praise God for saving us."

Stephen realized it was completely dark. "I had better get home. Father will want to hear the news." Stephen wanted to stay, but as his father had said the battle was not over.

The village was filled with the familiar smell of smoke from chimneys and baked bread, so unlike the soldiers' camp. The night was still and quiet; crickets chirped, and an owl occasionally announced its presence.

As Stephen pushed open the door to his parents' hut, an angry voice asked, "Where have you been? Mr. Hawthorn was here hours ago." Stephen was startled at his mother's angry tone.

"I was at Miriam's checking on Arelia."

"It certainly took you long enough," she retorted. "Dinner has been waiting."

From the look on his mother's face and the tone of her voice, Stephen knew enough to stay quiet. "It smells wonderful."

"It should. The girls and I have been cooking all day. It has been two years since we have seen you, you know," she said angrily.

His mother's manner was completely alien to Stephen. Two years ago, he had left a warm, loving woman who wanted his best interest. He didn't even know the woman he had returned home to.

His sisters seemed oblivious to their mother's sharp tongue. His father sat by the fire, reading a worn and often read New Testament. "Son, Mr. Hawthorn said you found a secret cave," he said in order to change the subject.

Stephen joined his father by the fire as the girls helped his mother set out the food.

"Several men went out today scouting for soldiers along the creek," he continued. "We should have ample warning in time for you and Arelia to hide."

"What did you say?" Mother's sharp tone chilled the room. Even his sisters stopped to listen.

"Stephen and Arelia will have ample time to hide," Father repeated.

"My son is not going to hide in a cave with some girl we do not even know. What will people think? There is *already* talk about their journey here and *that girl's blood-soaked dress*. I will not have it!"

"Mother!" corrected Father. "Stephen and Arelia are in danger. They will hide."

"Only the girl is in danger. Stephen can stay," reminded Mother.

Stephen was starting to get angry. He thought that he had left his angry, uncaring environment behind. "Mother, I risked everything to bring Arelia here. I will follow through with my decision. I have no intention of staying here without Arelia or of ever returning to the Fairchild Estate."

"You are right. You risked everything—for what?" she demanded.

"Time to eat," Father cut in, trying to distract the interrogation. "Mother, this is a feast. You have outdone yourself."

"And me, Father," said Jean, wanting attention.

"And you." Father hugged the young girl as she basked in his affection. "And Martha," he smiled her way.

Stephen looked at all the food and felt sick. He had eaten more than enough at Miriam's. Besides, the conversation with his mother had diminished any appetite he might have had.

Mother sat stoically during dinner. Stephen couldn't believe the woman she had become. The girls, on the other hand, laughed and talked loudly, vying for attention.

"Stephen, your mother has a very good point about you and Arelia being alone in the cave. That will never do. If Arelia is to be accepted here, we must honor basic rules of decency. We do not want her to be disgraced."

Joan fought to hold her tongue.

"But, Father," interrupted Stephen, "we must hide."

"You are right, Stephen," Father agreed. "But you do not have to hide alone. Martha can stay with you."

Stephen's mother jumped to her feet, showing her shock and disapproval. "Why should Martha be forced to hide in a cave? She has done nothing wrong."

Martha saw things differently. It sounded like an adventure to her. "It is all right, Mother. Stephen needs me now."

"And I need you also. This house is not easy to keep," insisted her mother.

"I will help you, Mother," offered Jean.

John was exasperated with his wife's reactions. She had always kept her family's best interest in mind. "That is right, Mother. There will only be three of us here. Jean will be able to help. Martha is going with Stephen."

Joan knew well enough to stay quiet when her husband used that tone.

"I will allow it, but I do not approve." She glared at her husband.

The only other time John had seen this kind of reaction from his wife was when Stephen had announced he was going to join the Fairchild army. She had ground her heels into the dirt and made her position known. It was only after weeks of discussion that Stephen had left the village. She had hugged him warmly when he left, with tears cascading down her worn face. Looking back on that occasion, John realized that her judgment might have been right. Here Stephen was back home, hiding from the very soldiers he had fought her to join.

Arelia spent her evening basking in the peace and tranquility of Miriam's home. She stood at the spinning wheel as Miriam spun the fine, soft, woolen thread.

"I do not see how you make such fine threads. My mother and I spun much of our own wool, but I have never seen thread like this."

"My threads certainly did not look like this when I first started. After my husband died, I spent many long hours at this wheel trying to sort out my life. My parents and almost everyone else said I was still young and should marry again." She stopped spinning and laughed softly. "By that time, I had been married long enough to realize that being married was not always easy. I did not want to get married just to have someone to take care of me. I was already useful for my knowledge of herbs and reasoned that I could take care of myself. No one understood my decision.

"Since that time, I have come to realize that you do not marry someone you can be happy with forever; you marry someone you can stand to stay with even when you or he is unhappy. I guess I never found anyone else whom I

336

loved enough to be happy with *and* unhappy with too. Life is about good times and bad. Young people do not always know that."

She smiled at Arelia, seeing that the girl was trying to make sense out of what she said. "I think that you are right. My parents were happy most of the time, but some of the time either one or both struggled. When a crop was bad or livestock died, my father would be nervous and irritable. Mother tried to make him feel better by pointing out the good things we had. She worked hard to stretch what we did have until the next crop came in."

"That is exactly what I mean," agreed Miriam. "You have to love someone enough to help him through hard times, because most of the time, his hard times become yours. You could marry *anyone* if your life promised to be happy all the time."

Arelia continued with her thoughts. "When Mother lost a baby, Father took over chores in the house when ladies in the village were not around. She was depressed for a long time and could not do things she needed to. Father sometimes cried with her and never complained about things that were not done."

"They must have loved each other very much," confirmed Miriam.

"When we got older, there were nights when I could hear them arguing. I never could make out what they were saying and did not want to. Some nights they would go outside so they would not wake us. Some mornings they would still be angry, and others they would be all right."

"You are fortunate to have these memories, Arelia. Not all children have good examples of marriage. Many children grow up in homes where their mother is not supported and has no right to address her concerns. There are many marriages where there is no respect for each other. I saw too many of these homes to want to remarry. I was fortunate that I married a man who loved me enough to stand beside me during bad times. I did not know if I would be so fortunate again,"

"Do you have children?" questioned Arelia.

"I was with child when Carl died. We were walking along the stream looking for a place for a picnic. He was picking up rocks to skim across the creek. He had skipped one four times and was looking for the perfect rock to skip five. We were so happy. He reached down to pick up the perfect rock and did not see a snake curled under the rock next to it. He was struck twice before we knew what happened. We started back to the village, but he fell. I started running, not realizing how far we had gone, but by the time I got back with help, he was dead.

"I guess my running and crying was too much for the baby. I got sick and lost the baby a few days later. I had only a few months left to go." Arelia saw that Miriam was still deeply grieved by her loss. "It was a girl."

"I am so sorry." Arelia didn't know what to say.

"Sometimes things happen that we have no control over. Our lives can change quickly without our permission."

"What did you do?"

"I did not want to stay here. My home, the people, everything was the same, but my family was gone. I could not face it. I was really good with the wheel and loom and had already sold a few pieces of fabric, and so Joan, who was my closest friend even back then, suggested that I go to a manor nearby to sell more fabric."

"Did you go?"

"Yes, I never worked in a castle like you did, but I did work in a manor house, Moreland Manor, for Sir Reginald Moreland and Lady Abigail. They were newly married, and Lady Abigail was setting up their manor house in grand style.

"When John brought me there to show my few pieces, Lady Abigail asked if I would stay to weave linens for the house. I spent the next three years there spinning and weaving.

"Sir Reginald traveled to France and London often and brought back elegant fabrics from all over the world, even from the Orient. I learned to copy some of the colors and, if I do say so myself, perfected my craft.

"By the time Lady Abigail became pregnant with her first daughter, she had enough linens for two houses, and there was not much left for me to do. Sir Reginald knew that I had lost my husband and daughter and asked if I would like to become nursemaid for the baby.

"I had already decided it was time to head home. He was such a nice man to all the servants. We laughed sometimes when he would go into the kitchen while we ate to see if all our needs were being met. We decided that Lady Abigail was so socially conscious that he worried she was working us too hard.

She would have been mortified to know he had set foot in the kitchen and actually spoken casually with the servants. Even though we were all about the same age, we tended to think of him as a father rather than our master.

"Anyway, I could not accept his offer. I declined when he and Lady Abigail were together, hoping he would buffer any response she might have. She was a good woman but was so concerned about how things *should* work that she often put her more caring feelings aside. Things do not always turn out as we would like.

"One old woman on the kitchen staff told me that a woman alone was worth nothing and that I would end up as a beggar on the side of the road or dead in the forest. I was thankful for Sir Reginald and Lady Abigail because they dismissed her comments as nonsense.

"He arranged an escort to take me home, and the morning I left, he gave me advice that set me on solid ground. He said, 'Being rich is simply knowing how to manage your resources. You will never do without if you recognize what you have and use it well.' It was so simple. On the way home, I thought about what my resources were: my family, my skill in spinning and weaving, my knowledge of Scripture, knowing how to read, and practice in using healing herbs. I realized that I had a lot of resources, and that I had people who cared about me and a God who loved me.

"Because he told me those few simple words, I had the wherewithal to take care of myself. Otherwise, if I had listened to that old woman, I may have seen myself as alone and helpless and ended up that way."

"That is what happened when my family died," agreed Arelia. "I was left alone with only memories."

"I am sorry, dear. I did not know. But you are still young. Was it the plague?"

Arelia related her story from the plague to the wolf attack. Miriam made chamomile tea while Arelia connected the events of her traumatic past. They sipped the hot, steamy brew, warming their hands on the cup and their feet from the heat of blue and yellow flames dancing off stout logs.

"Poor child. You have had a very difficult life for someone so young." Miriam was genuinely sympathetic, remembering the lives lost in their own village and the struggle in pulling families back together. She thought about the orphans in her own community who were so lovingly taken in by those who had lost their own children.

Arelia wanted to continue and tell Miriam about her life at the castle. She studied the woman's face, feeling that she could be trusted.

"Were you ever married?" Miriam asked casually.

Arelia was taken aback by this question. "No," she answered flatly.

Miriam took the cue. "Well, child. I do not know about you, but I am ready for bed. Tomorrow will be very busy for both of us."

Arelia could not understand how she could be sleepy after so much sleep, but she quickly put on her bedclothes, too. Miriam blew out the candles on the table, leaving only the glow from the fireplace to light the room.

"Good night, Miriam. Thank you for everything."

"Good night, child."

Miriam lay in bed thinking about the struggles this young girl had been through in her young life. *She has more to tell*, she thought as she drifted off to sleep.

CHAPTER 35

 "Captain, our men have found debris from a washed-up boat and scraps from a woman's dress. There is no sign of bodies; it seems the two have been washed out to sea."

Captain Hardgrave was excited to report the news and put the whole episode to rest. Since the disappearance, Sir Edward had become obsessed with the search; he showed a cunning and cruelty that the captain thought had come only from Marisa. Sir Edward hounded everyone about news or any clues they might have. He even took to asking servants what they knew. The dark circles around his deep-set eyes told of sleepless nights walking the floor, waiting for information. Hardgrave was put off and puzzled by the uncharacteristic behavior; the implication being that he did not trust the captain.

"And?" interjected Sir Edward.

"Sire?" The captain did not know what he was asking.

"And where are the bodies?" he insisted.

"We do not have bodies, sire," he repeated softly for a man of such great force, realizing he needed more proof he could not give.

"What did you say?" Sir Edward asked angrily.

"We do not have bodies, sire," the captain said more forcefully.

"Captain, I am worried about my army. Do you know why?" asked Sir Edward scornfully.

"No, sire," he answered, holding his anger in check.

"Do you want to know why?" he shouted again.

"Why, sire?" the captain asked the obvious question.

"Because you are an imbecile!" he shouted.

The captain stood his ground but wanted to drive his sword through the man's chest.

"How do you *know* they are dead if you did not find the *bodies*? We were tricked once by horse tracks. Do you think that he could not trick us again?" Edward's tone was acidic, standing in the captain's face, glaring into his eyes. It was all the captain could do to keep from pushing him. Hardgrave knew he was right, which upset him all the more.

Sir Edward gained his composure and walked toward the window. "Captain, let me explain something to you that you might be too dense to understand." He focused on the waves as he gathered his thoughts and then turned to face his subject. "Lady Marisa was a strong woman who wanted nothing more than the best for her children. She has two; one of them is my heir. I want my name to carry on, and it will through my son, my name and undivided property. It will remain that way unless there is another heir through Arelia. Do you understand?"

"Of course." Hardgrave resented the insult, veiled within the elementary lesson.

"I do not want my son to find twenty years from now that Arelia has produced a son who will threaten to take his inheritance. Marisa was most clear in this. I did not completely understand the significance at the time, but I have and will have only one heir.

"If I do not have her body, I do not have the confidence of knowing my heir is protected; therefore, I need a body, or we will continue to search. My estate is only safe if she is here within my walls or proven dead. There is no other option."

"What will you have me do?" the captain asked through clenched teeth. The captain's uppermost thought and desire was to put *this man* to his rest.

Sir Edward walked toward him. The captain could smell his breath and turned from its stench. "I will have you go to his village and bring them back. Do you know where he is from?"

"Yes, sire."

"Why are you not there now, Captain?"

The captain put his hand on the sheath of his sword. Sir Edward grabbed his hand. "If you are as stupid as I think, you will use your sword. But if you value your life, you will do the job ahead of you." Sir Edward spoke with a sick smile, almost wishing the captain would draw his sword.

The two men froze, each considering the challenge. The captain removed his hand from his sheath. He had no fear of Edward Fairchild, but he knew that Edward's father would not rest until his son's murderer was punished. "Will you join us in the search, sire?"

"Do you need me to do your job in the field, too?" asked Sir Edward again with his sick smile and sarcastic tone.

"My men and I are capable," came Hardgrave's seething response.

"Take enough men with you to send one back to report to me each day. I will expect the first soldier to return in three days. Is that clear?"

"You will get your report." The captain turned and left the parlor to go to the stable.

"Jacob, I need twenty horses ready to ride without delay. Prepare five more horses with rations for us for ten days. I will return immediately," the captain commanded.

"And where is your trip to, sir?" Jacob inquired casually.

"To Officer Wingate's village," he replied as he walked out of the stable.

Jacob thought for a moment and then called, "Joseph, come quickly. You must go to your Mother. Tell her about the captain's search. I will send you with the troop to tend the horses. Go and prepare your things quickly."

Joseph ran to the babies' room. Bethany was rocking one of the sleeping infants, and Sarah was stitching a tiny garment. "Mother, the captain is going to Stephen's village," he said as he burst into the room. Bethany and Sarah were startled by his news. The tiny baby boy began to cry.

"Is there some way to warn them?" asked Sarah nervously.

"There is no time, Mother. We are to leave within hours. I am going with them to tend the horses. I may not be back for weeks," Joseph explained.

"Sarah," interrupted Bethany, "Stephen is very smart. He got Arelia out of here. Surely, he must realize Sir Edward will search for them."

"That is true, Mother. I must pack my things quickly. They will need my help with the horses."

After Joseph left, the women sat quietly, considering the danger Stephen and Arelia would face.

"Do you think Arelia is still alive, Bethany?"

"I have thought a lot about it. She had several days to rest and had regained much of her strength. I think, with Stephen's help and encouragement, she has a good chance. Wherever she is now cannot possibly be as bad as life was for her here, Sarah."

"That is true. I wish there were something we could do." Again the women were quiet, thinking about what needed to be done.

"Bethany! I have Arelia's amulet!" Sarah remembered with a start. "I must get it to her."

"Joseph can bring it to her."

"Hopefully, he will see her. If he does see her, the captain will see her too," reminded Bethany.

Again, the women were quiet.

"If they go to the village, he could leave it with Stephen's mother. If Arelia is alive, she can give it to her," Bethany thought aloud.

"I will get the sack to Joseph." Sarah put her sewing aside and hurried to her room.

Joseph was already back in the stable, having gathered his few things. Sarah was not prepared for the confusion there. The captain was busy instructing servants about packing horses and checking supplies. A dozen soldiers were packing the horses' saddlebags. Jacob had brought out a small cart to fill with extra supplies, reasoning that a cart would slow the troop through the woods. The captain rejected the idea immediately but was rethinking his hasty decision, considering the load of provisions.

Sarah felt the small sack in her pocket. How would she get this to her son without the captain's notice? *Had he seen the bag before? He knew Arelia had the amulet.*

She turned quickly and headed toward the kitchen.

"Mother," Laura called as she entered the large, busy room. "The soldiers are going to the village to find Arelia." Laura was near tears again.

"Settle down, Laura. Quiet," cautioned Sarah. "I know. Find a small grain bag for me. Quickly!"

Laura hurried to a large pantry and returned with a small burlap sack.

"Good morning, ladies," Sarah greeted the women as she gathered a loaf of bread, a chunk of cheese, and some carrots. "You know Joseph is going with the soldiers. I thought he would appreciate an extra treat from his mother."

The women laughed. "You spoil him, Sarah. He is nearly a man, you know."

"Yes, and he will never be too much of a man to lose my motherly attention." Sarah laughed.

"You had better pack plenty. The way those soldiers eat, there may be nothing left for him; he may starve," one woman offered.

On the way to the stable, Sarah shoved Arelia's soft dark bag into the bottom of the burlap sack. She greeted Captain Hardgrave when she walked toward Joseph.

"Joseph," she called. "I have something for you." Joseph was preparing his own horse. The captain watched Sarah intently.

"What is it you have for your son, woman?" the captain asked suspiciously.

Sarah hoped that she was masking her nervousness. She opened the bag casually. "I have a few carrots, bread, and cheese. I am afraid while he tends the horses, he might miss a few meals. Now, Joseph, please do not eat this in one day." She laughed and then looked at the captain. "Sire, would you like me to prepare such a sack for you?"

The captain seemed put off by her offer. "My men provide my meals," he said arrogantly.

"Captain," Jacob called to distract him from Sarah. "Have you decided about the cart?"

"I am sorry, Captain. I will tell my son goodbye quickly and then be out of your way," Sarah reassured.

When Hardgrave left hearing range, Sarah instructed Joseph. "I know you will not see Arelia but watch for Stephen's mother. There is a small dark sack in the bottom of this bag with her amulet. Never let anyone see the bag but give it to Stephen's mother for Arelia. She should have it for their children. Explain that it is Arelia's Fairchild legacy."

"You can count on me, Mother," Joseph said as he hugged her goodbye.

CHAPTER 36

Arelia was not aware of all the preparations for their trip into hiding. Several women had brought bread, cheese, and vegetables for the young couple. Stephen's mother quickly announced to each of them that Martha would be with the couple the entire time.

Stephen and his old friend James packed horses with thick blankets with which to make up three beds as comfortable as possible, while John Wingate and Mr. Hawthorne packed supplies they felt the three would need: candles, a small shovel, live embers loosely wrapped in heavy leather, a sharp knife, rope, and a snare for catching small animals. The village seemed to have new energy as they plotted their scheme. As villagers were usually on the short end of the stick, there was little opportunity to get the best of royalty; now it was their turn. In light of the fact that Sir Edward raised taxes, even after hardship from the plague, there was great satisfaction in helping Stephen. Having been through so much together, they were willing to risk their lives for their neighbors. Only the children were left uninformed.

The men decided it would be necessary to have a funeral for Arelia after they left for the cave. Mr. Shoemaker reasoned that if any of the soldiers questioned the women and children, they could relate the story honestly with similar details. The children would witness the full scene played out without being aware of the plan. Fortunately, with so many minds, everything seemed to be covered.

"Father, have any of the scouts returned?" Stephen asked after he and James returned from the cave.

"No, I think you will be safe one more night, but after that, you cannot delay. We do not want to cut your escape close. Tomorrow is the latest for you to leave."

"Good. I want Arelia to rest a little longer. She deserves a good rest," Stephen reflected aloud.

"And what do you deserve?" his mother asked angrily, packing up supplies for them to load. Stephen ignored her question.

"Mother, thank you for organizing our food." Stephen tried to distract her from her anger.

"Martha handled the food. I have enough to do to take care of my own family without getting caught up with strangers."

"Come outside, son. We need to check on everyone's progress," Stephen's father deflected, trying to ease the tension.

Stephen turned to his mother when he got to the doorway. He wanted to talk to her but did not know what to say.

"Stephen, come here," called his father. "I have never really met your lady. Go with me to Miriam's." John smiled and patted his son on the back. With his father's support, Stephen's disposition changed as they crossed the clearing.

"Son, you must learn to keep your eyes on your goal. It will do you no good to stop and focus on where you are if that is not where you want to be. Right now, I am sorry to say that your mother is focusing on her disappointment. She has focused so much on the future she planned for you that she has turned your present situation into anger. I do not want you to return that anger. I do not approve of what she is doing. This is not like her, but she is creating it for herself. She could focus on your goal with you and be happy. It is most important that you keep *your* eyes on what you want, because things may become more difficult. Just remember, love is worth any price."

Stephen and his father knocked on the door to Miriam's hut. Arelia's face lit up when she answered the door. John was pleasantly surprised by the change a couple of days had made in the beautiful young woman. He smiled, knowing the feelings his son and Arelia felt for each other. *Nothing like new love.*

"Arelia, this is my father."

"How do you do, sir?" Arelia could see the resemblance between father and son.

"I am glad to see you doing well, Arelia." Something about her made him smile.

Miriam interrupted, "She is better, John, but not quite well. I want her to ride a slow horse to the cave. I have cautioned her about straining herself. Stephen, you and Martha must keep an eye on her."

"Is your sister staying with us?" Arelia grinned, excited by the news.

"Yes, Mother wants someone with us." Stephen's tone implied it was unnecessary.

Miriam interjected, "Stephen, you may not deem it necessary, but if you are planning to stay in the village, you have a responsibility to protect Arelia's name and keep her in good light. Almost everyone understands the necessity of traveling without a chaperone in order to escape, but do not expect any more than that from these people. This is something you must do for Arelia." Miriam offered her explanation to both Arelia and Stephen.

"I think it is wonderful." Arelia smiled. Stephen's father liked Arelia immediately. Her dark round eyes and wide smile overcame any concerns he had. He could even overlook the dark circles around her bright, happy eyes.

"We have one more night here. Then, tomorrow, we go to the cave. Father will come for us when it is safe to return to the village."

John added, "Martha is more excited than I have ever seen her. You would think she was making a grand journey." He laughed.

"I look forward to getting to know her."

"She will be your sister soon," Stephen said. Arelia was not sure why, but she was very embarrassed by his comment.

Miriam noticed her discomfort. "Arelia will spend her time resting until then. What time of day do you intend to leave?"

"Unless one of the scouts returns with news, I think it will be safe to leave midmorning. Stephen and James will take crates of food this evening, and then Mr. Hawthorn and I will escort them to the cave in the morning to bring the horses back."

"Arelia, I have set out two dresses for you. Hopefully there will be a creek nearby for you to rinse out your things if you are there for a time," Miriam offered.

Arelia did not like the sound of being away a long time, but she was excited to get to know Martha. Miriam gathered a few things she thought Arelia would need and even a few things for Martha and Stephen.

"Here is your cloak, child. I will hang it here by the door. Oh my." She laughed. "Do you have rocks in the pocket?"

"Oh, Miriam, you above anyone would love what I have in my pocket!" Arelia took her father's Psalter and handed to Miriam.

"A Psalter! What a treasure. Where did you get it?"

"Father copied every word. It is much like the Bible his father kept in their chapel." Her excitement showed. She was so happy to share the book with someone who would really appreciate its true value.

Miriam made no response to the clue Arelia unintentionally revealed into her past.

"Sir Reginald also had a beautiful Bible, which I read often over the three years I was with them." As she turned the pages, she asked, "May I read my favorite psalm to you? I feel certain you will understand and love it too."

They sat side-by-side on the bench as Miriam read Psalm 116.

I

1   I love the LORD, who listened
to my voice in supplication,

2   Who turned an ear to me
on the day I called.

3   I was caught by the cords of death;
the snares of Sheol had seized me;
I felt agony and dread.

4   Then I called on the name of the LORD,
"O LORD, save my life!"

II

5   Gracious is the LORD and righteous;
yes, our God is merciful.

6   The LORD protects the simple;
       I was helpless, but he saved me.

7   Return, my soul, to your rest;
       the LORD has been very good to you.

8   For my soul has been freed from death,
       my eyes from tears, my feet from stumbling.

9   I shall walk before the LORD
       in the land of the living.

III

10   I kept faith, even when I said,
       "I am greatly afflicted!"

11   I said in my alarm,
       "All men are liars!"

12   How can I repay the LORD
       for all the great good done for me?

13   I will raise the cup of salvation
       and call on the name of the LORD.

14   I will pay my vows to the LORD
       in the presence of all his people.

15   Dear in the eyes of the LORD
       is the death of his devoted.

16   LORD, I am your servant,
       your servant, the child of your maidservant;
       you have loosed my bonds.

17   I will offer a sacrifice of praise
       and call on the name of the LORD.

18   I will pay my vows to the LORD
       in the presence of all his people,

19   In the courts of the house of the LORD,
       in your midst, O Jerusalem.
       Hallelujah!

Arelia fell asleep praising God for placing her in the home of a lady who had also suffered loss of loved ones and her imagined future but deepened her faith because of it. She was oddly looking forward to the adventure ahead, knowing she would be safe with Stephen and that it could be fun to get to know a new friend.

In the dark, quiet night, Miriam wondered how Stephen had fallen in love and run away with a young lady who may, in fact, be a Lady Fairchild. *What has he gotten them into?*

The captain and his troop made good time. A hard yet uninterrupted ride along the rocky coastline brought them within hours of the scene of the wreck. They set up camp just before sunset, but Captain Hardgrave was frustrated that there was no sign of the fugitives. He was unaware of how close they were to the wreckage.

The soldiers rose before sunrise and were saddled before dawn. Within hours, they came upon the wreckage. The captain realized he should have sent horsemen to this area first. The stream that fed into the ocean at this point would lead directly to Stephen's village. *Maybe Fairchild is right. I am not thinking clearly. This should have been obvious.*

"Shall we head back, Captain? The boat is shattered. They are obviously dead," suggested one of his officers.

"And what convinces you of that?" demanded Hardgrave.

"The wreckage, sir, and there are scraps of her dress caught in the rocks. They could not have survived at night. The boat washed up, and the bodies washed out to sea." The young soldier made the comment casually, implying that his deduction was obvious to everyone but the captain.

"You have made a strategic error that betrays your lack of experience. Wingate is an officer with a keen mind. I will not be made a fool by his ruse. We have several more hours of light. It is going to be slow through the woods. There is no time to waste."

"How many days to the village?"

"One and a half to two days from this point," he answered.

"Watch for signs of their passage before us. Tomorrow, I will send the first messenger to report to Sir Fairchild. I want to have definite news to send back." They led their horses into the woods without noticing the remains of a campfire covered with loose branches just off the path.

A few hours into the woods, the sun began to set. They made camp along the stream and began to drink the strong ale which Jacob had conveniently loaded into a wagon. Joseph tied up the horses as the men settled around the camp. He was thankful for his mother's thoughtful sack. Even if it was to hide Arelia's amulet, he needed the food.

After too much drinking the night before, morning came before everyone was ready to ride. Soldiers rose slowly in spite of the captain's commands. None of them understood the pressure he was under. Sir Fairchild was expecting his first scout, and there was no substantial evidence of bodies to report.

"Men, keep your eyes open for any sign of the girl and Stephen. Sir Fairchild will want any information." Eager to reach the village, he drove the troop at a quick pace but was soon impeded by thick underbrush and a narrow path which was seldom traveled. Some men tried to ride their horses along the creek but lost their footing on loose rocks.

By the time they stopped to rest the horses and stretch their legs around noontime, Hardgrave was growing increasingly frustrated with their slow progress.

"Captain, come look at this," one of the men called out. He ran to an outcropping of rocks to find the remains of a campfire and emptied nutshells. "They must have stayed the night here, sir."

"Yes, I can see that. They are alive!"

"Sir, it may be old campsites of people running from the pestilence like we saw behind us," another soldier suggested.

Hardgrave picked up a nutshell and turned it over in his hand. "No, this is too fresh." He kicked the burned-out fire with his boot. "This campsite is no more than a few days old. There is no sign that they stayed any amount of time.

"Johnson, return the news to Sir Fairchild.

"We no longer need to keep up our pace. We'll proceed slowly and let them think that we have discontinued the search. They will be comfortably settled when we arrive."

CHAPTER 37

Stephen and James rose early to pack the remaining supplies to take to the cave; Arelia awoke early, sensing excitement as the men congregated to finalize their plans.

"Arelia, you must have a big breakfast this morning. I want you strong for the trip," Miriam suggested as she checked what she had packed the night before.

"Miriam, I would not call this a trip. Stephen says we are less than an hour away. It took several days to get here from Faircastle."

There was a loud, impatient knock on the door that startled the two women. Fear streaked Arelia's face. "Get in the bed, girl, under the blanket."

Miriam appeared calm as she opened the door. "Get Arelia up. We must leave quickly." Stephen announced as he hurried into the room. "One of the boys spotted a campfire in the woods last night. He rode all night, so the soldiers are about a day away,"

Arelia jumped out of bed completely dressed and ready to go. "Is this fast enough?" Miriam laughed, but Stephen just turned and hurried out the door, too focused to realize the humor. "Hurry!" Stephen shouted over his shoulder.

Miriam handed Arelia a small burlap sack. "Godspeed."

Having to squint in the early morning sunlight, Arelia realized that it had been days since she had been out of the hut to see the light of day. Stephen's father was mounted on one horse and holding the reins of another large horse. A young man was sitting on a horse next to him with a young woman seated behind him.

"Arelia, this is my friend James. Do you remember my sister, Martha?" introduced Stephen.

"No, I am sorry. How do you do?" Arelia smiled shyly, wondering what Martha and James and others in the village had heard about her. Seeing Martha match her smile and sensing her excitement, Arelia knew they would soon be friends.

James smiled at the girls and instantly understood why Stephen had gone to such great lengths to free Arelia and, now, why he was willing to hide out in order to ensure her safety.

"Stephen," John interrupted. "You have time for introductions later. We must leave *now*."

"Arelia, you are going to ride with me," Stephen informed her as he mounted his horse. He reached down and pulled her up behind him. "All right, Father. James, we will see you in about an hour."

The three horses took off in different directions. "Where are they going?" Arelia was confused.

"Because the soldiers are so close behind, we do not want to leave any obvious tracks. Different routes will throw them off."

"Who is going to ride the horse your father is leading?" Arelia stopped at that question. "Stephen . . . is that a coffin over there?"

"Yes," he answered.

"Who is it for?" she asked sadly.

"You," he answered flatly.

"Me! Did they expect me to die?" she asked in surprise.

"Oh, I am sorry. I thought I told you."

"You have not told me anything," she corrected, near tears.

"The men are going to fake a funeral for the sake of the soldiers. It will happen as soon as we are out of sight," Stephen explained. "Notice there are no children around; they will think you died. The women have kept them inside until we are out of sight. That way none of the children can slip the truth."

"I am glad I will not be here for that." She sighed.

As soon as Stephen left the village, he increased his pace.

"Stephen, why does your father have two horses?"

"The men thought the soldiers would track two horses. Father is going opposite us and then up the creek and over those hills. By that time, he will have thrown off their trail. Both he and James will return with two horses to throw them off. When James drops off Martha, he will lead my horse back with him."

"The men are brushing our tracks away but leaving Father's. They are having a grand time outsmarting the army."

As soon as the riders were out of sight, Mr. Hawthorne sent notice to begin the funeral. Children were finally let out of their huts from a late-morning start; everyone, young and old, attended. The coffin was carried to the burial plot and placed next to the hole already dug.

"Who died, Mommy?" asked one of the children.

Mr. Carpenter winked at Mr. Hawthorne, confirming that their plan was a good one.

Miriam noticed that although Jean was there, her mother was nowhere to be seen. If the children had had experience with funerals, they would have known that it was strange that there were no tears and only a short reading, and that Jean, John, Martha, and Stephen were not among the mourners. The last of those who died were consumed by the plague, and there had been nothing ordinary about the disposition of their bodies. Many children had never seen or could not remember a traditional Christian burial. The younger girls were instructed to pick as many flowers as they could find in order to cover the fresh mound of dirt piled over the empty coffin.

After a short time, families returned to their huts waiting to begin the next phase of the plan. All day, all eyes were open for any signs of soldiers.

Arelia was fascinated with the cave. She and her brother and other children in their village had often played for hours in caves near her childhood home. This experience took on a sense of adventure as she remembered all the times she and Daniel had hidden for hours from the other children. But this time, the hiding was not for fun rather for survival.

Martha and James arrived shortly after she and Stephen had begun to unload their supplies. They could hear Martha talking and laughing as the horse came over a small rise.

"This is the greatest adventure Martha has ever had. She has not been able to contain her excitement since Father spoke to her." Stephen smiled just thinking about his younger sister. He hadn't realized how much she had grown in the two years since he had seen her. She didn't seem so much like a little girl anymore.

"I know I am going to enjoy getting to know her," Arelia told Stephen. She looked forward to spending time with a normal girl. She and Laura had enjoyed what little time they had, but the circumstances were not conducive to having fun. Even though this was not intended as a fun adventure, Martha's laughter made it seem that way.

"I am going to start back right away," said James as he helped Martha dismount.

"Thank you, James. You are indeed a good friend," Stephen replied. The two men hugged stoutly.

Martha and Arelia were nowhere in sight, but he could hear them talking in the cave. Martha's laughter carried through the small opening.

Stephen squeezed his way into the second opening and knelt there until his eyes adjusted to the dimly lit room. "Stephen, this is so exciting," squealed Martha. "Thank you for inviting me."

"I am glad you are here with us, too, but you are going to need to be quiet. Your voice and laughter carry. We do not know when the soldiers are coming, and we would not want to give them a clue to our whereabouts."

"All right, Stephen," Martha whispered with a broad, mischievous grin.

Stephen couldn't help but laugh. "I really am glad you are here, Martha."

"It almost looks like the men plan for us to stay for months," Arelia remarked as she surveyed all the supplies the men had brought. They had dried meat, cheese, carrots, and loaves of bread in several bags near the opening of the cave, with blankets and eating utensils and large containers of water stacked in the corner.

"We won't be able to leave the cave or have a fire until we get word from the village," explained Stephen.

"No fire?" asked Arelia. "What about wild animals?"

"We may get a few small animals, but a bear cannot fit through that opening," Stephen assured, remembering their last scare.

"What about wolves?"

Stephen crawled to her across the low cave. "Arelia, Mr. Hawthorn and I checked for any sign of wolves or bears; there was none. But if it will make you feel better, we can stack rocks at the opening."

"I will help. Do you want me to find some now?" chimed Martha.

"All right, girls. We will go gather some large boulders." He smiled.

Martha was out first. "Look over there, Stephen," she shouted. "There are some big ones."

Stephen grabbed her arm roughly. "Martha, you really must be quiet, or I will have to send you back."

Martha's face fell. "I promise to be better."

Arelia jumped to her defense. "Stephen, do not scare her."

"Listen, girls. You must be a little scared so you will be careful. We have no escape if they find us."

Martha pointed at the rocks she had seen. "Look over there," she whispered with a mischievous grin.

Stephen and Arelia laughed. "Much better," he said. "Beginning tomorrow, we will stay in the cave. We can spend time in the front area where there is more room and light, but we must use branches to cover our tracks."

The girls spent the entire afternoon collecting nuts and berries. Stephen sat atop the cave watching the horizon for riders while keeping an eye on the two young women. Arelia had taken on a much younger appearance as she amused herself with Martha. He had not realized how close they were in age until now.

The three took advantage of sitting outside while they cracked nuts and tossed the shells into the brush. "We can entertain ourselves for days cracking all these nuts. Mother will be excited if we bring some home," said Martha as they watched the sun settle into the evening sky, admiring two bowls full to overflowing.

"I look forward to meeting your mother. I remember seeing her briefly, but I do not even remember what she looks like. If she is anything like the two of you, I know I will love her," Arelia said. Martha cast a knowing look toward Stephen. Neither of them responded to Arelia's innocent comments.

"What would you ladies like to eat this evening?" Stephen quickly changed the subject.

Martha ducked into the cave and came out quickly. "Stephen, we will need a torch. It's too dark to see inside."

"We must cover the opening when we light a fire. It will have to be small so we do not have too much smoke." Stephen began to gather brush to disguise the entry. "Arelia, gather some small sticks. We can start a very small fire for light once I cover this opening."

The cave took on an eerie but somewhat comfortable atmosphere with very tiny flames leaping from a bowl-sized fire. Cracks in the rocks overhead allowed little wisps of smoke to escape and hints of moonlight to push through, casting soft willowy shadows on the dark cave walls. After a satisfying meal, they sat around the fire quietly for a long time, tending their own thoughts; even Martha seemed mesmerized by the flames.

"Stephen, tell me about the castle and about being a soldier," Martha requested, breaking the silence.

The girls listened intently as Stephen related his stories about battles he had fought and military life. Stephen's memories reminded Arelia of hearing her father's stories years ago, stories that she thought were made up to amuse her, her brothers, and her sister, only to find them true. Her eyes filled with tears, knowing that her family was gone forever. She watched Stephen and Martha talking, smiling, laughing, and listening to each other, and she missed her own sister and brothers intensely.

Stephen heard the sniffles that accompanied her tears. Sensitive to her memories and loss, he suggested, "We should get some sleep. We must be prepared for tomorrow."

Stephen and James had arranged three bedrolls, one on one side of the cave and two on the other. Martha started arranging her things near the two bedrolls closest to the back of the cave away from the opening. Stephen and Arelia were both surprised by the obvious. They looked at each other. Stephen smiled and winked at Arelia, but she was embarrassed. Martha's simple assumption brought up the gulf between the two girls. Even though they were only a couple of years apart, they were infinitely different in experience. At fifteen, Arelia was very mature, and Martha, nearly fourteen seemed childlike.

Once the girls were settled under their blankets, Stephen smothered the fire. The cave was pitch dark. As Stephen felt his way back to his bed, he bumped his head on the cave's low ceiling, and Arelia and Martha giggled at his moans and groans.

"Very funny!" Stephen moaned, causing Martha to giggle all the more.

Martha fell asleep quickly, tired from the excitement of the day. In contrast, Arelia's life was passing before her.

"Stephen, how old is Martha?" Arelia asked in a hushed tone.

"I think she is thirteen. Why?"

"I was just wondering. Good night."

"Good night," Stephen answered her casually but wished that he were lying with her in his arms to keep her warm. He remembered watching James set up the double bedrolls and thought that he appreciated his friend's concern and understanding at making a bed large enough for him and Arelia. It never crossed his mind that lying with Arelia was an impropriety. He knew now how wrong he was. *What was I thinking?*

Arelia could hear Martha's low, deep rhythmic breath as she slept. *Martha seems such a child*, she reflected. *Could I have been so young and innocent when my parents died? How have I been thrown into such a life?*

The thought of her lost childhood brought tears to her eyes. She felt so lonely. Stephen was the only person who knew her as she had become. No one on earth knew her as a child. She couldn't even remember herself at that age. It seemed centuries ago.

"Arelia," Stephen whispered. "Are you crying?"

His voice startled her. She didn't want the intrusion, even from him. "No, I am fine. The dampness makes me sniffle." She wanted to sob. *Martha can be herself. She does not have to pretend to be someone else. She has no secret life. Even I do not know who I am.* Her thoughts flowed like waves crashing onto the shore, one after another with no relief. Finally, she slipped into a restless sleep.

Martha had been lying awake for a long time. The cave was dark, but she thought it was morning and was too excited to get back to sleep; sunlight was peaking between the rocks overhead. This was fun for her, and she was ready to start her day.

Stephen rolled over in his leafy bed.

"Stephen, are you awake?" she whispered.

"Arelia?"

"No, Martha," she answered quietly. She got out of her bed, careful not to disturb Arelia, and squeezed through the opening into the smaller, exterior cave.

Stephen lay in bed, amused at her enthusiasm. "Do not go out," he reminded.

Martha peaked out the blocked opening. The sun was much higher overhead than she had expected.

"Stephen," she whispered. "It is late. Get up."

He went into the outer cave. "And what shall we get up for?"

"It is daytime?"

"All right, I will get up, but let Arelia sleep as long as she needs to, and remember, we need to be very quiet," he reminded lovingly.

Before John rode out of town, he talked to the boy who had spotted the soldiers' campfire the evening before. They hadn't seen him as he had stolen away through the trees to warn the villagers. He had ridden through much of the night and expected the soldiers to arrive either at midday or late afternoon. John had an idea as he talked to the boy, who told him that the troops were about five miles down creek.

He rode off toward the soldiers. He had ridden at a good pace along the creek for the better part of morning when he spotted the column of men and horses.

He quickened his pace. "Captain," he called.

Hardgrave watched the older man leading an extra horse right toward him. "What can I do for you?"

"I was wondering if you might have seen my son," John answered.

"And who would that be?" was the captain's response.

"Stephen Wingate, sir."

The captain was genuinely surprised. "How is it that you think I would know him?" asked the captain cautiously.

"I believe he was with your troop, from the Fairchild estate. Am I correct?" asked Stephen's father.

"Yes, but how is it you are looking for him out here?" the captain pursued.

"Stephen arrived at our village two days ago with a girl he had saved from wolves. Unfortunately, the girl died shortly after they arrived, and Stephen left on foot just as he had come to the village. I assumed he was returning to the estate," John explained.

"He was with a girl? What was her name?" the captain asked.

"I remember it to be Arelia, although I am not really sure. Everything happened so quickly, and he was awfully upset."

"And you say the girl died?" the captain questioned suspiciously.

"Yes, sir, we buried her this morning, but Stephen was gone already. Did you see anyone?" John asked with forced concern.

Joseph listened to John and was heartsick about Arelia. He didn't know how he would break the news to his family and Bethany. He thought about the amulet in his sack and wondered what to do.

"Sir, do you mind if we ride back to your village with you? Your son has not gone in this direction, or we would have seen him. My men can use fresh supplies. Then we will head back to the estate," said Captain Hardgrave.

"Certainly." John smiled, thankful that the captain had taken the hook. "We should quicken our pace to arrive before dark. I will lead the way."

John rode ahead at a gallop, proud that he had outsmarted Fairchild's troops.

Dark was falling on the village when the children began to shout their arrival. The villagers were surprised to see John leading the troop. James and Mr. Carpenter hurried out to greet them.

"Go along with me," John said in a whisper as he dismounted and then loudly, "I did not see Stephen. I was sure he was going back to the estate."

"I am sorry, John," Mr. Carpenter said, following his lead. "He will probably make his way back by week's end."

"Are you men sure he was going back to the estate?" Hardgrave interrogated.

They looked at each other absently. "I do not know where else he would go, Captain. Was he with you when he found the girl?" answered John.

"No. He was ahead of us by a couple of days," Hardgrave answered. He was confused; this was not what he expected.

"Mr. Carpenter can help your men with the horses. We can have the women prepare hot food. We are honored to have Stephen's captain with us," John said with all the charm he could muster.

As he and James walked away, John said quietly, "Spread the word to treat them like royalty. We will kill them with kindness." The two men smiled at their own shrewdness.

"Sir," Joseph said to Mr. Carpenter. "Did I hear them say that Arelia is dead?"

"Yes, son, she died shortly after they arrived," he said casually. Mr. Carpenter noticed that Joseph's eyes became teary. "Did you know her, son?"

"My mother took care of her when she first came to the estate. She and my sister became friends," he explained sadly. Mr. Carpenter was tempted to tell Joseph the truth but busied himself with the horses, not trusting himself to keep their secret.

"Sir," Joseph interrupted. "Did Stephen really go back to the estate?"

"I just know he is gone, son. I do not know where else he would have gone," Mr. Carpenter explained.

Later, when Joseph was removing cheese and carrots from the sack, he saw the dark pouch with Arelia's amulet. He shoved it deep into the sack, not knowing what to do with it.

The villagers started coming to the camp with food for the soldiers. Several women went straight to the captain with warm bread, cake, and butter. "Share these with your men, Captain. Any friend of Stephen's is a friend of ours." In a short time, the camp looked like a festival with all the food and people milling around.

The captain was sincerely mystified by the entire occasion. He accepted the villagers' hospitality graciously, but he still intended to seek more information in the morning.

At first light, Miriam noticed him standing in the graveyard at the fresh gravesite. "Good morning, Captain. I see you have discovered Arelia's grave."

"So, this is where she is supposedly buried?" he responded suspiciously.

"Yes, this is where she is buried. She stayed with me. Poor child. She was in such pain."

"And what supposedly happened to her?" continued the Captain.

"She hemorrhaged, sir. We could not stop the bleeding. There was so much blood," Miriam explained. She shook her head sadly and sincere tears came to her eyes.

"I do not intend to offend you or your friends, madam, but we will need to open the coffin. My master wants solid proof," warned the captain.

Miriam cast her eyes to the ground and let her tears fall. "I understand, sir. She must have been well loved. I can give you proof short of opening the coffin. People here regard the dead highly. You would offend many. Come with me." Then in a conspiratorial whisper, "Forgive me, sir, but by now there would be a stench."

Miriam walked behind her hut to a pile of rocks and fresh dirt. "We buried her dress here, sir. Since the plague and the smell of burning flesh, the men decided we should bury her dress so as not to bring back painful memories of those we lost, whose bodies we burnt." Miriam hoped the dress and her tears would satisfy the stern, suspicious man. She began throwing rocks to the side. Joseph had been watching them from the camp and walked over.

"Help the lady remove these stones," the captain commanded. Joseph tossed the stones aside and then noticed a shovel leaning against Miriam's hut and began to dig through loose dirt. He soon reached a bag which he pulled from the hole. Miriam pulled out Arelia's torn and bloodstained dress along with several blood-soaked rags.

"How do I know that this is Arelia's?" the captain asked. Joseph pulled out the dress and looked along the neckline.

"Here, sir. These are my sister's initials. She must have made this for Arelia." Joseph handed him the dress.

"Sir, why would I mislead you? I know your master must miss the girl if he sent soldiers to find her. If it were within my power, I would restore her to him," Miriam reasoned convincingly.

Captain ordered over his shoulder as he walked away, "Help fill that hole."

Miriam noticed that Joseph held Arelia's dress with near reverence. "Did you know Arelia?" she asked.

"My mother and sister loved her very much," he responded. "Are you Stephen's mother?"

"No, I am his aunt. Tell your family I helped Arelia the best I could, but there was just too much blood."

Hardgrave stopped, stood quietly, deep in thought. He reasoned that there would be no apparent reason to mislead him. Obviously, no one knew the true reason Stephen had returned. Of course, Stephen couldn't have told them the truth about Arelia. Stephen's father certainly wouldn't have approached him hoping to find his son if he had known the truth.

"Madam, I will take the dress and rags with me. My master will want proof of her demise,"

"Of course, sir. I would like to write a letter of condolence, if you would permit. I will explain the situation and send my regrets," offered Miriam.

The captain nodded. "That will be very helpful," he accepted. "We will pack our camp and leave shortly." He turned and headed toward his campsite.

Miriam noticed the boy squatted quietly by the freshly dug hole. "Are you all right?" she asked.

"We thought she would finally be happy," he said absently.

"She is happy now," Miriam assured. She prompted Joseph to his feet. "Come back for the letter for your master before you leave."

Miriam returned to her hut to compose her letter of condolence. Like the other villagers, she reveled in throwing the soldiers off their path.

John came into the clearing as the captain was making his way back to camp. "Good morning, sir. How can I be of assistance to you today?" John offered.

"We will be leaving today, Mr. Wingate. I have spoken to the woman, Miriam. She has shown me the girl's dress, which I will bring back as evidence to Sir Edward. We will be leaving soon."

John was surprised that the captain was satisfied so easily. "We are sorry to have such bad news for you, sir. Please give our regrets to Sir Edward. I am sure the girl was of good service."

The captain looked surprised for a split second, and then laughed whole-heartedly. "Oh yes, of great service!" He turned and walked toward his camp still laughing. John watched him, puzzled by his response.

"You seem to have amused him," said Mr. Hawthorn as he walked toward John. "What do we need to do today?"

"Unless I am mistaken, our job is done, but we must not let our guard down. Somehow I thought it would be much more difficult than it was. We must continue to be careful. This was too easy; it could be a trick." John watched the captain walk back to the camp. He was laughing heartily with one of the men. Somehow, John was insulted by his laughter, but he didn't know why.

CHAPTER 38

Arelia awoke at midday. She could hear Martha and Stephen talking in the outer cave. "You know she will change in time," Martha consoled.

"How much time? I never thought she would act like this. Father said he would handle it, but I sure do not know how," Stephen said.

Arelia lay very quietly. *Are they talking about me?* she wondered.

"Has she been this way for long?" Stephen asked.

"Not this bad, but she has been short-tempered with everyone, not just you," Martha responded.

"I do not even want to be around her," he said.

"Nor should you. You should spend time with Arelia anyway. Are you going to begin a hut for the two of you?" Martha's voice was getting excited. Arelia smiled at the thought of her grinning expression and listened intently for Stephen's answer.

"Father said he has a spot for a hut picked out close to Miriam's. I know Arelia would like that, but he said Mother disagrees."

"Mother disagrees with everything!" Martha was disgusted. "Ever since you brought Arelia home, and her plans for you and *precious Madeline* fell through, she disagrees with everything."

"Madeline is of no interest to me anymore," Stephen said insistently.

"Have you even seen her since you have been home?" Martha asked curiously. Arelia's curiosity was also piqued.

"Only to wave across the clearing; we did not speak," he answered.

"Then, how do you know you are not interested in her?" Martha pushed for an answer.

"I just know!"

"But how?" Martha pressured.

"Martha, when you fall in love with someone, no one else interests you." Stephen crawled to the opening of the cave and surveyed the area, wanting to close the subject.

"Stephen, why do you love Arelia? I mean, *how* do you know?" Stephen could see Martha's question was serious, and she wasn't going to be satisfied until she had an answer. He sat down next to her and thought for a long time. Arelia strained to hear what he would say.

"Martha, this probably will not make sense to you, but when I shot the wolf and ran over to help the girl, I felt she was someone I already knew. She was nearly unconscious with pain, but I knew that one way or the other she would be all right, and it was up to me to save her. Her life at the estate was not happy, and neither was mine; it seemed like the only time I was happy was when I was with her. I just want to be with her all the time," he explained.

"Is that what love is? Wanting to be with someone all the time?" Martha asked.

"I do not know about everyone, but that is how I feel. All right, enough questions," he interrupted. "I am getting hungry. Let us see what we can prepare without waking up Arelia."

Arelia lay very quietly while they prepared the meal. She didn't want Stephen to know she had overheard their conversation. He was the only person she wanted to be with, too; but she didn't even know anyone else. After overhearing their conversation, she was determined to meet Madeline when she returned to the village.

Martha was going back into the outer cave when she hit her head on the low opening. "Ouch!" she shouted.

"Martha, quiet!" Stephen said in a loud whisper.

Arelia appreciated the excuse to finally wake up. "Are you all right, Martha?" Arelia said in a sleepy voice. She crawled through the opening to the outer cave and squinted at the light flooding through the opening.

Stephen inched his way to her and gave her a warm hug and kiss on the cheek. "Good morning, sunshine," he said lovingly.

Martha was glued to the scene. She had never seen her parents show such affection even though they were married. Arelia was painfully aware of Martha's gaze and gently shoved Stephen away. She wanted to return Stephen's affection but didn't feel comfortable in front of his sister.

"Time to eat," Martha announced, embarrassed.

The afternoon was spent listening to Martha tell stories the way only a thirteen-year-old girl can. Stephen had to continually remind Martha and Arelia to be quiet.

He watched as Arelia became more and more relaxed as the day went on. Even Arelia told a few stories about her brothers; her face came alive with happy memories as she spoke.

At dusk, they went out one at a time to relieve themselves and stretch their legs.

When Martha left, Stephen put his arms around Arelia. "Are you all right? We have not had a chance to talk since we arrived." He kissed her gently on her cheek.

Arelia was nervous that Martha would come in. "Stephen, this is improper."

"What? That I would hold you?" He seemed surprised.

"Yes, if someone would hold Martha like this, would you think it improper?" she asked.

He drew back. "Martha is thirteen and not betrothed! What is wrong?"

"That is just it! I do not know what is wrong and what is right. When we get back to the village, I have to know how to act." Her voice was frustrated and frightened.

"I see," he said. "Arelia, we are alone now, and we love each other. I will not do this in front of anyone if it makes you uncomfortable."

"I am sorry, Stephen. Remember, Miriam said that people would judge us by what they accept as proper. I do not think they would accept this, and then they will not accept me."

"You are right, but I do not know how anyone could not accept you," he teased.

"Stephen, look," Martha called. Stephen hurried outside.

"What is it?" Tension filled his voice.

"Look how beautiful the sky is. Come in the clear; you cannot see through the trees." Arelia came out to join them. They stood in reverent silence as the sky turned from orange to red and then to darkness.

Arelia was so moved by the majesty before them that she asked, "May I read something for you from Father's Psalter?"

As they settled on the ledge above the cave, she read from Psalm 27.

"I will not read all of it, but only the first part and a little of the end. I think you will understand."

I 1 The LORD is my light and my salvation;
whom should I fear?
The LORD is my life's refuge;
of whom should I be afraid?

2 When evildoers come at me
to devour my flesh,
these my enemies and foes
themselves stumble and fall.

3 Though an army encamp against me,
my heart does not fear;
Though war be waged against me,
even then do I trust.

II 4 One thing I ask of the LORD;
this I seek:
To dwell in the LORD's house
all the days of my life,
To gaze on the LORD's beauty,
to visit his temple.

5 For God will hide me in his shelter
in time of trouble,
He will conceal me in the cover of his tent;
and set me high upon a rock.

6 Even now my head is held high
above my enemies on every side!
I will offer in his tent
sacrifices with shouts of joy;
I will sing and chant praise to the LORD.

"I want to thank you both, because you have stood by me."

"And sat by you and laid by you." Martha laughed. Stephen shook his head at Martha's constant humor, knowing how hard it was for Arelia to express herself so personally.

"It is fine, Stephen. You have stayed with me in this tent"—she motioned toward the cave—"and tonight, we gaze on the Lord's beauty. I feel very blessed.

"But there is more at the end."

> 13 I believe I shall see the LORD's goodness
> in the land of the living.
> 14 Wait for the LORD, take courage;
> be stouthearted, wait for the LORD!

> Psalm 27:1-6 & 13-14

No one spoke for a while. Martha broke the silence in tears. "Arelia, I know you lost your entire family. I would die if that happened to me. I try to be funny because I want to make you happy. I have no idea why you must hide, but I know for certain that my brother will take care of you. I honestly believe that you will see the goodness of the Lord in the land of the living because you are with us!" She jumped up and enfolded Arelia in a big hug.

Stephen laughed and said, "So much for Martha's beautiful moment."

Arelia scolded with a smile, "Stephen, she did well. One day we will give shouts of joy and songs of praise, too."

Stephen interrupted with his hand on Martha's head. "But not now! Now we need to be very quiet and go to sleep."

When they settled onto their pallets, only slivers of light shone through the concealed opening. Arelia whispered to Martha, "Are you asleep?"

Martha shifted on the straw mat. Arelia whispered, "Would you like to pray the Our Father before we go to sleep?"

No response. Remembering reading the psalm on the ledge and Martha's response, Arelia hoped to keep the feelings alive a little longer with the prayer she and her family said every night before bedtime.

She heard Stephen shifting, and it sounded like he was getting up, but it was too dark to know for sure.

He knelt next to her pallet. "Arelia, give me your hand." She raised her hand, and they found each other in the darkness. "Our Father, Who art in heaven," he began in a soft, reverent voice.

She joined in, "Hallowed be Thy name. Thy kingdom come," Their words continued, burrowing so deeply into Arelia's soul that only tears could express the praise and petitions held within.

With the final, "Amen," Stephen's lips rested on the back of Arelia's hand before gently laying it by her side. She heard him settling onto his pallet, wanting nothing more from his unselfish act of love.

They both knew something beyond words had happened, something mystical. Their angels knew that the two hearts, joined together in need, were now joined soul to soul, resting within the loving Hands of God.

Earlier in the afternoon, when the soldiers were nearly ready to leave, Joseph approached the captain.

"Sir, should I get the letter from the lady Miriam now?"

"Yes, and make it quick. It looks like rain. I want to make camp before the rain."

Joseph ran to Miriam's hut with his hand stuffed deep into his pocket.

"Come in," Miriam called when he knocked on the door. "I have wrapped the dress in heavy rags. They are there in that bag." She pointed to a bag near the door.

Joseph stood nervously, not knowing how to begin his conversation while Miriam finished her correspondence.

"Lady Miriam," he began. Miriam smiled at his polite address.

"Yes?" she responded warmly. There was something she really liked about this boy.

"Do you know Stephen's mother?" he continued.

"Yes, she is my brother's wife."

"Oh . . . well," he stammered, "I have something that belongs to Arelia that you must give her. Mother wanted her to have it to give to Arelia, but now that she is dead, I am not sure what to do with it." He seemed to be thinking aloud.

Miriam stopped her writing. "You say your mother and sister cared for Arelia?"

"Yes, I think Mother loved her almost as much as she loves us."

Miriam studied his face for a long time. "And you care for her also?" Miriam continued.

"I did not know her well. I really only knew her from what Mother and Laura said. She seemed very nice."

"What is it you have for her?"

Joseph handed her the dark bag. "Mother said it is her legacy and is very important." Miriam didn't look in the bag but placed it in a drawer in the table.

"Thank you, Joseph. I have a note I want you to deliver to your mother for me."

"Madam, my captain is in a hurry."

Miriam finished two notes quickly and closed them with her wax seal.

"Godspeed," she said as he rushed out the door.

"Hurry along, boy," the captain hollered to Joseph as the troop pulled out of the village.

A gentle rain began that night and continued for two more, slowing the progress of the troops and isolating the young fugitives in their hideout.

The men in the village decided to give the soldiers plenty of time before letting Stephen and the girls return. Stephen grew restless in the cave not knowing what was happening in the village. He began to feel caged in the dark, listening to the incessant dripping through rocks overhead. Smoke couldn't escape through rain filled cracks, and there was no sunlight to lend even a little brightness to the gloom that engulfed him.

Martha, on the other hand, loved the time with her brother and Arelia.

Stephen couldn't imagine that any one person could have so much to say. At times, he wanted to gag her to have a little peace and quiet. She spent most of her time at the mouth of the cave cracking nuts, listening for Arelia to awake, and talking to Stephen.

Arelia spent most of the time sleeping. The sound of rain reminded her of days in her village when only her father would go out to tend the animals. For some reason, she couldn't seem to get enough sleep. Martha had taken the task of caring for her and anticipating all her needs. Arelia would awake to tea and cracked nuts and berries. She was overwhelmed at Martha's kindness.

Occasionally, Stephen would leave the cave to scout around and stretch his legs. During those times, Martha would tell Arelia about the boys in the village whom she found attractive. Arelia thoroughly enjoyed the opportunity for girl talk. She imagined that she and Martha had been friends for years and that her life had never been interrupted. It was a healing time for her.

Because of the rain, mud, and thick undergrowth, it took the troops four days to return to the estate. The captain was not looking forward to seeing Sir Edward with the news. He regretted leaving Arelia's coffin in the ground and returning without her body, although the thought of carrying a corpse back to the estate left him feeling ill. The search for Arelia was his commander's obsession, not his own. Hardgrave didn't care whether they found her or not; it was of no consequence to him.

It was a relief for him, and all the men, to return to their own camp with tents and fresh food. Although the captain wanted to change into dry clothes, he proceeded directly to Sir Edward's parlor when they arrived.

"What is it you carry in that bag, Captain?" demanded Sir Edward, just as rudely as before.

"This is the dress Arelia wore on her deathbed, sire. You see it is soaked with her blood." The captain dumped the smelly, bloodstained dress and rags onto the floor.

Sir Edward studied the pile of rags in astonishment. "And what else, Captain?" he demanded. "What a fool you are! Could they have butchered a pig and soaked these rags?" It was an accusation of ignorance.

"Yes, they could have. I am no fool! I saw her in her coffin," he lied. "I did not think you wanted a rotten corpse delivered to you." The captain was convincing, holding his gaze eye to eye.

Sir Fairchild met his stare. Hardgrave accepted the challenge. "You saw the body and knew it was the girl?" he questioned.

"Sire, I was extremely familiar with Arelia. Even though she was beginning to rot, she was still recognizable." The captain held his ground.

"And the soldier?"

"On our way to the village, we came across his father, looking for him along the creek. He did not realize we were tracking him. He told us that after the girl died, Wingate left without word," the captain explained. He was tiring of the conversation and wanted to get to his camp.

Sir Edward went to the window. His energy seemed to wane. "The soldier is of no consequence now. We will get on with our lives." His voice was flat and empty. It was as if the thrill of the chase had given him energy that was now lost.

"I almost forgot, sire. Here is a letter from Miriam, a lady in the village. She sent an explanation of Arelia's death. Everyone seemed to think you would be disheartened by her loss." The captain snickered as he handed Sir Edward two notes.

"One is for Sarah. In her haste, she neglected to write which note was which.

Edward broke the wax seal on the first note and read.

Dear Sarah and Laura,

The fabric you inquired about is being repaired. One of the pieces was torn in transport and needs repair. They will make a beautiful garment for the right occasion. Let me know if you would like to see them.

With high regard,
Miriam

He casually cast the note aside and opened the second letter.

Dear Lord Fairchild,

It is with our deepest regret that we inform you that your servant
Arelia has passed away in our village. The stress of the trip caused
a hemorrhage that could not be stopped. Please forgive me for
her demise. She was beyond my help.

We offer our prayers in your favor.

Your servant,
Miriam

Edward seemed to study the message for some time.

"That will be all, Captain. I feel the need to rest."

The captain made his way to his camp. *Who is the fool now? I hope this dead
girl haunts you to your death.*

Edward sat in his overstuffed chair looking at the sky. He felt an emptiness
that he hadn't felt since before he met Marisa. Since Arelia's disappearance,
he had been distracted from his loneliness and could continue toward the goal
Marisa had set; now he had to face life without her.

His manservant came into the room quietly and set a tray on the table.

"Harold, have Sarah and Bethany bring the twins. I have not seen them
since their mother died. I would like to see them now."

Sarah and Bethany were surprised to hear Harold's request. They dressed
the babies in the finest dresses Laura had sewn. "Hurry, lest he change his
mind," said Sarah.

Sarah knocked softly at the parlor door. Edward answered the door himself. "Hello. What do you have?"

"Your children, sire." Bethany's voice carried a tinge of anger.

Little Marisa smiled enticingly as he peeked into the blanket. "Is she smiling at me?" he asked surprised.

"Of course," Sarah answered.

He looked at the beautiful little baby with large dark eyes and an infectious grin. "She *is* smiling at *me*, is she not?" Sir Edward looked around for everyone's confirmation. Harold noticed a hint of a smile on Sir Edward's face for the first time in as long as he could remember.

"And the boy?"

Bethany showed him little Pearce sleeping soundly in the crook of her arm. "They are both very small."

"They are still babies, sire," Bethany reminded. "They will grow."

"I will want to see them like this each day now. You can bring them here each morning after they eat."

"It will be our pleasure, sire," Sarah was sincere in her response.

"I have this house and this estate and no one to care for it. I think I need to find a mother for these babies." He seemed to be speaking to himself.

"Sire, Sarah and I will always care for the children."

He seemed not to hear, lost in his own thoughts. "Oh, I have been remiss. Did Lady Marisa name the children before . . . ?"

"Yes, sire," Bethany, trying to calm her tone. "Marisa and Pearce."

"Pearce." He winced. "So, she named our heir after her own father . . . and herself." They watched as he walked to the window and stood for some time. In spite of everything, even Bethany felt a sense of loss for him.

"Sire," Sarah interrupted. "Bethany and I are honored to care for your children. We will continue with devotion as long as you allow us."

"Yes, and I can see you have done a good job, but this house is too empty now. I will wait a proper amount of time, but I cannot wait too long. The children need a mother, and I need a companion."

On the fifth day, the rain finally stopped. Although Martha seemed unaware of it, Stephen had become increasingly irritated with her continual prattle. By now, Arelia was tired of sleeping and wanted to leave the cave.

"How much longer do you think it will be, Stephen?" Arelia asked.

"The soldiers must have come by now, but I do not know how long they will stay," he responded wearily.

Shortly after noon, Stephen heard horses nearby. "Quickly, get in the back. I will sweep away these prints. Martha, stay very quiet. Not a word, no matter what!"

Within seconds, the three were hidden in the darkness. They froze as they heard men's voices drawing near. Arelia was so frightened she could hardly breathe.

"Stephen."

No answer.

"Stephen. Martha. Are you here?"

Stephen put his hand over Martha's mouth.

They could hear footsteps in the cave as the men felt for the second opening. "Stephen, I know you are here."

Stephen and Martha recognized their father's voice.

"Father?" cried Martha.

"Yes, and James. Come out here. It is time to go home!"

Martha ran out of the cave, jumping up and down, shouting, "Alleluia, alleluia, alleluia!"

Father and James watched, wide-eyed. Stephen placed his hand on his father's shoulder. "She is all yours now." He laughed.

Arelia and Stephen looked at each other and said at the same time, "Songs of praise."

CHAPTER 39

John and James related the events of the previous few days to the three former fugitives as they rode back to the village. Neither Stephen nor Arelia felt completely comfortable with the captain's easy surrender. Everyone in the village seemed to feel their plan was successful. John felt the same way, but Stephen had reservations. He knew Captain Hardgrave and Sir Edward too well to trust them.

After all the excitement of getting back to the village, with neighbors coming and going, the Wingate family finally settled in for the evening as the last visitor bid them a good night. With Mr. Carpenter having returned home, Mr. Robertson retold the entire plan with Stephen and anyone who would listen, to hoots and hollers of success and praise for a job well done. Each man in his own time had to relate his part in the ruse. Stephen especially enjoyed the camaraderie while Arelia began to feel fatigue settling in.

Miriam and Arelia returned to Miriam's comfortable hut, where Arelia felt as if she were finally home. Miriam was surprised with how excited she was to see Arelia. Since the morning Arelia walked out her door, her small home seemed to lose its radiance and life. In such a short time, she had developed a real affection for this young woman who had moved into her life as though she had been there all along.

"Arelia, I know you are happy to be here, but something seems to be troubling you."

"You are right." She hesitated, not knowing how much to say. "I know what Stephen's father and James told us about the captain, but I know him, Miriam, and I do not think he would give up so easily. He did not even look for us in the hills," Arelia answered.

Miriam responded, "Maybe we were so convincing, he felt no need to."

"Maybe, but . . ."

"Oh, I just remembered. Sarah's son gave me something for you." Miriam reached into the drawer and pulled out the soft, dark pouch.

Arelia's eyes opened wide and a shadow crossed her face. "Why did he give this to you? Did you look inside?"

"No, of course not. It is not mine." Miriam picked up a trace of relief in Arelia's face.

Tears puddled in Arelia's eyes. "What did he say?"

"I am sorry if it hurts you, child. I did not think this would be a problem for you. He seemed very concerned about your well-being and was deeply sorry that you had died. He said Sarah and Laura wanted you to have this because it was your legacy."

Arelia appeared startled for a trace of a second. "You did not look in the bag?"

Miriam sat next to her on the bench and put her arm around her shoulder. "Child, when the time is right, you will tell me what you want me to know. Until then . . ."

Arelia rested her head against the nape of Miriam's neck, and the tears began to flow. Miriam stroked her hair as she would a small child.

Stephen's homecoming was strained from the moment the door closed behind the last visitor. All the trite talk in the world could never cover the tension of his mother's silence. Jean was full of questions, which Martha readily answered with full animation and excitement, only adding to the tension. Stephen's mother listened to every word as she busied herself with dinner.

"Girls, enough of that prattle. I am not the only one eating here. I do not have the luxury of sitting about idly, and neither do you," Joan angrily interrupted.

John interrupted, "Stephen, come outside with me. The ladies will call us when dinner is ready."

Stephen and his father walked out to the livestock area. "See that little calf?" he said pointing to a wobbly-legged newborn calf. "That is going to be one good cow. I am giving that to you to start a herd for your family."

Stephen looked at the small calf in amazement. "The way I see it," John continued, "that little heifer is like your new life. It is a little wobbly starting out. It will need a lot of care and nurturing, but it can turn into a whole herd if treated properly.

"I don't think you have told us all there is to tell about Arelia, but I am going to trust your judgment. Martha certainly seems to feel the same as you do about her. Now, your mother is a different story. If you can think of anything you can tell her, you should do it now. She will not talk with me."

"Father, there is nothing to tell her." Stephen was genuinely concerned about his mother but didn't have the energy to confront her.

"Well, think about it, son. But, for now, we need to think of building a hut for you and your bride. How much time do we have?" John asked.

Stephen seemed puzzled by the question. "I guess I have not thought about it," he admitted. "I had so many other things to deal with. All I planned was getting here."

John laughed. "Well, now that you have her here, you need to decide what you intend to do with her. I doubt Miriam will keep her forever." He slapped his son on the back good-naturedly.

Stephen was embarrassed by his lack of a plan. "It is all right, son. You have done a really good job up until now, and I know you will continue. You and Arelia decide a good time and let me know. I will talk to your mother."

"How long will it take me to build a hut?" Stephen asked.

"About three months," John answered. Stephen seemed surprised.

"Three months?" Stephen repeated.

"Yes," John answered with a mischievous grin that Stephen recognized from Martha, "if you work alone—or one month if we all help you. Which sounds better?"

"I can sure use the help."

"All right then. In four or five weeks, we can have a hut for you and your bride. Why not choose six weeks from today for a wedding celebration?"

Stephen's face lit up. "I will tell Arelia tomorrow," he said.

Arelia awoke early to the smell of fresh bread and hot tea. Miriam was working almost soundlessly at her spinning wheel. It seemed like a completely different life to her. Arelia watched Miriam a long time before getting out of bed. She was mesmerized with Miriam's peaceful demeanor and soft smile. She had never seen anyone who had such a presence.

"Good morning, Miriam."

Miriam continued to hold the thread firmly, twisting it as the wheel coasted to a stop. "You have already had a visitor this morning," she said.

"Has Stephen been here already?" Arelia asked.

"Yes, and he said he has something very important to talk to you about. I suggest you dress quickly and find him." Miriam smiled as Arelia was already getting dressed as she spoke.

"Have some tea and bread before you leave. You must eat well now. You have to build yourself up," she instructed.

"There is no way I would leave without eating some of your delicious bread. The aroma woke me up." Miriam sliced a thick piece and slathered it with freshly whipped butter.

"Stephen brought the butter when he came to check on you, and eggs for lunch. He must intend to fatten you up." Miriam laughed.

"Well, between the two of you, you are going to do a good job. I could eat this whole loaf." Arelia savored every bit of the soft, warm bread soaked in creamy butter. She had one more piece before walking out into the fresh morning air. She was surprised to see Stephen and James clearing underbrush nearby.

"Good morning," she called.

Stephen lit up when he heard her voice. He leaned his sickle against a tree and walked over to her.

"Miriam said you needed to tell me something important."

Stephen pointed to the area they were clearing. "What do you see there?" he asked.

"I see trees and underbrush," she said, a little confused.

"Is that all?" he pressed.

"Yes. Is there more?" she asked, still confused.

"There is much more. Look closely."

Arelia squinted her eyes and looked from side to side. "What should I see?"

"You should see a lovely hut that says, 'The Home of Stephen and Arelia Wingate,'" he said warmly as he squeezed her hand.

Arelia looked at him and grinned. "Really? Our own home?"

"Yes. What do you think?"

She turned around, noting Miriam's hut nearby. "I love it," she said and gave Stephen a big hug.

At that exact moment, Stephen's mother stepped outside her door to empty water from the basin. She caught sight of Arelia hugging Stephen in full view of everyone in the village. Her eyes burned in anger.

"What can I do to help?" Arelia asked.

"I never thought you would help. This is my gift to you. You do not need to do anything. Father said once James and I clear the spot, all the men will help us build."

"Stephen, this makes me so happy. There must be something I can do."

"You can talk to Miriam and see what we will need inside. Maybe you and Martha and Jean can start preparing things to stock it."

Arelia jumped in delight. "What a great idea. Maybe your mother and Miriam will help, too."

Stephen ignored her comment. "Go talk to Miriam." As she was walking away, he called to her. "You only have six weeks; you better hurry."

"Six weeks!" Arelia smiled and ran into Miriam's hut.

She did not need to say a thing. "It seems Stephen has given you very good news," Miriam teased.

Arelia couldn't wait. "Yes, he is building our hut. He said I have only six weeks to prepare my part." Then she stopped. "What is my part?"

"No need to worry, child. You will have plenty of help."

"Miriam, I want Stephen's mother and sisters to work with us. Should I ask them?"

"Well, I know Martha and Jean will want to help, but they cannot neglect their duties at home. Now Stephen's mother has her hands pretty full. We can get it done with Martha and Jean's help," Miriam said to protect her from a confrontation. "We can ask the girls. Stephen said they are going to come by after their morning chores."

"What can I do right now? Today," Arelia asked, excited about something for the first time for as long as she could remember.

"The first thing you should do is collect herbs for cooking so they will have time to dry. Then we will start a garden plot. Six weeks is not much time. You certainly will not be ready to harvest, but you can get a start on it. We can collect herbs together after lunch. I need to replenish my supply too," Miriam suggested. "Another very important thing to consider is your wedding dress."

"A wedding dress?" Arelia responded like it had never crossed her mind.

"Of course, child."

"Oh, my." Arelia sat on the bench. In her village, it was a custom to wear your mother's dress. She suddenly realized that no family would represent her at the wedding. There was no one to give her away.

Miriam could read her thoughts. She opened a cedar chest in the corner by the fire and removed a package. "You may want to consider this instead of something new." She opened the package to reveal a delicately stitched dress with a finely embroidered neckline and bodice.

"This is beautiful." Arelia touched the soft, fine fabric. "Where did you get it?"

"My mother made it for my wedding. She spent as much time stitching this dress as Carl and the men took to build this hut. My daughter would have worn it one day. I hate to see it go to waste."

"Oh no, I could never wear your dress," Arelia stated.

"And why not? I will never have a daughter, and you have lost your mother. It seems right to me." Miriam lifted the dress from the box. "Stand up," she insisted. She held the dress up to Arelia's shoulders. "You can try it on tonight when we do not risk interruption. Everyone will be surprised." Miriam smiled warmly.

There was a knock on the door. Miriam wrapped the dress quickly and secured it in the chest. Arelia opened the door to Martha and Jean's smiling faces.

"Stephen told us to come over after chores. Here we are." Martha grinned her *only-Martha* grin. Jean followed close behind.

"Come in, girls. You are just in time," said Miriam. "We are going to be very busy the next few weeks."

"What are we going to do, Aunt Miriam?" Jean asked.

"We are going to prepare a new hut for a wedding."

Martha squealed. Jean looked puzzled.

"Who is going to marry?" Jean asked innocently.

"Oh, Jean, where have you been? Stephen and Arelia, of course," said Martha, with a know-it-all air.

"Arelia? Mother said Stephen is going to marry Madeline even if it kills her."

The room fell silent.

"Jean, you are so silly. That was *long* before Stephen brought Arelia home," Martha said a little too loudly.

"No—" Jean began.

"So," covered Martha. "What are we going to do?"

Arelia's brows were wrinkled, but she didn't want to pursue the conversation. She was afraid of what she would hear.

"The first thing we are going to do is collect herbs for drying," offered Miriam. "Arelia and I were just talking about that. Right, Arelia? . . . Arelia?"

"I am sorry. What did you say?"

"I said we are collecting herbs today," Miriam repeated.

"Yes, we are." Arelia's excitement was deflated. All her insecurities resurfaced. *Who do I think I am? Stephen deserves better than me.*

"Come, girls. I will walk you out," said Miriam. After the door closed behind the three of them, she said, "Girls, I think it would be wise that you not mention Stephen and Arelia's wedding to your mother. Let Stephen and your father talk to her first."

"Do not worry, Aunt Miriam. I surely will not want to tell her anything," agreed Martha.

When Miriam opened the door, she could almost see a visible shadow covering Arelia. "What is it, child?"

There were no tears in her eyes. "Stephen's mother is right. Stephen should marry Madeline. I am not right for him."

"That is Stephen's decision to make," Miriam suggested.

"Is it?" she continued.

"Only you know the reason that you think you are not good enough for Stephen. Even Stephen does not seem to know, and I suspect he knows you

385

well. Maybe he loves you enough to feel your reason is not good enough to stop him. Maybe he sees something good in you that even you do not see in yourself. I have only known you a few days, and I think you are perfect for him. Stephen's mother has never even spoken to you, so where does she get her judgment?"

Arelia looked down at her hands folded on her lap. "Maybe her judgment is a mother's intuition."

"Maybe it is," Miriam agreed. "And maybe it is a terrible mistake that can ruin both your lives. You should go outside now and gather kindling from the underbrush that Stephen cuts. You will need it to start plenty of fires in your fireplace," Miriam suggested. Arelia didn't move.

Miriam leaned down and looked into her eyes. "Listen to me, child. Stephen risked his life to bring you here. You may or may not have trusted him until now, but he did get you here safely. You owe it to him to trust him a little longer."

Arelia walked into the bright sunlight. Stephen and James were still working and had managed to clear quite a large space.

"Arelia, come over here," Stephen called when he saw her. He could see that some of the life had drained out of her. "What is it? Are you ill?"

"No, I am fine. I have come to stack kindling."

"Great. There is plenty here. We can keep a fire going for months."

Arelia felt better as she busied herself with the firewood. In no time, she had a sizable stack of kindling. Just as she realized she was hungry, Miriam called her in to eat.

Earlier, while the girls were at Miriam's, John had confronted Stephen's mother. "I will not have it," she insisted.

"You have no say," he countered.

"I am his mother. You cannot tell *me* I have no say about my son's wife-to-be!"

"Joan, what is it? What are you afraid of?" John pressured, yet again.

386

"John, are you blind? The girl had blood on her petticoat."

"Is that all? It was probably her monthly flow."

"It was too much; and what about all the dark blood on her dress and the rags? That was not monthly flow. The girl is a whore."

John was stunned and speechless. "The girl is a whore!" Joan repeated vehemently.

"You have never even spoken to her. She is a very nice girl," John defended.

"Then, she is a very nice whore," she said caustically. "And how has she fooled you, John? Did she smile sweetly at you?"

"What has happened to you, woman? Where has all this anger come from?"

"I do not want my son's life ruined," she shouted.

"Joan, quiet down. Do you think Stephen has some say? Do you think we have taught him good judgment?"

"I did until he brought this girl home and risked his life to do it," she answered angrily.

"You need to meet her," he suggested. "If the blood is what you think, maybe some soldier forced himself on her. Maybe Stephen has saved her from that."

"And maybe, dear innocent John, she smiled at a soldier to encourage him, and Stephen has been fooled by her also," she said in a sarcastic, sickly-sweet voice.

John stood up angrily. "Joan, it is not like you to pass judgment on someone you have never even spoken to. If you love your son at all, you will give this girl a chance."

"You mean the girl I saw hugging my son in the middle of the village for everyone to see," she continued.

John smiled warmly. "I seem to remember you hugged me when you agreed to marry me."

"But not so all could see. She does not even know what is proper. How will she teach her children and your grandchildren? Can you explain that?!"

"I know the girl's excitement was too great to suppress, and that is all I need to know," he said firmly. "Again, I beg you. If you love your son at all, you will give this girl a chance." He left her alone to rethink her opinion.

Moments later, the door flew open.

"Mother, Miriam said Stephen is going to marry Arelia, not Madeline. Is that true?" Jean blurted out.

"Jean, be quiet," commanded Martha.

"Are you defending the girl?" Joan asked Martha curtly.

"Mother, I like Arelia. She is like us. She was raised in a village, but she had the misfortune of losing her whole family. I will not turn her away. Besides that, Stephen deeply loves her."

"Everyone seems to feel as strongly in her favor as I do against her," considered Joan aloud.

"Mother, I really think you would like her, too, if you gave her a chance," insisted Martha, noting a weak moment.

"I strongly disagree with Stephen about what will make him happy. I think he has been misled. I think you have all been misled, but for Stephen and you, I will give her a chance. But not right away."

"When, Mother?" Martha pressed.

"Give me time, Martha. This is a new thought," Joan answered, with smoldering anger but without flames.

CHAPTER 40

Days seemed to pass with lightning speed. Arelia and Miriam sat on two tree stumps which Stephen set out for them in order to appreciate the work in progress. Men came and went, adding to the structure as it took shape before their very eyes.

"Miriam"

"Yes, dear."

"There is something that I have been wondering about which I would like to ask, if I may."

"You may certainly ask me anything. I will answer if I can."

"It is personal."

"Arelia, we have not stayed away from our personal thoughts and feelings; there is no reason to start now." She smiled, curious about what was on Arelia's mind.

"You live out here all alone, back in the woods away from everyone else."

"Yes. It is very quiet and peaceful, is it not?"

"Yes, but why?"

After having shared so much of Arelia's own life with her over the past several months, Miriam suspected the questions about her own secluded life would come about eventually.

She smiled, and then paused with a faraway look in her eyes. "This is not an easy answer, and it is a long story, similar to yours in some ways." Arelia leaned in as if to hear more clearly.

"My father, like yours, was an educated man. His training had been in London before he moved back to this little village, returning to his parents who had sacrificed to get him an education. Boys from villages are not formally educated, as you know, but my grandfather had a connection in London, someone who worked in one of the large estates. As a boy, my father worked as a house boy and sat with his charge and the tutor during the boy's lessons. Soon the tutor began to give my father lessons of his own, and he quickly excelled beyond the young lord's work. The lord of the estate supported him in his learning, expecting him to remain with the family in order to help with business matters." She paused, seeming to wait for a thought. "I cannot remember who the family was," she continued. "Because of his education, he never felt that he fit in once he returned."

"I understand that. My father was more educated and different from anyone in our village. I understand why now. Did your father stay?"

"Yes, to his parents' disappointment. He had never wanted to leave in the first place. His childhood sweetheart was here; she was to become my mother." She smiled a soft, wistful smile. "They had missed each other terribly when he went away to school, and he promised that he would never leave her again.

"My grandparents were disappointed because they had dreams of his being a man of substance in London, but everything he wanted in life was here: a wife, a family, friends, a small piece of land, and animals. Their dreams for him were much greater than his desire for himself. I have come to realize that he was a very quiet and introspective man by nature."

Arelia smiled. "I cannot say that about my father. He was actually rather outspoken, with a good sense of humor. People often asked his advice, and he gave it freely. My mother was also the love of his life, and his greatest desire was for a family. He gave up everything for that dream."

A sadness clouded Miriam's eyes. "My father had to give up everything but not by choice. He built a home for my mother before they married, near my grandparents' home. Even though my parents wanted children more than anything, it took several years for me to come into their lives. I remember being very happy and having many friends, but my parents seemed much older. When I was five, my mother gave birth to my little brother."

"Mr. Wingate?"

"No, not John. I have another brother who will always be in my heart, as will my parents. I will see them again one day, when my time comes."

They sat quietly as they both felt a longing for their families who had gone before them. Miriam took a deep breath before continuing, rubbing her eyes to push back tears. Arelia had never seen her like this, but Miriam had never spoken of her own past before today.

"I could see right away that there was something wrong with my brother, and I knew my father saw it too. The midwife tended to him and kept him from my mother until she fell asleep. I remember hearing she and my father talking in whispers, and I was very afraid. Before she left, she told me that I would have to be a 'very grown up girl' because my mother would need considerable help from me.

"As she gathered up a pile of blood-soaked rags, I looked at my mother's ashen face and wondered if this was what it meant to have a baby, and then I saw Father standing at the window with my little brother. He was quietly crying. I was overcome with fear."

Seeing the tears gathering in Miriam's eyes made Arelia regret that she had asked the question. "Would you like a cup of tea?"

Miriam just smiled. "Yes, that would be very nice."

They were happy to move from the stumps to a more comfortable place. Arelia went straight to the hearth to stoke the fire for water as Miriam settled into her rocking chair.

As she poured water from the pitcher into the pot hanging over the fire, Arelia stole a glance or two at this woman who had loved her so much. She had never seen sadness in her, only love, caring, and compassion. She worked quietly as the tea steeped, welcoming a chance to leave Miriam to her memories.

As she handed her the cup to warm her, she said, "Miriam, I am sorry to have asked about your past and caused you so much pain. You do not need to continue."

As she took the cup, Miriam took her hand. "Sit down, child. You have caused no pain for me. No one has ever asked me about myself, and this is only the first time to tell my story. The pain is from so long ago, and it is nothing compared to what you have undergone."

"Miriam, that is not true. I had no idea that you ever had any pain in your life. You are so happy and content."

Miriam's little laugh surprised her. "Oh, Arelia, with all you have been through, you still have innocence about you." As she took a sip of tea, Arelia's wrinkled brow prompted her to explain. "Everyone on the face of the earth has had some sort of pain, some greater than others.

"Jesus taught us that with His life. A Divine Man, perfect in every way, Love itself. And yet, look at His pain. I compared my pain to His, and I thank God that He is here for me. That is why I am happy and content. I have God's love and grace. He gave us angels, and saints who have also suffered. Why should I be any different?"

She continued, "My mother and father suffered greatly from the obvious discomfort of our neighbors. Do you remember what it was like when there was a new baby in your village?"

Arelia smiled at the memory of the steady stream of curious visitors and well-wishers who brought eggs, cheese, fresh vegetables, bowls of stew, and warm bread. "Oh, yes, it was wonderful."

"No one came to see my baby brother. No one visited my mother. My father told me that the midwife had probably told everyone about my brother, and they did not come, not even to see my mother. My mother's sister did not even come."

"Why? What happened?"

"My brother's lip looked like it had been cut or ripped in two and badly stitched back together. His lip went up to his nose which set his nose lopsided. He was not a pretty baby. He looked very different. Later, children said he looked like a monster." She sighed deeply. "After a few weeks, the midwife came back with a loaf of bread, and she apologized to my father. She said that she had never seen a baby with a face like his, and she had expected him to die. My aunt finally came over and after her, two other neighbors, but everyone else stayed away."

"What about your grandparents?"

"Oh, other than Father's mother, my grandparents were gone by then. My grandmother was very ill and nearly blind. She did not even know who we were anymore. Father had moved her to his sister's home in another village. We had not seen either of them since."

"You were only five. What about your friends?"

"I had no friends anymore. When Mother sat on the porch with Benjamin, I would play outside, but no one would come over. We saw them watching and whispering."

"What did your father do?"

Miriam smiled with a little chuckle. "Early on, I realized that Father disappeared every day for several hours while Mother and baby Benjamin slept."

"He disappeared?"

"Yes, just disappeared."

"For how long?"

"A few hours every day for several months?"

"Months? Where did he go?"

"Right here." She smiled as she motioned, palm up to where they were sitting.

Arelia shook her head as she looked around. "I do not understand."

"For months, Father cleared this piece of land and built this cabin. We knew nothing about it. He woke us up early one morning, as he placed blankets and clothes in a pile on the table with a determined look on his face. My mother asked what he was doing, and he said, 'Moving!'"

"We both said, 'Moving!?'

"'Yes. We are moving. They do not want to look at us, and I sure do not want to look at them. We are moving!' Mother and I were very confused. About then there was a knock, and two of our neighbors came in and closed the door. They were the husbands of the two ladies who visited my mother. Mother and I were very confused as they loaded my mother's chair and the table into a wagon, while Father wrapped Benjamin in a blanket. 'Do not ask any questions. Let me help you to the wagon,' he told us."

Arelia smiled. "I have so many questions!"

"So did we!" She laughed. "Mother had not been well since Benjamin was born, and the midwife was right; I had to grow up fast. Honestly, I do not think that I missed my friends because I was so busy with Mother and Benjamin. He had started smiling and entertained us with his cute expressions and smiles. But it was different with Mother; she needed a lot of help. Father and I cooked and cleaned, bathed Benjamin, and washed the clothes. Mother did not have the energy for any of it."

"Your life must have been very hard for such a little girl."

"I did not think it at the time. I guess I was too busy. We stayed in the house together almost all the time because when we went outside, people whispered. We were happy inside together.

393

"Father moved us into the woods, here, away from side glances and whispers. We could go outside whenever we wanted with no one looking. When Benjamin got big enough, he could go outside and dig in the dirt. He was my best friend."

Miriam reached out her arms into a stretch. "I need a walk. We should take time before dark and gather a few herbs. I need to move these tired bones. Would you like to join me?"

"Yes! I would love to learn about healing plants."

Miriam laughed. "Well, it took me years to learn, but I guess this is a good day for you to start."

Arelia had to laugh as she watched the small, wiry lady peek under bushes, circle around tree trunks, dig at roots, and look high into trees.

"What are you looking for, Miriam?"

"I keep only a few kinds of healing plants. Some I do not worry with because they can be very dangerous."

Arelia stopped in her tracks. "Dangerous?"

"Of course, child. Many plants are wondrous healers; some good in only small doses and many very poisonous. We do well to know the difference or to leave them alone completely. I have heard of healers who know the subtle difference between what is helpful and what is poisonous and how to measure them carefully to avoid harming someone."

"I know of what you speak." Arelia shuddered at the memory of the teas she was forced to drink.

Miriam walked over to her. "Oh my, yes you do. I have been careless in bringing you here."

Arelia reached for her hand. "You are never careless with me. You think of herbs in healing ways. There is no reason for you to be concerned. What others do in harming others is not what you do. I want to know the good of God's plants."

As Miriam tied the herbs in bundles and hung them from the ceiling to dry. The two women continued their conversation from before their outing.

"After we moved into this house in the woods, our lives seemed better. Mother seemed happier and healthier. Occasionally her two friends would visit, and they even seemed to develop an affection for Benjamin. It was always a treat for them to come with a cake or fresh vegetables. Father saw their husbands on occasion, working in the field or tending sheep.

"It was during this time that John was born. Happily, I had two brothers. It was a good life for us, except that Benjamin would seem to get sick with no explanation.

"His lip had kept him from nursing before John was born, and so the midwife advised Father to have Mother give him goat's milk. That was of great benefit for a time, but he never seemed healthy. Before long, both Benjamin and Mother did not seem well. The cold was especially hard for them. They spent some days under a pile of blankets from sunup to sundown. Father started feeding John goat's milk too. Mother could not nurse him either.

"Benjamin died before Mother, when he was only three."

"Miriam, I am so sorry. It is terribly hard to watch a brother die." Both women sat in teary silence until Miriam went on.

"Mother was never right after that. She seemed to get older overnight, and Father was carrying a great burden.

"One night, when they thought I was asleep, Mother told Father that he had to teach me to read and write in order to be able to take care of myself, because I had no friends and would never get married. I had never even considered my future, and I was completely taken aback. I remember their talking back and forth, but I do not remember anything they said after that. I was frightened. What would become of me after they were gone?"

As with so much of what Miriam had said, Arelia related it back to her own future. *What will become of me?*

"The next day," Miriam continued, pointing toward the corner of the room, "Father opened that big trunk, dug under the blankets, and took out a book. That was my first day of school. Because of Mother and Father, I learned to read."

"Father taught me to read also. Mother insisted because the boys were learning. We only had three books; one is the Psalter which my Father copied."

"Well, that makes us two of only a few women who can read."

"Miriam, one more question, please."

"Yes, but only one. I find myself very weary."

"Why have you never remarried?"

"Child, my heart was broken at my mother's death but healed when I met Carl. Losing him and my precious baby at the same time was more than I ever wanted to bear again. I could love everyone who needed help, but I was unwilling to risk such deep personal loss again." She looked into Arelia's eyes and smiled a soft smile. "That is, until now. I find I have opened my heart to you."

CHAPTER 41

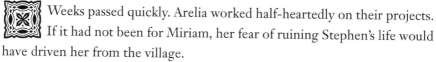Weeks passed quickly. Arelia worked half-heartedly on their projects. If it had not been for Miriam, her fear of ruining Stephen's life would have driven her from the village.

Stephen, on the other hand, worked with a vengeance. Joan noticed his conviction and high energy, realizing that she had never seen such determination in her son before. His fervor seemed to motivate everyone in the village. Some men were out building the hut; others were fashioning furniture in their spare time. Many of the women had begun preparation for linens as wedding gifts. Everyone seemed enthused, except Joan.

Finally, late one afternoon, she was worn down by everyone's enthusiasm and decided to take the first step. All eyes followed as she walked across the clearing to the edge of the trees and knocked on Miriam's door. Stephen and John interrupted their work to watch Joan in amazement. Although there had been less tension around the house, Stephen was nervous about what his mother would say. He put down his tools and started toward Miriam's hut.

"Stephen," his father interrupted. "Come here."

"I am going to Miriam's," Stephen responded.

"No, son. You need to let the ladies be. Miriam will intercede if necessary."

"Joan, how nice to see you," said Miriam when she answered the door. Arelia looked up from the spinning wheel and smiled at Miriam's friend, surprised that she was meeting one of her friends for the first time since her arrival. So many women had come by with best wishes. "Arelia, do you remember Stephen's mother?" Miriam noticed Arelia's smile quiver.

"Hello," said Arelia hesitantly. Her voice had a hint of a shudder. She felt tightness in the pit of her stomach. She wanted to stand up to greet her but feared her knees would buckle.

Joan smiled weakly. "I hope you do not mind if I drop in for tea. Everyone was out of the house, so I thought I would take time for a visit."

"I am so glad you came," Miriam was sincere in her statement. She had prayed for the right timing in getting the two women together, though she was surprised that the first move came from Joan.

"Arelia, put leaves in the kettle to steep. Time has escaped me." Arelia had stopped spinning and was hoping to gain her composure to join the two older women. Joan watched every move she made as she prepared tea. Miriam was amused at how intently and obviously Joan studied Arelia as they talked. Fortunately, Arelia was occupied and didn't seem to notice the woman's intense attention and penetrating stare.

Joan made note of Arelia's delicate features from head to fingertips. Martha had commented about how graceful she was, and it appeared to be true. Joan didn't want to be impressed with her and was watching closely for any flaw she could detect.

Miriam kept the conversation going, although it was clearly one-sided. "Is that not so, Joan? Joan?"

"I am sorry. What did you say?" Joan asked when Miriam finally caught her attention.

"I was saying that you and I were friends even before you and John met," repeated Miriam.

"That is right," Joan replied absently. She noticed that Arelia had chosen Miriam's nicest teacups and had laid out a finely embroidered tea towel on the tray. She certainly had learned proper decorum.

Arelia brought the tray with the cups and plates to the table. She was cutting and arranging a cake that Joan could not distinguish. She placed the cake on the table and poured tea, as if she were serving royalty.

"Arelia, Stephen said you worked as a maid at Faircastle," Joan said, hoping to start a conversation.

"Yes, I did." Arelia's answer was short and delivered with a nervous smile.

"Miriam, you have kept a recipe from me. What is this delicious cake?" asked Joan.

"That is Arelia's doing. Cakes have never been my strength."

"You baked this?" For some reason, Joan seemed shocked.

"Yes, my mother always prepared this cake when nuts were plentiful. I gathered the nuts just behind Miriam's hut. It is one of my favorites." Arelia finally was able to smile.

"I can see why," added Miriam. "I think this would be a great cake for a wedding."

Arelia nearly choked on her tea, and Joan ignored Miriam's comment altogether.

"Arelia, Stephen has said so little about you. How did you meet?"

Arelia ignored the little jab and went directly to the question, relating the familiar wolf attack and Stephen's heroic intervention.

She certainly is a pretty girl, thought Joan, *but a girl, nonetheless.*

"Martha seemed to enjoy you in your cave adventure. You two girls are about the same age, aren't you?" continued Joan.

Miriam cut in, "Two years can make a world of difference when one has had the experiences that Arelia has."

"And what kind of experiences have you had?" Joan asked pointedly.

Arelia looked into her teacup, knowing the implication of her question.

"Joan," Miriam admonished. "Sometimes you can be very insensitive. You know that Arelia cared for her family during the plague and lost them all. I know Stephen told you about her being orphaned."

Arelia was determined not to cry. She was not sure if anger or the loss of her family motivated her tears. Joan didn't know what to say. In seeing the girl's reaction, she was embarrassed by her own cruelty.

"I am sorry, Arelia. That *was* insensitive of me." The mood had become very tense. Joan regretted her visit.

"It is all right, Mrs. Wingate," Arelia began. "I can understand your concern for your son." A single tear crept down her cheek, which she casually wiped away with the back of her hand. "My mother had concerns about my brothers, too. I do not begrudge you yours. We have never met. It has to be a shock for you."

Joan didn't know how to respond. She had a million questions, but they all seemed inappropriate now.

"How does it feel to have your son home?" Miriam asked, hoping to change the subject.

"You mean Stephen?" Joan asked absently.

"He is the only son you have." Miriam laughed.

"I have not seen him much. He is either hiding, working, or over here."

"He should spend more time with you. He has been gone a long time," Arelia suggested sincerely.

Joan was disarmed. Maybe she had judged this lovely girl too quickly, just as everyone had said.

"There is a way to remedy this, Joan," offered Miriam. "You remember how we couldn't pry you and John apart before you married. If you have Arelia to your house on occasion, you know Stephen will be there."

Joan took the lead. "Well, that is actually why I am here." She cleared her throat nervously. "I came to invite both of you to dinner tomorrow night."

A smile crossed Miriam's face. "I know I will be there. How about you, Arelia?"

"Thank you, Mrs. Wingate. I would enjoy that. Thank you very much."

As Joan left the hut, she waved at Stephen and John with a smug smile. She was transformed.

"I told you those two could handle her," John said as he slapped Stephen on the back.

"What kind of magic do they have?" Stephen's question was serious.

"They are women, son!" came John's immediate answer. "You will see more in the future, but never understand." He laughed.

Arelia stood looking at the new hut, which was nearly ready for its occupants. *Has it really been a month since my first dinner with Stephen's family?* Arelia wondered.

That first dinner with the Wingate family was filled with surprises. First, when Miriam and Arelia opened the door to go to the Wingate's hut, they found Stephen on the other side of the door, ready to knock and holding a bouquet of colorful leaves and grasses. He presented Arelia the bouquet with such love and care, bringing tears to both women. Arriving at the Wingate's door was equally moving when Stephen's sisters greeted Arelia with warm hugs. John took the ladies' capes while Stephen moved the bench away from the table and helped the ladies to their places. Arelia couldn't tell if Stephen's mother was unwelcoming or too busy with preparing the dinner to welcome them.

John led a prayer of thanksgiving before passing the serving dishes—a delicious meal everyone enjoyed. It was then when Joan surprised everyone. "Arelia," she began, "I hope you are enjoying your dinner."

"Oh yes, Mrs. Wingate, thank you. Everything is delicious. You are a wonderful cook." She smiled.

"If Stephen has his wish, we will have many more meals around this table together." She smiled at Stephen without the usual irritation.

John interrupted. "That is also my wish."

Both sisters joined in at the same time, "And mine."

Arelia held her breath, not knowing what to expect next.

Joan was the first to speak. "Yes. It is obvious to see that my entire family loves you, as does everyone in the village. Which brings me to tell all of you that I had an unexpected guest yesterday morning when I went out to find herbs." She smiled.

Miriam asked, "Joan, who was it?"

With a soft chuckle, she answered, "Madeline."

Martha, true to her nature, loudly echoed, "Madeline?!"

Everyone laughed at Martha's surprised outburst, but Arelia still could not seem to take a breath.

Joan placed her hands in her lap and shared their conversation. "It seems Madeline has also come to enjoy having Arelia here with us." She looked over at Arelia with a smile, and Arelia was able to take a small breath. Everyone was quiet, not knowing what to expect. "Yes, we had a surprisingly long and very pleasant visit under the trees. Madeline and I have never had a conversation only between the two of us. I see why I have always liked her."

She looked at Stephen for a few seconds, and then asked, "Stephen, have you and James talked about Madeline since you have returned home?"

"No, Mother, we have had no time for casual talk."

"That is what Madeline and I both suspected."

John coaxed, "Joan, what is this about?"

"Well, it seems that Madeline is a very brave girl, and she is most appreciative of Arelia, because she wants Stephen to have someone significant in his life—someone he loves. She said she sees that Stephen *truly loves you*, Arelia."

All eyes turned to Stephen and then to Arelia. Joan continued. "Also,"—she paused with a smile, as if for effect—"it appears that James and Madeline have fallen in love." Everyone was speechless.

Joan laughed. "You all have reacted exactly as I did. I did not know what to say. Madeline told me that she wanted me to be the first to know because she believed that both she and Stephen would be happier if we all accepted Arelia into our family. I have given her words considerable thought and prayer, and I now see that she is right—and so are all of you."

Stephen wiped away a tear and, after a sigh of relief, said, "Thank you, Mother."

Martha laughed with joy, and Miriam stood up from the table. "I think we should celebrate with dessert."

John asked, "What shall we do next?"

Stephen nearly shouted, "Let us build a hut!"

Martha shouted, "We will plan a wedding!"

Arelia put her face in her hands and cried for joy!

Every household had contributed something to help the young couple start a home. A bench here, a table there, a bed frame, a blanket, towels, and cups. The furnishings came from everywhere. Even Madeline, Stephen's intended, had contributed a lovely rug that she had spun and woven herself. Arelia could see Stephen and his mother's attraction to Madeline. In fact, somehow she and Arelia were becoming close friends. Rumor in the village was that she and James were relieved that Arelia was in the picture because they had secretly intended to wed for some time. Now, they were free to announce their intentions without fear of retribution from their mothers.

Arelia, Stephen, and his family had spent the last two days arranging all the furniture in the hut. Arelia was as nervous as Stephen was excited. Martha and

Jean had stuffed the mattress as Stephen assembled the frame. Arelia watched in amazement, realizing that was the bed she would share with her husband.

All in all, the mood in the village was light and cheerful. There was an air of celebration as nearly everyone felt responsible for the young couple's betrothal by having tricked the soldiers.

The wedding was only two days away, and preparations were being made for a celebration afterward. A pig would be butchered and roasted. Pies and cakes were in the making. Miriam and Joan decided that Arelia's mother's nut cake would be perfect for the wedding cake. Several women had the recipe and would contribute to the whole.

It was getting dark when Miriam called Arelia in to dinner. "Only two more days, child. How is the hut coming along?"

"It feels like a dream, Miriam. I do not think I deserve all of this attention. These people do not even know me."

"That is right, because if they did, they would give you even more." She laughed. "They probably know you better than you think. Remember, Martha will be your sister-in-law, and she knows you."

"You know what I mean, Miriam."

"Yes, I do know, and I do not agree with your thinking. You are a lovely young woman who has been through more than most people experience in a lifetime. You deserve all your good now. Remember, this celebration is also for Stephen and his family. They are celebrating a growing family with your coming into their family, and do not forget the possibility of you and Stephen having babies in the future."

Arelia blushed.

"Arelia, you are thinking too much. The love you and Stephen share is the only thought you need to have now."

"I keep thinking something horrible is going to happen," admitted Arelia.

"Listen carefully, child. Your thoughts are more powerful than anyone knows. I have seen in my own life how my thoughts have affected my experiences. Get your mind off gloom and doom. There will be enough of that without your asking for it."

"I am not asking for something horrible. I said I fear it is coming," explained Arelia.

"Fear it, and it will come. Fear is a powerful magnet. For some reason, we attract what we fear. Focus on the opposite and expect good things. More good will come that way." Miriam seemed sincere in what she was saying, but Arelia couldn't understand what she meant.

"I do not understand. I have had so many bad things happen that I never thought about. I never could have imagined anything so bad," Arelia countered.

"Arelia, there are so many things we feel we have no control over and cannot understand. I do not understand either. I just know that when I fear bad things, they sometimes happen, and when I expect good, I see good."

"But I still cannot understand why all the bad things happened to me."

"I cannot say I really understand either. There are so many things that happen that we have no control over. No one saw the plague coming, and there was nothing anyone could do to stop it," Miriam agreed.

"I certainly had a lot of terrible things happen to me." Arelia thought for a long time. "Miriam, are you saying if I am not afraid, and I do not think bad things will happen, nothing bad will ever happen again?"

"No, I am afraid not." Miriam smiled at the girl. "I wish I could say 'yes.' What I am saying is that not as many bad things will happen, and when they do, you will see the good behind the bad experience. For instance, your wolf attack was a nightmare, but you would not have met Stephen if it had not happened."

"No," Arelia understood what she was saying. "I would never have come this far, and I certainly would never have gone to the castle and met my uncle." Arelia immediately caught the slip and looked away nervously.

Miriam heard the hint but ignored her unintended comment. "I say my husband's death is the best worst thing that ever happened to me."

"The best worst?" Arelia's wrinkled brow showed that she was confused.

Miriam laughed at her expression. "Yes, when Carl died and I lost my baby, I thought my world had ended. I wanted to die, too. I developed a reliance on myself that I never would have had. I turned to myself and to my Creator for direction. Since that time, I have healed many through knowing about herbs and have possibly even saved lives. I have come to know more people here and even in other villages. I would never have done any of that if I had been a wife and mother. That is not to say one is better than the other. It is only to say that I am very thankful for the short time I had with my husband, and I am thankful for the gifts I have now. I am thankful to have you in my life." She patted Arelia's knee.

Arelia took her hand. "I think I am beginning to understand. But I will really have to think about this."

Miriam squeezed her hand and released it. "Guard your thoughts as you would a fortress. Your mind and your free will are two of your Creator's greatest gifts to you. Go to sleep now. Tomorrow is going to be a busy day for us both." Miriam kissed Arelia lightly on the forehead. "This may sound selfish, knowing your tragedies, but I am happy you have been brought to me. 'May the words of your mouth and the thoughts of your heart find favor before the Lord,' dear Arelia."

Arelia smiled and added, "Psalm 19."

The day before the wedding was filled with activity. The village seemed to hum with excitement. The women talked about the last wedding in the village, between Arthur and Mary Hawthorne, who now had a four-year-old daughter. There was plenty of room for excitement. James and Madeline pictured their own celebration, which would be announced after the wedding, as they threw themselves into the activity. Even the threat of rain had not dampened the joyous mood.

Miriam had fitted her wedding dress to Arelia. The dress would be a surprise to everyone. Many of the women talked about how sad it was that Arelia couldn't have had time to prepare a dress, but none of them offered their own to the young woman.

Miriam admired Arelia at her final fitting. "I think we have it right this time. You look so beautiful."

"Thanks to you and your wonderful dress. If it were not for you, I would not have anything special to wear. In fact, if it were not for you, I would not even be here."

"Well, you *are* here, and this little village has a treat in store for them tomorrow."

The Wingates' household was busier than ever. Joan was very much in cadence with everyone else by now. This was her only son and the first wedding in the family, and she wanted it to be right. She sent the girls to collect colorful leaves and berries for decoration. The girls' good dresses had been altered and laundered. Even John's dress coat had been brought out for the occasion.

She had wanted to get a piece of cloth to make a new dress for herself but realized she would never have time with all the other preparations. Instead, she had remade one of her old favorites by adding ribbon and a finely embroidered collar. The dress was as good as new for the occasion and would be fitting for the mother of the groom.

That evening as she laid out her dress, getting caught up in the excitement, she realized for the first time that this must really be a time of mixed emotions for Arelia. On one hand, it was her wedding day, but on the other, her family's absence would be painfully apparent. She could actually feel the hurt in her heart and wondered how Arelia was handling the pain.

"I will be back, John."

"Where are you going at this time of night?"

"There is something I must give Arelia," she said as she dug through a chest and pulled out a small box. John simply smiled at his wife, who had changed so much in such a short time.

"Miriam." Joan pushed open the door without knocking.

"Joan? What in the world are you doing here this late?"

"I have something for Arelia." Arelia was putting away the last bit of dinner and cleaning off the table.

"Come sit with me, Arelia," Joan said, setting the small box on the table and patting the bench next to her. "I know this is a time of mixed emotions for you. My mother gave me these gloves to wear on my wedding day," she said as she opened a small, delicately carved box. "My grandmother had embroidered them for her. I would like you to wear these tomorrow as my new daughter."

Arelia's eyes were wide, and her mouth dropped open. The room began to blur as tears clouded her vision. "Thank . . ." She couldn't speak. *Where is my own mother? I have only strangers to give me away.* Miriam moved close to her.

"Child, Joan and I will never know your pain, but we wish we could ease it. What is lost is not retrievable. We can never take the place of your family, but we will try to fill the gaps if you let us."

Arelia reached for Joan's hand and put her arm around Miriam and wept. She was tired of pretending to be someone even she didn't know. These two caring and sympathetic women knew only a small part of her grief. The rest needed to stay hidden, maybe forever.

Neither Joan nor Miriam tried to talk her out of her tears. Both women knew from experience the healing that tears brought. No one knew why the three were brought together or what the future held for them.

CHAPTER 42

 Flashes of light and pounding thunder woke Arelia in the middle of the night. Rain fell so hard it began to drip through the thatch roof.

My wedding day. How will we get married in this weather?

Miriam was already up, checking that Arelia's dress was safely away from the drops dripping steadily through the leaking roof.

"Oh, Miriam, what are we going to do?"

"Do not worry. We have a long time until morning. As hard as it is coming down, it will rain itself out. Go back to sleep. You want to be rested for morning."

The next time Arelia opened her eyes, light was shining in from under the door. She listened for rain, but it seemed to have stopped. She could smell her mother's nut cake baking. *What time does Miriam get up?* "Miriam, do you ever sleep?"

"Occasionally," was her simple answer. "I talked to John earlier this morning. We are going to wait a few hours for the ground to dry. The men have chosen a place for the ceremony that is thick with leaves and not muddy. You can feel the excitement. The entire village smells like cake!" Miriam's own excitement showed in her eyes and infectious smile. "Get out of bed, child. I have water boiling for a warm bath."

Arelia lay in bed a minute or so longer watching Miriam. *How would my family have been? Whom would I have married?*

"Miriam." Arelia said her name almost as if she were thinking to herself. "You are the most wonderful substitute mother any girl could have."

"Well, this substitute mother says, 'Get out of bed!'" Arelia thought Miriam's eyes actually twinkled.

The two women had their breakfast of tea, bread, and boiled eggs.

"This is your last breakfast as an unmarried woman." Miriam noticed a hint of concern cross Arelia's face with her light comment. "Did I say something wrong?"

"I am so scared," Arelia admitted in a soft voice. "Everything has happened so quickly. I do not know if I can be a good wife."

"Did you agree to marry?" Miriam asked.

"Yes, I think so. I agreed to leave the estate with Stephen. He has been so wonderful to me. I think he asked me on the way here, but I was in so much pain and so afraid. I guess I agreed. Everything happened so fast—so much has happened since we ran away."

"Oh, I see." Arelia could almost see Miriam's mind ticking.

"What do you see?"

"I see a young woman who thinks she needs more time, and time has run out. Have you spoken to Stephen about your concerns?"

"What would I say? It is not that I do not want to marry *him*. I do love him. I just do not know if I want to *marry* at all."

"Oh," Miriam said again.

"What should I do?" Arelia pleaded for an answer.

"Child, there is no easy answer to this. Look at all the things that are possible." She paused. "One thing you can do is tell Stephen that you want to wait. Then he will tell his parents, and they can tell the village."

"Oh, they will hate me, and so will Stephen."

Miriam continued, "Another thing you can do is sneak out while no one is looking and hide in the woods." Miriam winked at Arelia's surprised expression. "Or you can go through with the wedding and tell Stephen your concerns and hope that he will be patient and understanding."

"Stephen is the most patient and understanding man I have ever met, but I think that I will hide in the woods." Both women laughed heartily at the thought of it.

"Seriously, Miriam, what should I do?"

"This is your decision alone, and I must say I am glad of that." She patted Arelia's hand and then moved to the hearth to fill the tub. "I think that what you should do right now is get into a hot tub of water and think about what you really want to do."

The warm bath relaxed Arelia, unscrambling her thoughts as she soaked in the hot, fragrant water. "Miriam, do you think Stephen loves me?"

"Like a bee loves flowers."

"What if I am not a good wife?" Arelia asked with deep sadness in her voice.

"Is that what this is all about? Are you feeling unworthy again?"

Arelia splashed water on her face but did not answer.

"Child, you will not know if you are a good wife until you become one. We are all frightened by change. I was scared on my wedding day, but I was excited too. Are you excited at all?"

"I think I am, but I am so afraid that I will disappoint Stephen and his family."

"Do you want to be a good wife?"

"Yes, very much," Arelia answered.

"Do you love Stephen?"

"I think I do. No other man is as good as he is, and I respect him and admire his courage. I am happiest when I am with him, but I do not know if that is love."

Miriam considered her answer. "No one can say exactly what love is. When I married Carl, I thought I loved him, but my feelings for him changed over time, and I realized that I did not even know what love was when we first married." Miriam laughed softly as if remembering something very special. She continued, "It sounds strange even to me, but the first time I really knew I loved him was after our first big argument. We had really never gotten that angry with each other before we married, but after a few months it seemed that almost anything we did made either one or the other of us upset." She smiled again thinking of a time long ago.

"Finally, we cleared the air with the most horrible argument. I cannot even remember what we fought about now." She smiled and shook her head. "We found out later that we had even been heard from the other huts. He shouted, and I cried. I shouted, and he glared, then dead, cold silence. I thought my hurt would never end. Then he said, 'If you were my mother, I would run away.' For some reason, that seemed so funny to me. I laughed until I cried. He was offended that I was laughing at first, but I guess my laughter and tears were so genuine and infectious that he caught it. After that, nothing that we

410

said to each other seemed to matter. We both knew we had spoken out of anger, so we apologized and made up. I am not sure why; whatever it was just did not matter anymore. That night, he held me in his arms, and I knew I was where I wanted to be. I knew I loved him enough to work to save our relationship even when things were bad, and I knew he would too. That is when I knew beyond a shadow of a doubt that I loved him."

Arelia looked down at her hands—a sign that Miriam recognized by now warned that tears were close behind.

"What is it, child?"

Her delicate hands covered her face, and the tears began to flow.

More tears. More hurt. More healing, Miriam observed. "Would you like to tell me?"

"I cannot tell you," Arelia choked out through her sobs.

"You are the cryingest girl I have ever seen." She stroked the top of her head. "Let me warm your water."

By the time Miriam added a pot of hot water, Arelia's tears were slowing down.

"Miriam, Stephen does not deserve to be married to someone like me. His mother was right. Madeline should be his wife."

"You forget Madeline wants to be with James, and she believes that you are the one who makes Stephen happy. Stephen's mother welcomed you as her daughter."

"But she does not really know me. No one knows me," she shouted.

Miriam was taken aback by her reaction. "And what is it that we should know?"

"I am a whore," she shouted as if she would burst.

Miriam did not even change her expression. She had suspected Arelia's past from all the bloody discharge on the first night.

"You have been with a man?" Miriam questioned in a kind, nonjudgmental voice in order to encourage her to talk.

"Many men," she whispered sadly but with relief that her secret was finally out.

"Does Stephen know?"

"Yes, he came to me as one of those men, but we just talked for hours. He was so kind."

"Then, what is the problem?" Miriam asked innocently.

Arelia looked at her as though she had lost her mind. "How can you not see the problem? I said I am a whore."

"No, what I heard you say was that you *were* a whore and that you have escaped that experience at great risk. Did you solicit those men?"

"Of course not." She sobbed. Arelia considered Miriam's question. "You do not understand." She sighed in resignation. *No one understands.*

"Yes, I understand too well. Stephen has forgiven you, but you have not forgiven yourself. It is not Stephen's disapproval of you that will keep you from being a good wife but your own disapproval of yourself."

"But he will expect things of me as his wife, and he has that right," Arelia countered.

"Stephen knows your past, and he loves you. He is a good man. I do not think that he will make unjust demands on you. You have said yourself that he is the most patient and understanding man you know. You seem to be judging him according to the other men in your past, not based on who you know *he* is."

Arelia looked at her hands again. "They were so horrible, Miriam, so cruel."

Miriam interrupted her thoughts. "Your past can ruin your present situation only if you let it. As long as you carry the past around with you in your mind, it will continue to affect you. It is only by leaving those memories behind that you can create a happy life here and now—in the present. Do not carry this weight with you. Put it down and walk away from it."

"I do not know how to do that. I cannot just forget," Arelia said sadly, with despair.

"Do you have good memories with Stephen during that time?"

Arelia smiled. "Yes, wonderful memories,"

"Any other good memories with anyone else?"

"Oh, yes, with my uncle and Sarah and Laura."

"Would that be Joseph's mother and sister, the young man who sent you the bag?"

"Yes."

"Would it be possible for you to force yourself to focus on the good during that time?"

"My favorite time was walks on the beach with my uncle and Stephen, the wind and waves. Stephen and I would sneak out at night in the moonlight. I had never seen anything like it before. It was so beautiful."

"I suspect you protected your mind before. Otherwise, I do not see how you could have withstood and escaped what you described to me. It appears Stephen had his hand in that."

"Oh yes. I would not have survived without Stephen . . . and Laura and Sarah, too."

"You do have beautiful memories of people you love. Again, guard your mind like a fortress. When fearful memories attack, bolt the door and look at the beauty in your past and now with your new home—in your new life. You will never forget those times. They will always resurface, Arelia, but you cannot allow yourself to dwell on them," Miriam cautioned. "I still think of Carl, the snake, and losing our daughter. That pain and grief is still with me, but it is a memory which I do not allow to destroy what I have now. It is because of what happened that I am with you now." She smiled.

"Is it really that easy?" Arelia asked. "I know I did it, but today it seems hard."

"I didn't say it was easy. Sometimes our memories can be our greatest enemy, but the rewards for defeating negative memories and thoughts are great. Arelia, gratitude is the greatest defense against regret. Be grateful for what you have *now*. Be grateful that you had an experience that brought Stephen into your life. Would you like to talk to Stephen before the ceremony to be sure that he understands your concerns?"

"No," Arelia said emphatically. "I do not want to talk about this with him now."

"It will come up soon," Miriam cautioned. "The longer you wait, the harder it will be."

"No, not now." Arelia was firm in her decision.

"Do we call off the wedding or proceed?"

"Proceed," Arelia said with a weak smile.

As Arelia was stepping out of the tub, there was a knock at the door. She quickly wrapped herself in a dry cloth. "Aunt Miriam," Martha and Jean excitedly called through the closed door. "We have flowers for Arelia's hair."

Miriam opened the door to two of the brightest and prettiest girls she had ever seen, each with a huge bouquet of flowers and brilliantly colored leaves.

"Are you taking a real bath?!" Martha squealed as they rushed into the room. "This is such an exciting day. Where is your dress!?"

"No, now, girls, you want to see her complete, do you not?" Miriam said as she ushered them to the door. "Run ask your father when the ceremony will be." The girls ran out as quickly as they had come in.

"How shall we fix your hair? Do you want it up or down—or should we do it half and half?" Miriam suggested.

They brushed her long, straight, silky hair until it shined. Miriam gathered the hair from around her face and fastened it on the top of her head with a white linen ribbon. Fine wispy locks of hair framed her face and accentuated her dark, round eyes.

"Shall we arrange some flowers?" Miriam asked.

"Of course. I cannot disappoint my new sisters." She smiled. They picked out the tiniest and brightest flowers to put in Arelia's hair.

Just as Miriam placed the last flower, the girls charged through the door again. "Father said we will meet in one hour. The men are adding straw to the leaves."

Arelia's stomach did a flip. "One hour!"

"Arelia, you are beautiful," both girls chanted.

"All right, girls," Miriam interrupted. "Be on your way. Arelia needs time to dress—and she needs privacy."

Just as Miriam was fastening the dress, there came another knock at the door. This time Joan slipped through before Miriam had a chance to open it. She stopped in awe to admire her new daughter-in-law.

"My, you *are* beautiful. Stephen is a very lucky man."

"Thank you," Arelia said modestly.

"Do you recognize the dress?" Miriam asked.

"Oh my, it is from *your* wedding. I had forgotten how lovely it is." Joan thought back many years ago. "I came early because we have forgotten something very important. Who will give Arelia away?"

Arelia looked at Miriam in dismay.

"I will," Miriam said.

"Not you; you are a woman." Joan laughed, not taking her seriously.

Arelia smiled. Even in the short time that she had known Miriam, she knew that being a woman was not enough to keep Miriam from doing what she wanted.

"My, you are very observant, Joan. I am a woman who tends my livestock and tills the soil. I cook, spin, weave, dispense herbs, milk cows, chop wood, and maintain this hut. I even heal people if necessary. *I will give Arelia away,*" she stated firmly. "It is exactly what Arelia wants, and no one else will do." She smiled confidently.

Arelia took it from there. "Miriam has cared for me since the first night I was here. I do not know any of the men well enough to ask, and certainly Stephen's father cannot do it. Miriam is the closest to family that I have."

"Oh, dear. I fear I am being outnumbered again."

"What you fear you attract." Arelia laughed.

"What?"

"Never mind, Joan. We will be out shortly. Gather the others," Miriam said.

"Do not forget the gloves," Joan reminded as she hurried out the door.

As Arelia pulled Joan's gloves out of the drawer, she noticed a small, dark bag pushed to the back. *My amulet,* she thought.

"What is it, child?"

"I have a gift from my father here," she said as she slipped it over her head and tucked it under the neckline of her dress.

Arelia gave Miriam a big hug. "This is perfect. Now I am ready."

Miriam could see everyone gathered nearby when she peeked out the door. "You have a big surprise, child. Let us go now."

When Miriam pushed the door wide open, Arelia stopped to take in a scene she could not believe. The men had laid a path of straw and brightly colored leaves from Miriam's doorway to the gathering place at the base of a cove of trees. Children had hung vines intertwined with flowers from the low branches, making a canopy of flowers lit by sunlight. Two men played flutes in the distance, competing with birds for music.

One of the children shouted, "There she is!"

Everyone turned toward the door. She and Miriam heard a few "oohs" and "ahhhs" as the villagers caught their first glimpse of the radiant bride standing in the doorway. A gentle breeze caught soft wisps of her dark tresses, giving gentle motion to a picture of beauty. Miriam's cream-colored dress hung delicately from her shoulders with tiny, embroidered, pink flowers nestled in variegated-green leaves, appearing as a garland gracing her neck and shoulders, accenting the small buds that Martha and Jean had provided for her dark, shining hair. Folds of soft fabric fell from a fitted bodice with pink buds falling like rain to another thick ribbon of buds and leaves encircling the hemline, giving the impression of standing in a field of flowers.

"This is like a story, Miriam. How is this real?"

"That is all life is, child, a story. Now, go to meet your groom."

CHAPTER 43

Arelia's knees were weak as she walked down the colorful leaf-carpeted path under the admiring gaze of the crowd, but she held her head high as she approached her groom. She noticed Madeline first, beaming as if she were the one getting married, and then Martha and Jean. As she and Miriam walked toward the canopied clearing, the crowd parted to make way for her, and there was Stephen. She felt as if she were seeing him for the first time. *In spite of that smile, is he as nervous as I am?* She felt herself grinning as she walked to his side. When his eyes caught hers, everyone and everything else seemed to fade away as he reached for her hand.

No one appeared to care or even notice that Miriam was giving her away.

Because so many clergy had died from the plague, there was no priest to perform the ceremony. Through mutual decision, Arthur Hawthorn had taken on the role as spiritual guide for their little community. His own ceremony was fresh enough in his mind to enjoy performing the service for this young couple and, in fact, for the entire village.

Stephen couldn't believe that Arelia and he would finally be together. He was caught between wanting to shout for joy and cry from relief. Each time he looked into her dark, smiling eyes, time seemed to stop for him; he had never seen a woman so beautiful both on the inside and in all that is pleasing to the eye. All the pain and risk culminated for him in this one moment of time.

Stephen and Arelia listened as if in a dream as Mr. Hawthorn read a passage from his family's handwritten, timeworn New Testament. "This passage is from 1 Corinthians 13:4–7," Mr. Hawthorn began.

"Love is patient, love is kind." Arelia smiled. She knew this to be true of Stephen and hoped that she demonstrated the same courtesy to him. "It does not envy; it does not boast; it is not proud." Arelia was fleetingly struck with a memory of Marisa and Edward but glanced up at Stephen, cherishing the nearness of him and wiping away any harmful thoughts.

"It is not rude; it is not self-seeking; it is not angered; it keeps not record of wrongs." John smiled at Joan and loved her all the more for growing to love Arelia.

"Love does not delight in evil but rejoices with the truth." Stephen gently squeezed Arelia's warm hand. He drank in her beauty with his eyes. She lovingly returned his gaze.

"It always protects, always trusts, always hopes, always perseveres." The words echoed in Arelia's head. *PROTECTS . . . TRUSTS . . . HOPES . . . PERSEVERES. This is just what Miriam told me.* She experienced warmth radiating through her body and felt as though she and Stephen were the only two people in the forest.

"Love never fails." As Mr. Hawthorn ended the reading, tears came to Arelia's eyes. Stephen gently brushed them away. *I will not fail you, Stephen*, she thought, wanting to say the words aloud as Mr. Hawthorn continued.

"There is little more to say about love than what we read here," Mr. Hawthorn began, "Patient, kind, rejoicing in truth, protecting, trusting, hoping, persevering, those are words about behavior. Love is a promise to actively work at caring for each other. Notice it does not say anything about feelings. It does not say 'Love is a warm, comfortable feeling,' or 'Love is when you want to be with each other for all time.' It does not say that you cannot get angry or bored with someone you love. In fact, the words patient, hopeful, and persevering would indicate that there will be hard times when you love someone. There was a time that I did not know that, and I had to read these words over and over until I understood.

"Immaturity suggests that love is an emotion which will always feel good, but that is not what Scripture tells us, and certainly real life does not suggest that either." The married couples laughed quietly in agreement, including Mrs. Hawthorn.

Arelia listened to the words of love and commitment of which Mr. Hawthorn spoke and resolved to never let Stephen down. It was a conscious decision that she made voluntarily and vowed to keep. She realized that she had never felt so strongly about anyone, not even her own family; now she would demonstrate her love for him in everything she did. She would continue to push her doubts of worthiness aside, not wanting to give weight to her fear. She would trust him and their commitment to each other; she would persevere in her struggle to turn from fear; and she would have hope in the future of a family as a wife and mother.

Mr. Hawthorn continued, "Stephen and Arelia, we are all aware that you have already been tested in your commitment to each other, and you have won. We stood by you then, and we will continue to stand by you in the future. You have given us a renewed sense of what it is to love and to protect someone, and we thank you for the example you have given us.

"Those of us who have been married for many years might envy the new love Stephen and Arelia have for each other right now, but I encourage those of you who are looking with a jealous eye to examine what you are doing to respect your own husband or wife. Are you appreciative? Are you speaking nicely and politely to each other? Are you thoughtful of each other? There are things you can do to show your love, beginning this day. We are reminded by witnessing the love and sacrifice Stephen and Arelia have shown for each other. Protecting, always trusting, always hoping, always persevering, this is what we are called to do with our spouses and with each other. Love never fails, but we can fail in our love for each other. We have been reminded how important we are to each other because of those we have lost over the past years. Today we come to appreciate our families and each other once again.

"Stephen, Arelia, as we see you here today, you have given us a new idea of what love between a man and his wife can be: starry eyes, soft smiles, and tender touches." Everyone nodded; a few chuckled and murmured. "Our prayer is that most of your days are filled with the feelings you have for each other today, and that on the days you are feeling challenged to practice the virtues of love for each other, you remember this day and this hour. You are a blessing to each and every one of us and a wonderful reminder of how to love.

"Arelia, I want to address you first. Stephen and I have known each other since we were young. I missed him when he left, but now I know it was in God's plan for him to meet you. We all know you lost your entire family, and I believe God wants us to become your family now. We are happy to have you here. I do not think being married to this man will be easy. I know him." Many of the men laughed, and Stephen's father patted him on the back. "But I do know he has committed himself to you at all costs.

"The words of Paul to the Corinthians are more than mere words; they are virtues. Actions filled with grace to help us survive. I believe that those virtues are instilled in your life already. I think that to get from your village to ours you had to have trust, hope, perseverance, patience, and you can rejoice in the truth that God loves you. You have within you all that it will take to be married to this man.

"And Stephen," as he addressed Stephen, Stephen and Arelia's eyes met, and they shared a look that knew the deeper, secret truth of Mr. Hawthorn's words. "You have certainly protected Arelia and persevered under difficulty, but as a soldier, you may have developed some attitudes that will not serve you in marriage. Pride, anger, record keeping; self-seeking actions befit a soldier but not a good husband. I encourage you to put away the influence of soldiers and pick up the virtues that Paul shares with us today.

"Once these vows are made, you are both committed to put aside your past in order to build a new life for the future. You will carry the old you with you, your memories and attitudes will remain, but you will take on a new existence together that will reestablish who you will become as husband and father and as wife and mother. God has given you the tools to build a new life together and a new family, and He has outlined, in these words from Corinthians, a way to evaluate yourselves when things get rough. And," he added jokingly, "He has given you a good group of people to help you stay in line."

Many cried as Stephen and Arelia exchanged the sacred vows to love, honor, and obey, and when the final blessing was said, everyone cheered. Each person felt a part of the young couple's lives, and in fact, they were. They had played their roles well in order to save them and then spent weeks preparing for the celebration and for their lives together. All the mothers and fathers were aware of Arelia's loss, and many of them tried to fill the gap, each in his or her own way. Several of them had lost daughters of their own, and Arelia was a blessed surprise rather than a loss; she represented a child who was a gift to them and their community, rather than one taken by the plague. It was hard for Arelia to imagine that in such a short time so many of these people had become like family to her. Today, only the marriage of Stephen and Arelia mattered to anyone. There was reason to celebrate.

Succulent dishes were arranged outside of John and Joan's hut on makeshift tables, amid flowers and greenery. Fragrant aromas of well-seasoned dishes mingled together to whet any appetite—large or small. Tables were covered with fresh breads, pies, potatoes, and carrots made in every imaginable way. Several ladies had arranged all the nut cakes in the center of the table and decorated them with fresh flowers and berries. It was hard to tell if the centerpiece was a wedding cake or a huge bouquet. Across from the tables, men had dug a huge pit where they roasted a pig and several chickens. The roasting had begun in the middle of the night, so the tantalizing aroma of pork had awakened everyone to anticipation of more than the ceremony! Several men gathered to carve moist, roasted meat.

Flutists began to play, and those who were not serving or eating danced to familiar tunes. Rarely had there been such jubilation in this small village. Other than Arelia's counterfeit funeral, the last gathering had been around bonfires as villagers burned their possibly plague-infested possessions and livestock. Now was the time for a much-needed celebration!

Everyone ate too much, and they danced until darkness signaled the end of the festivities. As each person, young and old, left, he or she went to both Stephen and Arelia and wished them the best of life. Arelia was moved by such an overwhelming outpouring of love; it was in stark contrast to the life she had so recently left behind.

Stephen's family was the last to give their best wishes. "Arelia, we welcome you into our family. We hope that all pain is behind you, and that there is only joy ahead." John spoke so sincerely that Arelia felt that she had truly found her right place. Her eyes filled with tears over the love and tenderness she felt for her new family as she allowed herself to accept the love they so freely extended.

CHAPTER 44

After the last well-wisher had gone home, Stephen and Arelia approached their hut for the first time as a married couple. They noticed ribbons of smoke billowing from the stone chimney. Stephen opened the door to yet another fairytale image: a roaring fire in the fireplace, steam billowing from a kettle hanging over the fire, candles lit on the table and bed stand, and a lovely tea service arranged for tea. Neither of them had seen the hut complete with contributions that everyone had made.

"This must be home," Stephen said with a big grin as he carried Arelia over the threshold, holding her as they took in the scene.

"Who was here?" Arelia asked as he set her down gently near the hearth.

"It is the best wishes of everyone, but I see James and Madeline's hand in the fire and candles."

"You are right. Look at this." Arelia held up a white nightgown that was neatly laid out across the bed, decorated with tiny pink, yellow, and blue flowers stitched around the neckline. "There is a note here from Madeline. 'We wish you and Stephen all the best in your lives together. We are so happy that he brought you to us, too.'"

"We are so blessed with friends like these," he said. "Would you like me to help you unfasten your dress, so you can put on your new nightgown?"

She hesitated for a second. "Yes, that would be helpful. Then I will put on tea."

Stephen was obviously nervous too—and excited! His large fingers fumbled with the tiny buttons and tight loops, spaced too closely together. "I am not doing a very good job," he said sheepishly behind her back, "but you will not be able to reach. Should I go for help?"

Arelia laughed at the thought of it. "Help? And who would you run to?"

"My mother or Martha," he answered seriously. Arelia didn't want to laugh for fear of hurting his feelings; he was trying so hard to be helpful.

"We have all the time we need. Let me put on tea to steep first; then you can try again." When she turned around to get the loose tea, she could see that he was sincerely concerned. "You are doing a good job. Did you get any of them undone?"

"Only three—I have about two dozen more to go." He seemed to be facing overwhelming odds.

"Would you like me to run over to Miriam's for help?" she offered.

"It *is* her dress. You could leave it with her." He was relieved at the suggestion.

"I cannot come back in my underclothes." She laughed. She grabbed her heavy wool shawl and new nightgown.

Stephen blushed. "I know that you can figure it out between the two of you."

Miriam was concerned to see Arelia at the door until she saw her big grin. "Let me guess. Stephen cannot unfasten the dress?" she laughed. "Turn around. Oh, I see that Stephen did better than Carl. He only got two undone before I ran to my mother." They both laughed. "Now hold still so I can get you out of this thing."

Arelia slipped out of her dress and into her new nightgown.

"How are you, child?"

"There is no time to be concerned for myself. Stephen seems so nervous, although we have been alone so many times before," Arelia explained.

"But never as husband and wife. Remember that this is his first time as your husband, and he is probably worried about you."

"I never even thought that he would have concerns. You know, he even fought off wild animals for me."

"But that is something familiar to him, dear. This is very different."

"He is so nervous."

"Remember, too, Arelia, this is your first time with someone you love and who loves you. In essence, you have never had this experience before. Keep your thoughts only on Stephen. This is *your* night together."

Arelia looked into Miriam's eyes. "You are so dear to me. How will I ever thank you?"

423

"The only way that you can thank me is by being truly happy."

They hugged goodbye before Arelia ran back to her hut, hoping no one would see her. Martha opened the door to throw out dirty water from the basin just as Arelia ran from Miriam's.

"Look, Mother. Arelia is running from Miriam's in her night clothes!"

Joan laughed. "It must be all those buttons. Grandma had to get Miriam out of that dress, too." John laughed from his chair by the fire.

Arelia smelled strong spice tea when she opened the door. The room felt and smelled like home. Stephen was sitting by the fire just as her father had done. She stood in the doorway taking in the scene, trying to realize that this was *her own home.*

"I am home," she said, cherishing the sound of those words as she hung her shawl on the peg on the back of the door, just as her mother had done so many times.

Stephen watched her in amazement. "I cannot believe we are finally here in our own home. It seemed forever, and I was not sure if it would ever happen. Now it seems to have happened overnight."

He rose quickly and extended his hand to her. "Here, sit by the fire." He led her to her rocking chair. "Tonight, I will serve you."

It was one of those perfect moments that happens so seldom—the fire, the aroma, hot tea, and Stephen—her husband. They talked for hours about their childhood experiences and their expectations for a family, just as they had the first night they met, but this time was different; this time included the future. Arelia suddenly realized that they were not pretending; they were making real, possible plans for the future.

"Arelia, I do have one question—one I have asked but did not understand your answer. I do want to know everything about you."

"What is it?" she wondered at the sudden change in conversation.

"Your maiden surname—Davidson."

Somewhat relieved by the question, she replied, "My father returned to my mother having run away from Faircastle in order to ask for her hand against his parents' will. Needing to appear as a villager, he could not reveal his Fairchild surname. Sir Daniel laughed when he put together what he believed to be my father's thinking in choosing the name Davidson. I think I mentioned that my mother's surname was Peterson, as in Peter's son." She smiled. "My father loved the psalms written by King David, and my uncle told me that Scripture and the psalms calmed his somewhat unruly disposition and guided his actions. Uncle Daniel said that my father was a fair child who chose to become the son of King David who guided him through life with his psalms."

Stephen laughed. "How clever! He must have been a very interesting man—a man who married for love, giving up Faircastle for your mother's hand. I think I would have liked him." He smiled.

"Oh, Stephen, he would have loved you. Now that I think of it, in some ways you are very much alike." Her love seemed to grow deeper in sharing. She felt that she had introduced the two men she loved, and they admired each other.

He stood from is chair and took her hand. "Come, sit on my lap." She blushed. "I want to tell you something.

"We will have children of our own, and you will share stories about your mother and father, and your sisters and brothers. You will carry on their memory with our children. The Davidsons will live on in the imaginations of our children, just as they live on in you, and I will have the benefit of learning about you and your family in the telling.

"But for now, I know that no one expects to see me tomorrow, and we can sleep in, but I am really getting sleepy. All the planning and building is finally behind us, and I am exhausted. Are you sleepy?" Arelia nodded as she yawned. "Shall we go to bed then?" he asked hesitantly.

"That is the natural thing to do when you are sleepy," Arelia teased. She stood from his lap and savored the sight of him simply stoking the fire and re-fueling with three more logs.

He turned and saw Arelia study him; he blushed at his own nervousness. He had heard soldiers brag so many times about their conquests. Lust and war seemed to be all they knew to talk about, but he had not been raised that way, and he was feeling very unsure of himself. Of course, his sexual tension was not unfamiliar, but the nervousness was. He had wanted to make love to Arelia so many times, but he had waited. Now, he could fulfill his desire, and he was nervous and unsure.

Arelia was already snuggled under the covers by the time he put his night-shirt on. *What's wrong with me? Maybe I should have listened and gone to a whore*

425

for my first time. What will I do? It never crossed his mind, for one second, that Arelia would have been that whore.

Arelia scooted to her side of the bed near the wall. "I warmed your place." She smiled.

"You sure did." When he saw her familiar smile, he realized he was lying next to his best friend and, now, his lover. He had no need for concern over their first night as husband and wife.

"Snuggle up here. I will get you warm," he said as he scooped her into the crook of his strong arm.

Only flames from the fireplace lit the room; crackling and hissing logs were familiar bedtime music. Stephen gently stroked Arelia's arm that lay over his chest, and within minutes, they were both sound asleep.

Cold woke Stephen from a deep sleep. He smiled to himself when he realized where he was and who was lying next to him. He slowly got out of bed so he wouldn't awaken Arelia. As he put more logs on the dying embers, Arelia sat up. "It is very cold in here. Come back to bed to warm up."

He ran from the fireplace and hurried under the covers. "Do you hear thunder rumbling in the distance? There must be rain on the way." New flames cast a golden glow over the room as they cuddled together.

"Stephen, did I ever thank you for bringing me here?"

"I am sure you did."

"I do not think I did, not really." She leaned up on one arm and stroked his chest, then looked into his eyes. "You have made my life so wonderful."

"No, *you* have made your life so wonderful. You are the one who made the choice to leave and took the risk with me. I should thank you, too."

Arelia was surprised. "Thank me?"

"Yes. I was unhappy there, too, but I would never have left for myself. I do not know why, but I know I would have stayed if not for you." Stephen thought for a while. "By helping you, I saved myself."

Thunder rumbled directly overhead. Each flash of lightning lit the cracks around the door and shuttered windows.

"Thank you for coming home with me." He leaned toward her and kissed her gently on the cheek. She turned her face and met his lips. She lay against her pillow as they shared a deep, lingering kiss.

Arelia felt something like butterflies in her heart and stomach. She accepted his kiss again, thinking only of the beauty of being alone together. He did not hesitate to respond to his own desire. He yearned to satisfy not only his emotional desire for her as he had done before but, now, his physical desire as well. Arelia freely accepted him into her warmth; her breathing became heavier as they kissed, and she held his taut, sure body. She was no longer frightened or confused but wanted to satisfy his strong passion and openly receive this perfect expression of love from the man who had restrained himself for so long. In fact, she longed for him.

Spent by their lovemaking, Stephen fell asleep as he lay at her side. She lay with her head on his chest and twisted his dark hair around her finger. Her thoughts brought her back to other men at other times; Stephen seemed like a different species altogether. His touch was gentle and electrifying and his look, warm and loving. There was nothing painful about being with him as his wife. Her eyes grew heavy as she thought about how wonderful he was to be with. God blessed them both.

She woke to soft whistling. Stephen was already dressed; the fire was blazing, and tea was steeping.

"Good morning, sunshine. I thought you were going to sleep the day away."

Arelia had never seen her mother in bed. She was always the first up in the morning with bread and tea ready on the hearth, and the last to bed at night. "I am so sorry. Let me pour your tea." She quickly jumped out of bed.

Stephen stopped her and held the covers back. "Get back in this warm bed. I will bring tea to you. Once this time is over for us, you will no longer have the luxury of staying in bed. You better take advantage of me while you can." He laughed as she quickly hopped back under warm, welcoming covers.

Their hut was much like Miriam's, except the furnishings supplied from different hands made it unique to them. Their table was larger than Miriam's, provided by his father with a wish for many grandchildren. Two families each provided rocking chairs which stood in front of the fire: one large for Stephen and a smaller one for Arelia. Two families had worked together to provide a small cupboard which everyone had filled with tea leaves, preserves, bags of potatoes, flour, carrots, and even a small parcel of sugar; hand-stitched linens sat clean and ready to use on a corner of the table. Each item spoke of welcome and acceptance. Firewood was stacked, floor to ceiling behind the door, keeping out even the threat of cold. There was no loom or spinning wheel, but every convenience Arelia could wish for was at her fingertips. No one would ever mention that the four china plates and cups and saucers, the tea pot, serving dishes, and forks and knives were remnants from families who had not survived the plague; some things were better left unsaid.

Stephen seemed familiar with the supplies in the cupboard as he quickly found tea leaves and sprinkled them into the steaming pot that hung over the fire, placed boiled eggs and hard bread on a plate, and spread a small cloth over the blanket, picnic style. They spent the morning in bed with a breakfast of hot tea, warm bread, and boiled eggs. "Mother would never approve of crumbs in bed," Stephen said as he dusted away a few stray breadcrumbs.

"Then I am glad we did not invite her." They laughed at the image of Joan sitting in bed with them in her nightgown.

"How long can we get away with being lazy before people talk?" Arelia asked.

"Not more than three days. I will replenish the firewood before then, but that will be the extent of my efforts."

After several hours over breakfast and kisses, Arelia put on her shawl and sat by the fire to embroider, using the finest thread that Miriam had taught her to spin.

Stephen picked up a beautiful piece of walnut that was sitting by the hearth. "See this wood?"

"Yes."

"Do you like it?"

Arelia wrinkled her brow and smiled curiously. "Should I? Is it special?"

"Special! You cannot see how special it is?" He pretended to be offended.

"Of course I can," she teased back.

"Do you know why?"

"No, I am afraid you are going to have to explain that to me." She laughed.

He proudly held up the large block of wood. "This is my wedding gift to you." Arelia was very confused now. She didn't know what to say. He laughed at her puzzled expression. He pulled his knife out of his pocket. "Between this knife and this piece of wood, you will have the most beautiful candlesticks in the entire kingdom."

"You can do that?" she exclaimed.

"Of course I can. I did not have time to build a hut *and* make candlesticks, too, and I thought that you would want the hut first."

Arelia jumped up and gave him a big hug. "How did I get so fortunate to find you?"

"If you remember correctly, my dear lady, I found you." He picked her up and carried her to bed. He laid her against her pillow and kissed her passionately. She unbuttoned his shirt and stroked his chest.

"I had no idea that you had found me for keeps," she said lovingly.

"For ever and ever." He stroked her hair. "If I kiss you again, you may never get your candlesticks."

"The candlesticks can wait," she said as she pulled him to her. They made love again, more passionately than before. Arelia pushed unpleasant memories aside as his passion mounted. She loved his soft, gentle kisses, which were common only to him, but unbridled passion brought traces of fear and painful memories.

Miriam's warning came to her. *Guard your mind like a fortress.* Stephen was unaware of her feelings as his passion peaked.

He lay next to her and touched her cheek, then her nose, and then her lips. She looked at the tenderness in his eyes, knowing she had nothing to fear from him, and she never would.

"I better get that carving started, or you will not have them before our first anniversary," he said affectionately.

Arelia lay in bed and watched as he carved the dark wood by the fire with the same focus he seemed to devote to every task he took on. *I must truly protect my thoughts*, she thought as she fought back her tears. *This is a good man whom I have vowed to be with—I will honor my vow. I will love him forever.*

"Would you like stew for dinner?" she offered, mainly to distract herself. They spent the rest of the day cooking, carving, and embroidering. Stephen whistled softly as the candlesticks began to take shape. The hut took on a peaceful air as they enjoyed their first day of marriage. Going through the motions of a normal routine helped Arelia become more relaxed.

After dinner, Arelia picked up her Psalter. Stephen lit the lantern in anticipation. "What do you have for me tonight?" he asked as he moved the lantern closer to light the parchment.

"I found this psalm today. I think it speaks for both of us. It is Psalm 100."

1   A psalm of thanksgiving.
     Shout joyfully to the LORD, all you lands;
2   serve the LORD with gladness;
     come before him with joyful song.
3   Know that the LORD is God,
     he made us, we belong to him,
     we are his people, the flock he shepherds.
4   Enter his gates with thanksgiving,
     his courts with praise.
     Give thanks to him, bless his name;
5   good indeed is the LORD,
     His mercy endures forever,
     his faithfulness lasts through every generation.

Stephen smiled. "That reminds me of Martha, jumping for joy and shouting 'Alleluia!'"

"It is a joyful psalm. Do you think our lives will always be as happy as they have been the past few days?"

"I would like to say yes, but we have seen so much hardship in our lives, and we may see more. I value every minute we have shared and will draw on these quiet, peaceful times if life ever becomes difficult again."

"That is what I think, too." Arelia sighed. "But I was hoping you would disagree." She smiled.

"Well, for now, my sunshine, we can shout joyfully to the Lord for carrying us through to this wonderful time."

After the second day, they were both ready to get out of the hut. Stephen went to visit his parents, and Arelia went to visit Miriam.

"Good morning, child. You are just in time for tea," came Miriam's pleasant greeting. "How is married life?" she asked as she poured tea.

"Wonderful. Stephen is a wonderful man. We really enjoy each other."

"That is as it should be. And how are you? Are you happy as a married woman?" Miriam knew the question was general enough to avoid—and specific enough to answer truthfully if Arelia needed to talk.

"Sometimes bad memories crept in, but I did what you told me and thought only of Stephen."

Miriam took her hand and looked at her closely. "I can see you are very happy. You are good for each other. Your job will not always be easy, but remember, the reward for winning against your memories is great."

"It is wonderful. Thank you for all the ways that you have helped me."

"Arelia," came a call from outside the door. Jean and Martha came running in. "Mother wants to know if you and Stephen and Miriam can come for our evening meal. Stephen said we would have to ask you."

Miriam laughed. "You have already trained him well."

Stephen and Arelia slipped comfortably into the routine of village life over the next several months. Stephen tilled and planted a garden and tended livestock during the day and carved at night. Arelia cooked and cleaned and worked in the garden most days and embroidered at night. Some of her days were spent with other women sewing or baking. Occasionally, she would go to Miriam's to spin thread and talk away the day—that was always her favorite day.

Miriam and Stephen were the only two people who knew Arelia's real past, and they both loved her. This was a time of true healing for her. The past seemed farther and farther away, and painful memories seemed easier to push aside.

One night as they sat by the fire, Stephen proclaimed, "I have your gift!" He held three intricately carved candlesticks up for her to see. "They took much longer than I thought. Here is your wedding gift, my beautiful lady." He bowed as he held them out for her approval.

She had watched him carving intricate designs night after night, but he wouldn't let her look. Now she could see his handiwork.

"They are beautiful. Oh my, you have carved pictures."

"They tell a story. Let me explain them to you. This candlestick represents before we married—these seven trees symbolize your family. The biggest tree is your father; then here is your mother, and the smaller trees are you and your sister and brothers. The little squirrel with a nut on the second candlestick is to remind you that nature will always provide. The cave on the hillside is a place of safety, and the groove all around it signifies the path that brought you here.

"The second candlestick has a picture of our hut."

"It looks just like it. You are amazing." He smiled at her more-than-generous compliment.

"Carving is my favorite pastime."

"What are the trees here?"

"There are only two trees. One is you, and I am the other. They are strong oak trees. The acorns carved around the base symbolize our family to come and the generations that will follow as the fruits of our love and labor grow."

Arelia's eyes filled with tears of unexpected love. "They are so beautiful, but the third candlestick seems plain in comparison."

"The third represents our future, and we do not know what that is just yet. I have work to do over the years on this one." He held it up with a smile.

"Oh, Stephen, they will always be my greatest treasure."

CHAPTER 45

 "Miriam, Stephen said he thinks I am with child, but I don't feel any differently than I have felt many times before when Bethany gave me the strong tea to start my life blood. I told Stephen it was just time to drink the tea. He insists that I talk to you."

Miriam studied her carefully and then turned toward the fire to start tea. "Child, how many moons has it been since your last flow?"

"I have had only three since the wedding."

"That has been many months," Miriam observed thoughtfully. "Are your breasts tender?"

"Yes, but just as they were at the estate. I just need to start my flow as Bethany did," Arelia insisted, but she looked worried. "Bethany said it is what women do."

Miriam busied herself with the fire. "You love Stephen, do you not?"

"Very much."

"Would you like a child?"

Arelia appeared surprised by her question. "Do you think I am with child? Bethany never. . ."

Miriam sat next to the fire.

"Come here, child." Arelia sat at her feet and rested her hand on Miriam's lap, afraid to speak.

"Arelia, when you love a man and lie with him as his wife, he plants a seed inside of you, just as a seed is planted in the rich soil of the earth. His seed will grow inside of you to be a lovely child, the fruit of your love."

Arelia smiled. "Miriam, my mother explained all this to me." She considered why Miriam explained this now. She sat quietly looking into the flames, beginning to realize the importance of her words. "Is this seed only planted by a man who loves you?" she asked, afraid to hear the answer.

"No, child. Any man can plant, even if the ground is forced."

Arelia's eyes grew wide with understanding, and her head fell into Miriam's lap. Tears began to fall slowly at first but then turned quickly into sobs. Miriam felt her grief as if it were her own. *More pain. More healing.* Miriam stroked her hair and wiped her tears and nose with the hem of her skirt.

Arelia jumped up and raced to the basin and vomited. Miriam dipped a rag into a bucket of water standing near the fire.

"Come lie on your cot, child." Miriam wiped her face with a damp cloth.

"Oh, God!" Arelia cried. Miriam sat on the edge of the cot and rubbed her back, unable to calm the shattering moans. Arelia soon cried herself to sleep.

Stephen knocked on the door at dark. Miriam placed her finger over her lips to caution him to be quiet. He grew concerned when he saw Arelia sleeping on the familiar cot.

"What happened?"

"I have been waiting for you. We must talk. Stephen, you are aware of Arelia's life at the estate?"

"Yes, of course I am. But what could be wrong? Arelia is free from all of that now."

Miriam had been thinking of how she would explain this to him. She knew there would be no easy way.

"Stephen, were you aware of times that Arelia was sick for several days at a time?"

"Yes. Is she ill again?"

"No. She is fine, but she is going to need more love and support from you now than ever before."

"I do not understand. We have been through so much."

"Let me pour you a cup of tea. We need to talk." He watched Miriam at the hearth, not knowing what to expect.

"Did she ever mention Bethany's tea?"

"Yes, she said after the bitter tea she would have horrible stomach cramps and be sick for days. Bethany had her drink it every few moons."

"Did you ever question why?"

"No. There was nothing in my control there except to get her out. That is what I was determined to do."

"I know you are familiar with the female life flow."

Stephen blushed. "Yes, of course. That is why I thought Arelia was with child and sent her to you."

"Stephen, that is the reason Bethany gave her the bitter tea, to start her life flow after several months without."

Quick realization crossed his face like a dark cloud. His jaw clenched and fires shown in his eyes, but he didn't speak.

"Do you understand what I am saying?"

"Only too well," his voice was sharp and angry.

"Who is your anger toward?"

"Marisa and Edward Fairchild, and Bethany. Oh, my dear God!"

"Arelia had the same realization this afternoon. It pained her deeply. A woman's feelings are different. She will experience grief, guilt, anger, shame, and confusion. You only feel anger."

"Why shame and guilt? She did nothing wrong," he declared. Arelia turned on the cot but didn't open her eyes.

"Quiet," Miriam cautioned.

"Miriam, I do not understand. She does not deserve to feel guilt or shame. She was a slave with no choice."

"You are right. She did nothing wrong, but wrong was done to her. You are going to be the only one who can truly help her through it. You and I are the only ones who know about her life at the estate. Your relationship is such that she will need your love and approval more than ever. I caution you to conceal your anger lest she think it is directed toward her."

He sat on the bench and hung his head. "I understand. Those animals! How could they do that to anyone?"

"You may stay now, or I will get you when Arelia awakens. *You* are also strongly affected; do not deny any of your own feelings. We can talk if you want to, but do not talk to Arelia about it just yet." Miriam knew she had a willing partner in Arelia's healing, and she welcomed the additional support.

Stephen left his tea only to return to his hut to start the fire and begin supper. He was unable to sleep and just sat watching the fire for hours, imagining Arelia's pain.

"I am not the first to plant my seed in her," he said aloud, his anger mounting.

435

There was a gentle knock at the door that startled him. "Stephen," Miriam called as she came into his dark hut. "Arelia awoke very distressed. I fixed her a very mild tea to relax her. She needs you."

When Stephen jumped from his chair to go to her, Miriam grabbed his arm. "Your anger is showing. She needs to see only your love. I told her I talked to you, and that you understand."

"But I do not understand!" he shouted. Miriam was taken aback by his violent reaction. "She is my wife," he continued. "Can I know this is my seed?"

"Sit down," she commanded angrily as she closed the door. "Take your mind off yourself and put it on the woman you love. Your anger is nothing compared to the flood of emotions she is experiencing. It is your seed! There is no doubt, but for her, it is her entire identity. I will not allow you to see her until you can put your self-concerns aside." She looked him in the eye, waiting for a response. He could not meet her gaze.

"Do you love the woman, or did you just want to be a hero?" she challenged.

Anger crossed his face. "You know I love her!"

"Then act like it! You can feel sorry for yourself later."

Shock, then anger crossed his face. He sat in his chair before the fire, put his elbows on his knees, and buried his face in his hands. "I did not think it would be like this," he said, shaking his head from side to side. "I thought we would be even closer when we discovered she was with child."

Miriam rested her hand on his shoulder. "We seldom know the challenges ahead of time, Stephen. If we did, we would avoid them. You have all the tools you need to work through this. Arelia needs you now more than ever. She has more wounds to heal."

"Will the hurt ever end?"

"It may not end, but it will heal. It will take love and compassion.

"Miriam, will you help me?"

"Of course. Can you see your lady now?"

"Yes, you go ahead. I will be there shortly."

When Miriam left, Stephen splashed cold water on his face and combed his hair. *The hurt is hers. I must be there for her.*

He opened the door to Miriam's hut slowly, without knocking. Arelia was in the rocking chair facing the fire. She appeared so tiny and delicate; all the life seemed to be drained from her.

"Arelia," he said softly. She faced him with teary eyes and quickly looked away, brushing a tear from her cheek. "There seems to be a cloud over my sunshine." He knelt by her side and stroked her hair.

Miriam was surprised and pleased at the gentleness this man showed, placing his fiery emotions aside.

Tears dropped onto the bodice of her dress. "I am so sorry, Stephen."

"Sorry about what? That you carry my child?" he asked as a reminder. She didn't speak.

He took her hand gently. "Look at me." She looked up with red, puffy eyes. "Arelia, I am the one who is sorry. I cannot understand all that was done to you, but I am here now, and you are carrying our child." She looked away. Fear gripped him.

"Do you want this baby?" His tone was tense and anxious.

She looked up and smiled weakly. "I want your baby."

"That is who you are carrying—*our* baby," he assured her. "Are you ready to come home, or do you want to stay with Miriam tonight?"

"She wants to go home with you," Miriam interrupted. Arelia and Stephen looked at her, surprised. She simply smiled and walked to her spinning wheel.

"Thank you, Miriam," Stephen said as he helped Arelia from the chair. They left Miriam's hut to return to their own home just a stone's throw away.

"Put on your gown and get into bed. I will rekindle the fire," Stephen said as he opened the door to their warm home.

Later, when Stephen got into bed, he patted Arelia's slightly swollen belly. "Are you a fine strong boy or a delicate little girl like your mother?"

Arelia smiled. "I hope it is a fine boy to grow into a wonderful man like you."

"We cannot forget what we have planted. This is our first fruit." Stephen truly seemed pleased. He held her gently in his arms as they snuggled under the covers. They were filled with the peace and comfort of love and belonging.

Stephen was dozing off when Arelia said, "Stephen, did I ever thank you for bringing me here?"

Stephen laughed. "Only a hundred times."

"Good. Now I want to thank you for bringing me to Miriam."

"I am thankful for her, too. I do not want to let her down."

Arelia smiled. "She said the only way I could thank her was to be happy. I will do my best."

"All right, sunshine. You better get some sleep. We have already lost most of the night."

Over the next several weeks, Arelia and Stephen struggled to keep past memories and images from discoloring their joy. He heeded Miriam's warning not to let Arelia see his anger. Chopping firewood was a good outlet for releasing his anger. Only Miriam knew the motivation for the piles of firewood that Stephen generously chopped for their neighbors.

Arelia distracted herself from her memories by spending more time with other women. Being so thin to begin with, several women noticed her girth and hinted at sewing baby clothes. Arelia had not confirmed their suspicions, but it was becoming obvious. Joan and John began to ask probing questions with little result. Finally, Joan invited them for Sunday dinner to get a definite answer.

"How long have you two been married now, Stephen?" Joan asked.

"About six months, Mother. You know that."

John winked at his son.

"Arelia, you must let me help you let out the bodice on your dresses. You must enjoy being able to cook in your own home."

"Mother!" Martha was shocked at her mother's implication.

"Son, is there something you want to tell your mother and me?" John asked outright.

Stephen looked at Arelia for permission, and she gave a gentle nod. "Yes, I guess there is. It seems Arelia and I are going to have a baby."

Martha squealed as only Martha could. Jean was out of her seat and hugging Arelia.

"A real baby!" she exclaimed.

"Yes. A real baby," Arelia confirmed.

"You two wasted no time." John laughed.

Arelia blushed.

"Father!" Joan corrected.

"Can we tell?" Martha was already at the door ready to spread the news.

"Arelia?" Joan asked.

"Yes, if Stephen approves."

"Yes, but do not shout it out. Tell people quietly in their homes."

The girls were gone in a flash.

"Arelia, are you well? Do you have morning sickness?"

"Except for a few times, I have felt well so far. Miriam is giving me an herb to build my blood. She thinks I am too pale."

"She usually knows. Do whatever she advises."

"Well, son, we may have built your hut too small."

"It is good for now, Father. I think we will be comfortable for a few more years."

"Not if you keep going at this rate."

"John, leave the children alone," Joan reprimanded.

The rest of the afternoon was filled with plans for new furniture and clothes. Joan was brimming with advice for the expectant mother.

As Stephen and Arelia walked back to their hut, villagers came out to greet them. They were showered with hugs and handshakes. Once again, Arelia was overwhelmed with the love and affection of her new family.

CHAPTER 46

 "Stephen, wake up," Arelia cried. "Get Miriam quickly!"

"What is it?" Stephen was alarmed.

"I am having sharp pains, and the bed is wet beneath me."

Before she finished her explanation, Stephen was out the door. It had only been two short weeks since their announcement, and everyone in the village was excited. Arelia feared the all-too-familiar pains.

Within seconds, Miriam hurried through the door still in her nightgown. "Stephen, put water on the fire, and then go get your mother. Send her back alone. You stay at her hut. I will send for you."

"Miriam," Arelia cried. "What is happening?"

Stephen stopped at the door waiting for Miriam's response. "Stephen, get your mother now," Miriam commanded.

Arelia grabbed Miriam's hand and cried out, "Oh, Miriam. These are the same pains."

Between the pains, Miriam dropped blue cohosh leaves in the steamy water. She pulled the covers back.

"Have you passed much blood, child?" Miriam's fears were answered. The diluted bloodstains indicated that the sack had ruptured. There would be no stopping the miscarriage now.

Joan rushed through the door still in her bedclothes.

"Is she all right?" The expression on Miriam's face spoke unwelcome news.

"Bring some rags, Joan," instructed Miriam as Arelia cried out again. The cries and pains continued for about an hour. The women were helpless to stop the loss of the newly formed child.

Arelia screamed when she saw the tiny fetus with clearly distinguishable features. For the first time, she experienced her pains without the drugged fog of Bethany's concoction. For the first time, she saw the results of her premature labor, resting fully formed in the palm of Miriam's hand.

"Oh, God, no!" she cried as Miriam laid the dead child in a small wooden bowl and covered it with clean linen. "No!" Miriam held her and rocked Arelia gently through her heartbreaking sobs.

Joan returned home just before sunrise. The bloodstains on her gown and her drained expression told Stephen all he needed to know. He had paced the floor all night, ignoring his father's plea to sit and pray with him.

"Mother,. . ." he began, but he didn't know how to ask. "Arelia?"

"She is sleeping. The baby is gone," she said as she sat wearily in her rocking chair by the fire. Her grief and exhaustion were too great for tears. She remembered her own experience so many years ago. The pain was as real for her now as it had been then.

"Stephen, many young women lose babies and have healthy children later," John consoled.

Stephen was out the door before his father finished his sentence. He opened the door slowly and crept into the room. Miriam was wadding up blood-soaked rags. A small, tightly wrapped bundle in a box on the table told the truth of the premature pains. The sight shocked him.

Arelia was sleeping soundly, her sweat-soaked hair plastered against her face and neck. Stephen went to the basin and dampened a rag, returning to the bed to wipe his young wife's brow. He sat at her side and wept. She didn't stir from a deep sleep.

Stephen didn't leave Arelia's side for days. Many kind people brought food, and all came by with condolences. Most women had lost children prematurely and knew Arelia's pain; death was a familiar visitor.

Arelia's depression was deep. Miriam understood the root of her grief better than Arelia did herself. Arelia felt guilt and shame over all the other induced losses, although they were not at her own hand. Only Miriam knew and understood.

Stephen felt helpless as he failed time and time again to reach her. Every attempt he made to comfort her was met with teary stares. He felt, like his father, that there were other healthy children ahead of them; he couldn't understand her inability to look to the future.

One morning, two weeks later, Miriam walked over to stay with Arelia while Stephen went to work the field and tend animals. "Arelia, I want you to walk with me today."

"I do not feel well enough to walk," she answered blankly.

"I have your shawl. Come with me." Miriam took her arm and helped her from her bed.

"Where are we going?" Arelia asked when Miriam opened the door. She squinted at the bright sunlight she had not seen in nearly two weeks.

"To the creek; not too far." The walk seemed far to Arelia. Her whole body was weak and unwilling.

"There it is." Miriam pointed to an outcropping of rocks near a small waterfall. "Look closely at those rocks and tell me what you see."

Arelia strained to see something unusual. "All I see is a fall and some rocks."

"Walk closer. Now look again." Arelia looked closely at every rock before seeing the two crosses tucked into the outcropping. One cross was large and one very small.

"Here is where my family was taken from me." Miriam pointed to the two weatherworn crosses.

"Come, child. Sit with me a while." Arelia couldn't move. Miriam coaxed her closer to the memorial. "I come here often to think. I know I am loved here."

"You said that this is where they left you. Is this their gravesite?"

"No, child, I placed the crosses here myself. This is the last place I was with Carl, the last place I saw him alive. Carl and our baby are buried in the burial ground on the rise. I find it more peaceful and private here in the trees, with the creek." She took a deep breath.

"Arelia, people live, and people die. We do not determine the time for either event. I do not think we want to. You have suffered so much tragedy in your life, but you have a lot of joy, too, if you will only see it. Do not give up now. You have brighter days ahead."

"I am too tired to go on," Arelia defended.

"You have lost your energy by seeing only sad things—things you cannot change. The only thing you can change now is how you will move ahead with your life."

"I do not want to move ahead."

Miriam walked to the small cross and rubbed the dust off it with the hem of her dress. "I remember the time when I did not want to move ahead either. My father pleaded with me to get out of my grief, but I was not ready. I had lost both my husband and my baby." Miriam turned toward her. "Arelia, have you forgotten you still have a husband?"

Arelia covered her face. "I thought it would be better here."

"Is it not better? Do you come and go as you please? Do you have all the food you wish to eat that you can prepare for yourself? Do you have the love of everyone in the village? Do you have your own hut and garden and livestock? Do you have a husband who loves you?" Miriam seemed to be growing impatient.

"Miriam, you do not understand. You cannot possibly understand." Arelia moaned.

"You are right," she said lovingly, tucking frustration away, as she sat next to Arelia on crackling leaves. "I do not fully understand. Everyone's pain is her own. Can you look at the two crosses for my husband and daughter and say you understand me? Our life experiences are different; no two of us is exactly alike, . . . but our feelings are the same. Grief is grief. Pain is pain. Loss is loss. Do not turn in on yourself and concentrate on the hurt. If that is your focus, that is all you will see. Concentrate on your garden, and you will see new growth. Concentrate on your spinning, and you will see new threads with the promise of beautiful cloth. Concentrate on your husband, and you will see love. Concentrate on your home, and you will see a family. Be grateful for the good, and you will be given more."

Arelia didn't respond. She sat quietly for a long time. "Where is my baby?" she finally asked.

"Mr. Carpenter built a small box. He, Stephen, and his family and I buried him not too far from your hut in the graveyard."

"Why did *I* not go?"

"We asked, but you chose not to hear us. Sometimes in deep grief we do not hear much of what is said," Miriam explained.

"I have not been listening to Stephen because he seems so cheerful. He does not understand."

"Do not be angry with Stephen for trying to bring you out of your grief. You are right—men cannot completely understand. But do not forget that Stephen has also lost his child."

Arelia appeared surprised by that comment. "Oh, Miriam. I never even thought about Stephen. He was so excited about having the baby. Oh, my dear God, he lost his son. "

"Yes, and all the dreams that went along with him. Whether it was a son or a daughter, he lost his child just as you did. Although you have not seen it, he has grieved. I have seen him cry, but he does not want to add to your pain. I think it is time to tell you about Stephen the day you lost the baby." Miriam took a deep breath and sighed before continuing. "Joan had gone home to tell the family about the losing the baby. Stephen was frightened he would lose you, too. He ran right home, and when he peaked through the door, he saw you were sleeping. Child, you were a sad sight. Neither of us talked. He pulled his chair next to the cot and lifted your hand so gently and then kissed it, resting it on his leg while he took a damp rag and wiped your forehead. I had never witnessed such love and gentleness from a man.

"After a while, he asked about the baby, and I handed him the child, wrapped in a tea towel. He opened it so slowly and then just gazed at his lifeless, premature son. What he did next moved me to tears.

"He placed the boy on his little tummy over your heart, completely covering the baby with his big hand and then, almost in a whisper, prayed the Our Father and the Angelic Salutation."

"Miriam, I feel guilty for being so selfish. I thought he did not care," Arelia confessed.

Miriam continued, "He left for a while and asked if I could wait with him, in case you needed me, while Mr. Carpenter build a little box for the baby's burial. Of course, I wanted to stay. He took your Psalter by the fire and stayed for quite a long time reading psalms."

They sat quietly for a while, with only the sounds of nature filling the silence. Arelia rested her face in her hands and let the tears fall, freely and abundantly.

Miriam rubbed her back. "Waste no time on guilt, child. Just fix what has been done. If you spend time on guilt, you compound any selfishness by concentrating on yourself again and drawing others in to console you, in order to convince yourself of your innocence. Guilt is the most selfish of emotions unless it moves you to mercy and reconciliation. It often gives you an excuse not to move forward."

"But I am so sad."

"Of course, you are. You have lost your child and all the dreams of life with him."

"Miriam," she paused, seeming to catch a fleeting thought. "Do you ever think about Mother Mary? My mother talked about her the night before she died. I have been thinking about her lately."

"Oh yes, child. It was by contemplating her losing Jesus and Joseph that I was encouraged to move on. I think she actually helped me. I would wake up at night thinking about how we suffered the same pain."

Arelia wiped her eyes and sniffled. "But she did not suffer in the same way. She got to hold her son and watch him grow into a man."

Miriam was little surprised by her response.

"Yes, and she grew to love him deeply, but then she watched him die a most horrible death. She saw his flesh shredded in a flogging. She saw him mocked with a discarded royal robe and crown of thorns. She saw people he loved call for him to be crucified rather than to convict the man who was guilty of crime. She saw him carry his cross alone. She saw him nailed to a cross. Arelia, she understands more than anyone about grief and sorrow."

"Oh, Miriam, I think I may have had a dream about Jesus and Mary's suffering. How have I been so blind?"

Miriam walked over to the creek and floated a large colorful leaf downstream. Arelia watched her closely, and then turned to study the two crosses before her.

At least I have Stephen. Poor Miriam. She walked over to Miriam, watching the leaf float out of sight. "I am so sorry, Miriam."

"About what, child?"

"About your family."

Miriam smiled and squeezed her hand. "I am, too. But now it is time to head back to the village. Stephen probably wonders what happened to you."

They walked back quietly, each having experienced the same grief and the same pain of losing loved ones.

*

Stephen noticed a difference in Arelia the moment he opened the door at the end of a long day. The smell of fresh stew told him all was well.

"That smells wonderful. Did you fix it?" He couldn't disguise his surprise.

"Yes. Now I want you to sit down while I finish preparing dinner. I will get you some tea."

Stephen watched in amazement while Arelia busied herself with dinner. Although her step was slower than usual, there was a glimmer of light in her eyes that he had not seen for a long time.

"What did you do today?" he asked, hoping to put the pieces together.

"Miriam and I walked down to the creek to her family's memorial. We had a long talk." She smiled.

Miriam, he thought. *What kind of magic does she have?*

When she brought his tea, she sat by his side. "I have something to ask you."

"What is it?"

She hesitated, before looking into his eyes. "I want to go to our son's grave."

Stephen met her gaze but couldn't speak.

"Will you take me, Stephen? Please."

He took her hand and pulled her onto his lap. "Of course, I will take you." He buried his face in her hair and let out a deep sigh.

"Well, let me serve dinner now so it will still be light."

"No, let dinner wait. Grab your Psalter."

The young couple walked a short distance from their hut past a gathering of trees and up an incline. Situated on top of the knoll was a gravesite with three dozen or so graves, reminiscent of the site where her brothers and little Prudence were buried. "This is a lovely spot, Stephen." Arelia began to get teary.

Stephen looked down at the tiny mound of fresh dirt and rocks. He put his arms around her and cried. They held each other and shared their grief for the first time since they had lost their baby.

"I want to read something to you." She handed him the Psalter. "This is from Psalm 139." He smiled as she watched him in wonder.

1   LORD, you have probed me, you know me:
2   you know when I sit and stand;
       you understand my thoughts from afar.
3   You sift through my travels and my rest;
       with all my ways you are familiar.
4   Even before a word is on my tongue,
       LORD, you know it all.
5   Behind and before you encircle me
       and rest your hand upon me.
6   Such knowledge is too wonderful for me,
       far too lofty for me to reach.
7   Where can I go from your spirit?
       From your presence, where can I flee?
8   If I ascend to the heavens, you are there;
       if I lie down in Sheol, there you are.
9   If I take the wings of dawn
       and dwell beyond the sea,
10   Even there your hand guides me,
       your right hand holds me fast.
11   If I say, "Surely darkness shall hide me,
       and night shall be my light"
12   Darkness is not dark for you,
       and night shines as the day.
       Darkness and light are but one.

"That was about us. Now, I want to read about our baby."

II 13   You formed my inmost being;
   you knit me in my mother's womb.

14   I praise you, because I am wonderfully made;
   wonderful are your works!
   My very self you know.

15   My bones are not hidden from you,
   When I was being made in secret,
   fashioned in the depths of the earth.

16   Your eyes saw me unformed;
   in your book all are written down;
   my days were shaped, before one came to be.

III 17   How precious to me are your designs, O God;
   how vast the sum of them!

"Arelia, God knew him and loved him. God himself will take care of him until we meet again." He threw his head back and laughed. "Do you think he is with your family as we speak, and your mother is holding him right now?!"

Arelia jumped and hugged him. She cried, but this time, tears of joy. "Oh Stephen, I have missed you."

He calmed her within his arms, searching her soul. "We will have more children, but for now, we have each other," he said with confidence.

"I know. Stephen, I am so sorry for losing sight of you and our future." She smiled. "Have I ever thanked you for bringing me here?" He laughed.

They basked in the peace of the moment until Arelia noted, "There is no marker."

"I wanted you to help me decide what to put there. I did not want to make that decision alone, and I wanted to ask what you want to name our son."

"Stephen, of course."

"I thought you might want to name him after your father," *and uncle*, he thought.

"No, there is no one he should be named after but you. Now he will have a marker. Oh! Could you carve something?" she suggested.

He thought for a minute. "Yes, I know exactly what to make."

CHAPTER 47
Faircastle—1352

As many changes had occurred at Faircastle as had occurred in the village during the passing months. Because there was no longer a diversion with the possibility of Arelia providing another heir, Sir Edward had taken an active interest in his two young children who were now approaching their first birthday. Specifically, his interest was focused on baby Pearce as his heir, but Sarah and Bethany made sure that baby Marisa received her share of his attention, too.

News of Marisa's death had brought inquiries from all over the countryside about Edward's intentions of finding a mother for his heirs. Lords and ladies often dropped in with their daughters, always unannounced, supposedly in transit. With the first anniversary of Marisa's death approaching, the respectable time for grieving was drawing to a close.

Sarah and Bethany had no idea there were so many available young ladies in all of England. They were very careful to study each woman and engage her in conversation when she met the children. They felt that they should have a rightful say in choosing any woman who would become little Marisa and Pearce's mother. A young woman named Katherine met their approval and, curiously, drew Edward's interest also.

With the formal grieving period ending soon, Edward requested that Lady Katherine visit again, as she was the only one who even slightly interested him, mainly because of her youth and cheerful disposition. He felt that she could keep up with two toddlers and help to lift the dark shadow that shrouded everyone. Sarah was pleased with his choice, but Bethany reserved her comments. Sarah knew that Bethany secretly hoped no one would fill the role of mother, and she continually reassured Bethany that it would be in name only, and no one would take their place in the children's hearts.

Edward called Harold, his valet, "Summon Sarah and Bethany. I would like to speak to them."

Edward had no desire to actively court any of the ladies who had been paraded before him, but he didn't care to spend a solitary life either. The children filled a void in his life at this point, and so he only wanted a wife to mother his children.

Harold ushered the two servants into Sir Edward's parlor. "You requested to see us, sire?" Bethany asked.

"Yes, please sit down." Edward's wrinkled brow indicated that he was thinking about something important. "You know we have only a few short months until Marisa and Pearce's first birthday. If you recall, my father is due to return at that time."

"Yes, sire," Sarah responded.

"And you also know that the children need a mother."

Bethany cleared her throat and shifted uneasily from foot to foot.

"Of course, it is not for lack of care from the two of you," he continued. "But I am lonely. I have no desire to spend unnecessary time courting. That is for the young and foolish. Lady Katherine will return here with her father within days of the children's birthday to meet Sir Daniel—tradition requires that our fathers meet. At that time, I will ask her to be my wife. We can wait a respectable amount of time, possibly another year for the wedding. That will give her father time to prepare a dowry."

Bethany cleared her throat again to cover a startled gasp. Sarah smiled at her indiscretion.

"We can save my father a trip," Edward continued, "by having the birthday celebration and announcement at the same time."

"That would be wise," Sarah agreed. Bethany looked at her disapprovingly. "What can we do to help, sire?" offered Sarah.

"That is why I called you. Lady Marisa always handled such things. Now, everything is up to me, and I have no idea what to do. Would you ladies be able to take care of the celebrations without neglecting the babies?"

Sarah answered quickly, "Of course. The kitchen staff has prepared many celebrations under Lady Marisa's supervision, and so they will know what is expected for such an occasion. I will ask Laura to help with the babies' wardrobes. She can begin sewing right away."

"That will be fine. Do whatever you need to do."

"Sire, will you want a new wardrobe for the festivities yourself?"

He smirked at the idea. "No, that will not be necessary. I will only need one outfit for the actual wedding. I will wear what I have for the birthday celebration and announcement. Of course, the children will need clothes for both occasions and my father's stay. People may stay for days, and I want the children presentable as Lady Marisa would require."

"We will be limited by cloth. Since Lady Marisa is gone, I have not bought cloth, and I understand Laura has already used most of what we had for the children."

"Excuse me, sire," Sir Edward's servant interrupted.

"What is it?"

"The note, sire," Harold reminded.

"What note?"

Harold opened the drawer of Edward's desk and handed him a note.

"I had forgotten all about this. This may be a solution, ladies. Follow through with it if you desire." Edward handed the note to Sarah while Bethany looked over her shoulder as she read aloud:

Sarah and Laura,

The fabric you inquired about is being repaired. One of the pieces was torn in transport and needs mending. They will make beautiful garments for the right occasion. Let me know if you would like to see them.

Miriam

"This could be helpful, sire. But where is the note from?" Sarah was puzzled.

"Joseph brought it back from the soldier's village when they went for Arelia."

Once again, Bethany gasped, then cleared her throat, and faked a cough to cover her surprise.

"Bethany, maybe you should stay away from the children if you are sick. That cough could be serious," he observed.

"Sire, can we go to the village to see if the fabric is appropriate for our needs?" Sarah interjected.

"Who will tend the babies?"

"I will stay, sire. Sarah and Laura can go. Joseph can take them," Bethany suggested.

"That will be fine, but do not waste time. Buy as much fabric as is available. I am sure Lady Katherine will want new dresses in preparation for the wedding, and I can supply fabric for her, too."

Sarah tucked the note in her pocket. "We will leave immediately, sire."

Sarah and Bethany hurried down the hall. "What do you think it means, Bethany?"

"I think we are thinking the same thing, but we will not know for certain until you arrive there."

"Laura and I will leave early tomorrow. What will I do if there is no fabric? How will I explain that?"

"Do not get ahead of yourself. If she suggested fabric, she must be able to supply it."

Sarah decided not to share the note with Laura lest she be too excited and leak the news to the other women.

Joseph had the horses saddled and a small cart filled with supplies ready when Sarah and Laura arrived at the stable early the next morning. Jacob was briefing Joseph on a quicker route to Stephen's village and introducing him to two housecarls and two soldiers the captain had sent to escort them. Sarah was very nervous when she saw the warriors.

"What are these men doing?"

"Mother, we need an escort. It is not safe to travel alone for such a long distance," insisted Joseph, who was not aware of their true mission.

"Sarah, you and Laura cannot go without protection. I see no reason anyone would interfere with you, but just in case, these men will be a deterrent," Jacob added. Sarah had spoken with her husband late into the night about her concern for finding Arelia, and although he supported her, he knew all too well the danger that awaited unsuspecting travelers. Since the plague, too many stories were told about ambushes and assaults.

She had not explained her belief that it was really Arelia awaiting her, and so he did not understand the threat soldiers posed. Although she wanted to object, she didn't. Laura mounted a horse with Jacob's assistance, while Sarah rode in the cart. "Then, let us be off. We have a long distance to cover."

In no time at all, the small caravan of seven began their journey. The ride was long and tedious. The trail was narrow, and both women often rode together in order to get the cart through the trees and ruts. Sarah couldn't find time to separate herself and her children from the soldiers to share with them what she thought could be good news.

Late on the third day, one of the men spotted a clearing and shouted, "The village is ahead."

Sarah could see an opening in the trees. As it was still daylight, she was concerned that one of the soldiers might recognize Stephen if he were out working.

"Joseph, you run ahead and determine if this is the right village. You have been there before," Sarah suggested.

"As have we, madam. This is the right village," one of the soldiers insisted.

"Ride ahead anyway, Joseph, and locate a place to camp. I am very weary and need to settle quickly." Sarah was persistent in her intent.

With that, Joseph quickly rode into the clearing. Several men who were working in the field looked up to the sound of a racing horse. John was the first to recognize Joseph.

"Stephen, that boy was with the captain. Get in your hut quickly."

Stephen turned to go with James at his side. "Do not run, son. You will be too obvious. Just look away. I will block his view of you." Stephen tried to appear casual. He had not seen the rider's face and was curious.

"Do you recognize the rider, James?"

"Yes, he was with Fairchild's men when they came searching for you."

"But not a soldier?" Stephen questioned.

"No, he came along to tend the horses."

Stephen wanted to look. "Was his name Joseph?"

"I do not remember. Be quiet and get to your hut."

When Stephen closed the door behind him, Arelia looked up from her sewing. "What has brought you in at this time?" she asked when she saw the concerned expression on his face.

"There is a rider from Faircastle."

The sewing fell from Arelia's lap as she jumped up. "Oh no, Stephen. You must be mistaken."

"Father recognized him. James thinks it is Joseph."

Arelia's tension released. "Then, it must be." She seemed excited. "Is he alone?"

"Yes, he seems to be, but we must stay in until we know for sure. Someone must be with him," Stephen cautioned.

"What does this mean?" Arelia asked nervously as she put water on for tea.

"It simply means we wait until Father comes."

Although it was only a short time, it seemed hours before the knock on the door. Stephen was relieved to see his father's calm expression.

"You must be careful," he cautioned. "It seems to be small group with four escorts. Even if we do not recognize them, they must not see you."

"Why are they here?" Stephen asked.

"It seems Miriam sent a note with the boy saying she had fabric for a special occasion. Evidently, their master is planning to remarry soon, and they need cloth," John explained.

Arelia was surprised. "Edward sent a stable boy and four soldiers to buy cloth?"

John laughed at his omission. "Oh no, the boy's mother and sister are with them to choose from Miriam's cloth."

Arelia's face lit up. "I must go to Miriam's to greet them." She hurried toward the door as Stephen grabbed her arm to stop her.

John immediately understood. "No, you and Stephen must stay here."

"Father is right. This is Miriam's business, not ours." Stephen suspected a trap.

"Please, Stephen. You know it is Sarah and Laura. Only Laura sewed."

"You cannot take any risks now. From what I understand, we cannot discount trickery from Sir Edward Fairchild," John reminded in complete agreement.

"Sarah and Laura would never do that to me." Arelia was offended at the implication.

John sensed her deep hurt. "I am sorry, Arelia. Certainly the women are not here to find you, but they could be used as a trap for you to run into. You and my son have come so far. You cannot take any chances now. We will bring supplies to you as long as necessary until they leave."

Arelia turned to tend the fire. She didn't want Stephen and his father to see her broken heart. Sarah and Laura had been her only support and lifeline at the estate; they were as close to family as she had before marrying Stephen. Other than Stephen, they were the only link to her past, no matter how bad that past had been.

Stephen stood behind her at the hearth and wrapped his arms around her waist. Not until the door closed behind John did she turn to face her husband.

"I am sorry, Arelia, but I cannot risk losing you. Let Father determine if it is safe, and then maybe you can see your friends."

Joseph tied his horse to a tree not far from Miriam's hut and began to unstrap his saddle as the remainder of the caravan arrived. "This is a good place to camp. The lady with the cloth is in that hut." He pointed to Miriam's small home, noticing a new hut nearby.

Sarah was eager to talk to Miriam. She sensed that her note was not without special meaning. "I will go talk to the woman now. Laura, will you join me?"

"Mother, there is no hurry. We can see the fabric tomorrow. I am very hungry and tired now," Laura objected.

"Then you rest. I am going now."

Miriam had heard the noise of horses and opened her door just as Sarah was approaching her hut.

"Lady Miriam?" Sarah called out.

"Yes," Miriam responded curiously at the unfamiliar women calling her name.

"I am Sarah from Faircastle." Miriam smiled broadly at her announcement.

"I have been expecting you, Sarah." When the door closed behind them, Sarah was relieved that Laura had stayed behind.

"I understand you have fabric for me to see," Sarah explained with a twinkle in her eye.

"Yes, in fact, I have two pieces."

"Your note said one of the pieces was damaged. Were you able to mend it?" Sarah continued.

"Yes," Miriam continued the ruse. "It is more beautiful now than ever."

Sarah laughed, and tears of relief filled her eyes. "When can I see it?"

"You are very anxious, Sarah."

"Lady Miriam, I have worried for so long. I only received your note four short days ago."

"Oh," Miriam said with a laugh. "That explains your late arrival. Let us go see it now."

Miriam knocked lightly on the door of the nearby hut. It was beginning to get dark, and Stephen was stoking the fire for Arelia to prepare dinner.

"Come in, Father," Stephen called out as Arelia went to open the door. Miriam walked in and closed the door behind her.

She placed her finger over her lips. "Be very quiet," she said as she opened the door.

Arelia covered her mouth and let out a muffled scream when she saw Sarah. The two women rushed into each other's arms as their tears fell freely. "Sarah! It is you! This is hard to believe!" Arelia cried.

"I cannot believe it myself, child. I was afraid you were dead."

Thunder rumbled overhead with that proclamation, announcing a storm building on the horizon.

"On the contrary," interrupted Stephen. "We are alive and well. What a surprise to see you." Stephen was concerned that Sarah was unknowingly setting a trap, but it was too late now.

"Stephen's father said Laura is here. Where is she?" Arelia asked.

"How did you know we were here? Does Sir Edward suspect anything?" Stephen interrupted.

Sarah was quick to cut that train of thought short. "This is how I know." She pulled the note from her pocket and handed it to Stephen. "I only received this four days ago."

Stephen smiled at Miriam when he read the note and handed it to Arelia. Arelia laughed. "A torn fabric?" she laughed.

"It did the job. Here she is," Miriam defended.

"Yes, and I had better get back before someone comes to get me," Sarah said.

"I cannot let you and your daughter sleep in the elements. Please be my guest," Miriam offered. "Tomorrow, we will bring Laura over to visit you, Arelia, but for now, let the ladies rest."

"Come early," insisted Arelia. "There will be no sleep for me tonight. I will have breakfast ready for the three of you at sunrise."

"Count me in," said Stephen sheepishly.

Miriam escorted Sarah to the campsite to retrieve Laura and their things, as if they had been friends forever. Laura was more than happy to move into a hut and under a roof as thunder and lightning flashed and rumbled overhead. She took little time to prepare a sleeping pallet next to the warmth of the hearth with blankets she brought from her own bed. Within minutes of lying near the warm, crackling fire, she fell asleep.

"Good," said Sarah, checking on Laura. "Now you must tell me everything that has happened since the youngsters arrived. I see they are married now."

As Miriam relayed all the details to Sarah, the two women shared laughter and tears, reliving all the events since Stephen and Arelia's arrival, both happy and sad. Miriam didn't realize how late it had become until the room became chilled against dying embers. Clouds shed a gentle rain, bringing a sense of calm and tranquility.

"We have an early breakfast. I suggest we get some sleep. After such an exhausting trip, you must be worn out." Miriam set three thick logs on the fire to warm the room.

"My mind may not let me sleep; I am so excited for Laura now. She has no idea what she has in store for her tomorrow. Miriam, I sincerely thank you for your note and your hospitality to both Laura and me, and especially to Arelia. I have a suspicion she would not be as happy as she is if it had not been for you. In fact, I suspect she would not even be alive."

CHAPTER 48

Morning couldn't come quickly enough for Arelia. She had difficulty falling asleep and woke early but then couldn't fall back to sleep. By the time she had fresh baked bread already cooling on the hearth, the sun had not even come up. Stephen woke to the fragrant aroma just as there was a knock on the door.

"Joan thought you might need this for your company." John laughed at Arelia's surprised expression as he put the pitcher of fresh milk and bowl of eggs on the table. "She wants to have all of you over for dinner this evening. I do not know how we will get you to the hut without the soldiers seeing you, but someone will figure it out."

Stephen was dressed and refueling the fire in an instant. He was surprised to see the bread cooling on the hearth and wondered how he had slept through all of Arelia's preparations.

Miriam slipped quietly through the door. "The ladies will be here shortly," she laughed. "Good morning, John. I did not expect to see you so early."

"I thought that I should come over before the soldiers start their day. The rain gave them a soaking. Hopefully, they will sleep in."

"He brought fresh eggs and milk. We are going to have a feast." Stephen was excited at the prospect of such a hearty breakfast. "Where are the ladies?"

Miriam grinned. "Sarah is having a time trying to explain to Laura why they need to see the cloth so early. She told us to go alone, and she would see it later. It may be a while before Sarah gets her here. Is there anything I can help you with?"

"No, but you can have a cup of hot tea while we wait," Arelia invited. "I will boil the eggs, but everything else is ready."

"If Sarah is not successful soon," Stephen told Arelia, "you may need to go get Laura yourself."

"Sarah is very persuasive. Laura will be here." Just at that moment, there was a knock at the door. Arelia stopped short of opening it to gain her composure. When she opened it, Laura's sleepy eyes opened wide and she shouted, "Arelia!" Sarah shoved her in the door and slammed it behind her.

"I told you to be quiet, Laura. We do not want to wake the soldiers."

The girls were laughing and hugging, oblivious to Sarah's reprimand.

"I thought you were dead!"

"You were supposed to, and we must keep it that way."

The next knock startled everyone. The girls stood frozen. John whispered, "Arelia, Stephen, stand in the shadow behind the door. It could be a soldier. Miriam, answer the door."

Miriam answered the door calmly to Joseph and one of the soldiers. "Yes? Are you looking for your mother?"

"Excuse me, madam. We heard Laura shout. Is everything all right?" asked the older soldier.

Laura stepped forward. "I am sorry if I concerned you. My mother did not tell me this was an old friend of the family." Sarah cast Joseph a cautioning glance.

"Madam, I thought you called 'Arelia.'"

Laura paused, off guard. Miriam laughed, "You listen well, sir. My name is Marelia. It is not common. Do you know someone by that name?"

John sat quietly by the fire ready to respond, if necessary. The soldier said, "Please excuse us, sir."

"Think nothing of it, Officer."

Sarah interrupted, "Joseph, will you stay? Marelia has not met you yet. It has been so long since I have seen her. You were just a small boy."

Miriam addressed the soldier, "Sir, I will prepare a treat for you and your friend. Joseph will bring it when he returns."

"That is very considerate. Please accept my apologies."

When the door closed behind him, Sarah placed her finger over her lips and whispered, "We must be very careful. We cannot afford to make another mistake."

Just at that moment, Arelia and Stephen stepped out from the shadow. Joseph jumped at the motion, then gasped when he recognized Arelia.

"You are not seeing a ghost, Joseph. It is I, Arelia." He stood in shock.

Laura laughed and shook his arm. "Wake up, Joseph. This is not a dream."

"Arelia?" he whispered, "How can this be? I saw your grave and the bloody rags."

"Our plan worked well, did it not?" commented Miriam.

"And Stephen?" Joseph asked, still in a daze.

"Yes." Stephen laughed and slapped his back. "Snap out of it, man."

Laughter took over as Arelia set out the food. John excused himself from the group to get home to Joan. Stephen and Joseph couldn't get a word in edgewise as the four women related stories from the past several months. Stephen ate and left quickly to tend his livestock while Joseph listened quietly in disbelief. Stephen was not concerned that the soldiers would recognize him in the dim morning light; they were huddled around the campfire, clutching warm mugs of tea, unaware that he was in their midst.

While the women continued to talk, Miriam prepared a plate for Joseph to bring to the soldiers. "Remember, my name is Marelia. Do not talk much, lest anything slip. It would be better if you did not spend much time with them," she coached Joseph.

"Thank you, Lady *Marelia*." He smiled. "I may make an excuse of checking out the livestock and spend a little time with Stephen."

Just as the night before with Miriam and Sarah, the morning was spent in laughter and tears.

"Bethany sends her love," Sarah told Arelia. Arelia looked away with mixed feelings.

"Tell her 'thank you,'" Arelia said politely.

Sarah understood Arelia's conflicted emotions, and so she talked about the babies and the plans for the wedding without referring to Bethany again.

"Lady Katherine is nothing like Marisa. She will make a good mother for the children, although Bethany is afraid she will lose her place as 'grandmother.'" Laura laughed. Again, Sarah noticed Arelia's reaction.

"Arelia, Bethany has changed so much. She really is a grandmother to the babies. Marisa caused her to do things against her nature," Sarah offered in defense of her friend.

Arelia changed the subject by asking about the new bride-to-be.

Laura was interested, too, as only her mother and Bethany had been given a chance to spend time with Katherine and the babies. "I actually think you would like her, Arelia." She stopped with a surprising realization. "Seeing you here happy and healthy, I see a resemblance between you and Lady Katherine now. She has dark hair, much like yours, and a similar smile. Do you see it, Laura?"

Laura was wide-eyed with the same realization, wondering how they had not seen it before. "I certainly see it now, Mother."

"She—"

A knock at the door startled them. Arelia ran to the corner behind the door before Miriam opened it.

"Aunt Miriam," Martha said, "Mother said to invite you to dinner, too, and for all of you to come over at dark. Mr. and Mrs. Robertson have invited the soldiers to their house before dark, so they will not see Arelia and Stephen."

"What a wonderful plan, Martha. Tell your mother we will all be there."

Miriam and Sarah went back to Miriam's hut so Arelia and Laura could have time alone. "Arelia, I am so happy for you. You did the right thing," Laura said as she noticed how peaceful Arelia's hut was once the others were gone.

"Yes, but it is not all perfect."

"Did you think it would be?" asked Laura.

Arelia considered her question. "In all honesty, I think I imagined a fairy tale. But Stephen is a real man, and I am still just me."

Laura laughed at her observation. "I thought Stephen was a knight in shining armor, too." The two giggled over their own apparent innocence.

"I wonder why we always think life will be perfect when we change this or that?" Laura questioned. "But it is good for you now, I hope," she prompted.

Arelia smiled. "Most of the time it is better than good. But I lost a baby," she said, choking back tears. "I still get very frightened sometimes."

"Oh, Arelia, I am so sorry. You have plenty of time to have more babies," Laura consoled. "This is better than living *every* day frightened for good reason. At least you can enjoy your life here and know that you are with people who love you and will not intentionally hurt you," assured Laura.

❀

Stephen spent the day in the farthest field with James and Joseph. Arelia didn't even notice when the midday meal and tea came and went and Stephen didn't come home. She and Laura were too busy talking and having fun. Madeline took care of Stephen and James. Since she and Arelia had become such close friends, she was anxiously awaiting an invitation to meet Laura and Sarah.

Stephen returned to the hut shortly before dark to clean up and escort them to his mother's for dinner. Arelia couldn't believe the entire day had passed so quickly.

The Wingate house was filled with so many people. John had rigged an extension to the table for the happily unexpected guests. Even with the extension, the table was crowded. Joan and the girls had spent the entire day preparing a feast, not to mention the delicacies some of the women had prepared for the family and their guests.

John seemed to be the only one to notice that Martha and Joseph didn't seem to mind sitting at the far end of the table together. Nor did anyone else seem to notice that Martha was not a giggly child that evening; she was wrapped in serious conversation with the young man.

Arelia caught Laura's eye several times during the dinner, and the two silently shared their conversation about being happy, confirming that, indeed, Arelia was happy and was in the right place.

Joan was very excited to meet Sarah and Laura. She had to continually remind herself that this was not Arelia's family, but that these were the ladies Arelia had worked with at Faircastle. After dinner, the men moved to rocking chairs in front of the fire, and the women settled around the table to cut the nut cake which Madeline had so considerately provided. Sarah and Laura were delighted to hear that Arelia had a family recipe to share, and that she had a new friend her age. Jean ran over to invite James and Madeline for dessert.

When Arelia walked to the hearth to bring each man a slice of cake, she turned and saw the room filled with all her family and friends; it was all she could do to hold back tears but, now, tears of joy.

Before she knew, it was time for the caravan to return to Faircastle. As Miriam packed up the cloth she had for Sarah, Sarah pulled Arelia aside. "I will give Bethany your regards, Arelia."

"Yes, that will be fine." Arelia's polite response revealed her hurt and confusion.

"Child, I can see you are still hurt by Bethany's part in your life at Faircastle; in some way, I am too. But we must put it in the past. She has changed so much without Marisa's influence. I see you have too." Sarah smiled warmly, hoping that Arelia would get the point.

"There are some parts of my past that I am still working on. Bethany is one of them."

"I really do understand, but remember how strongly Marisa controlled everyone. I just wish you could see Grandma Bethany now." She laughed.

Arelia laughed, in spite of herself. "I cannot in any way imagine that, but for you, I will try."

"That is more than I can ask."

Before the small caravan pulled out of the village, Arelia's tears fell, already missing her friends.

Bethany was the most excited to hear the group had returned. It seemed months rather than days since their departure. She ran to meet Sarah in the stable. "Did you see the mended cloth?"

"Yes." Sarah smiled.

"Is it the one we thought it would be?"

Sarah nodded. "Come upstairs with me to my room, and I will show you what fabric we have to work with and tell you everything."

"Joseph, would you carry that box up to my room, please?"

Joseph walked over to Bethany. "I saw the fabric, too. It is really beautiful." He winked.

When they were in the privacy of Sarah's room, Bethany asked, "Did you give her my love?"

"Yes, of course, I did."

"Did she say anything?" Bethany prodded hesitantly.

"She said 'thank you.'"

"Did she send her regards?"

"Of course, she did. You worry too much," Sarah consoled.

Sarah and Laura had, in fact, brought back beautiful fabrics. The three women began planning a new wedding tunic for Sir Edward and outfits for the babies. They had such a short time before the festivities were to begin. Laura had plenty of sewing to do in order to prepare an appropriate wardrobe for the babies in celebration of their birthdays, Sir Daniel's return, and Sir Edward's engagement announcement.

Edward was none the wiser, only knowing the women had purchased abundant fabric, just as planned.

CHAPTER 49

Not long after her friends' visit, Arelia noticed that her monthly flow had stopped again. She didn't want to face what she feared was ahead of her. Miriam now coached her on what to eat and how to care for herself. Stephen had been given explicit instructions by Miriam to cease all sexual activity for the sake of the child. Other than what she absolutely had to do, Arelia was instructed to stay off her feet and rest as much as possible.

Only John, Joan, and the girls were told the news this time. Joan and the girls immediately stepped in to help with all the chores Arelia was no longer able to do. Both Stephen and Arelia enjoyed having his family more involved in their lives. In fact, Stephen realized that although he thought he had always wanted to be a soldier, he could never live his entire life away from family as many of the officers did. Arelia had come to enjoy Martha so much from their cave-hiding days that they fell right in step from where they had left off.

Of course, Martha could not go without telling anyone the news, and so she and Arelia invited Madeline over to tell her, swearing her to secrecy. Arelia and Madeline had become friends and had so much in common in their lives: growing up in a farming community, practicing the same Catholic traditions, surviving the plague, and being close to the same age. No one thought anything of the time the girls spent together; no one suspected they were sewing clothes for a new baby.

Arelia's life seemed to be at a peak. She was expecting a child again, but this time with thoughtfulness and planning. She had made contact with her past and left herself open to Sarah and Bethany's knowledge of her existence. And for the first time in many years, she felt like a woman with a destiny who had a loving and supportive family to help her. Yet with all this, she had an uneasiness, a feeling that something was about to happen.

465

✳

"Miriam, I have such a strong feeling of uncertainty, almost fear." Arelia sat at Miriam's loom making a length of fabric from the fine threads which Miriam had spun.

Miriam responded without interrupting her spinning. "Child, all our lives are uncertain. We must just live one day at a time, making the best decisions we can as need arises."

"But my greatest fears come from my past, not so much from what is happening to me now. In fact, I never thought I could be this happy."

Much of what Arelia had said from time to time showed Miriam that Arelia was covering a big wound that needed to be healed before she could move on with her life. She worked quietly, studying the young woman, knowing that she had to proceed cautiously. "Sarah and Laura were really wonderful people. Were others at the castle as pleasant?"

Arelia answered with great tension in her voice. "No one was pleasant except for them."

Miriam stopped the wheel and walked over to the fire, settling into her comfortable rocking chair. "Time for a break. Put water on for tea, and then come sit by me." Miriam studied the beautiful young woman, remembering the tortured child who had first come to her. After hanging the pot over the fire, Arelia assumed her comfortable and familiar spot on the floor at Miriam's feet. Miriam stroked her long dark hair. "It seems some of these unpleasant people caused you a great deal of pain."

"You know the pain I have been through. You have seen the results."

"Yes, I have seen the results, but I do not know how you came to be in your situation. I do know about the wolves and that you were forced by many men, but seeing Sarah and Laura confuses me about how you ended up there."

Arelia's eyes were teary and her voice angry. "It was my cousin and his wife."

"You had family there?"

"Oh, Miriam, I found my father's family. Nothing that happened to me after that makes any sense to me."

Miriam remembered that Arelia had accidentally mentioned her uncle

466

from the castle, but they had never continued that conversation. "You mentioned an uncle once. Was he also cruel?"

"I did not think he was, but he left me." The weight of hurt was so heavy, it was almost tangible.

"I am sorry, child. Can you tell me more?"

Arelia stood to tend the embers and put more wood on the fire. "Sometimes I hurt so much, I think I would break. I have not allowed myself to think about it."

"Arelia, have you ever seen a very deep cut that healed over on the surface, but was infected underneath?"

"Yes." Arelia was confused by the direction of their conversation.

"That kind of wound is not pretty. Around the scab, it turns red and inflamed and is often full of puss."

"Miriam, that is disgusting."

"Yes, it is. I have tended such wounds, and they take much more time to heal than a new wound that is cleaned properly in the first place. If those injuries are not opened up and cleaned, the person can actually die from the infection.

"Our emotional lives are very much like that. Many times our feelings are wounded, and we go on with our lives without cleaning out the hurts. Soon we find that we change, we get angry with those we love, we become fearful for no apparent reason and never really feel joyful. If we continue to let the emotional wound fester, we can, in fact, die from the filth that eats away at our lives and destroys the love we feel for ourselves and for others.

"Soon we are operating outside of the element of love, and we begin to feel frustration and distress in our lives. In a sense, that frustration is there to get you to change directions, because you can no longer handle what you are feeling. It is the same with a sore on your body; once the infection is too great, you must clean it out, or it will actually kill you.

"Arelia, your emotional wounds are great. The infection has not spread noticeably yet, but it will. The feelings of uncertainty and fear are simply signs of the problem. You seem to fear attack."

"I have been attacked before. It could happen again if my cousin finds out I am here!"

"Who is this cousin?"

"Edward Fairchild. He and his wife put me in the servants' quarters and had me drugged with strong herbs so they could send men in to rape me. It makes no sense why they did that to me. They were my family." Her tears began to fall. Miriam was relieved to see the wound opening up so the cleaning could begin. "If Sarah tells Edward she has seen me, he could come for me."

"You are right; he could. Do you believe Sarah came all that way to betray you?"

Arelia looked down and seemed to consider the question. "No. I suspect she came to see if I was all right. I really believe she loves me."

"Then she would not jeopardize your life," Miriam added.

"She could tell my uncle when he comes for the festivities," Arelia continued.

"Yes, she well may do that, and what do you think he would do?"

"I do not know," she answered honestly.

"Do you think he loves you?" Miriam questioned.

"That is what I really do not know. He would not see me the last time he came to the castle. He promised he would, but he left without talking to me."

"Do you know why?"

"No, there seems to be no reason."

"Could he have found out about the men?"

Arelia's shocked expression showed that Miriam had presented a new idea.

"Oh, Miriam! He must have. I was so foggy the whole time, I did not even know he had come and gone." Gradually the story started to fall into place—all except Edward and Marisa's motive for her destruction. "This is all so confusing. I never would have treated my family like that."

"Did you have other family besides Edward and your uncle?"

"No, Father and Uncle Daniel were the only two children, and Uncle Daniel only had one son."

"So that would make Edward the heir to the entire Fairchild estate. Edward was in a very comfortable position before you came along." Miriam watched as the picture became clearer to Arelia.

"But I am no threat to him. I am a girl."

"Yes, a girl who your uncle loved very much, the discovered daughter of a younger brother who he regretted losing."

Arelia considered all that was being said. "Miriam, that is insane. I do not want anything of his."

"Yes, and what they did to you was insane. People who see things insanely think insanely and act insanely. It is a natural reaction for them. Thank God that we do not think with their minds! Now, think carefully. What is the worst thing that could happen to you if your family found you were alive?"

"They would come to get me."

"And?" Miriam prodded.

"And what?!" Arelia was becoming exasperated with Miriam's questions. "Just tell me!"

Miriam laughed. "I am trying to get you to realize that you are worrying about nothing."

"Am I?" asked Arelia sarcastically.

"I think you are, but maybe you are not. I do know that all your worry will only make things worse."

Arelia sat quietly. "Miriam," she asked pensively. "What do you think could happen?"

"I have only known Sarah briefly," Miriam began. "She is clearly a good woman who loves you as a daughter. She would never do anything to hurt you. She may tell your uncle about you because she was so concerned about how you were hurt during his last visit. Although I have not met him, he sounds like a reasonable man who loves you."

"He is not the one who concerns me—my cousin Edward frightens me," Arelia stated.

"You fear him because you have not forgiven him."

"Forgiven!" Arelia shouted in astonishment. "I fear him for what he has done to me. He could do it again."

"Do you really think anyone in this village would let that happen? You are no longer an orphaned child trapped in a room unknown by anyone. You have many friends, including Sarah and Laura. Certainly, you know that Stephen would not let that happen."

"Yes, but Edward could certainly destroy my name."

Miriam laughed wholeheartedly. "I personally would not believe him because I know you, but from what I have heard of him, I would believe what you have to say about him. It looks like he should be the one to be concerned after treating his family as he did, especially if his father were to talk to you, Stephen, Sarah, Bethany, Laura, or even some of the soldiers.

"Your fears have given Edward too much power. You have failed to realize that people are basically good and want to help those who need help. Do you really think anyone here would care about his lies?"

Arelia shook her head. "I cannot say. You know people like to talk."

"Yes, and they always will. But those who love you will stand by you. They would certainly not allow you to be injured by any man. Besides, I think he may probably be smart enough to not want to lose his father's favor.

"Once you are more peaceful about all of this, I think you and Stephen should visit your uncle. I am sure he would love to see the new baby." She gestured toward Arelia's expanding girth. "He would be a great-uncle." Her smile was infectious.

Arelia smiled but shook her head again. "I do not know how to even begin to feel peaceful!"

"You must begin by forgiving Edward."

"How can I forgive him? That is impossible."

Miriam calmly studied the changing colors of the fire. Her eyes reflected the flickering flame. "I am not sure how you will forgive a hurt as deep as yours; the offense is surely there. I just know you will never be peaceful until it is forgiven."

Arelia seemed angry at the suggestion. "You cannot possibly understand what I have been through to ask such a thing. You just want me to pretend it never happened."

"That is not at all what I said. Unfortunately, we can never erase our experiences or the hurts associated with them, but we can place our memories in a different perspective."

"What are you saying?" Arelia was confused.

"Have you ever done anything you regretted?" Miriam asked.

Arelia nodded.

"Have you always asked forgiveness or apologized?" Miriam asked.

"Not always."

"Why not, if you knew you hurt someone?" Miriam pushed.

"Sometimes things are better left unsaid than discussed. But that has nothing to do with my cousin," Arelia defended.

"How do you know what is in his heart? How do you know what fear motivated him to act the way he did?"

"Cruelty and greed are what guides his heart!" Arelia stood firm.

"Yes, he certainly acted that way. Do you ever wonder why?"

Arelia was stumped this time. "No. There is no reason that his actions can be justified."

"Of course not. But we are not thinking with *his* mind. He had some fear or insecurity that caused his insane behavior. That is not to say that what he did was right in any way, but that there must have been something great to cause such cruelty—some kind of fear or misperception. If you continue to hate him, you tie yourself to him for eternity. Let him go . . . through forgiveness."

"It is not fair." She moaned.

"Oh, dear child, you are so right. Life is not fair."

Arelia's eyes were wide. "I do not know how I could ever forgive him."

"You do not forgive the actions in the sense of condoning or justifying what he did to you. What he did will never be right. Understand that he was reacting to a hurt or fear in his own life, and then wish him healing for his own hurts and a life of love and happiness in his future," Miriam explained.

"Arelia, you must understand that your cousin's only power over you is the power you give him through your memories. He is not here now, but you still allow him to hurt you. You are still frightened. Put aside that part of your life. Do not give it, or him, any more time than he has already taken. Realize that what happened in the past is just that, the past, and it can have no effect on you unless you allow it. Instead, when those thoughts creep in, think about how much your parents loved you. Think about the way they raised you to value and appreciate the family you have now. Thank them that the love and guidance they gave you provided you with the strength and perseverance to survive extreme hardship and made you the person you are today. Focus on Stephen and the family that you will have together." Miriam smiled as Arelia's tension seemed to lessen. "When you realize that your cousin no longer has any effect on you, you will be able to forgive him."

"That is forgiveness?"

"That is how I have forgiven my hurts. I do not have to associate myself with those who have hurt me, but when I think about them, I do not think about past hurts; I simply pray for their healing. By concentrating on healing the hurts inflicted on *them* that caused *their* behavior, I forget my own hurts and sever our hurtful ties." Miriam continued, "Until you come to some point of forgiveness, you will always fear him. Arelia, are there others who have hurt you?"

"Miriam, the list seems long right now."

"I would encourage you to do this exercise with everyone you know, even those you love," Miriam explained.

"You cannot mean Stephen?" Arelia was surprised by her suggestion.

"Yes, especially Stephen. He is the one closest to you who would be most harmed by any grievances."

"But he is good to me. He has never hurt me." Miriam's laughter offended Arelia. "He *is* good, Miriam, and you know it!"

"Child, even those who are good to us cause us injury. None of us here are perfect." Miriam rose from her rocking chair to drop loose tea into the hot, steaming water. She carried the pot to the table.

"I know Stephen would have more need to forgive me than I him," Arelia said, almost to herself.

"Yes, you may be right. You have been hurt deeply. Do you see how we hurt others out of our own hurts?"

"Why I act the way I do sometimes I do not know," Arelia said. "I know he gets hurt and impatient. He deserves to get mad at me."

"Anger is never justified. That kind of thinking is a trap. We are usually angry because we do not understand why others do or say what they do. Just be determined to correct any thoughts that separate you from Stephen," encouraged Miriam.

"The thoughts I have that cause trouble are not about Stephen; they are about those other men, and Stephen gets mixed into it," Arelia explained.

Miriam asked, "Whom do you need to forgive in order to stop those thoughts?"

"Do not even say it. I never will!" protested Arelia.

"And who is hurt by holding back forgiveness? You and Stephen or those men?" Miriam was persistent and unrelenting in her lesson. "And does your relationship with Stephen deserve to be hurt because of the anger you hold for others? Your anger comes out toward Stephen. Those men are not around to receive it."

Arelia watched Miriam strain the tea. "I think I would be weak if I forgave them. It would be like saying what they did was all right."

"What they did was not right and never will be. You could never agree with it. Remember that you forgive them by hoping their hurts are healed and their lives become happy. That is all," Miriam reminded.

"All!" Arelia scoffed. "That may be easy for you, but it sounds too hard to me."

"Come here, child." Arelia stood by Miriam at the warm fire. Miriam took her hands into her own and looked lovingly into her troubled eyes. "You are not alone once you choose to forgive these people. Inside each of us is a Spirit that helps us with our thoughts but for the asking. Every time you feel the tension of a bad thought, you simply ask the Spirit of God to direct your mind. You will be amazed at the miracles that will happen if you do this sincerely. Ask God to give you the desire to forgive and then allow Him take over; you must step out of His way."

"Miriam, it would take a miracle to do what you are saying."

Miriam laughed again. "And a miracle is what you will get if you sincerely ask. Remember that you are going to forgive the men to make your life with Stephen happier. You do not have to do it for them, but you must do it for yourself. You must do it for your baby too." She smiled.

In spite of herself, Arelia knew that Miriam was right—she always was. A part of her wanted to hold on to the hurt because it was a big part of who she was. But a greater part wanted to be free of the hurt and anger and fear that seemed to be growing inside and influencing her thoughts and behavior. She would do anything for Stephen—anything to make him happy—anything, including letting go of the anger and hurt she felt. She could see how her anger was sometimes turned against him, and she feared Miriam was right—that it would get worse. She would not let that happen, and she could never let it affect their baby.

"I know you are right, but it will be awfully hard. I do not know if I can do it."

"Hard!" Miriam laughed. "You have been through much harder. Working to forgive people will be nothing compared to what you have already been through. Do you remember what Jesus said from the cross?"

Arelia wrinkled her brow. "'Into Thy hands I commend my Spirit.'"

Miriam smiled. "Yes, what else?"

"John, here is your mother."

"Anything else?"

Arelia shrugged.

"How about, 'Father, forgive them for they know not what they do.' Who do you think He was referring to?"

"The Scribes and the Pharisees?"

"How about the men who scourged Him?"

Arelia nodded yes.

"Or the men who placed the crown of thorns on His head and spat in His face?"

Arelia was taking it all in, in mind and spirit.

"How about those who yelled, 'Crucify Him'? How about the Apostles who left Him? Or Judas Iscariot? How about those who jeered at Him as He carried His cross alone, or the men who drove the nails through His flesh? Or the man who drove the sword through His heart?"

Arelia was speechless. Tears began to form in sad eyes, under wrinkled brows.

Miriam took her hand. "I think you understand."

Arelia released a big sigh. "He wanted to be free of them before He died. Is that what you are saying?"

"Yes, child. I know you cannot do it by yourself. That is why you must call on the Spirit of God and His love. Turn your hurt and anger over to Him to handle and forgive all those who have hurt you." She studied Arelia with soft, tender understanding.

"Child, I think you are looking for *perfect*. After what you have been through, I do not blame you, but unfortunately, perfect does not exist in this world. The good and bad often go hand-in-hand." A mischievous twinkle lit her eyes. "I would like perfect, too, you know."

"How are you so wise? God certainly led me to you. Thank you, Miriam."

They were interrupted by a familiar knock on the door. "Am I in time to have tea with my two favorite ladies?" Stephen greeted them with a big smile on his face.

"Your timing is perfect." Arelia gave him a welcoming hug.

"I hope I am not interrupting important women talk."

Miriam laughed. "I think we have talked more than enough for one day."

"I do not want to embarrass my sunshine, but Miriam, how is it that Arelia gets more beautiful with each passing day? Some days she shines brighter than others."

As Arelia prepared tea for Stephen, she looked around the small hut at the spinning wheel and the loom, the warm fire, the dried herbs filling the room with their fragrance, the tiny cot in the corner where she had been nursed back to health, Miriam's cot next to the fireplace with the beautiful, well-worn quilt, the rocking chair which held the woman Arelia had come to love as her mother, the heavy wooden table and bench where they had spent so many hours enjoying each other's company, and, most importantly, the two people who had saved her from her prison. She knew she was where she belonged. Remembering,

Thank you, Father, for bringing me home.

CHAPTER 50

Weeks had passed since Miriam had spoken to Arelia about forgiveness. She *forced* herself to offer a prayer for Edward when he came to mind the first few times. "Father, forgive him. He did not really know all the harm he was doing. Heal him and save his soul." After that, it seemed a little easier, but she still hurt inside, and she knew she would need to be persistent in her prayer. She also knew that it was easier now because she wouldn't see Edward face to face, but she feared the thought of ever seeing him again. She hadn't thought about all the soldiers since she and Stephen hadn't had relations because of the growing baby inside.

One quiet, still afternoon, she walked to their baby's gravesite. She and Stephen had picnicked there every Sunday since Mr. Hawthorn had begun a weekly prayer and scripture service. Jean and Martha joined them on occasion. Jean had commented that the baby wasn't *finished*—she couldn't bear to say that the baby was *dead*. Arelia had begun to think of it that way, too, and so had Stephen. The baby was awaiting them in heaven.

Each night when they lay in bed together, before going to sleep, Stephen would put his hand on her expanding belly and pray for their child. "Lord, give this child the warmth and protection of Arelia's loving body until Your creation is finished." Arelia smiled, thinking of the creation at hand.

But this afternoon, she sat at her first child's gravesite. She leaned against the huge oak tree that shaded the tiny grave and noticed acorns littered the ground. She thought of the candlesticks that Stephen had so lovingly whittled for her as a wedding gift, with the tiny acorns symbolizing the family that they would have one day. And now, here was one child planted in the earth and one still rooted firmly inside of her. She rested her hand on her belly and felt deep peace with the flow of life inside and around her, changing and growing, revealing itself in so many ways—one child in the ground, unfinished, never to have a chance to grow, and the one inside carrying on the process of creation. The baby inside moved under her loving touch.

She realized that *she* would have been the child in the ground if she had not chosen to leave with Stephen, but because of her choice, she was continuing creation—not only the creation of the life inside her but creation through her own process of growth and healing. How sad it would have been if she had given in to the horrors of life and not had a chance to experience the love that surrounded her now.

Moments of peace like this filled her with hope for the future. She knew that she was a long way from being free of fear and from truly forgiving all those who had hurt her, but she was determined to try. She had faith in Miriam's good counsel and in the healing power of prayer and time.

Her mother came to mind, wondering what kind of grandmother she would have been—a role Miriam would fill for her children now. *Green pastures will come again if you and John survive.* A smile crossed her face as she noticed slender blades of green grass pushing through the sun-warmed earth.

She sighed as she thought about how innocently she had hoped for a fairy-tale life when she escaped Faircastle. She pictured nothing but happiness in those few moments when she forgot about Edward and his threat as Stephen rowed across the dark water during their escape, with the wide-open sky as a guide. She wondered if her fear of what Edward would do to her was just as unrealistic as her fairy-tale image of her future with Stephen. One image was serenely blissful and the other sheer terror. Could the truth be somewhere in between the two? Could both realities contain a mixture of good and bad? Maybe this was the green-pasture fairy tale she had prayed for after all.

Her life with Stephen was happy and close to perfect but not heavenly. Could it be that if Edward found her, she would have the love and support of her new family, and he would not be able to completely destroy her, as she feared? Could the threat of him help her to realize the love which surrounded her? Had her hell vanished forever now that she had experienced redemption?

Miriam once told her that life was just a story, and that she had the opportunity to help determine how her story would play out. She understood now that her story was one of happiness and joy *and* fear and sorrow. She was content to live out her story while trying to make choices that were based on love, not fear. It was such a choice that had brought her to Miriam, Stephen, and her new family, and with the same thinking, she would consciously try to make her choices in the future. Her choices had finally led her to a place of safety, peace, and comfort. She had chosen love instead of fear.

She was home.

Afterthoughts

This story is for anyone who has ever been hurt by family, friend, or stranger. Things haven't changed much over time. The scenery changes. Our clothes and speech and the way we get around change, but human relationships stay pretty much the same. We love each other; we hurt each other; and the prescription for healing remains the same—love and forgiveness.

The hardest and most meaningful thing we can do in this life is to develop and nurture truly loving relationships. We aren't always successful, but we can never stop trying. We get so caught up in our own problems and hurts that we often end up hurting ourselves even more deeply than others have hurt us by holding on to offenses and grievances. We can cover or deny our hurts, but until we confront them, they will never give us peace. We will never truly love.

We must each take personal responsibility for our own lives. Just as with Arelia, no one can save us unless we are willing to save ourselves. There are no quick fixes or magic potions—no Prince Charming or fairy-godmother—but there are people who are willing to help us through our pain if we look hard enough and accept the helping hand.

There are many people who lose their personal choices, as Arelia did, at the abusive hands of people such as Marisa and Edward. There are no quick fixes for those caught in the sex-slave industry. We need to be vigilant and prayerful, and loving and protective of those around us—and supportive of those courageous people who risk their lives to free victims of abuse.

I hope and pray that we can all learn the lessons of love and forgiveness that the Messenger and Miriam teach and that we will eventually "live happily ever after."

WE INVITE YOU TO ENJOY THE FIRST CHAPTER OF
THE SEQUEL

To Love Again
The Fairchild's Story

SEQUEL TO

To Live Again
Arelia's Story

Chapter 1
Havenshire, Norwich County—1356

Arelia dug into cold, fertile soil, breaking clods of dirt to prepare the ground for spring planting. She let the loosened soil fall from her fingers. *How long has it been?* she wondered.

Angela was born just a little less than two years after Stephen had carried her into his parents' hut following their escape from Faircastle. Now here was a playful three-year-old chasing leaves and gathering acorns for her make-believe stew, while baby John, hobbling and falling, tried to keep up with his big sister.

With Stephen's enduring love and Miriam's counsel to them both, the years had passed quickly. Angela had turned one shortly before Arelia realized that John was on the way. Miriam had warned Stephen after John's birth to avoid getting Arelia pregnant again and had spoken to each of them, though separately, about when it was safe to enjoy their marital embrace and when they needed to stay apart. Stephen had told his father that he felt like a bull being kept in a separate pasture.

But Stephen really didn't mind. He never spoke of his restraint to Arelia. She had been so good to him even during those times when he knew grief overwhelmed her. He watched memories wash over her like clouds in a thunderstorm. He seldom asked which thoughts darkened her normally bright eyes and overshadowed the sunshine of her smile. She had so much to grieve—the loss of her family in the plague, the unexplained loss of her uncle's affection, the loss of babies that were born too early to live, and abuse at her cousin's hand. He knew how hard she worked to heal her grief and fear, and he loved and respected her through her struggle.

But today the sun was bright as she turned the soil. The last flake of snow had melted weeks earlier, and it was time to plant. Although Stephen and the other men would plow large sections of land for food for the village, Arelia always turned her own small patch of ground, mostly for relaxation. Miriam and Madeline often joined her to visit but mostly to play with Angela and baby John.

Madeline and James had married shortly after Stephen and Arelia, but Madeline had been unable to conceive. Arelia wished that she could pass on some of her fertility to her friend.

"Angela, what has baby John put in his mouth?" Arelia shouted.

Angela put her chubby little hand on her brother's forehead, almost knocking him over, and scraped a handful of dirt and leaves out of his mouth, "Momma, her eats everything. Her a mess," Angela's tiny little voice carried back. John started to cry from having his leafy treat removed and from nearly being knocked to the ground.

His wobbly little legs held him as Arelia stood to pick him up. "*He* is a mess," Arelia corrected.

Arelia heard horses approaching from a distance and caught a glimpse of a familiar flag nearing the edge of the village. It was the Fairchild banner—an emblem that she had not seen in several years, and one she tried desperately to forget.

She ran to scoop up baby John and grabbed Angela's little hand. "Hurry, children. We must go inside." Her heart pounded as she ran to her hut. "Oh, dear God, where is Stephen?" She watched through the small window as a procession of only four soldiers stopped at the outskirts of the village, right in front of Miriam's hut.

Miriam was standing at the door as one of the soldiers dismounted and approached her. After speaking to him for some time, Miriam pointed to the field where the men were working. The soldier mounted his horse and rode to the field.

Tears filled Arelia's eyes as panic overcame her. *Surely Miriam knows Stephen is in the field. What is happening?* She watched as Miriam chatted briefly with the other soldiers and then walked casually toward Arelia's hut.

Arelia stood behind the door as she opened it for Miriam, staying out of view of the soldiers. "Miriam, what do they want? Why did you direct them to the field?" Miriam knew the panic Arelia felt. She had felt it herself when she saw the soldiers come to her door.

"Everything is all right, child. The soldiers are not looking for you or Stephen."

"But how could you send them to the field? They will see Stephen," Arelia chastised.

Miriam took Arelia's trembling hand into her own as she had done so many times before. "Arelia, you know that I will not jeopardize your safety or Stephen's. The soldiers are looking for men who are willing to work at Fair-castle. It seems there was a fire that burned down the stable and part of the house. They are looking for men whom Sir Edward Fairchild will pay to rebuild what was lost. I directed them to Mr. Carpenter. You can rest easy. I saw Stephen and James go into James's hut."

Her dark eyes brimmed with tears. "Oh, Miriam, will I ever get over this horrible fear? Will there be a time when I can live normally?"

"Now, child, do not do this to yourself. You have overcome so much. You are more peaceful than ever before. Seeing the soldiers surprised you, that is all. They will not see you or Stephen. They are not even looking for you." Miriam pushed the black-silky hair away from Arelia's tear-stained face.

Angela climbed on the bench near the cupboard and stretched for a sack of tea. "I put it in the water, Grandmother Miriam."

As Miriam helped Angela, Arelia stood to the side of the window shaded by shutters and watched the soldiers mill around as they waited. She recognized two of the men from the soldiers who had often ridden along the beach with Stephen. "We must not let them see Stephen," she said absently, almost to herself.

"Arelia, come away from the window. Stephen has the good sense to stay out of sight. You must do the same."

They were interrupted by a knock at the door. Arelia stood behind the door, heart pounding, as Miriam opened it. "Where is Arelia?" James asked as he came into the room.

"I am here. Where is Stephen?" she asked, the tension returning.

"Everything is fine. Stephen will stay with Madeline until the soldiers leave. Mr. Carpenter, Mr. Hawthorn, and three others have volunteered to leave with the troops as soon as possible. We do not want to draw attention by being uncooperative," he said.

"Thank you, James. Do you know when they plan to leave?" asked Miriam.

"Martin said they will be ready before sunup tomorrow. Until then, Arelia, you must stay inside."

Arelia nodded. "You do not have to worry about me. I may never go out again."

"The water is boiling, Grandmother. Put leaves in now?" asked Angela.

After tea, Miriam took baby John and Angela to find Grandmother Joan. It was much too beautiful a day for the children to stay inside. Arelia spent the afternoon at her spinning wheel, trying to distract herself from looking out of the window, but she could not stop the thoughts that poured through her mind like a river carrying her to her death. Images of her cousin Edward as he dragged her by her hair and kicked her until her ribs cracked. Captain Hardgrave unbuttoning his trousers and climbing into her bed, his eyes burning with sick desire; unfamiliar soldiers waking her in the middle of the night to satisfy their drunken lusts; Marisa, whose lips smiled with friendly acceptance but whose eyes told the truth of her hatred; and the bear that attacked her and Stephen in the cave as they escaped to his village. It became more than memory. It was real. She wanted to scream, but her tears fell silently on the threads that she pulled from the wheel.

When will the pain go away? Why has it returned?

Lady Katherine! Why would they even bother to give me a title? I am little more than a governess for his children, Katherine Fairchild thought as she watched the twins play in their large room filled with every amusement available—two painted rocking horses, two child-sized wagons, blocks, and ostentatious miniature furniture. *The children have their toys for their amusement, and I have* the children *for mine.*

Katherine's mother had warned her not to complain. After all, Edward had been completely honest about his intentions: he wanted a mother for his children. But Katherine had been young when they married, only sixteen, and she had imagined so much more. Of course, her mother had borne Katherine by the time she was sixteen, and so she couldn't understand what Katherine had to complain about. But Edward was much older. There had been many visitors after Edward had officially announced that his grieving time was over; and after the parade of eligible women of all ages, he had chosen Katherine.

She had thought it strange that their courtship involved so much time spent with the servants Bethany and Sarah and with the twins. She had begun to wonder whether Edward had chosen her or if Bethany and Sarah had. Now she knew.

But her mother had warned her. The very wealthy Edward Fairchild had chosen her eldest daughter over all the others who vied for his attention. So Katherine did not complain. They would think her ungrateful, even though Edward was nearly twice her age.

And after almost five years, she had come to appreciate Bethany and Sarah. What little she knew about Edward had come from them. She knew that Edward had been given Faircastle, the Fairchild estate, when his grandfather had died shortly after the plague and that his father, who was a charming man, had moved to the grandfather's estate. She knew that Edward's first wife, Marisa, had died the night the twins were born. No one seemed to feel kindly toward Marisa except Edward. In fact, there wasn't much said about her at all. Sometimes silence says more.

The person she knew nothing about, but wanted to, was Arelia. Bethany and Sarah had mistakenly called Katherine by that name almost constantly when she first moved into the estate. The most she could draw from the servants was that Arelia was Edward's cousin and that she was dead. The one time she mentioned her name to Edward, the look in his eyes was all the warning she needed not to pursue the inquiry with him. Helen, Katherine's maidservant, often hinted that Arelia had been mistreated by Edward, but she never really said enough for Katherine to fully understand. Katherine was under the impression that, for some reason, the servants didn't really know or weren't allowed to talk about what they knew.

So here she was, years later, with little or no life of her own, watching Edward's children play, day after day, hour after hour. Her mother told her that she could entertain, even throw magnificent balls. She knew everyone would attend, but when Katherine mentioned it, she was met with Edward's all too familiar glare. Entertaining was out of the question—an issue her mother did not understand.

But, again, she was not complaining, *Edward had been honest*. Even though her parents had pressured her, she really had wanted to marry him. Before her marriage, she had a fairy-tale image of living in a castle with all the finery that went along with it, including the handsome prince. And the finery was there. Even before the wedding, Edward had Sarah and her daughter Laura make as many new gowns as any woman would ever want, in every imaginable color. She had the hair ribbons and capes to match if she wanted. She imagined herself wearing a different gown to every social occasion, near or far. Unfortunately, the gowns sat wasting in a massive wardrobe, and they would probably never be worn.

She had a lovely room just down the hall from Edward's. He encouraged her to choose bright tapestries to bring light and warmth to the drab, cold, stone walls and heavy rugs to cushion the floors. Her oversized mattress was stuffed with feathers and covered in fur, and the massive four-poster bed was draped with expensive fabric. She had everything—except a husband.

Katherine often thought about Charles Reynolds. Charles was the boy she had always thought she would marry. They had grown up together. He was her best friend. She had no idea that her parents had other plans, and she had no idea that her younger sister Regina would one day marry Charles.

Now she was living a fairy-tale existence in everyone's eyes but her own. She had begun to feel ugly and frumpy. Edward had dutifully made love to her on their wedding night, but it had not been what she had imagined. He seemed strained and preoccupied, and his breath smelled of liquor. Katherine had felt that she was somehow disturbing him—an obligation and imposition rather than a pleasure. When morning came and the effects of the drink from the night before allowed him to awaken, he almost seemed surprised to find her in his bed. After several weeks of nearly ignoring her, he suggested that Bethany and Sarah prepare a room for her with any and everything she could possibly want. Katherine was far from disappointed by the suggestion. She had already grown tired of his sad, blank stares, and she was continuously disappointed that after hours of dressing to interest him, he did not even notice.

But she did not complain to anyone. Young Master Pearce and little Marisa had filled her time, if not her life. They had just had their second birthday a few months before the wedding, and, once again, Edward had been honest with her about wanting a mother for his children; but Katherine had thought he wanted a wife and a friend, too. She had waited an entire year for the ceremony and had seen him only twice during that time. He had followed all social protocol and was hospitable to her and her family, causing her mother to worship the ground he walked on.

The wedding ceremony itself was right out of the fairy tale she imagined her life would be. Her mother had made all the arrangements; all Katherine had to do was show up. Women commented for months after the event that they had never seen a dress more beautiful nor seen so many flowers in one place. Katherine seemed to glide down the stairs on her father's arm and down the long aisle to Sir Edward's side as their royal guests watched in admiration of the beauty before them.

Afterwards, servants bearing trays of tempting delicacies proceeded through lords and ladies of class and distinction until it was time to imbibe in a gourmet meal of particular flair. The ballroom floor appeared mirror-like with crystal chandeliers reflecting rainbow colors from floor to ceiling. Guests danced until dawn as violinists and harpists serenaded lovers on the dance floor and throughout the gardens.

Since returning to day-to-day life at Faircastle from that fairy-tale night, Sarah and Bethany had tried to fill the all-too-obvious gap, but no one could. Occasionally Katherine's mother and her sister Regina would visit for a few days and tell Katherine over and over again how fortunate she was to have so much. It hurt to hear Regina complain about how little her husband Charles provided for her in comparison.

Every month or so, Edward would steal into her bed after having his typical bottle or two of brandy. She always awakened with a start, but she allowed him to satisfy his husbandly desires. She would rise early, leaving him in her bed while she tended to the twins. Poor Helen was always surprised to see him and embarrassed when she brought the water basin in the morning. Katherine was no longer embarrassed; she had become somewhat numb to what the servants thought. She felt invisible, and it didn't seem of any consequence one way or the other.

Young Katherine had wished for a child of her own before she married. Her father told her it was not necessary to go through the pains of childbirth because Edward already had an heir. She still wanted a child, but not from Edward. She could not imagine him as a father even though she cared for his two children. He had so little contact with them and never even asked to see them. In fact, unless Bethany and Sarah brought them to him, he would probably never see them at all. The times he did see them, the children seemed to be afraid of him.

She was startled from her thoughts by a knock at the door. "Lady Katherine," Bethany greeted. "Sir Edward wishes to see you in the parlor."

"What does he want?"

"I do not know, my lLady. He simply said to summon you."

Katherine couldn't conceal her concern whenever Edward summoned her. He did not call for her often anymore. During her first year at the estate, he often called to chastise her for not managing the servants properly or for not managing the household as he wished. But she learned quickly to consult with Bethany or Sarah before making any decisions or giving instructions, and so she and Edward had not had that sort of discussion in years.

Katherine knocked gently. Harold, Edward's manservant, answered the door. "Come in, Lady Katherine. Sir Edward is waiting."

The parlor seemed darker than Katherine remembered. Edward's chair was facing the window, and he didn't even turn to greet her. "Come here, Katherine. How are the children?" His interest seemed sincere.

"They are fine, sir. They are growing. Would you like to see them?" she replied.

"No, that is not necessary. But I do want to talk to you." He had not yet looked at her, although she was standing directly in front of him. "Have you heard that we are having workers come in to rebuild the stable and kitchen area?"

"Yes, sir. Helen has informed me that the soldiers should be returning in a few days. I have arranged for the men to stay in the large room over the servants' quarters. I understand there will be about six. I have had cots set up," Katherine explained.

"You mean Arelia's room?"

"I do not know which room was Arelia's, sir."

Edward looked at her for the first time since she had entered the room, but he hesitated to talk. He simply stared, lost in thought.

"What is it, sir?" she coaxed.

"I do not want these men talking to the servants. There will be more than six men, probably closer to twenty. There are men coming from several different villages. Have makeshift arrangements set up in the courtyard. That will serve them well enough," he instructed.

"But, sir, it is still cold and rainy. The men will be of no use to you if they become ill, and then it will take our people to care for them." Katherine realized that he did not want them near the servants' quarters and wondered why.

He seemed to consider her response. "You are right. How many men can you fit into Arelia's room?"

"Pardon me, sir?"

"I said, how many can you fit into Arelia's room?" he repeated impatiently.

Katherine reminded, "I do not know which room that is."

Edward looked away, suddenly remembering. "It is not important. Put as many as you can in the large room over the servants' quarters, and since Jacob died in the fire, you can use his space too. But do not make them too comfortable. We want them to work quickly and be gone."

"I understand."

"You may go."

As Katherine turned to leave, he reminded, "Remember, I do not want these men to talk to the servants."

Edward sat quietly watching the door after Katherine left, realizing that he knew very little about the young woman—his wife. Of all the girls and women he had considered to be his wife, she was the one who had caught his attention. There was something about her—an innocence and excitement—her smile. She was the one he had thought would return the spark to his life, and he had wanted someone young enough to keep up with the twins. He had wanted someone different from Marisa, someone who would not remind him of her. He couldn't stand to be reminded of Marisa; the grief was too great.

He had thought that Katherine was that woman. She looked nothing like Marisa. Although she was pleasant to look at, she did not have Marisa's striking appearance or her visual perfection. And, of course, she was nothing like

Marisa in attitude or action; no one was. Marisa had been focused and driven toward power, property, and wealth; nothing stood in her way. Katherine, on the other hand, was pleasant but quiet. She would allow Edward to be in charge, even though he was not sure he wanted to be.

Yet watching her at the wedding celebration was like watching a mere child. He was sixteen years her senior but could have been fifty. She made him feel old. He knew from watching her that he would need strong brandy to consummate his vow. It was expected of him. At the time he didn't understand why he'd had so much trouble in bed their wedding night. Maybe it was the veiled fear in her eyes—a fear he had seen before—a memory he could never erase.

Did Katherine really look so much like Arelia, or was his mind playing tricks on him? When he could no longer distinguish the two and the memories had become too plentiful, he had instructed Bethany and Sarah to prepare a separate room for her.

"She has a manner of someone I know," his father had remarked at the wedding celebration. Neither of them could place the resemblance at the time, but it became painfully apparent to Edward as the days went on. Maybe that's why Bethany and Sarah seemed to favor her.

Years had passed almost without notice since then, and yet nothing had been accomplished. His days were spent mostly sitting in his chair in the parlor by the window and his nights sipping brandy or whiskey until Harold helped him to bed.

Even Captain Hardgrave rarely reported to him anymore. Edward often wondered how his troops were doing, but he rarely had the energy to find out. On the occasions when he had made his way to the camp, the disgust in the captain's eyes seemed to mirror all too accurately how he felt about himself. He did not want to see that reflection again.

Besides, Sarah and Bethany appeared to be perfectly competent in running the house. At times Harold helped them with the more important decisions. Edward frequently overheard them talking when one of the women came to the parlor to bring a problem to Edward. They would mistakenly think he was asleep in his chair, but Edward was relieved by it. He listened to them express their concerns to Harold, who always gave excellent advice. Edward saw no reason to get involved. Marisa had always made decisions without him, and he allowed Harold to do the same.

But Katherine—if the children did not love her so much, he would have her sent away. How could he not have seen the resemblance earlier?

To Love Again
The Fairchild's Story

is due for release January-February 2022.